Highland Heart

Emma Baird

VINCI

BOOKS

Vinci Books

vinci-books.com

Published by Vinci Books Ltd in 2026

1

A CIP catalogue record for this book is available from the British Library.
Paperback ISBN: 9781036711191
The EU GPSR authorised representative is Logos Europe, 9 rue Nicolas Poussion, 17000 La Rochelle, France contact@logoseurope.eu

By Emma Baird

The Highland Books

Highland Fling

Highland Heart

Highland Wedding

Highland Chances

Highland Christmas

List of Characters

Katya
A freelance writer and unofficial Pilates teacher with little money and too much time on her hands to mull over things such as…
Her relationship with an American workaholic, *Dexter*, a man who says super-awesome a lot.

Zac
Posh, blonde and one of the world's most flirty guys.

Gaby
Katya's best friend, newly moved to the opposite end of the country and totes loved up.

Jack
Gaby's boyfriend. Mean, moody, magnificent. Also bears a resemblance to Jamie Fraser stroke the actor Sam Heughan. His much better-looking younger brother, as Jack would tell you.

Mena
A fabulous, and fabulously spoiled cat.

Mhari
A 'friend' of Gaby's and a potential flatmate. Only move in with her if you don't mind every bit of your life being examined.

Dr McLatchie
A GP who has a side hustle as a psychic, one she freely admits is a complete fraud.

Caitlin Cartier
A 'self-made' reality TV star billionaire at the age of 21, thanks to the beauty company she set up. Some of you might think she is based on a real-life person. The author refers you to the front of her book where she tells you everything in this book is fiction and any resemblance to real-life characters co-incidental. Entirely.

Lois and Angeline
Two m'wah, m'wah lovey types who cannot be trusted.

Jolene
A pregnant New Zealander with weird taste in boyfriends.

Stewart
Said boyfriend of the above. Part-time coder, full-time bore.

Scottie
His dog. Loves food, walkies and watching humans do Pilates.

Ashley
The owner/manager of the Lochside Welcome, where you can find the world's most Instagrammable toilet.

Jamal
Owner of a general store in which you can buy anything and everything.

Enisa
His wife, runs a mobile beauty service and specialises in hair removal from anywhere and everywhere. Doesn't draw the line at anal bleaching.

Madeline
A mentor who wants to help young women succeed in whatever they do. Goes above and beyond.

Lachlan
An international man of mystery. Dodgy.

Laney
A woman who hates oysters.

Chapter One

"Hey, what a coincidence! I was about to call you! There's this totally amazing, beyond awesome announcement the Blissful Beauty board made today at work—"

Katya zoned out, mouthing the all-too familiar words to herself. Beyond awesome. Totally amazing. When she'd first met Dexter, she found his hyperbole irritating. Then it became cute and now it had zinged back to making her want to scream.

She put the phone on speaker and opened her laptop, deciding to finish a blog she'd been working on for a client. Dexter multi-tasked all the time, anyway. Doubtless while he phoned her, he was checking his emails, updating his Outlook calendar and making an appointment with his over-worked dental hygienist. Those super-white American teeth didn't stay that way by accident.

"So what do you think? Isn't it the most exciting thing ever?"

Whoops. Caught out not listening and with Dexter, the 'most exciting thing ever' could be anything or nothing. The man was an enthusiasm machine, ratcheting it up to levels so high she often worried about his blood pressure. Mind you, Dexter also tempered his enthusiasm with plenty of suggestions. He could declare anything as awesomely amazing and add ten ideas for changes which would make the said thing 'beyond brilliant'. And Katya believed you should use hyperbole sparingly. If a person routinely came out with the words 'amazing', 'fantastic' and 'utterly brilliant', where were they left to go?

She let out a sigh. "Sorry, the phone cut out there. You know what the reception is like in this place." Fine most of the time, seeing as Great Yarmouth had its fair share of masts. The reception excuse was the one everyone used when they pretended they'd been listening all along.

"What were you talking about?"

Go to the bottom of the supportive girlfriend list, she told herself. *And do not leave there until you are a much nicer person.* He sighed back, or it might have been a harrumph. Had he put her on FaceTime and spotted the lack of attention? In case there was a sneaky tech way of spying on someone she hadn't worked out, she turned her phone face down. And to be doubly sure in case he could still see her, she plastered on a smile so wide her jaw ached.

"Blissful Beauty's UK launch was such a success," he said. Work talk once more. "Caitlin wants to conquer Asia and specifically South Korea. South Koreans spend $13 billion on skincare and make-up every year. I mean, man— what potential. It'll be super-amazing if we crack that market."

Amazing, she said to herself. *Do not say 'super amazing'. It's up there with beyond awesome in terms of phrases I loathe. When they make me the Prime Minister—and any like-minded person would agree it's a position I'm overqualified for—I will make it death by firing squad to anyone who ever adds qualifiers to amazing, awesome, brilliant and all those other words that are fine on their own.*

Even though the thoughts remained unsaid, Katya guilt-tripped. Was she too horrible to be someone's girlfriend? Her best friend Gaby was the sweetest person in the world. As someone with the aforementioned dislike of hyperbole the opinion served as proof she didn't use the words lightly. Which was why Gaby was loved up and blissfully happy, and Katya sour and discontent, too busy picking holes in her relationship and quibbling about other people's use of language.

Katya knew her friends envied her too. Dating the UK-based marketing manager of reality TV star Caitlin Cartier's Blissful Beauty make-up and skincare company did that to girlfriends. "The freebies!" they said, followed by, "Um, so can you get us that glow serum/sparkle bronzer/lip plumper? I tried online and it's sold out at the moment."

Her handbag, propped on the desktop next to the laptop, spilled its contents—said glow serum and lip plumper among them. The bright pink and silver packaging, stars and all, seemed to wink at her—a sign the products themselves realised how desirable they were. Every single twenty-something wanted them in their handbag, beside their bed and tucked away safely in a locked bathroom cabinet. When the glow serum first came out, it crashed the Blissful Beauty website.

When that happened Dexter was, to quote, "beyond stoked".

"So… this weekend?" His enthusiasm quotient ratcheted back down, and she tensed. Once upon a time, she'd attributed Dexter's almost permanent keen tone to his American upbringing. Now, she wondered if it was unique to him, or something ingrained in marketing managers.

They needed to show a strong belief in the product they were put on earth to promote. Still, no mistaking that change in tone, which signalled…

"I know we were supposed to meet up this weekend, but I gotta work. Make a start on what we will promote and where. South Korea is a whole different ballgame. We gotta think much smarter than we did for the UK launch, and if I don't get going on it, some dude in the LA office will wing his or her way in there with beyond awesome plans that will blow Caitlin—"

Enough already, to borrow American phraseology.

"You're cancelling." Someone had to be direct in this relationship.

"No! I'd love for us to meet in London, but it would need to be for one night only. And I'd have to catch a later flight than I planned, and to get away super early on the—"

"It's fine, Dexter. Let's cancel." No one could accuse Katya Bukowski of not being able to take the hint. A weekend where she spent several uncomfortable hours on an overcrowded coach to get to London from Great Yarmouth, and then another few grabbed hours with a man too distracted to pay her attention? No. Thank. You. And *I did not sign up for this.*

Long-distance love. Gaby's grandmother, a woman people ought to elect as the leader of the UK *and* the US so overqualified was she, had lots of homilies about relationships. If she contradicted herself with them, she didn't care. So, if the wise old bird said, "Absence makes the heart grow fonder," one time, she had no problem uttering the words, "Out of sight, out of mind," another day.

Dexter was based in Scotland, Katya in Norfolk. For the first few heady months of their relationship, Katya couldn't believe her luck. Years of disastrous dating and now this guy she clicked with straight away. They did crazy stuff. He got the train to Newcastle, as did she, giving them three hours together. Then, she paid well over the odds for a last-minute flight to Glasgow from Stansted, and they spent two days tucked up in a hotel room, totting up a bill that continued over seven pages. If specified, it might have outlined weird things done with Mars bars.

Ahem.

Another time, he met her in Exeter when Caitlin's private helicopter dropped him off at an airfield. There, they decided that qualification for the Mile High Club included doing it in a hangar while pilots and small aircraft came and went, awkwardness, giggles and the world's most intense orgasm (Katya's) turning it into one of those stories destined to achieve urban myth status, talked of enviously by others for years to come.

Heady days? And now already bygone days?

"Babe, I'm sorry," he said now. The flip side of overuse of hyperbole was never knowing the truth of sincerity. She weighed up every word. 'Babe' wasn't her nom de plume of choice, but the 'I'm sorry' had substance and gravitas. Still, did a girl ever find it flattering when her still-recent beau decided his work was more interesting than her?

They ended the phone conversations with those kissing sounds. M-wah, m-wah, as the mouth widened and moved to goldfish open and closure. Katya hovered above herself and shook her head. *Really, Katya?* Her forehead and nose wrinkled, and the dreaded list materialised in front of her.

Katya loved pros and cons. As the oldest of four girls, organisation—her sisters would call it bossiness—came naturally. Or perhaps the pros and cons thing was thanks to an e-book she'd written for a life coach once upon a time.

"Detach yourself from the situation and write out the

yeas and nays to help you make your mind up when it wobbles," the expert on sorting yourself out advised.

Dexter: Reasons to dump him.

- If he says 'beyond awesome' one more time, I'll bite off his ~~tod~~-tongue.
- He can do the lotus position with his knees on the floor AND get his feet flat doing a downward dog. (And a man doing yoga; it's wrong of me to despise it, but... jeez, yuk.)
- He's a workaholic. ~~Times one hundred~~. Times one thousand.

Dexter: Reasons to keep going out with him.

- The 'thing'. I've never felt this strongly about anyone before.
- When I see him in front of me, my body forgets ANYTHING my mind says. (Hyper-flexibility is a handy skill for a bloke to have.)
- The hangar. Newcastle.
- When I get over the hyperbole, our conversations entertain me. Like, enough not to want to make me put my phone down.

And the 'thing'? Most people would agree. What made people attractive to others was undefinable. And individual. Katya couldn't explain Dexter and why her mind and body reacted so positively to him to her best friend, the aforementioned super-sweet Gaby. The two of them had been friends since they were kids, so close their thought processes synced all the time. And yet, the relationship Katya had with Dexter still mystified Gaby.

"But he's such a…" she would say and then shut up. Their fifteen-year friendship wouldn't survive complete honesty on both sides. Katya, after all, had maintained a heroic silence throughout Gaby's ten-year relationship with her ex, douche bag Ryan.

So far, Katya gave Dexter's boyfriend criteria on the pro side heavier weighting. Given her low boredom threshold, a fascinating guy was a must—and Dexter surprised her all the time. But it was only a matter of time until the points slid down. And then, then Dexter ended up the way of every guy she'd ever dated since discovering the joy of boyfriends at the age of thirteen. Dumped.

She doodled their names next to the list, enclosing them in a heart, and then shook her head. How teenage!

Making herself a cup of tea and taking it into the living room, Katya sighed at the mess. The flat's tidying rota, drawn up by Katya, had been ignored yet again. Dirty cups littered the coffee table. Next to the sofa, empty pizza boxes stacked up, a tower of cardboard that threatened to topple over any time soon. Beer cans lay on their side rolled into the back of the sofa. She moved them to the table and sat down gingerly, hoping not to sit on spilled lager or worse.

She switched on the TV and flicked through the options. Too many choices, hmm? Click, click, click—flicking through programmes like they were Tinder profiles. Watching a series for one or two episodes before boredom set in. Choosing the next one and hoping this time it might work out… Her mother was on marriage number three. Katya didn't blame her. Her father was a loser and her sisters' sperm donor no better. The memories of him still made her shudder. Now, her mum's third marriage looked as if the end was nigh, her mother muttering that Danny bored her to tears these days.

I don't want to be like my mum.

Dexter didn't bore Katya. Wasn't ennui impossible when someone's job kept snatching him away from you? The everyday details about Dexter eluded her. On an ordinary night when he finished work—what did he do? Where had he gone to school, or college for that matter? How long had he worked for Blissful Beauty? How come he could get his feet flat on the floor when he did downward-facing dog? Not many people could do that.

Whirlwind dates. They allowed no time for the exchange of mundane information.

Her phone went. Dexter again.

"Hey, you!" he said, those silky vowels of his soothing to the soul. "I'm sorry I had to put you off, but I've been thinking. It's time I visited Great Yarmouth, right? We've been dating, what, eight weeks and I've never been."

"Er… I suppose so."

Her surroundings did not lend themselves to romantic rendezvouses. She looked at the view in front of her and sighed. But as Dexter started to detail what he'd do to her when he visited, she forgot the mess, the shabbiness and the lack of privacy. And him coming here. A big step. She reorganised the pros and cons list once again, the cons slipping down once more.

"And you promise?" Lightly said, heavily meant.

"Hell, yeah." Her phone beeped—pic coming through. "I can't wait. And it's only seven days away."

She hung up, checked out the picture he'd WhatsApped her and stared at it far longer than necessary. Dexter blowing her kisses and winking so suggestively she blushed, miles away. Her message back—"I'm counting down the days." In her head, the weekend took shape. Perhaps she might even introduce Dexter to her mum and sisters…?

Another ping. A second WhatsApp message caught her eye. Madeline. Its contents so unexpected, she had to read it five times to be sure. The evening that had started with disappointment ended with promises on all fronts.

Katya grinned. Her life was about to change for the much, much better.

Chapter Two

Madeline's WhatsApp message had been brief. "Can you get to London on Monday? I've fixed up an interview for you with a literary agency who want to discuss ghost-writing?"

Too right she could. Madeline owned a huge online recruitment agency and she mentored people on the side. A few weeks ago, Dexter mentioned her to Katya and suggested she get in touch. Madeline needed someone to mentor, he said—a young woman, preferably.

"How do you know her?" Katya asked. Then, "Does mentoring work?"

Dexter whacked up those enthusiasm levels. "Oh yeah. I was mentored at the start of my career. It's super-useful, especially if you need a neutral outsider to talk to. Madeline mentored one of my marketing assistants and I've promoted her a coupla times since. Awesome, huh?"

He forwarded Madeline's email address before Katya said yes, but when the reply came back Madeline said she was specifically looking for a freelancer to mentor.

"Freelancing creates its own particular challenges—not least the isolation. I started my recruitment business from scratch, so I know how difficult it is to push yourself."

Too right.

So far, Madeline had made lots of useful suggestions. She wasn't able to speak on the phone or meet face to face —"too busy, so sorry"—but she was always at the end of an email. And she told Katya she wanted her to succeed. She had plenty of contacts too.

Such as the talent and literary agency she suggested, a satellite office to a much bigger operation in the US. "Go see them! Edmund Morris & Co are awesome and well connected."

Two days later, Katya found herself at the agency—a glossy, glitzy place in the centre of London. Earlier that year, she'd ghost-written a celebrity self-help book. The first few chapters of it, anyway. The job fell through, mostly because the celebrity had no idea what she was talking about. CeCe had heard about it and loved the few chapters Katya had written.

Could Katya do it for another client of theirs, so far unspecified? An American client this time.

"Don't you want a more experienced writer?" Katya asked. The world of celebrity ghost-writing was new to her. She wasn't familiar with the ins and outs, but practicalities suggested someone in the same country would be better placed to do the job.

The woman—CeCe—shook her head. "Our client specified it had to be you."

Katya almost fell off her seat. "Me?" Did she have some parallel secret life where she befriended A-listers and if so, why did she still live in Great Yarmouth in a grotty flat-share, existing on packet noodles and beans on toast? In her secret life, was she part of Taylor Swift's squad and the woman Justin Bieber called upon when he wanted to discuss the finer points of his lyrics and poetry?

(He should. She'd improve them no end.)

CeCe refused to tell her any more. Client confidentiality and all that. When she mentioned the fees for the project, Katya decided she didn't care. She'd started copywriting and PR freelancing two years ago when she was made redundant from the firm she worked for. Since then, she'd never needed to bother the tax authorities with revenue as she'd yet to reach the heady threshold of earning £11,500 a year. If this project worked out, Her Majesty's Revenue and Customs would want words with her next year. She'd be able to buy her own flat—heck, maybe even move to Glasgow so that she and Dexter didn't have to do the long-distance relationship thing.

CeCe got to her feet and extended her hand. "Thank you so much. We'll be in touch once we've drawn up your contract and then we can go into more detail about how the process will work."

Katya returned the handshake. *Sure, and thanks ever so much for just offering me this opportunity, oh good grief this is amazing...*

CeCe saw her to the door where one of her minions escorted Katya out of the building. They appeared to distrust visitors' ability to find the exit. Or perhaps they were worried she'd nick something on her way out. The office was jam-packed with expensive equipment and people wearing suits they didn't buy in the Marks and Spencer's sale. Unlike Katya's. She left the place in a daze.

Edmund Morris & Co's offices were in Soho, and Katya made her way to Regent Street, as she had a few hours before she needed to get the train back home. London was always a shock to the system, its crowds and noise relentless, and she watched a death-wish cyclist zig-zagging his way through cars and buses as the drivers honked their horns at him.

The bus that had just overtaken him featured a huge advert for the new Blissful Beauty shop in London that had opened that week. Curiosity stirred, so Katya made her way there. If she couldn't be with Dexter in person, she might as well check out the company he worked so hard for.

Once she reached one of the quieter streets, she decided to phone someone to tell them her good news. Lovely, shareable news didn't happen often enough. Dexter's number went straight to voicemail. As the UK's marketing manager of a beauty brand planning a high-profile launch in another country, taking personal calls in the middle of the day had to be a no-no.

She tried Gaby, and the same happened. Less explainable. Gaby was a graphic designer, and she lived and worked in Lochalshie, a tiny village in the Highlands. Her phone was always next to her iMac, and she loved any excuse to stop working. "I have news," Katya messaged her —usually persuasion enough for a work break—and walked to Regent Street.

Blissful Beauty's only UK shop—it was an online company in the main—was on one of the side streets off the main road. Thanks to girlfriend privileges, she needed nothing, but it would be interesting to see how busy the place was. It sat between an achingly hip bar and a sandwich shop that promised everything from gluten-free to vegan and every special dietary requirement in between.

The shop came as a surprise as it was smaller than she'd imagined. No mistaking the branding, though—pink and silver stars ran riot, and a queue of overexcited teenagers and twenty-somethings waited outside. A bouncer guarded the front door, arms folded and expression dour. When the queue surged forward every time someone left the shop, he extended an arm and barked at them to wait. Katya got in line, resigned to extended downtime. The two women in front turned to face her.

"What are you after?" one said, eyeing her speculatively. Working out what she needed, Katya guessed. Concealer, glow serum?

"I just want to see what it's like," she said, and then, because she couldn't resist the one-upmanship, she threw in, "I met her earlier this year. Caitlin, I mean."

Suddenly, they were all over her. What was she like? What does she look like in real life? Is she the best ever? Did she have any pictures she took with her, and if so, did she think if they flashed the photos on her phone at the bouncer he would let them queue jump?

A movement caught Katya's eye—a figure coming out of the front door and the bouncer moving aside letting no one else in.

Dexter.

The man too busy to see her because of (his words) super-important marketing meetings.

The jolt she got when she'd spotted him rapidly turned from sending her heart to the skies to plunging it to the ground. Did standing outside the shop like a groupie make her look too keen or desperate—or probably both? It was too late to do anything now. He turned right, heading straight for her.

"Katya!" Dexter the enthusiasm machine. He said her name now the same way he did whenever they met up. And yet. Something flitted across his face the second he caught sight of her, and she didn't think it was delight—more, *Yikes, I'm gonna have to think up a good excuse for this one.*

Katya's two new friends stared, and she introduced them. Dexter earned their lifelong friendship by offering to move them to the front of the queue. Job done, he returned to her and asked if she wanted to see the shop.

She shook her head. "No. I didn't realise..."

"It's so amazing to bump into you!" It was said so quickly, she guessed he'd used the time he took those two women to the front of the queue to rehearse the words in his head, so they sounded sincere. "Um, did we arrange to get together?"

Ah. The polite bit of him wondering if he'd forgotten to cancel, and the thought horrifying him. Mortifying.

"No, no!" she said, overdoing the fake bonhomie. "You're busy. I was in London for a meeting about a potential writing job and thought I'd take a look at the shop."

She deciphered a brain mulling over everything she'd said, trying to work out the good and the bad. The queue moved around them, delighted customers surging forward as the bouncer generously allowed two more people in.

"The meeting!" Dexter exclaimed, reaching for her hand. "Yes, of course. Edmund Morris & Co. Great guys. Do you wanna go for a drink?"

Why not? The 'so amazing to see you' line still sounded lame, but they were here now and two hours in London was two hours in London. He suggested the achingly hip bar next door that turned out to be attached to a boutique hotel—the Staffordshire. Questions swirled in her mind as they headed in, but she kept quiet, and Dexter said nothing either.

The doorman tipped his hat at them, and Dexter's preoccupied air vanished. Inside, he turned and flung his arms around her. She surrendered to the bliss of a man's heartfelt squeeze. London hotels and bars, used to endless meetings, didn't mind two people hugging. The groups of people coming and going moved around them seamlessly, reinforcing the moment's bubble feeling.

Despite the city's usual preference of disinterest, two women sat at the central bar sipping coffee from gold-rimmed china cups had spotted them. They nudged each other, exchanging whispers, their mouths rounded into 'o's of envy.

Katya had grown used to it. Dexter often attracted stares, his height, dark hair, intense eyes and hollowed out cheeks making him model-like. He favoured skinny-fit suits, and the one he wore now was a three-piece cobalt-blue version moulded to his body. She didn't blame the coffee drinkers. Dexter's appearance often lit her up, making her body glow and her mind fast-forward to what might happen next.

Could they, should they do that thing she'd always fantasised about, where they booked a hotel room for an hour, disappeared upstairs and tore each other's clothes off, returning to the foyer afterwards to the smirks of the reception staff?

"Just a quickie," Dexter said, stepping back from her, "I've gotta go in twenty minutes—real sorry but I need to head out to LA to meet up with the international marketing team."

Ah. Dexter's quickie wasn't hers. Even if she pulled that ice-cube trick Dexter often said made him see stars, they might manage it in twenty minutes, but she doubted the hotel would grant them a room for that tiny amount of time. She fanned her face, willing her libido back into its cave.

He steered her towards two of the armchairs next to the windows and asked the waiter who hovered nearby for a glass of champagne to celebrate. The two women watching them 'aah-ed!' in further appreciation. The champagne arrived, tiny bubbles drifting to the top of creamy-yellow liquid in frosted crystal glasses. She took a sip and watched his eyes. They didn't move from hers, and they were far and away her favourite part of Dexter. Yes, even more than *that* bit.

He leant forward. "So, tell me more about that meeting. Did Edmund Morris & Co agree with me—you're the most awesome, amazing, wonderful writer out there and they'd be insane to pass you up?"

Woman number one, her mouth still rounded, sighed even more at his words. Dexter's voice was liquid chocolate, the silk of it wrapped around you in blissful, comforting warmth.

"I got the job," she said, and whispered the ballpark figure they'd suggested, the figures still unreal-sounding.

Dexter clinked his glass against hers. "Well done."

"But I can't tell you the company name, what I'm doing, what I'm writing, when I start or anything. And I think it…"

Something struck her. "Oh God, you know the company name! So much for my discretion."

He touched his glass to hers again. "I won't say a word. Here's to you, anyway. It sounds like a super-awesome job. Have you signed the world's scariest confidentiality papers?"

"Too right. But as my friend Gaby always says, buried at the end of every non-disclosure agreement are the two sentences, 'We expect you to tell your best friend stroke boyfriend. Just make sure they keep their gobs shut.'"

He laughed, the sound causing further swoons from their audience, the women she'd nicknamed Beryl and

Madge in her head. "Better not tell me anymore," he said. "And I've worked with your best friend. She's an awesome graphic designer but I wouldn't trust her to keep quiet about anything."

Katya opened her mouth to object and shut it. No, discretion wasn't part of Gaby's make-up.

"When are you back in Glasgow?" she asked instead. Dexter had talked about a kick-off meeting to start the 'Caitlin conquers South Korea' campaign and then returning. This must be it.

He took another sip from his glass and glanced up. Dark eyes didn't give as much away as lighter ones. Gaby's green eyes expressed so many emotions it was as if the words happy, sad, dismayed, angry or whatever popped up in a speech bubble above her head. Dexter's eyes only changed when he hovered above her, hair hanging forward and beads of sweat running down his forehead. Then, they were magnificent—black intensity that felt almost frightening.

"A few days' time," he said, "though it depends on what the LA team say. And Caitlin."

Of course it did. Caitlin Cartier, youngest member of the world's most famous reality TV family and the creator of Blissful Beauty, though Katya doubted the twenty-one-year-old did much more than say, "Hey, should we have a light pink lipstick as well as a dark one?" while minions scurried around her and did all the real work. And unlike most people, Katya had met Caitlin—a teeny-tiny fizz-bomb of energy. Despite everything, she was likeable, despite her vast wealth and annoying, continuous social media presence.

Did Dexter sound evasive? There had been a pause before he said when he'd be back. A few days' time was open to interpretation. She glanced at the clock, an over-sized vintage skeleton model, its hands splayed at ten to two.

They were already half-way through Dexter's allotted twenty minutes, and she had run out of things to say. Dexter had too. Did words hover between them, one person wanting to say something the other had no wish to hear? This, the unexpected meeting, should have been brilliant. Katya half-wished he'd go. He hadn't resorted to foot-tapping, but Katya sensed someone else sneaking peeks at that oversized clock.

"Can I have another glass of champagne, seeing as Blissful Beauty are picking up the tab?" She might as well make the most of it. Dexter's expenses account was legendary. A measly bottle of booze, no matter the hefty mark-up smart hotels charge, only dipped in the ocean of what the world's fastest-growing beauty and skincare company could afford.

Dexter did that skilful, sexy thing, a soundless, commanding gesture that brought waiters all over the world running, and at the same time managed not to be patronising. The bartender materialised in front of them, white napkin neatly folded over one arm and poured Katya another glass. He held up a strawberry, and she nodded a yes, watching him drop the berry in the glass, bubbles gathering at the top to surround it. She raised it in a mock salute to Beryl and Madge, who both grinned back, lifting their china cups.

"Katya." Dexter slid forward, placing his hands on the armchair either side of her. Looking at him this close up made her squirm. She only recognised that black intense gaze when it... no need to spell it out, eh? Here, in a bar in central London, its intensity bored into her brain. She shifted on the chair, trying to move back so that the laser beam wasn't so focussed.

"I think we need to talk."

19

Uh-oh. A sentence that never preceded good news. It must be serious too. He'd left off the awesomes and amazings. Despite Katya's determination to play it cool, her eyes watered. Was this the 'it's not you, it's me' conversation? She blinked.

"The next four or five months will be insane," he said. "I'm sorry I didn't tell you about the LA meeting, but I only got the summons this morning. You and me, it's—"

"I know. Launches are a lot of work." She moved her gaze away from his before he glanced upwards or showed any of those other tell-tale body language signs that signalled someone was saying words they knew would hurt, frustrate or anger. "And you need to go. Your twenty minutes are up. That flight to LA can't be kept waiting."

"But—"

Speechless Dexter wasn't someone she was familiar with. In his mind, did he whirl through and discard hundreds of sentences? *"It's not you, it's me. You're mind-blowingly lovely"* (and she allowed the hyperbole here) *"but I've gotta move on. C'mon, Katya—LA and South Korea versus Glasgow? No contest. Your average ambitious guy can't say no."*

She stood up. The ability to style out a bad situation came naturally to someone who had three younger, inclined-to-take-the-mickey sisters. "Good luck!" she said, the breezy voice a remarkable achievement. "Can't wait to hear about all the exciting work you will be doing."

She managed not to make it sound sarcastic. Just.

He grabbed her hand. "You're gonna be busy with that new job too, huh? I'll see you when I'm back, right? When I come to Great Yarmouth?"

She said yes, and off he went, darting out of the hotel, arm held up ready to hail a taxi. Not a backward glance, either. Beryl and Madge mimed sadness, pouting after him and mouthing "Too sad, too sad!" at her. She hurried out of the hotel, preferring her love life not to have an audience.

A day that had started brilliantly. "Think of the money, Katya! You are going up in the world."

But there was always next weekend when Dexter visited her in Great Yarmouth. What was eight or ten days in the scheme of things?

Her phone beeped, a missed call from Gaby and a message too.

"You have news. I HAVE NEWS!!!!! News you'll want to hear!!!!! Phone me NOW. PS, sorry about all the exclamation marks."

Chapter Three

A week later and by some miracle, or rather bribery and the odd threat, Katya's flatmates had cleared out for the night, which meant she and Dexter would have the place to themselves to celebrate his return from LA.

Dexter's first visit to Great Yarmouth. So far all their meet-ups had taken place either in London or Glasgow, or midway points in between. It had taken her three hours to get the flat half-way decent looking.

The thought of showing him around made her nervous. The guy was returning from LA. Wouldn't Great Yarmouth's shabby 1950s seaside charm be lost on him? But on a clear sunny day Caister-on-Sea beach was heavenly, and she had a sneaky fondness for the Merrivale Model Village. As a child, her mother had taken her and her sisters there all the time. The four girls found the perfectly formed tiny houses, castle and cricket pitch fascinating, and they speculated endlessly on the imaginary inhabitants of the place.

Nerves and excitement fizzed together. *I can't wait, I*

can't wait, I can't wait... She moved to the fridge. Dexter was due in another couple of hours, which gave her time to rustle up something to eat. They could go out, but so far they had spent their time together in hotels. Katya had never made a man a meal in her flat before. Besides, if you ate something in your home you didn't have too far to go if lust hit you half-way through the main course. And she had Gaby's news to share too. What would Dexter make of it?

Katya took the food out of the plastic bag she'd dumped next to the sink. She'd bought the stuff the day before, but storing choice items in a communal kitchen was a mistake. Thanks to the cold weather, she'd been able to keep the food, well-wrapped in linen bags, outside. She peeled butternut squash and chopped onions, ginger and garlic for a Thai-style curry. Dexter shared her food views—responsible adults who cared about the planet should eat a plant-based diet most of the time. Even if both of them cheated occasionally, sliding down the slippery slope of cheese, chocolate and cream.

Half-way through cooking—the kitchen filled with the warm, toasty smells of dry-roasted cumin, coriander, and garlic and ginger—her phone buzzed.

Dexter. Fab. He'd arrived early and wanted the directions to the house.

"Katya."

Funny how much information you got from a single word. This one told her instantly she was not about to hear good news. And that the guy who delivered it was about to utter an all-too-familiar excuse. She beat him to it.

"You can't make it."

"I'm stuck in LA. A meeting dragged on and on and on, and now there's another one planned for the next day. I

23

haven't had a moment to myself to pee, let alone phone my girlfriend."

Multiple sorrys followed. And a harking back to the warning he'd given her when they met up in London the week before. The launch of a beauty brand in a new country was A Big Thing. All employees were now in lock-down, working every hour of the day and night. You needed strategies and plans for everything—from social media to digital ads, YouTube videos, celebrity ambassadors and more.

The flurry is short term, he added, but short-notice delays and cancellations were to be expected.

Great. Her American boyfriend had integrated himself so well into British culture, he sounded like an all-too-regular announcement at a railway station.

I will not cry.

The burnt-bitter smell in the air reminded her she'd taken her eye off the curry. She took it off the gas ring and hoped that she could rescue the top. Good job only one of them would be eating it, as the bottom half appeared to be inedible. She'd given flatmate number four £20 to clear off for the evening. Was it too late to phone him and say, "Hey, you can come back if you want. There's some burnt, left-over curry if you like. And... um... can I have my twenty quid back?"

Dexter promised he'd make it up to her. How about a long weekend in Glasgow as soon as he got back? He would organise and pay for everything—her train fare, the hotel, a meal in the best restaurant the city offered. She resisted the urge to yell, "It's not good enough!"

"I'm sorry," he said. That word again. "I've got to go. I'll see you super-soon!"

And that was it. Goodbye, Dexter. His haste to leave her was beginning to feel unnervingly unflattering.

———————

Later, having finished the unburnt portion of curry and washed it down with an ice-cold lager she'd 'borrowed' from the fridge, she phoned Gaby.

When she'd spoken with her on the train back from London the other week, the first question she'd asked had been, "How sorry?" in relation to Gaby's apology for all the exclamation marks she'd used in her text message. "There is a special place in hell for people who use too many of them."

"Oh, shush your fussy self!" Gaby said, her voice light and joyful. "My news is worth that many exclamation marks. It might make even you consider using one or two of them. So… drum roll, here goes, Jack has asked me to move in with him."

"Congratulations," Katya said, genuinely pleased. Though if Gaby moved in with Jack that meant she was staying in Lochalshie. Until eight months ago, Katya and Gaby had lived five minutes from each other for most of their lives. When Gaby's long-term relationship imploded, she'd needed to get out of town fast and ended up cat-sitting for someone in Scotland. Katya missed her like a limb.

The less noble part of her couldn't hold back the bite of mean, green jealousy at the moving-in-together news. Gaby escaped a ten-year relationship scar-free and moved seamlessly on to another one with another (much nicer) guy. Whereas Katya wasn't even able to persuade her boyfriend she was worth missing a stupid marketing meeting or two for.

"That's not the real news—oof, oh, yes it is," Gaby continued. "Jack, stop it! That's—"

Katya held the phone away. Other people's love lives should be conducted in private.

Gaby came back on the line, breathless and spluttery with giggles. "The not real, real news, then! If I move in with Jack, Mhari needs a flatmate. And Lochalshie is far closer to Glasgow and Dexter than Great bloomin' Yarmouth."

"Mhari," Katya said, her tone dry but her heart fluttering with the possibilities such a move presented. "The universe's nosiest woman. Who once shared a video of you with the world where you emerged from the loch, a full wardrobe malfunction on show via your nipples standing to attention?"

"Best video on YouTube," came a shout in the background. Jack. "I knew then Gaby was the girl for me. I coined the Nora Nipples nickname, by the way."

"You didn't!" Gaby's outrage made her smile. No, he didn't. He'd figured out early on that one of the wonderful things about Katya's best friend was that she was too easy to wind up. It was like taking candy from a baby.

Gaby wasn't distracted for too long. "Heart of gold, Mhari," she said. "You'll have fun. Plus the flat is three hundred times better than the one you're in—El Crappo Villas."

'El Crappo Villas' counted as a fair description. She shared it with four others. Plus the additional tens of thousands if Katya tallied up the cockroaches, dust mites and mice that occupied the building, thanks to landlord neglect and neighbourly slovenliness. The wallpaper peeled from the walls, the furniture came from Ikea's 1999 catalogue, and streak marks covered the double-glazed window, which looked out on an overgrown garden and bins that hadn't been emptied for a month.

It was the norm for people their age these days. No possibility of getting on the housing ladder unless the happy accident of birth provided you with wealthy parents able to sell off one of their city properties or cash in their final salary pension to provide you with a 50-percent deposit. A flat-share somewhere else wouldn't propel Katya into home ownership, but it might mean more cubic metres for her rent money. And soon, soon much more money was coming her way.

She scrabbled for the sensible excuses. *"I'll need to see it."* She had—when Gaby moved in a few months ago, she insisted on a house-warming party, and invited Katya. The flat was a 60s-style two-up two-down pebble-dashed building with a communal garden at the front and back, and its rooms far more spacious than the ones she was used to.

"What about work?"

Well, what about it? As a freelancer, all she needed was an internet connection. When Gaby first moved to Lochalshie, the connection had been problematic depending on where in the village you were situated. She'd had to move into Jack's house to work. And look where that had led. Nowadays, Gaby assured her, Lochalshie was as fully mast-up as every other place in the country. Flip, if she wanted proof, Gaby only needed to turn on FaceTime and show her…

"No thanks," Katya jumped in. God knows what she would see. Gaby and Jack cuddled up naked or something.

She wouldn't put it past her best friend—a big believer in share and share alike with one's closest acquaintances.

"I'll think about it and let you know."

As she stared out the kitchen window now, one of the neighbours' dogs wandered in front of the over-filled bins and pulled out the contents, scattering rubbish everywhere. Lochalshie was much closer to Glasgow than Great Yarmouth. She pictured herself nipping down to the city every weekend, maybe even on the odd evening. Much, much, much better than the present situation. She and Dexter would have time to find out the ordinary bits of each other. It would allow her to reassess the pros and cons list again and work out if her scoring was correct.

It had to be easier than the current situation where he travelled to London or she went to Glasgow and too many of their supposed weekends together got cancelled at short notice because of Dexter's work commitments. But did it mean something—Katya upping sticks and moving to be closer to Dexter when they'd only been together a few months? Might he see the move as threatening, one person pushing fast-forward on a relationship when the other was still taking it slow and steady?

Ah well. No need to tell him yet.

"Okay," she said when Gaby answered the phone, "I'd like to move to Lochalshie."

Gaby cheered so loudly Katya had to hold the phone away from her ear.

"When can I move in?"

Chapter Four

Was this the daftest thing she'd ever done? The question kept popping up in Katya's head. Her mum had thrown her hands up in horror when Katya told her she was leaving the metropolitan magnificence of Great Yarmouth and heading for the wilds of Scotland.

"But it rains all the time up there!" she said. "And they don't like English people. They've never forgiven us for decapitating Mary Queen of Scots."

"Good job I'm part Polish then," Katya replied. "And I think the Scots have probably recovered from the queen's unfortunate demise, given that she was executed more than 400 years ago. After Scotland booted her out of the country in the first place."

Her mother might be right about the rain, though.

Madeline expressed caution too. She'd sent Katya an email after the Edmund Morris & Co interview, saying CeCe Green had been "blown away by your brilliant writing style and professionalism. Could you afford to move to London now? It would be much more practical for you to be in the big city. I could set you up with some work to tide you over until the writing job starts."

"I'm moving to Scotland," Katya typed back, "for personal reasons. I'm sure I'll be able to work remotely and can conference call clients in London any time."

A long reply came back, detailing that personal reasons were none of Madeline's business but was Katya absolutely, one hundred percent, totally sure a move to such a remote place was wise? By this time, Katya had told her flatmates and landlord she was leaving, her flatmates had found her replacement in record-quick time, and she no longer had a choice. She specified this. Madeline came back with a luke-warm response but wished her well and said she'd try to advise accordingly.

Waiting for the next flight to Glasgow three days later, her worldly goods piled into a suitcase and a rucksack, Katya pushed away thoughts of jumping on the Stansted Express and returning tail between the legs to Great Yarmouth. Madeline's wariness had reinforced every single doubt.

No, this was the right move, she told herself. Gaby was in Scotland, the best friend she'd always lived so close to until this year. And moving closer to Dexter wouldn't make him less of a workaholic, but at least she'd only be a few hours away. Meeting up with him would no longer be an epic journey.

By some miracle, Katya had wrestled her deposit back from the landlord, which meant she'd enough spare cash to buy something at the airport—well, something small. Airport shops didn't have a reputation for bargains. Blissful Beauty displays featured prominently in the duty-free shop and the saleswomen waved the glow serum in her face.

"Look who it is!" a voice cooed behind her. "Didn't I say

to you this morning, I wonder what happened to that girl and her gorgeous boyfriend?'"

Katya spun around, startled. Madge and Beryl from the hotel, the women who'd stared so hard when she'd had her snatched twenty minutes with Dexter in London. They went by the real, much better names of Lois and Angeline, and, having introduced themselves, decided she ought to tell them all about what happened the other week. Other people's love lives were too, too fascinating.

"Can we buy you a drink, darling?" the Lois one asked. "In the first-class lounge?"

A new experience for Katya, the first-class lounge was worlds apart from the bog-standard bit of airports—harsh overhead lights, plastic chairs and people lugging around oversized bags. Most people in the lounge wore business dress, and uniformed waiters glided among them offering glasses of wine and champagne and little nibble-y things. She sat down. Lois and Angeline placed themselves either side of her, boxing her in.

She told them the names she'd made up for them in her head. They burst out laughing and said they needed to rethink their outfits if a stranger gave them such terrible nicknames.

"You told me this was trendy," Lois accused Angeline, pulling at the waistband of her paper-bag tied midi skirt. "I said, didn't I, that elasticated waists strayed too far into little old lady territory, ones you might call Madge and Beryl!"

She winked at Katya. Katya knew they didn't give a stuff. Lois's skirt was bright tangerine, a loud clash with her scarlet lipstick and the pink streaks through her bobbed dark hair. She spoke loudly, the voice of someone who'd never considered her opinions uninteresting, controversial or otherwise not worth airing.

The waiter brought over a bottle of champagne, and Lois and Angeline dived in. Katya accepted a glass too. Freebies in her world were few and far between.

"We love shampoo, don't we, Angeline?" Lois chortled. "We pretend to be Edina and Patsy from time to time. I'm Patsy, obviously, even if I've never managed the art of smoking three fags at one time."

More chortles. Katya knew the programme—Absolutely Fabulous hadn't done her PR profession's reputation any favours. And despite protestations otherwise, Lois was pure Patsy, Joanna Lumley—thin, seedy and ready to weigh up every situation and work it to her advantage.

"So," Angeline said, her voice a soft purr compared to Lois's strident tones. "Your delicious American boyfriend! Delectable, desirable and yet you finished on a low…"

Her hand moved to cover Katya's, a comforting squeeze. So comforting, she told them who he was, what he did and why his job kept him so busy promoting Blissful Beauty's stuff left, right and centre.

Lois raised her eyebrow. "Blissful Beauty? Isn't that the company Caitlin Cartier set up? Her glow serum is a miracle product."

Katya helped herself to a bowl of something. Bombay Mix at a guess. "Sure is. Dexter works all the hours God sends for her and he's devoted to her—though not in that way. I hope she realises just how much. But he's promised me a long weekend in Glasgow when he returns from LA."

Champagne on an empty stomach made you too talkative. Lois topped Katya's glass up.

Angeline tipped her head. "Did he? How splendid. We can recommend all the best places in Glasgow, can't we, Lo-ee-lo? I found this place once where I ate the best fish and chips I've ever had. Part of a chic hotel in Merchant City for discerning clients. What are your plans for when you get together with this chap again? Long-distance relationships are the pits."

She sighed, shrugging her shoulders right up to her head and screwing up her face.

Katya gave in to the urge to confide. Secrets were often easier to share with strangers whose advice wouldn't rely on previous knowledge of her.

"As it happens, I do. I'm moving to a small village in Scotland because it's nearer Glasgow where Dexter is based, so it should be easier for us to see each other."

"Where?" Lois asked. When Katya said Lochalshie, a look flashed between Lois and her sidekick.

"Do you know it, then?" The village was tiny. No one in Great Yarmouth had heard of it before Gaby moved there.

"Yes," Angeline said. "Beautiful spot. Now, tell us all about how you met the splendid Dexter."

By the time Katya rolled out of the lounge half an hour later, she was pie-eyed. And too aware she'd told them too much, wittering on about how she felt about Dexter and her disastrous relationship history. She'd spent the half an hour doing the opposite of the British stiff upper lip, a concept she believed made people better, not worse. Lois and Angeline hadn't said where they were going, but her guess was somewhere exotic and expensive. At least she would never see them again.

The announcement went out over the tannoy that Flight 349 to Glasgow was boarding. Unlike Lois and Angeline, Katya was flying Ryanair, and that airline did not supply lounges, free booze and nibbles. She made her unsteady way to the gate, its space crowded with bodies. The steward at the front called out those who'd splashed out on the aisle and front seats to get those precious extra inches of legroom. Katya wasn't going to board anytime soon.

One seat remained at the gate, but by the time she got there someone had beat her to it, dumping his own bag on the ground.

"Oh, sorry! Do you want the seat?"

As quickly as he'd sank into the plastic chair, he leapt to his feet just as she moved forward, so they were only inches apart.

"Whoops!" He took a step back, hands held out in supplication. The opposite of Dexter, Katya took in dark blonde hair, greasy at the roots, which framed a broad face and large blue eyes, his body squat and muscular. He was taller than her, but only just, the eyes meeting hers in frank appraisal.

Ryanair's staff invited the next lot of people to board.

"Off to Scotland, then?" he said, moving with her towards the queue.

Hampshire, or Hereford, Katya guessed—a home counties chap for sure, his English plummy and privileged, whatever the scruffy chinos and dog-hair-covered fleece said about him.

"Yes. You?"

He reached over and took the rucksack from her hand. "Allow me. I am. I hate flying. Do you promise to sit by me and hold my hand when the turbulence hits? I'm Zachary Cavanagh, by the way, though everyone calls me Zac."

"Katya. What if there's no turbulence?" she said, as they walked down the hallway that led to the plane. "Or we land up in the hands of Ryanair's best pilot, a flight so smooth he or she sends us to sleep the instant our bottoms touch the seats?"

His eyes sparkled. "I'm gutted you think me so cheap I

sleep with a woman on the first date." He turned his head back so he could look behind her. "Even one with an arse as perfectly rounded as yours."

She rolled her eyes. It had been a while since she'd encountered someone as full on as this. On the other hand, the over-the-top flirtation cheered her up. And he did tick a few of her 'before Dexter' boxes. Blonde, blue-eyed and... confident.

Once on board, Zac persuaded the businessman who was supposed to be sitting next to Katya to swap, the incitement easier as Zac had splashed out on an aisle seat at the front of the plane. He heaved her rucksack into the overhead locker and sat beside her.

The air hostess ran through the safety instructions as the plane taxied down the runway, ready to take off. Zac slid his head next to Katya's. "Do you want to know what I'm thinking?" he whispered.

"Don't tell me," she said, betting Zac's imagination didn't stretch to original. "You're picturing her standing in front of you in a hotel room, naked, as she gestures to the sides with her beautifully manicured hands and repeats the words 'brace, brace'?"

He laughed. "Close. But I imagined you instead."

He plucked at his seatbelt, hands shaking as the aircraft began to lift off.

"Usually I cope with flying by getting blind drunk, but I've got to drive the other end so my usual coping strategy's out the window. Please keep talking to me and stop me thinking about how unnatural flying is."

Ah—was that what the flirting was really about? He'd fixed his eyes on the seat in front, trying to avoid the window view. If you hated flying, when the plane took off a window view showed the ground vanishing under the plane, buildings, houses, roads and fields rendered tiny in seconds. Thoroughly unnerving.

"You're a hedge fund manager or some other equally unspeakable profession," she said, settling back in her chair. "I've no idea what that is, but you work in that field because daddy and mummy paid for a very expensive education, and you're connected to all the right people. The clients trust you to do magical things with their money, multiplying it so much they can live in huge mansions and holiday in the Caribbean three times a year.

"You're flying Ryanair because from time to time you enjoy slumming it. Once you get to Glasgow, you're off to the Hilton where you will meet your chums for a stag party which will involve three days of macho-style trips to the surrounding countryside where you will shoot things and then drink too much in stately homes. How am I doing so far?"

Zac, his face still sheet white, nodded slowly—a small smile escaping.

"Mmm. Not bad on the distraction front. Hopelessly wrong on everything else."

She'd done it deliberately, so no surprises there, but she still reckoned the guess about his education was spot on.

The plane levelled off and he let out a sigh of relief, reaching for the rucksack in front of him.

"Do you want to share my crisps?"

He plucked the bag from his rucksack and rattled it at her, eyebrows raised.

"No thanks."

"No? Don't you like the flavour? Or are you worried it commits you to something—such as me taking you out for a drink when we get to the other end to thank you for saving me from turning into a blubbering wreck when the plane took off?"

The single Katya wouldn't have hesitated. She'd met plenty of Zac types before. *"A drink? Don't be silly. What you mean is to get me tipsy enough that I say 'yes' to your later suggestion we go to bed together when I don't believe in wasting time and money, so I suggest we skip the drink bit altogether. Right?"*

The woman prepared to uproot herself from one country and move to another to take her closer to her man, didn't bother.

She took the bag from his hands, turning it so the ingredient list faced them. "I'm a vegan," she said. Well, ninety percent of the time. "Salt and vinegar crisps almost always have flavouring in them that's made from milk powder."

"Do they?" he asked, examining the ingredient list in turn. "You don't mind if I eat them, do you? No lectures about my questionable ethical choices?"

"Nope. What you eat is up to you."

"Up to me?" he said. "I might change my ways if a good woman suggests I do so."

Another sly wink. The obvious, flirty reply would be. *"Shame you're sitting beside a wicked one, then."* Again, she held back, the flirtation suddenly distasteful. If Dexter's LA flight included a glamorous actress who simpered and smiled at him (as she suspected they already did) and he responded, Katya would want to cry.

Still, Zac didn't give up. The questions came thick and fast. Where was she from? Was she off somewhere on holiday or was it a business visit?

Was she seeing anyone? She chose not to answer that one.

"Is Glasgow your final destination?" he said, as the plane began its descent. The plane tilted from side to side as it dropped height, and he grabbed her hand. "Please, please keep talking."

"No it isn't. I'm moving somewhere you won't have heard of. It's this tiny little place in the Highlands."

"Oh? What is it called?" The question came through clenched teeth.

"Lochalshie."

At that, his face relaxed and he grinned, the smile showing off white teeth and a slight overbite—the contrast to Dexter's perfectly straightened American ones.

"How fabulous. That's where I'm heading too. Are all the residents as gorgeous as you?"

Chapter Five

The delectable and desirable Dexter—who never applied those words to thoughts of himself—took in the flat and smiled at Marcia, another Texan.

She shivered. "I promise it's got an amazing heating system. Only takes half an hour to warm up." She pulled her coat around her and folded her arms. Like Dexter, adjusting to the British weather was an ongoing process. Blissful Beauty's Yammer site included plenty of tips on life outside the company's LA home. Getting used to UK weather, she told Dexter, was meant to take a year. Dexter kept his thoughts to himself—*A year? You've gotta be kidding.*

Used to American spacing where people got much more bang for their buck, the flat felt cramped. But, all things considered, he liked it. Two bedrooms, one of them en suite, the other right next to the bathroom, a dining kitchen and a huge living room with a bay window. The high ceilings intrigued him. Coving joined the walls to the ceiling, the plaster work intricate and delicate. In the living room, a once-upon-a time old fireplace that had been boarded up was now a feature, its centre taken up by a convincing fake wooden stove.

He took a photo with his phone almost automatically. He should send it to Katya, who would… No.

Marcia shivered once more. "I send thanks to the Lord Almighty, Dexie," Marcia had picked up Caitlin and his family's name for him, something Dexter wasn't comfortable with, "that our CEO wants to move the British operation to London. Can you beat it for convenience?" she said, sticking her arms out and pointing downwards. Under the flat was office space. Below that, Blissful Beauty's only UK bricks and mortar shop.

"You'll be the only guy in this city whose commute is less than five minutes!" she added.

True. Dexter knew about working here. He'd done the research. Thanks to exorbitant costs, most people were forced to rent flats way, way out and travel jam-packed in the Tube's sardine tin cans to get to work. You were lucky if it only took you an hour.

Marcia joined him at the window. They watched the queue of people waiting to get into the shop. "Does that ever go down?" Dexter asked. She shook her head. "Nope. I guess it's great for you. If you need to do market research just pop downstairs and ask. Or get them to pose for an Instagram pic." On cue, two girls coming out of the shop held up their pink and silver bags and posed for a selfie.

"Still on for the Forbes list?" Marcia asked, her eyes twinkly. An old joke between them. Something he'd said at his interview, one she'd been at as the HR director for the British operation. Was it his imagination or had she moved closer? His nose twitched. Marcia always wore one of Blissful Beauty's perfumes, this one sickly sweet. Jewel, he guessed, and the one still in development. Katya described it as the love child of vanilla, cinnamon and vomit when he gave her a sample.

Marcia never looked less than immaculate. Katya met her once and said she must have got her ideas about what being a professional woman meant from the TV show *Suits*. Pencil skirts, blouses tucked in, tights all year round, red lipstick, rigid hair and stiletto-heeled court shoes. If she turned her foot up, Dexter was willing to bet the sole of the shoe would be red.

Sure enough. He caught a glimpse of it as she headed for the bigger of the bedrooms and he followed. One of the main reasons Marcia tolerated London, she told him, was Meghan Markle—one-time *Suits* star and now married to HRH The Duke of Sussex and Earl of Dumbarton, otherwise known as Prince Harry. Sometimes, she headed out of the office, turned from Warwick Street onto Regent Street, and made her way to Westminster and Buckingham Palace. Where Meghan waited at the gates—*"Marcia, Marcia, over here!"* In her dreams. He told himself off for inner bitchiness.

"Still got that Brit girlfriend?" Marcia asked, the question idle, her face too intent.

"Yeah," he said. The bed in the room was king-sized and heaped with cushions. What was it with women and cushions? You had to throw them off the bed to get into it and presumably pile them back on again the next morning. Artfully.

"Long-distance relationships. They suck, right?"

Super-duper did. He blew out air and regretted it. Marcia's expression changed from sympathy to predatory. Scarlet lips licked. Eyes boring into him.

He pushed a hand through his hair and took a step back. "Who knows? So, gonna show me the office, Marcia?"

Chapter Six

Zac was on a mission, he told Katya as they headed for Lochalshie in his rented car.

Gaby's call came through as soon as Katya turned flight mode on her phone off. "I'm so sorry. I know we promised to meet you, but Jack's mini-bus has broken down. There is a bus you can get to Lochalshie. It, er, takes a while."

Shamelessly ear-wigging as they headed inside the terminal, Zac offered her a lift. She wasn't sure spending any more time with him was a good idea, but he insisted. If she went for the bus option, it would take her twice as long to arrive.

"And you can tell me all about the village, seeing as I'm heading there to start a business."

Outside Rent-a-Car, she opened the Audi's passenger door. Zac hadn't bothered looking at any of the cheaper option the hire company offered, opting for the boy racer red Audi TT Coupé straight away.

"You flash git," Katya remarked, eyeing the car. "Just don't break the speed limit, right? The road to Lochalshie bends and twists a lot, as I remember. I don't want to end up another road casualty."

He drove fast anyway, taking every corner as if it presented a personal affront to him. Fear of flying didn't translate to caution in any other area. Katya's mind kept flashing up images of those bunches of flowers people left on the hedgerows of country roads marking the final resting place of an unfortunate motorist or passenger. The drivers they overtook must have called him every name under the sun as the car sailed past. A few times, she spotted them flicking him the V-sign and worse.

"What's the business?" she asked, hoping conversation might distract her and slow him down.

"I'm planning to set up an online food business, offering local produce to high-end hotels and restaurants, and the public. I'll sell oysters, langoustines, venison burgers and that kind of thing. And I want to scope out the place for future restaurant possibilities. The place is crying out for decent food."

What might the locals say about that assessment of their foodie charms? As part of her 'please come to Lochalshie' pitch, Gaby had told Katya the village's Lochside Welcome was number one on TripAdvisor for restaurants in Lochalshie. Fair do's it was one of only two places where you could eat out in the area, but its wood-fired oven pizzas and chocolate decadence dessert were divine.

And Katya had fond memories of the place. The first night she'd spent with Dexter was in the Lochside Welcome's rooms. They'd finished off an... energetic evening with room service, the food as sublime as what they'd just done. Almost.

She found herself drifting back to the first time she'd met Dexter, at the Lochalshie Highland Games that summer. She'd experienced something she didn't believe in —instant attraction. Usually it took intelligent eyes, an intimate stare and a conversation where the guy made it clear the look in his eyes wasn't the only bit of him that was smart. This time, the universe placed Dexter in front of her. Her body responded and when the games finished, they took advantage of the rooms Blissful Beauty had booked out at the Lochside Welcome to drink, chat and do what they'd both spent the afternoon fantasising about.

Afterwards, she lay in his arms and wondered if she'd ever been this happy. And she, who billed herself as a wordsmith, copywriter extraordinaire, SEO content marketing expert or whatever else, didn't think such statements lightly. Dexter said, 'beyond awesome' and 'utterly amazing' a lot that night. She took him at his word.

"When can I see you again?" he asked, propping himself up on one elbow so he could tilt his face towards her. He put out his hand, using one finger to gently brush the hair from her face, fanning it out on the pillow.

"Chocolate," Gaby said, "that's what Dexter's voice sounds like. It's a lake of the stuff that washes over you. A girl can forgive him anything for that voice, even when he is telling her for the five hundredth and fiftieth time to re-do the already perfect designs she's given him." At the time, Gaby had been working on Blissful Beauty's UK website. Dexter's pickiness was legendary.

"Tomorrow!" Katya told him and laughed. Tomorrow was already here, seeing as it was three minutes past midnight. He bent to kiss her, soft and lingering.

"Can't." Regret, sorrow, pain. "I've gotta get back to Glasgow for tomorrow afternoon. But in the meantime, do you wanna to stay up all night?"

And they did, Dexter dragging himself into the shower

at five to twelve the next day as a maid banged on the door and reminded them the official checkout time was eleven o'clock. He handed over the £50 extra without a quibble and promised they'd meet up as soon as possible, even though that involved a four-hour-plus trip for him and two hours for her to meet in London for less than one day.

"An online business, then. Will enough people buy that kind of food? Isn't it awfully expensive?" Katya asked Zac, snapping out of pleasant memories.

He met her eyes in the mirror. "What did you say earlier about mummy and daddy ensuring I had an expensive education? I know a lot of people I can target—those eager to shell out for top-of-the-range meat and seafood."

"Why Lochalshie?"

He fingers tapped the steering wheel. "A friend recommended the place—said you could find great local suppliers and the start-up costs would be minimal. I'll do the set-up work now and hopefully the online business will be ready by the New Year."

Katya checked her phone discreetly, hoping for something from Dexter—a text, a WhatsApp message or even a photo on Instagram where Dexter had tagged her. "Missing you, LA terrible without you", or something. Nothing. If the Katya of a few months ago had known that heady excitement would tail off so quickly, would she have bothered with him in the first place? And now she had moved to the opposite end of the country (felt like) to be nearer him. The 'this is a mistake, mistake, mistake' chant in her head grew ever louder.

The car ate up the miles. The enveloping darkness of the October night meant the glorious countryside that marked the way to Lochalshie wasn't visible. Gaby often sounded as if she worked for VisitScotland when she talked about the place to others. The habit was contagious. Katya wanted Zac to be impressed, to see the village and stare in awe at the gently lapping waters of the loch, the hills and mountains that encircled it and the hundreds of shades of green you could pick out in the fields, trees and bushes.

Eventually the headlights caught the sign—*Welcome to Lochalshie! We love careful drivers.* "Ahem," Katya volunteered. Zac barely slowed, the villagers' safety on the streets saved by the lateness of the hour.

"Where can I drop you? A nice little cottage somewhere a weary traveller can grab a cup of tea and a sandwich?"

"Nice try. Here will do. I'm staying with my best friend this evening and she's only five minutes away."

He'd stopped outside Kirsty's house. Otherwise known as Christina the Dating Guru, the famous YouTube star (and former resident of Lochalshie) owned a big house next to the Lochside Welcome and right on the shores of the loch. Thanks to disappointment in love—the irony!—she'd left the place months ago, and the house was now on the market.

"How about if I offered the passenger a divine, vegan-friendly sandwich, a drink and the best way in the world to warm up and put colour in your cheeks?"

It shouldn't be attractive, that overwhelming, cocky confidence but Katya laughed again. Flattering to find someone so determined to spend time with her. She filed it under 'possibilities for the future', adding the proviso 'only a distant one'.

"I've got make-up that can do that just as well." Thank you, oh Blissful Beauty glow serum. "Have you bought this house?"

She pointed in front of her. Modern, open plan, filled with expensive furniture and located right next to the loch, it didn't surprise her that the property had sold. And if the Audi TT and the posh accent hadn't already given it away, Zac must be a very rich young man—capable of stepping onto the property ladder much further up than most people their age.

He got out of the car, and she followed. The two of them faced each other across the Audi's bonnet. "Be serious," he said. "How on earth could I afford it? So, tomorrow. Do you want to show me around the place?"

"I'm new here too, remember? I've no idea where anything is," she said, heaving her suitcase and rucksack out from the back of the car. "Thanks for the lift."

She ignored the call that came after her that she ought to give him her phone number.

"Hello, about-to-be-my flatmate. So, who's that and why is he at Kirsty's house?"

Katya stifled a groan. So much for the walk to Jack and now Gaby's house in peace and quiet, time to rearrange her thoughts and mull over everything that had happened that day. Mhari fell in step beside her, hand on her phone and thumb hovering in the air.

"How do you do it?" Katya asked, marching as briskly as she could while dragging a large suitcase behind her. Mhari puffed alongside her. "Is there a sensor on the road that's linked to your phone, so you get an alert when strange folks come to the village?"

Mhari faked hurt but forgot it quickly enough. You couldn't sulk and persuade people to part with information at the same time. "I just like a bit o' fresh air, is all. I'm out and about at all times. Not my fault if I see people doin' things they shouldnae be, such as getting out of posh cars with cute-looking guys who dinnae look like the cute-looking guy they're meant to be dating."

Mhari, Katya knew, would have questioned Gaby extensively, wanting to find out everything about her about-to-be flatmate. And Gaby's mouth ran away with her all the time. Everything she'd ever told her friend, Mhari now knew. It was a good job Katya didn't confide in Gaby half as much as Gaby spilled the beans to her.

"He's all yours, Mhari," she said, pointing at Zac, who was now letting himself into the house and too far away to hear them. "We met at the airport. He was flying to Glasgow. I was flying to Glasgow. When we landed, we discovered we were both heading to Lochalshie too."

The brisk march brought them to the end of the High Street and Jack's house, its lights a welcome sight. And it had taken Mhari out of the way of her own flat. Oh well, if she loved fresh air as much as she professed, she wouldn't mind. Few people could say that being nosey kept them so fit and healthy.

Katya raised her hand to knock on the door. Mhari showed no sign of leaving.

"What's he here for, then? And why is he in Kirsty's house? Has he bought it? Oh, I know! Is he the bad boy billionaire Kirsty went on about when she was trying to win Jack back? That car looks the part—the kind of nob vehicle a bad boy billionaire would own, driving it too fast doon the street to make all the lassies swoon."

Kirsty had dated Jack briefly before he had the good sense to dump her. And go out with Katya's best friend instead. At the time, Kirsty had tried to persuade Gaby to help her with a ten-step plan to 'hook a commitment-phobe', having mistaken commitment-phobia for active dislike on the part of the guy. Kirsty and her agent cooked up a book idea, Jack the case study and her methods tried out on him.

One of the dafter of the ten-plan steps—and they were all bonkers—was pretending a billionaire bad boy had fallen in love with Kirsty. She claimed it incited jealousy.

Given that Jack ended up with Gaby was proof that online dating gurus rarely delivered reliable advice. The book plan fell through.

"Goodnight Mhari," Katya said, making a mental note to share her words with Zac the next time she saw him. Just in case he thought his Audi TT boy racer tactics worked on women.

The door swung open, and Gaby beamed at her. "Katya! Mhari too! Do you want to come in and get to know each other better? And who were you talking about? I heard Kirsty's house has been sold? Is that true? I'm so glad you're here!"

———

Three days into her new Lochalshie life and she discovered Gaby was right. Mhari made a good flatmate. Katya hadn't expected that, but she was a vast improvement on the four others she'd lived with in Great Yarmouth. Once you got used to the non-stop questions, she liked the same shows on Netflix and spent the bulk of her time off in the pub, at other people's houses or visiting her ma and pa to get her washing done and a cooked dinner.

So far, Katya hadn't seen her that much. As the oldest of four sisters and then a flat sharer with three others, she wasn't used to the peace and quiet and revelled in the silence.

Nothing further had come from Edmund Morris & Co about the ghost-writing job, but her other clients kept her busy. Madeline seemed to have gotten over her dismay at

Katya's move and had already found her two clients based in the nearest big town, Oban.

"Caledonia Brewers," she messaged Katya, "loved that website copy you knocked up for them. Can you do more work for them over the next few weeks?"

She'd seen nothing more of Zac. Whatever setting up a food supply business involved, he did it invisibly. Villagers sidled up to her. Who was the new guy in Kirsty's house, and what was he doing in Lochalshie? She shook her head. It was Zac's job to tell the villagers his ambitious plans— especially anything that involved setting up a restaurant or pop-up business that might rival the Lochside Welcome. She suspected they wouldn't go down well.

And when Dexter called, voice dripping with exhaustion, she kept schtum. No need to tell him about the relocation yet. That could wait till they met up in person. She suspected he wouldn't like the Lochalshie thing one little bit.

Chapter Seven

"Hey! I'm back in Glasgow. Wanna come for the weekend in Glasgow I promised and celebrate Halloween?"

The phone call surprised her. Dexter had arrived back in the UK sooner than expected and was now suggesting they meet up in two days' time. Katya stared out of the living room where a bus had pulled up at the stop. She didn't have a car and rural transport made it more of a challenge to get to Glasgow than she'd imagined. Still. It was easier than coaching or training it from Norwich.

"What time are you able to get in to Glasgow?" he said, and when she replied 6 p.m. he asked if she could get there any earlier as it would be 'super fantastic' if they could spend even more time with each other. The sides of her mouth stretched into a wide smile. Take that, pessimism. He really wanted to see her. If she re-juggled her schedule for the next couple of days and worked her socks off, she could get the bus at lunchtime instead of a few hours later.

"And I've got something to tell you," she said, fingers

EMMA BAIRD

crossed again that telling him she'd moved to Lochalshie wouldn't send him screaming for the hills.

"Oh? Me too..."

"Good or bad?" she asked, noting the tiny hesitation before 'good'. Still, he ended the call telling her exactly how they'd spend most of the weekend and that wide smile returned.

A dirty weekend needed prep—and immediate action. She left the flat and popped into the pharmacy where Mhari worked. How the place made any money was another of Lochalshie's mysteries. Nothing on its shelves looked younger than five years old, and the villagers didn't supply it with that much pharmacy business. Mhari ran an operation on the side where she ordered up stocks of Avon Skin So Soft for its anti-midge properties, selling them at a 100 percent mark-up, but otherwise her days in there must drag.

Sure enough, when Katya stuck her head around the door, Mhari was glued to her phone. As well as non-stop WhatsApp updating, Mhari rated as one of the best players of Candy Crush in Scotland. Practice made perfect.

"Hiya, Katya!" she exclaimed, putting the phone down —a huge honour.

"I need your advice."

Mhari's face lit up. There was nothing she liked more than a spot of confiding. The wise woman did this at her peril, not unless she wanted it shared with all and sundry. Katya would rather not have asked Mhari anything personal but needs must. The woman knew everything and how to get anything at short notice.

When Dexter specified where and what his hands would do on Friday night, Katya decided to make the effort. For the Halloween Glasgow meet-up, she wanted a hair-free

52

body—the underarm shaving, full leg and bikini wax, eyebrow and top lip threading. So far, she hadn't spotted a beauty salon in the village.

She checked the street outside. It didn't look as if anyone was about to come into the pharmacy and interrupt an embarrassing conversation.

"I need to find a beautician. Where's the nearest place?" She could always pass it off as a manicure or a facial.

"Depends," Mhari said, holding out her own nails for Katya to admire. Mhari loved false nails, and hers were so long, they made a racket clacking over her phone screen. "There's a bit in Ardlui where ye can get the works, but Enisa, Jamal the shopkeeper's wife, does a wee bit of mobile beauty therapy on the side. She's awfy good at hair removal. Lot of Indian and Pakistani women like getting the lot whipped off, and I mean she's seen her fair share of fann—"

"Okay!" No need to dwell on the skill Mhari had at working out what a person really wanted when they asked about salon services.

"So, d'ye want Fancy Bodies in Ardlui or Enisa?"

"Enisa," Katya replied, and Mhari made a quick call— mostly ayes, no's, hair and nails.

The woman arrived at their flat that evening, armed with a foldable table, a double boiler and muslin strips.

"Aye, aye," she said, her accent a contrast to her appearance—full Hijab, and a veil that covered her hair though not her mouth. Over the top, she wore a white lab coat. At the door, she put down what she carried and eyed them both.

"You." She pointed at Katya. "You're the one needin' your body hair whipped aff, and the yin behind you wants me to dae her nails."

"Spot on!" Mhari said. "Enisa, meet Katya. She's awfy hairy and needs you to make her smooth as a baby's bum, so when her man edges his fingers up her——"

Katya whisked the woman in, cutting Mhari off. Enisa said she'd set her table and equipment up in the living room. She'd start with Katya and told Mhari to sit in her bedroom while she waited. Mhari tried to protest. Katya wouldn't have put it past her to take pictures of her undergoing bikini waxing and share them with the WhatsApp group, but when Enisa threatened to withdraw her mates' rates discount for Mhari's nails, she agreed to leave.

Alone, Enisa lowered her voice to a whisper—obviously aware Mhari had her ear pressed to the wall in the other room. "So, I've got a wee offer on at the moment—everything for fifty quid. Full leg and bikini wax, underarms, top lip and 'tache threading. D'ye fancy it?"

Katya nodded.

Enisa pulled out a pot, waving it in front of Katya's face. "I do anal bleaching too. Gives you a nice blonde bumh——"

"No, no! No need."

One eye-watering hour later, every hair follicle smarted in protest. Enisa stopped at points and asked, "Shall I just whip the hair off here too?" when she encountered stray hairs on toes and the like. Katya swallowed embarrassment and said "Yes, please". Her body felt oddly bare, as if the waxing had taken off several layers of skin too and she resembled those hideous pictures in medical journals that show musculature structure.

Mhari done—long pink plastic nails exchanged for jewel-encrusted purple talons—Enisa took their money and left, muttering about a job she needed to do for the local GP. Katya and Mhari changed into their pyjamas—an all-too easy habit they'd established only two days into living together—and searched for something to watch on Netflix when the doorbell sounded.

"Don't answer it," Katya said. She was make-up free for a start and rarely left the house without foundation, powder, blusher and eyeliner. Too late. Nine o'clock visitors presented too much of a temptation for Mhari. She was out of the living room before Katya had the chance to bolt to her bedroom and hide.

"Katya," Mhari's voice sing-song as she ran back up the stairs, "visitor for you!"

Zac, blonde hair much cleaner this time and blue eyes sparkly with mischief, stood at the door. Terrific. Who wanted visitors when you were make-up-free, bra-less and wearing an old pair of pink velour PJs? Zac's smirk told her the bra-less bit worked fine for him.

"I'm here to ask a favour."

Mhari made no move to leave, answering on Katya's behalf. "Aye, what is it?"

"This weekend," he said, "I've got guests coming, and I was looking for help entertaining them—someone to show them round the place?"

"That's a pity," Mhari piped up. "Katya's off tae Glasgow tae see that man o' hers. Just had her tush tidied up for it an' all."

"Mhari," Katya hissed. Any hope the tush reference went over Zac's head was dashed when his eyes dipped to her crotch almost automatically. But behind his smirk she sensed disappointment.

"Oh, that's a shame. Maybe next time."

"Who are your visitors?" Mhari asked. "Are they of the male variety? If you've got your posh boy mates coming, mebbe I could help. Mind, the fast car thing doesnae impress me. I dunno why men seem to think we lassies drop our knickers the instant someone revs their engine."

Zac stared at her, bamboozled. Katya's turn to smirk.

"Two women," he threw in hurriedly. "Katya's met them before, which was why I thought it would be nice for them to see a familiar face."

"Who?" she asked, astonished.

"Lois Manson and Angeline Berringer. You met them at the airport?"

So she had, and the weird coincidence struck her. How did they know Zac and why were they visiting him in Lochalshie? Her mind returned to their meeting. When she mentioned the village, they said they'd heard of it. They didn't mention, though, that they'd be visiting the place in the very near future.

"Why are they visiting you?" she asked Zac, watching his eyes duck away—perhaps too wary of Mhari and her nosiness. Oh well. A question for another time.

She saw him to the door.

"So," he said, dropping his voice. "Off to Glasgow for a dirty weekend?"

"Yes." No excuses, no explanations. She didn't owe him anything.

Zac tucked a lock of her hair behind her ear.

"You look beautiful without make-up. He's a lucky guy," he said, and with that he was off, leaving her to wonder why the prospect of not being there at the weekend was a teeny bit disappointing.

Chapter Eight

Katya added frothy underwear to the rucksack she packed on Friday morning. The kind that didn't cover all that much and allowed herself to imagine Dexter's hands sliding up and down the smooth skin she'd gone through agonies for. She dug out the smart trousers she'd borrowed from Gaby and put the velour pyjamas to one side. It was not a pyjama weekend. She planned to spend most of it wearing as little as possible.

"Have a lovely weekend, tiger!" Gaby's text message read. "You'd better come back knackered and bow-legged!"

When she got on the bus to Glasgow at lunchtime, Katya breathed a sigh of relief. Nothing had gone wrong so far—no phone calls, emails or text messages calling it off. Surely, surely her two-and-a-half days were bulletproof now? The next time she saw the loch, she'd be on the bus bringing her back on Monday afternoon, happy, content and with a great big grin on her face.

She arrived at Buchanan Bus Station in Glasgow several

57

bone-rattling hours later. Her back ached but the sight of all those buildings and people cheered her up. As a recent village convert, she was still adjusting to the quiet and stillness of the place. The bus station hummed with noise and activity as buses pulled in and out of stops and people got on and off.

She was making her way towards the taxi rank when her phone beeped. "Soz!" the message started, a word Katya loathed. "Emergency meeting re marketing strategy. Book yourself into the hotel and I'll be there soon as." He'd left an apologetic voicemail too, its wording the exact same words. What happened to "Get the earlier bus! It will be super fantastic if you get to Glasgow earlier"? She counted to ten and told herself this offered an opportunity to relax and refresh in comfortable surroundings.

Glasgow seemed busier than normal even though it was only mid-afternoon. The cab driver who took her to the hotel said the weekend closest to Halloween had replaced Hogmanay as the taxi industry's busiest night of the year. Already, people in fancy dress packed the streets—from elaborate costumes so professional they must have hired them, to the home-made. It seemed people still did that ghost thing with sheets, where they cut out eyes, drew on a mouth and threw it over themselves. Pubs and clubs advertised *Happy Halloween*, and the fancy-dressed smokers and vapers stood outside chatting to each other as they puffed out smoke or fruit-scented smells.

At the Radisson on Argyle Street, the receptionist shook her head when Katya said Dexter's name. She tried her own—he might have booked it under that—and got the same response.

"We don't have any rooms, I'm afraid," the woman, her hair neat and her nails and lipstick matched to the hotel's corporate colours, sighed regretfully. "Funny isn't it, how Halloween is now the busiest night of the year when it used to be New Year's Eve."

A by-now-familiar story, Katya phoned Dexter, her fore-finger stabbing at the phone's keyboard in irritation. Straight to voicemail. The words sang out, "Hey, this is Dexter! Gutted I can't talk but leave a message and I'll get back to you soon as." She wondered if it counted as a crime to stab someone for their answer phone message. She imagined herself in court—putting the phone on speaker mode and holding it up for the jury to allow them to listen themselves. They shook their heads in sympathy, and returned the verdict, 'not guilty'. She danced out of the Old Bailey a free woman.

Writers. They had trouble reining themselves in. She was just lucky that unlike her best friend, 95 percent of what happened in her head never made it beyond there.

"Do you know any places that might have a vacancy?"

The receptionist rolled her eyes. "Oof, you don't ask for much! Isn't it funny that Halloween is now the busiest—"

"Hilarious. Any places nearby you recommend I try?"

The receptionist whipped out her own mobile and put it on the counter so Katya could see the screen. She clicked on her 5 p.m. bookings app, and held the phone up, triumphant.

"You're in luck—the Rennie Mackintosh in Blythswood Square has its presidential suite free! And it's only ten minutes from here."

The hotel was in a small square on one of Glasgow's hills, its sides dotted with smart office buildings that all advertised law and/or accountancy firms situated within. Its rooms spread over four floors, and the presidential suite took up the whole of the top floor. The ground floor housed a bar stocked with craft beer and artisan gins, a gym and an in-house masseuse who promised her he'd iron out underlying tension in seconds and was available 24 hours...

The staff welcomed her with open arms. Well, they would. At £908 a night (VAT included) and a 50 percent non-refundable deposit required upfront; no wonder they greeted her like the return of the prodigal daughter. Would Modom like a glass of complementary champagne in her room? Yes, Modom jolly well would.

A porter who insisted on carrying her rucksack took her to the top floor. He was silent a second too long when she handed over a tip—five pounds was all she was able to afford—as if it was a note he had never seen before. Then the customer service instinct kicked in and he thanked her profusely if not sincerely.

Upstairs, the room's luxury soothed her rage. A huge four-poster bed draped in black and silver star-decorated curtains took up most of the space in the bedroom area. In the living room bit, a large sofa, two armchairs, a coffee table complete with an ice bucket, a bottle of champagne tilted at a jaunty angle and two crystal flutes, and a giant-sized plasma TV screen added to the opulence. The en-suite bathroom had a free-standing bathtub featuring copper taps and a power shower that would pummel you mercilessly. The toilet was one any normal person shrank to sit on, too scared their butt cheeks would leave a permanent stain.

Money bought all kinds of things. If Dexter didn't turn up in the next hour, she promised herself she'd book Mr Masseuse and if he asked, "Anything extra, Modom?", she'd explore that massage cliché in full. No point in wasting all that body waxing. And she would send the bill for all this straight to Blissful Beauty's office.

Grabbing the TV remote control, Katya flung herself on the suite's sofa. Seconds later, she padded her way across super-soft spongy carpet to the fridge. The golden rules of hotel stays included Never Help Yourself to Anything in the Mini Fridge, thanks to its extortionate pricing. She took out the 70 percent cocoa solids artisan truffles, the mini bottle of Prosecco, the tonic and the craft gin mini. The coffee table included a room service menu. Mindful that the receipt for tonight's visit was to wing its way straight to Blissful Beauty, she opened it and laid back on the sofa, crystal flute in hand. Yep, this was the kind of place where you could order lobster. On toast. She made that last bit up but decided to try it out.

"Hello? Can you mix me some lobster with home-made mayonnaise and put it on a lightly toasted bagel?"

The person at the other end of the line didn't baulk. "Certainly, Modom. Can you allow us half an hour or so?"

As she agreed thirty minutes was acceptable, her phone pinged. Dexter. "Ten mins! Promise!"

Exclamation marks did not make you any more forgivable. She poked her tongue out at the phone.

The bagel arrived at the same time as Dexter, the hotel having a better sense of time-keeping than he did. When the 'room service' cry at the door went, she opened it to find him holding a silver dome-covered platter and murmuring "Sorry, sorry" over and over. Tiredness added to Dexter's sex appeal. It painted black smudges under his eyes that made him look vulnerable and further hollowed out the planes under his cheekbones.

He took in the size and grandeur of the room without batting an eyelid and told her he'd pick up the tab—something Katya had already decided for him. Her card would be refunded in the next twenty-four hours, and he did not understand what happened to the original booking.

"When I checked with my PA, she swore she'd—"

"Your PA?" Katya cursed herself as her voice rose to a squeaky whine.

"Yeah?" he said, putting the plate on the table and offloading his rucksack on the bed. Unlike hers, his didn't look out of place in the room. No stranger to a five-star hotel, then. "You know I've got one?"

But not that you use her to sort out your personal life. Oh, what was the point explaining the distinction? Mr Workaholic wouldn't know what she meant. Or why it bugged her that he used someone else to book a hotel when she'd pictured him taking the time to phone the hotel himself. *"Hi there, can I book a room for Halloween? Yeah, I know... our favorite night of the year, and we can't wait to spend it together!"* She even allowed him the American spelling of the word in the scenario where he booked the Radisson himself. Because he thought it was that important. Hey ho.

She longed to reach out and touch his face, stroking comfort and muttering daft endearments that got him to close his eyes and sigh. But irritation and the time she'd waited for him to arrive had allowed fury to build. Did Dexter imagine he could waltz in late, flop on the bed, drink champagne and that was that?

Bored and restless after a long day travelling and having to move hotels, Katya wanted to dress up and go out. Perhaps they could rescue the night. A few drinks, some Michelin-starred food and hours spent rediscovering how the bits of him and her worked together.

"Shall we go out for a drink?" she said, aware they hadn't yet hugged or kissed. Pride held her back.

The 'yes' came after a pause; he wanted to flop on the

bed. But then, was it her fault he didn't say 'no' to that meeting? He worked for a make-up company. Short of news leaking that the company tested their products on bunny rabbits (and they didn't; Caitlin went on and on about their cruelty-free policies), or poisonous ingredients turning up in their skin creams, Katya doubted anything could be that important. She asked if either scenario had happened to double check, and he shook his head.

"I'll just get changed," she said. Gaby's black velvet trousers worked well with her pink silk jumper, and she dressed the outfit up with another layer of make-up and gold hoops. The presidential suite had one of those old-fashioned dressing tables, bow legs and an oval, ornate mirror. When she sat at it to apply make-up and brush out her hair, Dexter took the brush from her and pulled it through the strands at the back, his hands gliding gently through. Later sans clothing, he'd find out the hair on her head was the only stuff left. Their eyes met in the mirror; another person fast-forwarding. *Shouldn't we just…*

Say sorry, Katya, the nice bit of her argued, *for being such a grump. Say you're cross he was late, but now you have a whole two nights ahead of you and you will enjoy it. But first, you're going to remove that jumper and those trousers and jump on top of him.*

The words refused to budge from her head to her mouth.

He took her hand as they headed for the lift. "Where do you want to go?" The giveaway sign he was exhausted right there. Tonight, hyperbole was too much of an effort even for Dexter, the world's most enthusiastic person.

"I saw a bar down the road that looked cool. And they were advertising some kind of green monster cocktail."

The night had turned chilly, its coldness a stark contrast to the overheated hotel room. Beside her, Dexter shivered violently. A Texan, he still wasn't used to the Scottish weather; the damp windy autumn days were a particular challenge.

Geta's sat at the top of the hill, a basement bar with its entrance reached by stairs. The staff had strung white gauze cobwebs over and across the stair rails. By the time they reached the door, the stuff clung to their clothes. Lord knows how she would remove it from black velvet trousers. Still, it made Dexter laugh and gave what they wore a Halloween air. He squeezed her hand. The night began to look up.

The smokers gathered at the tables outside, with ghoulish faces, fake fangs and face paint. Inside, a DJ played whatever she guessed suited the night. It sounded as if the entire Rocky Horror Picture Show soundtrack would boom out at some point. The noise drowned out any chat, but now they were here, Katya couldn't suggest leaving. It had been her idea and her suggestion. Perhaps the green drinks would make it all worthwhile.

"What's in them?" she yelled at the barman dressed in a skeleton costume. Better than his poor colleague in a Hermione Granger school uniform. He had to shout in her ear to be heard. "Peach schnapps, Midori and Baileys!" he said, leaving her none the wiser. She and Dexter held the glasses and gulped them too quickly, the awkward silence far more deafening than the music.

Katya cursed herself. Why hadn't she found them some-where more suited to quiet conversation—a tucked-away booth in a quiet dark venue where she would say, "Dexter, guess what? I've moved to Lochalshie, so we'll be able to do this much more often."

In that scenario, his eyes lit up, and he grabbed her

hand across the table. "Amazing! I'll be able to get up there to see you too. We're gonna have such fun!"

Two cocktails later and she started to feel queasy. Those drinks had to be much stronger than they seemed. She tilted her head, alarmed at the way the floor rose to meet her.

"Letsh... Let's get shumething to eat." Oh dear. Katya's rules for relationships included never drinking too much in front of a guy. She hated the loss of control. This called for a large helping of something starchy and stodgy, and no more cocktails. Dexter said 'yes' quickly, marching them out of the place in double quick time. Outside, the fresh hair slammed into her, but the stairs proved tricky, the spindly heels an unwise choice.

"We could go back to the hotel," Dexter suggested. "The deal includes dinner, bed and breakfast."

What a relief.

The dining room on the ground floor screamed opulence. Dark red and gold embossed wallpaper was complemented by a carpet and well-upholstered chairs in similar shades. The waiters glided between tables, discreetly topping up wines and delivering plates of food as if they were competing with each other to do it as silently as possible. Music drifted through from the lobby where a man in a tuxedo played the grand piano.

The maître d' took the room number and ushered them towards a table in the middle. He pulled the chair out for Katya, and she sank into it with too much of a thump, her movements making the cutlery and glassware on the table rattle. The other diners raised heads and eyes in disapproval.

"Bread?" the maître d' barked, and she nodded vigorously. Her stomach churned alarmingly. Those two bites of lobster mayo bagel had done nothing to fill her stomach, and the thought of seafood made its contents swish and gurgle.

"Are you okay, Katya?" Dexter asked. His words... such pretty words, and that lovely liquid chocolate sense of them... Liquid chocolate—a lake of the brown stuff and the overwhelming vanilla scent of it.

Oh heck, no. No.

Her mouth flooded with saliva, the all-too ghastly tell-tale sign one glass of champagne, two mouthfuls of lobster bagel, four truffles and two dubious green drinks were about to make their way back up her gastrointestinal tract.

Dexter must have guessed it too. He leapt to his feet, grabbed the empty ice bucket on the table next to theirs, and handed it to her. Just in time too. The spasms started and up it all came, a virulent green half-chewed mess. To her relief, she managed to get all of it in the bucket.

Friday evening at the Rennie Mackintosh took on a different slant. Here, people paid good money not to bear witness to the stereotypical Glaswegian night out. Most of the other diners looked at them in horror. Three of them got to their feet and stormed out. The maître d' and two waiters hurried forward, their pinched faces radiating disapproval. No, this was not the kind of place where diners drank too much and threw up.

The queasiness returned—the bucket no longer in easy reach. Too late. Up came yet more green stuff, this time most of it covering the maître d's shoes.

If Katya could have listed the top three things to do in public that gave her nightmares, being sick was up there, way ahead of comedy slips on the ground. It topped finding yourself naked in a busy park. At least then you could hide behind a tree. Even Gaby, her daffy best friend, had never done this. If she weren't so ill and white, her face and neck would have taken on 50 Shades of Scarlet.

"Seafood poisoning," Dexter told the maître d', his expression daring the man to disagree. The £908 a night price tag must have allowed for a spot of carpet cleaning. "I'll take my girlfriend to our room. Send up some ice water for us."

She hadn't the strength to object when he took her hand and gently pulled her to her feet, half-carrying, half-dragging her out into the hallway and to the lifts. In the room, he lowered her onto the bed. The movement made her feel sick once more and she only just made it to the loo in time. When she emerged, pale and shaky, Dexter handed her a glass of water.

"Dexter, I…"

"Shush. Lie down. Another couple of hours and you'll feel much better."

He was right. She drifted off, awaking at 2 a.m., the full horror of what had taken place the night before hitting her afresh. The lights in the bedroom were off, but she could see the TV on in the living room through the arched doorway.

"Mid-November? That's earlier than we discussed." Dexter's voice was only just audible above the TV.

A minute's silence, though she heard squawking at the other end.

"Yeah, I know. It is mega important and there is tons of work to do. I assure you; I am one hundred percent committed to this project."

More sentences at the other end.

"No, it won't take me long to pack up. I travel super-light. Is the London flat available?"

"Better make it a twelve-month lease, not six. Yeah, amazing. I can't wait to get started. Goodbye."

Who wanted a grumpy girlfriend you took out for dinner and who then disgraced you by throwing up in public? Not Dexter, by the sound of things. He'd gone on and on about the launch of Blissful Beauty in South Korea and its 'all hands on deck' urgency. Sounded as if he wanted to start afresh by moving to London, just when she'd moved to Lochalshie to be closer to him.

What the heck?

Chapter Nine

Katya got out the bed, the noise making Dexter turn. His face fell.

"Excuse me." Yet another visit to the bathroom to throw up. The face that greeted her in the mirror wasn't one she recognised, eyes too dark in a white face, tiny spots of red on her cheeks and hair limp, clinging to her skull. The bathtub sang to her—lock the door, fill me up with warm bubbles, sink in and don't come out for hours.

"Seafood poisoning for sure," Dexter said when she emerged, mouth rinsed out with half a bottle of mouthwash. "That lobster bagel wasn't super fresh." He'd moved from the living room to the bed and patted it. When she got in beside him, she was hit by a bout of violent shivering. He pulled her close.

"I had it years ago. Oysters in a restaurant in Maine. It goes through your system faster than a speeding bullet. It makes you feel like hell for twelve hours, but you recover miraculously quickly. That's if it doesn't kill you."

Almost dry. Almost British irony. And yet, he was willing

to give her a ready-made excuse for shame. No, Katya's keenness to pour champagne and Green Monster down her neck wasn't to blame for the all-too-public vomit shaming episode. Instead, A Lobster Did It. She didn't buy it. The lobster mayo bagel tasted fine when she ate it.

"Dex," she said, and the word stretched out sitting in the space between them. It was what a person said as a gentle preface to the more important. A question, say... *do you love me?* Or, as it was about to be: "What were you talking about just there?"

She could spot dissembling a mile away—the guy working out what he thought she knew, trying to figure out an excuse that got him out of whatever. The final arrival at the answer: *I need to tell some version of the truth.*

"Yeah? The stuff about London?"

Katya nodded, the effort compounding an already brutal headache. "Sounds like you're moving there soon." Once upon a time, her first-generation Polish grandfather talked to her about what it was like living in a country where you spoke your second language. "Katya, I am always straight. What I say, I mean. But the bloody English —they edge their way around words all the time. And none of them understand grammar. I find myself explaining to them how their language should work all the time, and they maul it anyway."

Twice as true for Americans?

"So... this launch I've been talking about? The 'Blissful Beauty hits South Korea' thing? That market is worth—"

"$13 billion," she cut in. "You said."

"So super crucial to the company's plans for expansion. The vloggers and beauty journalists over there are hugely influential. Anything they rave about will have knock-on effects on the US and UK markets too. And Glasgow's just too…"

"Far away," she finished for him. "Makes no sense to have your company HQ here."

"And I need to be nearer Heathrow too," he said, "so I can fly to LA at the drop of a hat."

"Shouldn't that be Seoul?"

"Not in the early stages. We've got to put the research together and plan a long-term strategy. It's not definite yet. I need to get there asap, there's so much work to do. And the thing is…"

This was the bit where he dumped her, wasn't it? She didn't blame him. Who wanted a grumpy woman who wasn't able to handle her drink or didn't know how to behave in public?

Whatever he was about to say, he got no further. There was a discreet tap on the door and a voice called out, "Ms Bukowski?"

She struggled to get up. "Stay there," Dexter said, jumping out of bed. He wore a tee shirt and boxers, more respectable-looking than Katya in last night's obviously slept-in clothes.

The door was far enough away for her not to hear the whole conversation though she made out the words 'profound apologies'.

Dexter shut the door and got back into bed, resting his hand lightly on her head. "They've just 'fessed up to seafood poisoning. A few people had the lobster last night and there have been vociferous complaints. They've offered us another night, free of charge. Damage limitation, I guess, and so we don't write super-rude reviews on TripAdvisor and Yelp."

"I don't want to stay another night." Luxury meant

nothing when your head ached, your stomach rattled with emptiness and your mood refused to lift off the floor.

A sigh, so soft she couldn't be sure.

"What was the thing, then? What were you about to say before?"

The hand didn't let up stroking her head, fingers applying gentle pressure. As this was Dexter, doubtless he'd done an Indian head massage course at some point, and this was what he did now—touching the bits where he knew tension gathered.

"I need to move to London next week," he said. "And then I'll be back to LA for a coupla months, probably longer. Kinda crucial if I want to be part of the South Korean launch, and I do. I want that global marketing manager job before I hit thirty-five."

"Six years, then," she said, squeezing her eyes shut. If she cried now, she'd never forgive herself. None of that little speech included her. Nope, it was all about Dexter, and Dexter's wants. *And he doesn't want me.* Even though the words stayed in her head, she hated herself for how feeble she sounded.

"We could—"

This was the bit where he suggested a long or longer distance relationship—her travelling to London once more on the rare occasions he made it back from LA, Skype calls and telephone sex. She'd witnessed such relationships at university, where girls and guys who'd moved greater distances than she did in the pursuit of higher education tried their best to stay in touch with childhood sweethearts. It almost always ended in tears.

"No."

The stroking stilled, and he curled that tall, lanky body around hers. His hands moved to her breasts, but it didn't seem like a come-on. More a man saying a fond farewell to old friends. The tiny kiss that landed on the back of her neck suggested the same thing—finality. And despite it all, the tumbling emotions and the lingering queasiness, exhaustion overwhelmed her once more, and she fell asleep.

Sunlight streamed in the window, waking her again. It was one of those rare Scottish autumn days where frost touched the trees and grass and the skies were clear. As she moved, Dexter stirred behind her.

"Do you feel better?" he asked.

"Much." If you discounted the achy-breaky heart bit. "I'll take a shower."

Dexter often joined Katya in the shower—soap, hot water and an enclosed space offered tons of fun. The shower in the en suite was made for sharing too. If you straightened your arms out from the shoulders, you wouldn't hit anything if you turned 360 degrees. And it was jammed with expensive shower gels, shampoos and lotions that cost more than she earned for a day's copywriting. But as she got to her feet, legs still wobbly, Dexter stayed where he was.

The hot water ran over her hair and strengthened her resolution. *Keep it light. Keep it cool and make this easy.* She wrapped herself in a fluffy white towel and admired the colour the hot water had put back in her face. Now that her eyes were no longer bloodshot, the face in the mirror was recognisable once more and the grin, while manic, at least didn't make her look sad. She'd taken her clothes into the bathroom with her, so the Katya who unlocked the door thirty minutes was immaculate—hair blow-dried, foundation, blusher, waterproof mascara and lip-gloss in place.

Dexter had dressed too.

"Do you want breakfast?" he said. "I mean, I gotta——"

"No. I'm still too queasy to risk it." Not true, but why prolong the agony? She'd spotted a Pret at the bus station. They did vegan wraps and flapjacks. Stuff the cost.

As they checked out downstairs, the general manager came out to apologise once more, promising a full-scale investigation would take place. They were welcome to book their free night anytime in the next six months. It stung. She never wanted to see the inside of the Rennie Mackintosh hotel ever again, but knowing she'd never share another hotel night with Dexter made her eyes water once more.

In the street, he hailed her a black cab and then grabbed her, pulling her tightly to him. "Good luck in London," she said, standing on her tiptoes and kissing him lightly on the lips. They parted beneath hers, an almost automatic reaction—two mouths that knew the power of the perfect kiss and itched to do it in spite of hurt, anger and despair.

She broke away.

"Goodbye, Dexter. I hope the launch goes well and you get that promotion."

And then she got in the taxi, ordering the driver to take her to Buchanan Bus Station, the black tears running down her cheeks proof that Blissful Beauty lied on the packaging for its waterproof mascara.

She didn't look back.

Chapter Ten

"You're back early!" Gaby exclaimed.

So much for keeping her early return to Lochalshie under the radar. Mhari, who would have wheedled the story out of her, had gone back to her parents for the weekend, leaving the flat empty. When the bus had dropped Katya off on Saturday afternoon, bone-rattled once more, she'd managed to get back to the flat unnoticed. Even a talk with Gaby was out of the question—her happiness too stark a contrast to how Katya felt.

By the time Sunday morning came round, she needed fresh air and exercise. She let herself out of the flat and walked to the far side of the loch where she'd be too far away to bump into any of the villagers. It was a cold, blustery day, and the low winter sun didn't rise above Maggie Broon's Boobs, the locals' affectionate nickname for the two hills on the far side of the loch. Cheeky climbers added stones to the cairns on top of them every year, heightening the illusion.

And breathe... In one, two, three and out for six counts. If you concentrated hard enough on it, deep breathing banished thoughts. In theory.

She headed back, giving the dog walkers and strollers a wide berth. No one raised their hand to wave and the High Street didn't have its usual complement of people standing in small groups chatting. It was safe to risk popping into the general store for bread.

"I thought you were supposed to be away until Monday morning?"

Foiled. Jamal's general store was easy to hide in thanks to its narrow, jam-packed aisles. At least until you went to pay for your shopping. Gaby had come in, needing to buy Mena (the world's most spoiled cat) yet more smoked salmon.

Mena, Katya reflected to herself, had a diet far better than most humans.

Jamal, in his usual position of leaning over the counter, raised his head. He too dealt in the village's most valuable currency—gossip. Katya shook her head imperceptibly and Gaby nodded, knowing she needed to wait until they got outside. Goods paid for, they headed back outside.

"Monday morning was the plan," Katya said, "but it turns out a beauty launch makes you so busy you have no time for anything. Or anyone."

Gaby put down her shopping bag and threw her arms around her. "I can't believe that stupid workaholic can't see that you're the best thing that ever happened to him. When are you seeing him again?"

Ah. "I'm not," she said, congratulating herself when her voice didn't crack "I don't want to, Gaby. He's moving to London and will be in LA for the foreseeable future. A relationship won't work."

Gaby stepped back, holding onto Katya's arms so she

could look at her properly. "What an idiot he is. I can have him killed. That dodgy friend of Jack's, Lachlan Forrester? He could do it in return for some free website copy where you write euphemisms about the services he offers—*I'm in the business of tidying up the world's gene pool* and *Need your licence plates changed in a hurry* kind of thing?"

For a nano-second, Katya wanted to say yes. *Please, Lachlan, take your sharpest knife to Glasgow and kill him slowly and painfully and then perhaps Dexter will know how this feels.*

For a nanosecond.

But Gaby's terrible joke did its work. Once more, Katya managed not to blub or wail about how much she'd liked him and how she'd thought that this time, this time she'd found a keeper.

"Tell you what," Gaby said. "We're doing Sunday lunch. Jack's mum is popping over. You could get her to read your horoscope."

Jack's mum was the village's GP. She doubled up as a psychic stroke fraud, freely admitting to Gaby that she used a combination of social media accounts, body language, universal questions and vague recommendations to make herself sound authentic.

Unbeknown to Gaby, Katya worked for her. Psychic Josie's website got tons of traffic—90 percent of it people desperate to find out if their partner was The One or if their late grandmother forgave them for being a rubbish grandchild during her life. Psychic Josie sent Katya bullet points for articles, and Katya wrote them up. Clients who paid well and on time, Katya told herself, had the right to ask her to write whatever they wanted. But taking the woman's advice?

"Yeah, maybe not," Gaby said. She only trusted her

almost-mother-in-law's medical advice and even then, that came with a side helping of dire warnings.

"But please come," Gaby added. "Jack's a fab cook. He can rustle you up something plant-based."

Katya's stomach let out an almighty rumble, making them both giggle. She had eaten little since the disastrous lobster bagel incident.

"Well, that's settled," Gaby said. "Go home, get tarted up and we'll see you in an hour?"

———————

Gaby might have ordered Katya to tart herself up, but she hadn't bothered herself. When she opened the door to Katya, she wore sweatpants that should have gone to the great clothing wardrobe in the sky years ago, no make-up and her hair in a messy ponytail.

Taking it in, Katya marvelled at it. She longed to get to that stage with a guy—the bliss of being able to slob out in front of someone in your never-seen-outside-the-house clothes and make-up free. Especially if the guy still gazed at you adoringly, as Jack did Gaby. He teased her a lot, but Katya put that down to the way Scots men showed affection.

Waving a 'hello' to Katya, he left them to their girl chat and retreated to the kitchen. As a tour guide who spent his summers ferrying people around the Highlands in a mini-bus, he relaxed in the winter by cooking and painting. The oil landscapes that decorated the walls of the living room and hallway were all his. At one time, a painting of his ex-girlfriend, Kirsty, hung in the hallway. Not anymore. Gaby must have persuaded him to sell it or store it in the loft.

In deference to their soft southerner status, Jack had whacked the central heating up and lit the wood-burning stove in the living room.

He stuck his head around the kitchen door as Katya and Gaby settled on the sofa. "Mushroom and pearl barley risotto okay for you?" he asked Katya. "I've got some nutritional yeast to sprinkle on the top that can do instead of Parmesan."

Sometimes, Katya's treacherous mind put Jack on her dos and don'ts for a boyfriend list. His dos outnumbered anyone else's.

The front door opened, and Gaby rolled her eyes. "My almost-mother-in-law," she whispered. "She's got her own key. I think I might try to persuade Jack that's not a good idea. Can you imagine?"

She sniggered, stopping when she saw Katya's face. Too much of a reminder of Katya's own single status. It would be a long time until anyone burst in on her in a compromising position.

"Sorry," she said, and got up to say hello to the doctor and her husband, Ranald—a farmer who nodded briefly at them before going into the kitchen to speak to Jack.

The doctor bustled in, armed with plastic bags, clinking bottles and a cake tin. She didn't look much like her startlingly good-looking son, but they shared the same face shape and eyes, and those eyes picked Katya out straight away.

"Katya, have ye registered with my GP practice yet? And bare feet!" she said, putting her bags down so she could put her hands on her hips. "D'ye know the risks of going around unshod? You might step on glass, cut a tendon and then end up—"

Gaby leapt to her feet and laid a hand on the doctor's arm. "Don't worry, I'll give Katya a pair of my thick socks. Jack asked if you would mind helping him when you arrived? He's in the kitchen with Ranald."

Blatant tactics carried out, Gaby grinned at Katya, who smirked back. The good doctor needed careful managing.

"You don't still call her Doctor McLatchie, do you?" Katya asked. It seemed too formal.

"I don't call her anything," Gaby said. "She told me to call her Ca-Ca-Caroline—see? It's too much of a struggle to say it, so I try to address her directly to solve the issue. Anyway, enough about me. I wanted to ask you about Zac, the new guy. He gave you a lift here when you first arrived, didn't he? What did you think of him?"

She dropped back down on the couch, accidentally sitting on Mena's tail. The cat yowled in protest and stalked off to the kitchen to mooch for food. Today's vegan option was bound to disappoint.

"Loves himself," Katya said, "and a total flirt."

"Oh," Gaby said, her voice crestfallen. "We met him the other day in the general store. I thought he was nice. Fit, as well. I thought you loved blonde hair and blue eyes on a guy?"

"I do," Katya said, "but my don'ts list includes guys with an over-inflated opinion of themselves."

Gaby twisted toward her. "That blasted list of yours! He asked us lots of questions—wanting to know all about the villagers and the Lochside Welcome. And how long you and I have been friends. He didn't seem big-headed to me. You're too fussy."

"But better fussy than not, right, Gaby?" Katya flung back at her. "I mean, Ryan for heaven's sake…"

Gaby pouted and then began to giggle. She dropped her voice, mindful of their other guests. "I never told you this at the time..." Katya raised her eyebrows. Gaby believed in a no-holds-barred best friendship.

"... but he used to call it Little Ryan."

"OMG! I can't believe you held back on telling me that until now. How on earth did you keep a straight face?! Promise me you never, never called yours Little Gaby, or Gaby's flower or, or, or..."

The resulting hysterics made Jack poke his head around the door in alarm, worrying that his beloved or her best friend was fitting. The story cheered Katya up. Yes, she might have moved to the ends of the earth but at least she had Gaby and the regular contact they were used to.

Mena returned from the kitchen, slinking her way across the floor and leaping onto Katya's lap. Once Kirsty's cat—and the reason Gaby moved to Lochalshie—Gaby now spoilt her far more than Kirsty ever did. Gaby, the one-time cat hater too.

Katya tickled the little thing under her chin, and she purred, while Gaby made cooing noises and told Mena she was a very clever girl.

The doorbell sounded once more, and Gaby jumped up to answer it.

"Are ye sure? I dinnae want to intrude."

'I dinnae want to intrude' was the least truthful statement out there. Gaby gave Katya a rueful smile when she returned, the visitor in tow. Red-cheeked from the cold and wind and wrapped in a fake-fur-lined parka, scarf and hat leaving only the top of her face visible, Mhari peeled off her outer layers and plonked herself down on the armchair opposite the sofa—faking surprise at Katya's presence.

Katya knew she knew of her return. And here she was, ready to ask a hundred questions.

"So, a nice wee Sunday roast, then?" Mhari said. "Has Jack made Yorkshire puddings too?"

Gaby's mouth twitched. "Hundreds of them. Roast potatoes by the dozen and tons of gravy too."

From the kitchen, they heard a snort of laughter and the back door opening. "Thanks, mate. Are they the shiitake ones? They'll be perfect," Jack said to someone, and the doctor began a lecture on the perils of eating raw veg. When she returned to the living room bearing a bottle of wine and glasses, Katya suspected Jack had just booted her out.

The doctor poured wine into the glasses and sat down on the other armchair. Katya shook her head when offered, Friday's mortification too recent.

"I'm thinking of joining Tinder," Mhari said, startling all of them. After extensive debate on the subject, Katya and Gaby had decided Mhari was asexual, finding others' love lives far too interesting to bother getting one of her own.

"Do you remember that guy you met on Tinder?" Gaby asked Katya, starting to laugh once more.

"Oh aye?" the doctor piped up. "Were ye not always worried that these fellas would hae some nasty wee rash—"

"No, no. Tinder is safe enough," Gaby threw in. She'd told Katya the doctor tended to fixate on other people's genitals.

"Which one?" Katya asked, causing the doctor to round her mouth in astonishment. Surely it didn't shock her someone might try Tinder more than once?

"There was the one that Katya turned up to meet at Norwich train station, but when she got there, it was obvious he'd not used his own picture on the site, so she about-turned when she saw him waiting outside WH Smith's.

"Then, there was the bloke you met in that restaurant who was so boring you fled to the loos and escaped out the window in there. Or that guy you shared a coffee with. You went to pay and when you came back, you caught him on Tinder trying to line up his next date!"

Ah. Gaby hadn't remembered that one correctly. The person caught on their phone seeing who else was available had been Katya.

"And then there was that agency waiter, remember?" Gaby continued. "He kept smuggling you into events where he was working so you could—"

"Okay, okay," Katya cut in. The latter story did her no favours. Nor did the few Gaby had already shared. They made her sound either fickle or a bad judge of character. When Gaby—thank the stars—finished with Ryan just before moving to Lochalshie, Katya had jumped for joy. Almost ten years of struggling to keep her mouth shut about the man's many failings took their toll.

"Promise me," she'd said to Gaby then, "I vet every boyfriend of yours from now on to make sure you date no more duds." Did Katya need the same service? Her past record and perhaps even the present showed that might be right.

"And what about Mr Tory?" Gaby was still banging on about Katya's past love life. "Katya once dated this guy for two weeks. Fell head over heels in lust with him, then discovered he was a member of the Young Conservatives, and he kept going on about foreigners taking over England without putting two and two together about Katya's name —her being second-generation Polish."

The door to the living room opened once more.

"Duh," Zac said, that broad grin of his taking up too much space on his face. "And how delightful you're part Polish too. I love people with interesting backgrounds."

Katya swore to herself, wondering how much of that conversation about her less-than-glorious past Zac overheard. He was as ruddy-cheeked as Mhari had been earlier, the redness emphasising those clear blue eyes. The back door opening must have been him. "Never judge a book by its cover, right?" he added.

Thank heavens for Blissful Beauty's colour corrective moisturiser especially formulated to tackle redness. The heat in her cheeks might burn but it would not show.

"What are you doing here?" she asked. "And I hope you've made plenty of food, Jack? You appear to be feeding five thousand today."

Gaby shifted in her seat. She and Jack hadn't been discreet enough for Katya to miss the look they exchanged. A set-up. No wonder Gaby was so keen to know what Katya thought of Zac.

"A kind invite," Zac said, "to a lonely bachelor and the newcomer to the village."

Gaby clapped her hands. "Let's eat," and she and Jack moved the seats as far back as possible so they could set up an extendable dining table. It took up almost all the space in the room. Zac positioned himself opposite Katya. The lack of space meant their knees touched. He raised his glass and an eyebrow.

Jack placed a huge casserole dish in the middle of the table and Mhari leant forward, murmuring excitedly about roast potatoes and gravy.

"Mushroom and pearl barley risotto," Jack said as he

took the lid off, straight-faced. "It's a vegan dish to suit Katya."

The way Mhari's face fell, eyes crinkling and nose screwing up, made everyone laugh.

Ranald, the doctor's husband and a farmer, muttered something about how pearl barley should only be used for whisky or cattle feed and never, ever eaten. Like Mhari, he looked like he'd just changed his mind about lunch.

"All that fibre's awfy good for you," Dr McLatchie said, scooping up ladlesful of the risotto from the large casserole dish into bowls and passing them around. "But ye can hae some wine to help wash it doon."

Mhari took her first forkful, wrinkling her face. Her expression changed the moment she put it in her mouth, eyes rounding in wonder.

"That's all right," she said. "Mebbe I might go vegan."

A pause.

"Bacon," Jack said, holding one hand up and using his fingers to tick off items. "Sausage rolls, cheesy chips, Ashley's meat-feast pizza, Dairy Milk."

Katya had yet to see her flatmate eat anything green. Her daily diet favoured foods with a shelf-life of a year and more.

"Aye, right enough. But I dinnae like mushrooms most o' the time. These are quite nice."

"I got them from Zac," Jack said.

Katya held up a mushroom on her fork.

"Are you growing them yourself?"

"No, I got them from a local grower who supplies top-end restaurants in Edinburgh and Glasgow."

"How's setting up the new business going?" Dr McLatchie asked, topping up his wine. "You're doing some food thingy? What is it exactly?"

"Connecting customers with fantastic local food suppliers—an online business mostly," Zac said, digging into the risotto and telling Jack the dish showed off the mushrooms superbly. He didn't look at Katya so she couldn't call him out on that bit of fudging of the truth. What about the scoping out the area for restaurant possibilities bit?

A hand squeezed her thigh under the table. Gratitude for keeping her mouth shut? She jerked her leg away.

Risotto and plates cleared away, Jack brought in a cheese board overflowing with farmhouse cheddars, an oozy local Brie and a mound of creamy, speckled blue cheese.

"Another present from Zac," he said, placing the plate down with a flourish. "All from local dairies, organic and made from unpasteurised milk."

"Unpasteurised milk!" About to reach for a plate and the cheese knife, Dr McLatchie whipped her hand back. "Are ye out of your mind? Salmonella, E. coli, listeria, campylobacter—d'ye want to spend tomorrow bent over the toilet bowl, or sitting on it, your guts—"

"Parmesan," Zac said, picking up the packet on the table Jack had left out for those who skipped the full-vegan mushroom risotto experience. Dr McLatchie had grated herself a mound of it to top hers.

He flipped the packet over where the ingredient list clearly stated, 'made from unpasteurised milk'.

"Aye, well—dinnae say you have nae been warned."

Along with chocolate, cheese was Katya's vegan nemesis, and the sharp-sour creamy tang of the blue cheese tickled her nose. But why give Mr Know-it-all the satisfaction?

The internal struggle must have shown on her face. "Want some, Katya?" Zac asked, telling her to suit herself when she said no. He cut large slices of cheese for Gaby,

Jack and Mhari who all tucked in. More wine appeared on the table, and Zac filled her glass up. She gave in and crossed her fingers it wouldn't upset her still-fragile stomach. Or disconnect her mouth from her brain.

Jack disappeared into the kitchen and re-emerged bearing a plate of shortbread. "I made it especially for you," he said, placing it in front of her. "With olive oil margarine instead of butter. See what you think."

Katya took a mouthful of buttery sweetness and smiled at him. "I think you ought to enter the Great British Bake Off. This is fabulous."

The doctor, also avoiding the cheese, took a slice and bit into it. "Aye, no' bad son. But no' a patch on Ranald's."

The farmer, who seemed to be the least likely baker in the world, blushed and said Jack was the better shortbread maker these days, and the two of them exchanged complicit smiles.

"All I need now," Zac said, helping himself to another enormous slice of cheese and putting it on an oatcake, "is someone who can write sublime copy for my website. Does anyone know any writers who can help me?"

Katya glared at Gaby, guessing it had been her less-than-subtle idea to invite him.

"Goodie!" Gaby said, ignoring Katya's 'keep your mouth shut' vibes. "My friend is the best writer in the world —the best friend too. You can't go wrong with Katya. Hey, that could be your slogan, Kit-Kat!"

Anything more than one glass of alcohol turned Gaby into a gibbering wreck, overwhelmingly sentimental and deciding she was the wit of the century.

"Do you fancy the job?" Zac asked.

He lingered on the word 'fancy', flirting once more. "We'd need to spend plenty of time together, so you could get a feel for what I do and the food I'm producing. I'd make you sample everything, feeding you every delectable morsel so you tasted me, I mean the food, yourself."

Katya kicked him under the table and mouthed 'see?' at Gaby. She'd said full-on flirts weren't her thing. Jack's barely suppressed snort told her he got the taste reference.

"I'm plant-based, remember?" she said. "Remember? It rules out venison burgers and langoustines. Some people argue oysters don't count because they don't have a central nervous system or brain, so they don't feel pain. But I wouldn't, anyway. It's like eating snot."

"Aye," Mhari joined in. "They give me the dry boak."

"Not the way I do them," he said. "Oysters fried, paired with a spicy mayonnaise and stuffed into brioche rolls. Plus, they're packed with zinc—vital for your immune system. And a healthy sex drive."

"That's true!" the doctor chipped in.

That old cliché, hmm?

"Who's for pudding? Or coffee?" Jack said, getting to his feet. Katya took that as her cue, pushing the glass she'd only taken two mouthfuls from across the table to Ranald, who accepted it gratefully.

"I've got something to finish for a client," she said. "Thanks for the food."

There were protests, Gaby's the loudest, but the set-up made Katya uncomfortable.

She was half-way back to the flat when she heard someone call her name.

"Hey! Wait up. You're one fast walker."

Zac, his cheeks ruddy once more and panting, came to a halt beside her.

"Um… do you want a drink? A coffee? Back at my house?"

Not half as cocky now. Perhaps he expected women to drop at his feet and hadn't worked out how to behave when they didn't.

"No thanks. I've got work to get on with." True—an email from Madeline had come in, suggesting two other potential clients in Scotland she could approach.

She kept on walking, Zac panting at her side.

"How are you finding it here?" he said, pointing at the streets and houses around him. "The silence at night—it's hard to get used to."

There were at her flat. She held the key in her hand, pointing it at him like a weapon. Come no further. Still, they were two outsiders attempting to establish footholds in a new place—the attempt made trickier because of the close-knit community nature of Lochalshie.

"The two-a-day buses that count for public transport."

"I can give you a lift anywhere any time you want," he said. "And I'll drive carefully." He must have caught her shudder; the memory of the time he'd driven her up here.

"I like you much better when you don't flirt." Oh—the said-out-loud sentence surprised her. Too impulsive to be the norm for Katya.

He beamed at her. "Do you?"

"Not in that way. I'm seeing someone, remember?" The lie was easy enough.

"No, you're not," he laid a hand on her arm, the one holding the gun-point key. They both looked at it as if trying to guess whether Katya might stab him with it. "Gaby told me. He's an idiot."

Curses on Gaby.

"Good for her. I've got to go."

Katya opened the door. As it closed behind her, he

called out, "But is it okay if we meet up to discuss you doing some writing for me?"

He could wait. Besides, she'd Googled him after they'd first met. It took a bit of digging but she found information he hadn't volunteered so far. So much as Gaby meant well shoving the two of them together and however persistent Zac proved, it would not work.

Chapter Eleven

As Dr McLatchie had crow-barred the importance of registering with a GP into the previous day's conversation four times, Katya had taken the hint. On Monday morning, she made her way to the surgery, arriving in time for its opening.

Which was more than could be said for the good doctor, whose car squealed to a halt outside fifteen minutes later. By which point, Katya was soaked through. The rain had started up in earnest yesterday evening and was yet to let up.

"Aye, sorry about that, Katya. I had tae help Ranald. His flamin' sheep escaped from the top field. Thanks for that last article ye wrote for the website, by the way. I've got bookings for telephone consultations right up until Christmas. Come on in."

The doctor's office didn't resemble a typical GP's room. She favoured a softly-softly approach; all the better for folks to confide their inner-most health secrets. A low-slung coffee table and squishy armchairs took up most of the space. In the corner, a small computer sat on a desk and the room's large windows allowed in plenty of light. Even though that didn't count for much at this time of year.

Checks carried out—lies told on the registration form, *I hardly drink, and I've never smoked*—the conversation took an unexpected turn.

"Ye're awfy fit, aren't ye?" the doctor said, tipping her head to one side and surveying Katya. "When I listened to your heart, I could tell as it's slow and steady."

"I… suppose," she muttered, unsure where this was heading.

"What fitness stuff dae you do?"

Katya listed spin classes, running, hill walking and Pilates. Well, that *had* been the case. Lochalshie didn't have a gym, and the morning chill meant you needed huge stocks of willpower to force yourself out of the door to run.

"Our regular Body Combat teacher cannae do the classes on a Wednesday night anymore because she's pregnant. Nae point doing spin, as we don't have the bikes but what about you teaching us all Pilates? You could make some money on the side."

"I'm not trained!" Katya squawked, fast-forwarding to unpleasant scenarios where people lay on the floor, having suffered heart attacks or put their backs out attempting the bow and arrow move.

"Not to worry," said the doctor. "Jolene wasnae trained in Body Combat either. Strictly speaking, she wasnae meant to call the classes 'Body Combat' either or that Les Mills bloke comes after ye. But we didnae mind. Everyone who went to her class signed a disclaimer. Get them to do the same for you and ye'll be fine. And I'm a doctor so if anyone goes into cardiac arrest, I'll be on hand."

Wishful thinking on the doctor's part. Katya was willing to bet she'd relish an emergency First Aid situation.

"The villagers need exercise," she muttered darkly. "D'ye know what a ticking time bomb type 2 diabetes is? Tell Mhari to put a notice of it on the WhatsApp group," she said. "That'll bring the punters in."

And with that, she dismissed her. Katya headed back to the flat wondering why she'd allowed the woman to bamboozle her once more. She would need to spend the next two days on YouTube researching Pilates classes and how to run them.

On Wednesday evening, she arrived at the village hall an hour in advance. It didn't look promising. When the janitor who let her in turned on the radiators dotted around the hall they creaked and groaned in response. Would an hour be enough time to take the icy chill off the room?

The hall had been much more expensive than Katya had budgeted for. And when she'd set a cost for the classes, she'd made it as cheap as possible. She wasn't a real Pilates teacher, and no one would come if she charged city prices. But it meant she'd need at least twenty people to attend to cover the costs.

When she'd told Madeline she planned a side hustle, thinking her mentor would approve, another lukewarm reply came back.

"Hi, honey—how are you feeling? Okay? I don't know if it's a good idea to spread yourself so thinly when you should concentrate on growing your writing business. Isn't it going to take off soon? Still, Pilates is super-good for strength and flexibility, and if you spend lots of time hunched over a laptop, it can help."

Tacit approval, Katya decided. And nice of her to ask how she was.

She put out mats—again, the cost of them had come out of her pocket—found yoga-type music on Spotify and crossed her fingers.

Gaby had promised she'd come, and when she let herself into the hall ten minutes before the class started, Katya let out a sigh of relief. She'd brought Jack too. A reluctant attendee by the hangdog look of him. Mhari had been happy enough to broadcast the new class on What-sApp as she loved being the bearer of new news, but when Katya asked if she would come, she shuddered.

"No. Exercise doesnae agree wi' me."

However, when she pushed the door open minutes after Gaby and Jack, Katya hugged her, ignoring the protests of "Gerroff me!" The doctor followed her, along with Jolene, the one-time Body Combat teacher now pregnant, and her unlikely life partner, Stewart, more often to be found propping up the bar of an evening.

"Er... Jolene, how nice! Is it safe for you to do Pilates?" Katya eyed her belly, a neat bump, nervously.

"Yeah," she said, the New Zealand accent as strong as ever despite her years of living in the village. "And the doctor's on hand, anyway."

They waited another ten minutes after the class's scheduled start to allow for village time-keeping. The clock on the wall above the small stage ticked on loudly, emphasising the place's emptiness. Great. A total of six people and their fees not even close to covering what she'd spent.

"Okay," she smiled as brightly as possible, masking

disappointment. Or perhaps it was relief. She wasn't a qualified teacher. This might go horribly wrong.

"Let's get started."

Katya had been doing Pilates since she was sixteen. She knew most of the moves off by heart. It was still a big ask, though, standing in front of people watching you intently— even if there were not that many of them.

"Okay everyone. Start with your legs together and let's take several deep breaths."

In front of her, five people closed their eyes and inhaled and exhaled noisily. The sixth person, Mhari, still hadn't put her phone down, holding up a finger to Katya to signal 'one sec' while she checked her million social media accounts, WhatsApp messages and Candy Crush status.

Stewart didn't see exercise as an impediment to talking— squeezing out words between noisy exhalations. Gaby had warned Katya never to fall into conversation with him. You'd be lucky to escape in less than an hour. He specialised in coding. The world's most interesting subject. Not. She'd need to make future classes far more difficult to keep him quiet.

As a bonus, he'd brought his West Highland White Terrier, Scottie, to the class. The dog flopped on the floor next to the biggest radiator, watching them all through half-closed eyes. Katya fancied he viewed their activities as further proof of human idiocy.

"Porridge," Stewart said now, eyes still closed. "That's just the thing tae eat before you do any exercise. It's sets ye up good and proper. And I add a few chopped prunes for the natural sugars."

Argh. The porridge monologue was another of Stewart's favourites. He started most conversations with the porridge dedication. Next, it would be the best way to make it and how coders all ate it. It set them up nicely for a heavy session on the binary.

Katya started the class on the roll-down, ordering everyone to come down to the floor vertebrae by vertebrae, walk their hands out to front support and then push back into the downward-facing dog position. Proof of Stewart's fibre-packed breakfast made itself known as he let rip with a loud fart. Behind him, Gaby hastily slid herself and her mat to the side.

"Stewart!" Jolene bawled. It was another of Lochalshie's giant mysteries what someone as beautiful and talented saw in Stewart. Jolene's pregnancy showed she also viewed his dubious genes worth passing on.

"Dinnae worry," Stewart called out, his head between his arms. "It's no' one of those silent but violent yins—mair an all mouth nae action pump."

Next to Gaby, Jack's head shook, stifling laughter. The new Lochalshie Pilates class offered an advantage over other classes up and down the country. Laughter during Pilates made it much harder, thanks to the taxing effects on the stomach muscles as you exercised at the same time. It worked on Katya. Trying to keep control of farting exercisers stopped her descending into a pity tailspin.

All that money spent on the classes. All the hope and expectation she'd put into the relationship with Dexter. Waste, waste, waste.

She ordered the class onto their backs, and set them up for the hundred, Pilates' second-most notorious exercise.

An excited yelp came from the sidelines. Mhari, phone in hand once more, waved it.

"OMG! Wait till ye see this, Katya!"

"Mhari. You're supposed to be concentrating." Another

mental note for future lessons. Confiscate phones at the door.

"No, but this is MEGA. The Pop Glitter site's got pictures of Caitlin's latest boyfriend and ye'll never guess who he is!"

From the way Katya's ears burned and her heart sank, guessing would not be a problem. Still, when Mhari said, "It's your ex, that American bloke. Dexter! He didnae take long to move on, did he?", the revelation punched her in the guts.

Everyone looked at Katya. She smiled, trying to summon up the words, "I don't care". Even if they wouldn't ring true.

"We've both moved on. And let's get on with the class. How about the roll-up?"

The roll-up required someone to use their stomach muscles to pull them up to a seated position from lying down. Katya demonstrated the move, pointing her toes to lie down and sticking them up in the air as she rolled up, the benefit of having done Pilates since her teens. The class looked at her askance. They were about to discover Pilates' most notorious move.

The roll-up needed fierce concentration, and a complete focus on peeling the spine off the floor. It left no time for the mind to linger in places it didn't want to go. Such as boyfriends who forgot you at the drop of a hat. Katya got everyone to start and did the move with them. One, two, three, four...

"Katya!"

The wail cut through. Six pained faces faced her. She must have lost count, making the class work through far more repetitions than people not used to using their stomach muscles to haul their bodies from the floor liked.

"Oh dear." She didn't bother with sincerity. "But you'll thank me for it—perhaps not tomorrow when it hurts to cough but in a few years' time when you need to—"

"Aye, that's right," Dr McLatchie chimed in. "Pilates is awfy good for your pelvic floor muscles. She means you'll no' need to worry about accidentally peeing yourself when you cough or sneeze. And another thing, ladies. If ye've got good pelvic muscle control, your man knows about it, and he thanks his lucky stars because when he's inside—"

"Okay!" Katya jumped in, sparing everyone the doctor's colourful descriptions of the sexual act. From the way Jack blew out his cheeks, he was desperate not to hear his mother elaborate too. "Let's do some cat stretches."

Half an hour and a few deep breaths while lying flat out on the floor later and it was all over.

"D'ye want to see the Pop Glitter stuff, Katya?" Mhari asked, struggling to her feet. Again, everyone looked at her.

"No thanks. Do you want to stay behind and help me clear up?"

"Eh, no!" And with that, she was out of the hall in record time followed by Jolene, Stewart, the doctor and Jack, all no doubt petrified they'd get roped in. Watching them go, Katya hoped they'd awake tomorrow with their quads so tight sitting down on the toilet would hurt every time for the next three days.

Gaby stayed behind, sweeping the floor while Katya rolled all the mats up and turned off the heating. The janitor had said he'd lock the place up. He didn't seem to be in a hurry to return. As there was nothing in the place worth nicking, she saw no point in waiting for him.

Gaby's broom moved back and forth. Katya sensed someone bracing herself to ask tricky questions.

"Um, so Dexter and Caitlin. That's... sudden, isn't it?"

"Yes," Katya said. 'Sudden' didn't cover it—more like, heart-breaking, hideous and horrible. What about that excuse he'd used—*I'm too busy for girlfriends,* etc., etc.? When Dexter attended his millionth marketing meeting, Caitlin would be there. It must be easier to be with someone you worked with when work was where you spent all your time.

And how could he not fall a bit in love or at least lust with her? Mhari wasn't the only one who spent too long on Pop Glitter's website, even if Katya never admitted it to anyone. Caitlin's body felt as familiar to her as her own. Caitlin's Instagram feed featured non-stop pictures of it, semi-naked, bronzed skin glowing. That was when she wasn't telling her millions of followers that the latest Blissful Beauty sparkle bronzer was 'THE BEST, you guys, THE BEST!!!'

The special place in hell for people who used too many exclamation marks counted double for billionaire reality TV stars who spent too much time shoving their arses at a camera.

"I thought…" Gaby said, the broom stopping. "Well, I didn't understand it—you and Dexter. I mean, I know you are God's gift to men, and he was punching way out of his league."

Best friend loyalty. Worth its weight in gold.

"But I thought he'd see sense. If he took a few weeks to think about it, he'd work out you were the best thing that ever happened to him."

Gaby's phone pinged. She pulled it out and grimaced at Katya.

"God, sorry. That's the Pop Glitter app. I get notifications too. I hardly ever look at them, though."

So far, they'd taken it for granted that Mhari, who had only seen Dexter twice, was right.

Katya stuck her hand out and Gaby gave her the phone, mouthing "Sure?" as she did so. The Pop Glitter app welcomed you to the world of THE best showbiz gossip— up to date, and all the latest on your fav celebs. Its main story was Caitlin's Instagram feed. The most recent picture showed Caitlin stretched out on a sun lounger beside a pool, her head propped on her hands, smug smile in place. A man sat next to her, rubbing sun cream on her back. The bikini top was nowhere to be seen, her folded arms protecting her modesty but only just.

The man wore sunglasses, but there was no mistaking that smile. One she hadn't seen at all when they'd met up in Glasgow last week.

"JUST WHO IS CAITLIN'S NEW MAN???" the headline screamed.

"He's only rubbing sun cream onto her back," Gaby said, peering over her shoulder to see the screen. "That means sod all. In her world, her employees have to do that. It's written into their contracts—be Caitlin's slave at all times. I bet she has someone whose only job it is to polish her sunglasses."

Kind of Gaby. Pop Glitter had drafted in a body language expert, seeing as Caitlin had said nothing useful, such as, "You guys! Meet my new boyf—Dexter Carlton is the BEST ever. #inlove!"

Dr Anna LeStrange said, in her opinion, you only had to look at the way their bodies angled toward each other. Caitlin's head tipped upwards so she could see him. His smile wasn't forced. The chemistry between them sizzled. "I'd say Caitlin has met THE one," the doctor added. "We'll be hearing wedding bells before too long!"

Katya gave Gaby her phone back.

Gaby set her broom aside and hugged her. "They're

welcome to each other. And you'll find someone amazing, I know you will."

Behind them, someone cleared their throat.

Zac. And yet again, he'd eavesdropped on her disastrous love life.

"Sorry," he said, his face straight. "Didn't mean to interrupt, but I really need you to do some writing for me. It's urgent. I know it's late, but we could…"

Gaby nudged her. "Go on, my son!" she whispered, and left winking at Katya over her shoulder.

"Okay then," Katya said. "But not too late. I want an early night."

That smirk again as Flirty Zac came into play. "Ideal. So do I."

Chapter Twelve

"I'm only writing for you if you promise to take it seriously," Katya told Zac as they headed back to his house, Katya vetoing her place where Mhari would ogle them and update the Lochalshie WhatsApp group any time either of them said anything.

"How much rent are you paying for this place, anyway?" she asked as he opened the door, struck afresh at its size and space. The rent on the flat she paid was much cheaper than Great Yarmouth, but payments for a house this size had to be impressive. Zac tapped the side of his nose, and she rolled her eyes in frustration. Most people their age had no compunctions about sharing financial information.

Inside, he'd given Kirsty's house a single-guy make-over. The immaculate interior now lay under coatings of dust. Dirty plates piled up in the sink and littered the low coffee table, and empty crisp packets and carry-out boxes from the village's tiny Chinese take-away coated the floors. Zac must be too used to people clearing up after him.

When he spotted her eyeing the dirty plates, he screwed his face up. "Sorry. I should have tidied, but it turns out starting a new business keeps you busy. Can I get you a coffee?"

"Do I get it in a clean cup?" One of the dirty mugs on the coffee table sported a blue and white interior coating. He grimaced. "I haven't got round to buying washing-up liquid yet. Do you want to grab something to eat the Royal George?"

She stared at him, astonished. Kirsty's house was right next to the Lochside Welcome, the Royal George an old-fashioned hotel at the other end of the village favoured mainly by the hunting, shooting, fishing set. The locals rarely bothered with it.

"The Lochside Welcome's number one on TripAdvisor for food," she said, "and much cosier."

He shrugged. "I wanted to try it out. See what their food is like. But you're right. Let's go next door."

"Your treat," she said, following him back out the door into the Lochside Welcome, which blasted out heat thanks to a roaring fire in the public bar area. Stewart sat at the bar undoing all the good work of the earlier Pilates class, Scottie asleep under his stool. He nodded a greeting and patted the stools next to him.

"I wouldn't," Katya whispered, "you risk an ear-bashing. All he talks about is porridge or coding."

Gaby had saved Stewart's life once. Sometimes, she told Katya, she wasn't sure if she'd done the world a favour. Zac grimaced and headed for the other side of the bar. The rest of the Wednesday night customers did their best 'You ain't from these parts, are you?' impression. Eyes followed Zac as he walked to the bar. The woman there kept her arms folded and her eyes narrowed.

"I've heard this is the best place in Scotland to get pizza," Zac said, posh-boy voice audible to all. Katya debated speaking up. Her Polish-tinged Norfolk accent would provide a neat contrast to home county, perfectly pronounced vowels and consonants. *Not worth it*, the inner voice said. *You're still English, still an outsider.* She kept schtum.

"Can we get two of them and a couple of beers as well?"

He glanced back at her. "Katya—you're a vegan, aren't you? Do you eat pizza?"

The questions made her cringe. More loud and clear emphasis on the outsider status. They'd just confirmed it, even if the locals didn't already think it.

"No, that's fine. The Lochside Welcome moves wi' the times," the bar maid said, pointing at the blackboard to the side that listed the pizza choices. "We offer a vegan pizza too—roasted vegetables topped wi' vegan cheese. That do you?"

Katya nodded gratefully. Zac ordered the meat feast and chips, and he headed for the table she'd picked out bearing two bottles of craft lager.

She slid into the booth and retrieved her notepad from her handbag. As she hadn't been expecting a writing job at 8 p.m. on a Wednesday night, that and recording the conversation on her phone would have to do. The pub had filled up, meaning the phone audio was unlikely to be clear. The frequent glances in their direction were impossible to miss. Words drifted over now and then—*Aye, new guy, food business, oysters, writer,* and *she's a friend of wee Gaby, ye ken.* Katya hoped the Gaby friend thing put her in good standing.

Zac took the bench opposite and smiled, a tentative one that lacked his usual cocky confidence. If he kept it that way throughout, so much the better.

"Thanks. I'm so grateful you can help me out."

"What are you after? And why the urgency?"

"I need articles about me, what I'm doing, bits about the producers I'm working with, etc., that I can use to publicise my business. If I give you info, can you write it up for me asap?"

"How asap?"

By Sunday, it turned out—ten articles in total, including interviewing suppliers he had the phone numbers for. Katya's heart sank. She'd had plenty of experience interviewing farmers from her Norfolk years—salt-of-the-earth types and all that, but they stuck to yes and no answers. Squirrelling details out of them was murderously hard.

A big, urgent job then. What would Madeline the mentor advise? She would tell Katya to charge the guy a fortune, and the sooner she got the job done, the sooner it put money in her pocket. Edmund Morris & Co had yet to confirm the work she was to do for them. And extra Scottish clients aside, Katya needed the income. When she'd started freelancing, Katya had found the conversations about money excruciating. Experience and her mentor's advice changed that. Nowadays, it was the first thing she brought up.

"I'm very, very expensive." Not true, but the money the London company promised suggested she was. Years of scraping together a living had made her determined to overcharge from now on. She thought of a figure, tripled it and added another fifty percent. Madeline's advice—expensive rates stopped the time wasters.

"Wow, that's a lot of money." His mouth twitched. "On one condition, though."

"Condition? You don't get to impose conditions." Back to Flirty Zac already. Public-school boys, as she knew this one was for sure, could never be accused of lacking confidence.

"Yes, I do. I'll pay the price, but if the articles you write about me and what I'm doing don't get picked up by one of the Sundays or the lifestyle sites you go out with me."

She spluttered with laughter at that. "Okay. I'm confident enough to promise you that you won't spend an hour weeks from now asking Google its best tips for a first date."

"Too right I won't. I'm a legendary first date. There's nothing Google can teach me."

"Whatever." She picked her pen up. "All about you, then. Let's start there."

It was also a good opportunity for him to tell her what she'd discovered about him herself. If he said nothing, the alarm bells would ring loud and clear.

"Have you done this before, then? Set up a business from scratch?"

A brief nod. "Yes."

Ooh. That invited no further questions. Whatever he'd done must have failed miserably.

She fired off general queries—what experience did he have in the food business, what were his qualifications, where did he plan to find the supplies for the online business and how would it work logistically, packaging and delivering to customers?

The answers all sounded pat—the words someone prepared to persuade bankers, old college chums and rich maters and paters to part with money to fund a venture.

"What made you go into the food business?" she asked. "Notorious industry for failure."

"Isn't it the same with writing?" he replied. "My father was a journalist, and he was always talking about the good ol' days when you could write one decent feature and you'd get a week's wages for it."

They exchanged rueful smiles at that—Katya, thinking of the number of articles she'd have to write a week to make the minimum wage.

"And why Lochalshie, apart from the proximity to suppliers?"

"In somewhere like this, the overhead costs are so tiny compared to the cities it makes the venture low risk, and this is a God-given opportunity…"

The lager foam left a white coating on his top lip, distracting her and focusing her attention not on the words but the sound of his voice—lips that mouthed words polished and confident. And his eyes never left her face. She missed the end of the sentence.

"And moving so far away from your friends and family," emphasis on the latter. "That must be hard."

The eyes flitted away. And back again.

"You did it," he raked his hands through his hair. "Look, one reason I came here was because I was offered the house rent-free. And I don't have a lot of money to spare. The owner and I share the same godmothers—Lois and Angeline."

Katya's jaw dropped. "You and Kirsty? You know the whole Kirsty-Gaby-Jack story, don't you?"

Zac nodded. "Yes. If it helps my cause, I think Jack and Gaby are well suited."

Katya's mind boggled as it tried to process information she hadn't expected. Zac kept his eyes on her face, a hopeful look there.

"Your godmothers are Lois and Angeline?" she said. "And they visited you the other week. When I told them I was moving to Lochalshie, they didn't say they knew someone who was moving here at the same time."

"They can be a bit secretive."

True. Katya recalled that airport meeting all too vividly. She had prattled on about herself and they had told her nothing.

"So, yeah... Lochalshie. This area is a brilliant place to start a food business," he carried on. "It's all artisan this, organic that and customers wanting to know provenance. They want good, local food that has lived and died well. Lochalshie cries out for it."

"Your vegan pizza?" Ashley stood at the side of the booth, pizzas held in both hands and frown in place. From the look on his face, Katya gathered he'd caught the end of the conversation. She shifted in her seat. How would Ashley take such an insulting sum-up of the local food scene?

On cue the pub fell silent, everyone straining to listen in.

Zac got to his feet, taking the pizzas and the bowl of chips, and extending his hand. "Ashley, is it? My name's Zachary Cavanagh—though everyone calls me Zac. You'll have heard I plan to start a food business here? I wanted to pick your brains, and I've got a few ideas about how we can work synergistically—I mean, together."

Ashley eyed him up and down and then slid into the booth next to Katya, his bulk causing the table to tilt back and the lagers to slide towards her. He grabbed them before they could spill foamy liquid everywhere.

"Fish," Zac said. "I want to specialise in fresh fish and venison as there is so much of it around here. I plan to set up supply lines for restaurants and an online business where customers can buy their meat and fish straight from local suppliers."

"I don't do fish," Ashley said, pointing at the chalk

board behind him that also set out the day's specials—pizzas, baked potatoes and the new house speciality, deep-fried haggis and chips. It seemed to be a Scottish thing. While the loch and the nearby sea had fresh seafood and fish in abundance, the locals shunned them.

"No? But I'll be working with fresh-produce suppliers too, so you can come to me for meat, fruit and veg, and it'll be best quality you can get. I've also got contacts with wine merchants, and I can arrange heavy discounts."

Ashley's eyes lit up. The mark-up on booze exceeded that on food by a long shot. If he was smart, he'd buy in bottles of plonk and charge massive amounts.

"There's also the pudding option," Zac continued, winking at Katya discreetly. "You do the legendary chocolate decadence cake, don't you?"

"Made in honour of lovely wee Caitlin," Ashley said, and Katya ground her teeth together, wishing she could push the tiny boyfriend-stealing minx face-down into the cake. But yes, when Blissful Beauty's creator used Lochalshie as the place to launch her skincare and make-up brand in the UK for reasons anyone out with the village struggled to understand, the local hotel rustled up a calorie-laden treat in her honour.

After the reality TV star also used the Lochalshie Welcome toilets during her visit, Ashley installed a sign in the cubicle telling everyone the world's most famous bottom had parked itself on its very seat. To date, the loo was one of the world's most Instragrammed toilets, folks flocking to it so they could settle their cheeks where Caitlin had been. The pudding did well too, photos and hashtags of it appearing in social media feeds all the time.

"Why not consider a frozen version of it?" Zac said. "I

bet people would be more than happy to order slices of that with their meat and fish packs."

Ashley nodded. "Aye, I s'pose. Well, keep me informed."

As he got to his feet once more, the table wobbled again. He patted his belly. "Might hae to go on that vegan diet you do, Katya. What is it you're no' allowed to eat?"

As she listed its restrictions, Ashley's face fell. The plant-based diet was unlikely to get itself another convert any time soon.

"Slick," she said, as Ashley left.

Zac reached across and gripped her hand. "I want to make a difference here," he said, the voice at its sincerest. "Bring more money into the area but work sustainably too. I'm not just the rich idiot you think I am."

She raised an eyebrow. It had to be a ploy. Disarm the opposition by admitting you are what they suspect. Though with all that Polish and English vocabulary at her disposal, 'idiot' wasn't the word she would have chosen for Zac. Twat perhaps, or dziób.

He took a giant-sized bite of pizza, the far edges of his jaw moving from side to side as he chewed. Mesmerising once more and too easy to imagine how that jaw might feel underneath her fingers when they kissed.

When? If. And not likely.

"So, the PR consultancy bit?" he asked, still chewing. Normally, Katya would have found it repellent. When Zac did it, she thought it… oh, never mind. "Is that part of your exorbitant fee?"

She nodded. Madeline always said make your fees super-expensive, but let clients think they are paying for more than one skill, in this case copywriting and PR.

"The online business should be up and running by the spring, but when should I publicise it?"

"The Hogmanay ceilidh," Katya suggested, enjoying the feel of two still-unfamiliar words. "Gaby told me about it—it's the winter equivalent of the Lochalshie Highland Games. Designed to attract a few visitors and bring in the New Year with a bang. I don't know what the catering arrangements are, but why not give away free samples of the food your online business is offering and create some buzz?"

Hark at her. Madeline would be proud of her. Dexter too, Mr Marketer Extraordinaire, come to think of it, but she stamped down thoughts of him as firmly as possible.

"There's a meeting about it in the library next week," she added. "Why not go along and tell people about your plans?"

Gaby had already suggested Katya attend. "You'll meet everyone you need to know in the village," she'd said, "and I promise it's good fun."

Katya would be the judge of that—a village committee meeting was unlikely to feature in the top ten of anyone under the age of 50's list of fab ways to spend an evening. But it would have benefits. Zac could bang on about sustainability and working with nearby farmers. She could wax lyrical about how much she loved the place, mention that she could write promotional stuff for local businesses and iron out posture problems with her new Pilates class.

Zac greeted the suggestion enthusiastically.

"Brilliant idea."

He'd finished his pizza already, eyes fixed on the rest of hers. "Here," she said, pushing her plate towards him.

"So… the American," he held up a slice and bit into it. "He's no more and you're definitely single?" More talking, chewing and mesmerising jaw movement.

"Yes. And not looking for anyone to fill the vacancy."

EMMA BAIRD

Especially someone who's not telling me everything. She kept the last statement to herself, waiting to see what he would volunteer.

"Pity," he said, "it's such a waste, you're gorgeous—and clever too, the perfect combination. I couldn't believe my luck when I—"

Whatever he'd been about to say was cut off. Katya's phone bleeped at the same time as Mhari appeared, taking in the scene with a sly grin.

"Aye, aye Katya," she said. "I came tae find you because your laptop's been going mad—someone trying to get you on Skype. LA number, I think."

Katya's phone offered the same information—missed call from LA and a voicemail message. She leapt to her feet, heart thumping. There was only one person she knew in LA.

"Bye, Zac," she said. "I'll get that writing you need to you for Sunday."

She was out of the pub before she remembered she'd forgotten to thank him for dinner. Or asked him about what she'd found out about him online.

Chapter Thirteen

"Dexie, Dexie—it's so brilliant to see you!"

To show her excitement, Courtney bounced on her feet, punctuating every word. Dexter's older sister had given him five nieces and nephews, ranging in age from three to sixteen, and they crushed varying sized bodies to him, all desperate for a hug.

"I'm so glad you're back in the States," Courtney said, threading her arm through his. "It's been too long."

Not that long, Dexter mused, only a year, but Courtney depended on him. Two years older than him, she acted more like a younger sister than an older one. Despite all those children, Courtney was a kid herself. With three feckless husbands behind her she needed the support more than ever. Jamie, or was it Joe? The last one left her four weeks ago, and Courtney had done what she always did in times of trouble—phoned her younger brother, begged him to drop everything and return to the US to help her cope.

Lucky for him that the Blissful Beauty board decided now would be a good time to look at launching in other countries. And that he had enough money put by to fly Courtney and her kids from Michigan to LA when he returned. The rag-tag bags and battered suitcases told their own story. Courtney and her family had always lived on the breadline. Any money he sent their way vanished in record time, sucked into clothes, education and healthcare-shaped holes.

The sun struck him afresh, bright light beaming through the airport building. Outside the terminal, he took his sunglasses from his jacket. Cars, limos and buses crowded the area outside and he heard sirens, the ever-present background to the city.

"Did you bring any samples?" his oldest niece, Flower, asked him. When you worked with the world's fastest-growing make-up and beauty company and one headed by a 21-year-old, sixteen-year-old nieces decided that made you their favourite uncle.

"Not on me," he said, "but next week I can get you whatever you want. Make me a list."

"Awesome! And can I meet Caitlin? She's like the coolest person there is. Plus, I told my friends I've met her already, so I need details."

"You lied?" he asked, raising his eyebrows.

"Uncle Dexie, you're a marketing guy," she replied. "You lie, like, all the time."

Parenting at its finest—okay-ing your offspring's lies and a distinct lack of respect for their elders and betters.

"So, where have you found us to live?" Courtney asked. Blissful Beauty let Dexter use of one of the company's apartments in the Loz Feliz part of the city near Griffith Park. He'd used it in the past—a three-bedroom place with a spacious kitchen dining area and a living room with all mod cons. If Courtney saw it, she'd hint madly about moving in. Devoted brother and all, he couldn't cope with Courtney and her chaos. The ramshackle house he'd found for them out in Angelino Heights didn't compare well. Guilt threatened, but for the sake of his sanity and their future relationship, he needed to keep Courtney away from his new apartment. Besides, hadn't he'd bunged her enough money over the years?

He told her and said he'd drop them off. "I can't hang around, though. Sorry, guys. I need to go to the office. Make a start on working out how we make the launch of Blissful Beauty mind-blowingly brilliant.

"Do you wanna come, Flower? Caitlin won't be there, but I can show you around."

Flower was a smart girl. She had the potential for a marketing career or anything that rescued her from the dead-end jobs her mom favoured. Flower told him frequently she'd no intention ending up like Courtney, permanently broke and saddled with five children.

Flower shook her head, saying she needed to help her mother sort out their new home, and get ready for starting a new school after the weekend. He breathed a sigh of relief. Well-meant family intentions and all that, but he craved the calm peace of the Blissful Beauty HQ's offices, shutting the door and flinging himself into work. Plans, emails, Excel spreadsheets and everything else which would take up so much of his time, he'd have no opportunity to dwell on the UK.

He'd been in LA for three days now, and it was beginning to look as if he wouldn't return to the UK, or at least not to work. And the Courtney thing had reminded him of the ties he couldn't cut loose. Brought up by a single mother who'd died of cancer when they were both in their teens, Courtney and Dexter clung together. His sister opted for terrible relationship after terrible relationship, and he devoted himself to work and ambition.

Then he met Katya. Life offered other possibilities. He'd tried—flinging himself into mad ventures such as travelling up and down the country at the drop of a hat and hinting she moved to London, which would work out easier in the long run once the South Korean thing was over. But then there'd been that overheard phone call. Desperate to explain, to say she'd misunderstood his intentions, he'd held back instead. The Courtney cry for help had come the day before. What else could he do?

Him and Katya. Just another of those relationships that couldn't make it. Like a vacation romance, he told himself, the magic depended on the place. Best to put it aside as experience, even if the excitement of those early days still made his body tighten and tingle, its response matching the words he came out with all the time—amazing, beyond brilliant, staggeringly awesome.

And back in LA at the heart of the work that would put Blissful Beauty on the South Korean map, and increase its profit margins tenfold, who couldn't fail to be excited? He wanted this campaign. It tied into every goal he'd made for himself over the years. If he made global marketing manager for Blissful Beauty as the success of this campaign might do for him, his salary would double.

Sure, the money would be amazing, but ego drove him too. Nine months until his thirtieth birthday. The Forbes list of the Biggest Influencers Under 30 came out in July.

Dexter would be on it.

———

"Babe, you wanna come to the beach with me?"

November was rainy season in LA but so far, the skies were cloudless. The weather forecasters promised a day of glorious sunshine and temperatures of 78-85 degrees Fahrenheit.

Caitlin had grown up with minions. Her family's mega fame and wealth had come a little later to her older sisters, but as the youngest of the family she'd had staff around her all her life. Dexter's marketing career began in a large pharmaceutical corporate where employer/employee relationships bordered on the excessively formal. Caitlin treated all her staff like bosom buddies. Except that she kinda expected you to jump when she uttered the words. So if Caitlin wanted to bunk off to the beach for the day, that's what you did.

She'd turned up at the office this morning super early, demanding Dexter accompany her to a yoga class—the kind it cost more money than the average American earned in a day to attend. Her treat. It did the job. As his chest melted to the floor—as per the instructions of the teacher who banged on and on about spirituality while raking in around $400 an hour—Dexter visualised the tension leaving every bit of his body. Off it floated, from his feet, up along his calves, his quads, the lower back, the neck... the head. Okay then, it didn't quite leave there, but the over-heated room sweated so much out of him that it was too exhausting to dwell on anything.

English girls who forgot you too easily, say.

"I've got a ton of work to do," he said to Caitlin as they left the class, flashes going off to the left of them as they made their way to Caitlin's car. Photographers hung out here waiting for that oh-so-valuable unflattering shot. Caitlin was wise to them. She always spent ten minutes in the changing room afterwards ensuring she looked as if she'd worked out but not that much. A glow was nice. A usually glamorous star dripping with sweat, hair plastered to her head and eyes piggy because she'd left off the false eyelashes, brightening eye drops and expertly applied kohl less so. Her tee shirt advertised Blissful Beauty's Glow Serum, promising it gave you that fresh-from-a-yoga-class glow.

She yanked open the door to her pink-and-silver SUV, its size directly disproportionate to hers. Did she choose these things to make her look super-frail and feminine?

"What's that saying—it's an English one so you should know it, right? All work and no play makes Jack or Dexter a dull boy?"

He tried to argue that if he didn't push on with work for the South Korea launch, yoga classes this expensive might disappear. Unlikely, though. Forbes might label Caitlin the youngest self-made billionaire, but her family's combined wealth was vast. She shrugged, a super-cute move on one so tiny, sitting so close to the steering wheel it stuck to her chest.

"Dexie…" She shot him one of her killer under the (false) eyelashes looks. "Please come to the beach with me. I've got something I need to tell you. Like, crucial? It's something I've wanted to tell you for so long."

She stuck her hand out, resting it on his arm—tiny fingers topped with long nails exquisitely decorated with varnish and crystals studded in the tips. Was it his imagination but did the hand appear to hint at wanting to move elsewhere? His body—the bones, muscles, skin and flesh Dexter thought he knew inside out—tightened in response.

There was, though, this final thing he could do. "Caitlin, I've been thinking about how to further your brand. An autobiography would be a great idea, right?"

Caitlin's mouth rippled—it was the thing she did when she didn't agree with you but accepted you meant what you said. "I'm twenty-one. And a stupid Instagram star. Who's gonna care?"

He loved her, really. Despite everything, Caitlin knew what she was and didn't mistake herself for anything else.

"I can't write it," she said. "I didn't even graduate high school. And I don't want any old dude doing it."

"Too right. You need someone who understands every fibre of your being, right?"

She nodded slowly. "Do you know someone who can do it?"

"Yeah, I do," he said. "I'll pass on the contact details."

She fired up the engine. "Okay, if that's the boring work stuff done with, let's hit the beach. I'll even buy you an ice-cream."

Chapter Fourteen

By the time she got back to the flat, Katya's breath came in gasps. The caller had left a message, and she listened to it while letting herself into the flat, jaw dropping open as she battled overwhelming disappointment and stunned disbelief. Did she really want to call back?

She played the message again.

"Katya, Hiiiiiiiiiii! Hey, you don't know me, but this is Caitlin Cartier here."

Cute, telling Katya she didn't know the caller. Everyone in the world knew Caitlin Cartier. If they didn't, they lived in a remote village in the Scottish Highlands and never ventured online. But then, everyone here knew Caitlin anyway, seeing as she'd turned up at their Highland Games and displayed far more flesh than was wise to do anywhere north of London.

"My agent wants me to do my autobiography," the message continued, "and Dexie said you're the best writer in the world. He's the greatest, isn't he? So, anyway, can you call me back and we can talk about it? M'wah, m'wah!!!!!!"

When she'd listened to the message the first time, the unexpected offer took all her attention. Now, she zoned in on what Caitlin said about Dexter. "He's the greatest, isn't he?" Greatest what? Recommender of people for jobs? Marketing manager a gal could have? Or, and this was the most likely, boyfriend? The thought made her hot and cold. She had to stand at the bottom of the stairs for a few minutes taking deep breaths in and out to process it. What if Caitlin wittered on and on about him when Katya phoned? She might even—shudder—ask for advice.

"Hey, you're his ex, right? Can you pass me on any tips? I dunno what to get him for Christmas and I've only got $50,0000 to spend on him."

Any hopes that Mhari might stay behind in the pub were soon quashed. She hadn't run back like Katya had, but she opened the front door seconds later and squeezed herself in beside Katya. The two of them stood facing each other across the tiny landing at the bottom of the stairs.

"Someone important, then?"

"It's not Dexter, if that's what you're asking," Katya said flatly. "Um… I've got to make a work call? An important one?"

Hint dropped and ignored, Mhari marched up the stairs ahead of her. "Go ahead. Don't mind me."

So much for the 'work call' description putting her off. Anything that hinted at secrecy and confidentiality set Mhari's finely tuned news radars flickering from side to side. Katya moved toward her bedroom.

"The reception's better in here," Mhari called out as she headed for the living room, something they were both aware of.

Oh well. Katya might as well make the call in front of

her. It was that or have Mhari listening in outside her bedroom door.

"Are you going to put the phone on speaker, then?"

Katya sat down. "No, it's a private conversation—or as private as you can have when your intrusive-as-hell flatmate refuses to leave the room."

Mhari pouted. "I'll do the washing up for a week. And I'll tidy this place up too."

That made the two of them take in their surroundings. Katya had drawn up a rota when they first moved in, the sheet pinned to the cork-board in the kitchen by now curled up and marked with unidentifiable stains. She was the tidier of the two, but neither of them had taken the vacuum cleaner out of the cupboard yet.

"You'd better. And you are not to make a single, solitary sound when I make this call, right?"

Mhari mimed zipping her mouth shut, and Katya placed her phone on the table.

"I'm going to be talking to Caitlin Cartier."

Wise to warn Mhari in advance—otherwise she might shriek too loudly when she heard the tiny one's American drawl and ruin Katya's reputation as a professional. Or as someone too cool for school who routinely took calls from celebrities.

"Oh aye! D'ye think she wants tips on what Dexter likes in bed?"

"No!" Katya gritted her teeth. Trust Mhari to repeat what she'd worried about earlier but make it a thousand times worse. "She wants to talk to me about doing some ghost-writing for her. Say nothing, nothing at all."

Her intrusive-as-hell flatmate mimed the mouth-zipping thing once more.

"And turn your phone to silent. That wretched thing bleeps all the time."

Instructions obeyed by her flatmate, Katya rang the number, crossing her fingers Caitlin wouldn't take up too much of her time. Her phone package wasn't generous.

"Caitlin? It's Katya."

"Hiiiiiiiiiiiii!!!! So excited you phoned me back!" Caitlin's voice boomed out, that instantly recognisable Texan twang even more surreal as it came from a phone rather than the TV. She yelled at someone in the background and the thump of gangster rap cut out.

"You want me to write your autobiography?"

"Totes!" More conversation in the background. Caitlin must be another one of those multi-taskers. Phone conversations, in-real-life chats, dancing to rap music, muscling in on ex-boyfriends and—and going to the loo too, judging by the flushing sound.

"My agent's been badgering me for ages. Felicity Medina at Edmund Morris & Co?"

Ah, it all began to make sense. That meeting in London weeks ago and the hint at the big name. It still astounded Katya that the agency had picked her—an unknown. She had Madeline to thank. And she and Katya were now exchanging regular messages. The woman took her mentoring responsibilities seriously. She passed on details of prospective clients all the time, suggesting approaches that might persuade them to take her on board. Katya had landed five new accounts thanks to her.

Funnily enough, when Katya had tried to look Madeline up, she found very little about her. Her Gmail account featured a small head-and-shoulders pic—a smart, attractive woman in her 50s, Katya guessed, but there was little else online. Even the recruitment company she owned didn't have details of its staff.

"I'm old-fashioned, honey," she emailed back when Katya asked. "And I get most of my business through word of mouth."

"I want someone I connect with, y'know?" Caitlin put in now. "It's important to me that person understands every fibre of my being."

Katya swallowed, stifling a fit of giggles as Mhari curled her lip and mimed a rude gesture. How on earth had Caitlin hit on the idea that she and Katya had anything in common?

"Dexie tells me you're the best, most amazing writer in the world."

Was the hyperbole his or Caitlin's? Katya liked it anyway. Or did until another thought popped up. *Most amazing writer but not good enough girlfriend, Caity-waity…*

"And y'know, people can be mean," Caitlin continued. "I want to prove my haters wrong—a book that touches everyone. Shows I'm just an ordinary girl who put her head down and worked hard but who just wants to help people with her super-cool skincare and make-up."

Mhari pretended to vomit, and Katya felt her mouth twitch again.

"I have all these ideas you can write about—starting with my humble beginnings."

Humble beginnings? When the accident of birth put someone into an already wealthy family who then became wealthier thanks to the mother's idea to beam their lives into everyone's homes? Humble wasn't the word Katya would choose.

"And you can write stuff about my early life on television."

Caitlin had been a TV star for the last eight years. People knew when she'd started her periods, for heaven's sake. Katya doubted she could add anything new there.

"My struggles with fame."

Mhari mimed playing a violin and Katya coughed to choke off more laughter before it escaped.

"And then when I created Blissful Beauty—why it's so important to me that my company is cruelty-free, suitable for vegans, affordable and full of products I use. Every. Single. Day."

Not true. Dexter once admitted Caitlin never used her own stuff. She preferred creams that cost upwards of $500, Chanel make-up, injectable lip fillers, Vampire facials and Photo-shop stroke filters for every picture she or her team posted on Instagram.

By this point, Mhari lay on the floor doing what looked like the dying fly act. The sooner this call ended the better. The giggles gathered in Katya's stomach, threatening to make themselves known to the caller at any moment. And so far, thank goodness, no mention of Dexter the might-be boyfriend.

Alas, the conversation that followed killed off the giggles and replaced them with ghastliness. She got through it, grateful Mhari was there. At least her presence stopped Katya breaking down into a tearful tantrum. Before the giggles and the ghastliness combined and exploded, she leapt in with the practicalities.

"And the money?"

The conversation ground to an abrupt halt—someone incredibly rich battling with the unfamiliar idea that other people needed money.

"Yeah, you met with Edmund Morris & Co, yeah?"

Caitlin whispered something to someone. "They said what they'd give you as an advance?"

When she'd taken her first ghost-writing job—the one that didn't result a book but nevertheless got her this contract—a later examination of the contract revealed all the royalties went to the celebrity. She only got the advance. It didn't matter as the book never surfaced, but Katya vowed never to make the same mistake. She pressed her phone to record the rest of the conversation so she would have evidence.

"And a percentage of the royalties?" she said. Verbal agreements might not count but it was worth a try.

Mhari nodded sagely and mouthed '10 percent' at her —double what Katya had been going to suggest.

"Ten percent."

"Yeah, fine. Ten percent." Caitlin's instant response made Katya and Mhari screw their faces up. They should have asked for twenty.

She hung up, promising her agent/lawyer/perhaps even her mum would be in touch to sort out the 'deets'.

"Wow," Mhari said. She held up her hand for a high five, and Katya smacked it back, adding her thanks for the negotiation help.

"What are royalties anyway?"

Churning emotions aside—the prospect of writing the autobiography of the person who appeared to be her ex's new girlfriend—Katya loved how Mhari had upped the fees without knowing what she was talking about.

"A percentage of the sales of each book. Every time one sells, I get 10 percent of it."

"I wouldnae buy it," Mhari said, giving up on supportive mate mode. "But plenty o' eejits will. Mebbe a million folks? And if it's priced £10, say, that means…"

Arithmetic, it turned out, didn't figure in either of their skill sets. The minutes ticked by as they tried to work it out.

"A lot," Katya said finally. "Enough to buy a house outright, I'd say."

"Is that so?" Mhari's face lit up. "And your first tenant will be me. Paying mates' rates rent too, i.e. nothing. What do ye reckon?"

Chapter Fifteen

Zac appeared at their door the following week. Mhari opened the door, her delighted cry of "Katya! Somebody at the door for ye!" a giveaway it wasn't Gaby.

"Thanks for the articles you wrote for me. They're brilliant," he said when she came to the door. He'd opted for tight jeans and a thick fleece, replacing the usual scruffy chinos and hoodie. The denim clung to his thighs and... bottom. Katya did her best not to focus there. *I do not fall for someone just because they have a bottom I could take a bite out of.*

"Tonight's the Hogmanay Ceilidh committee meeting, right?"

Behind Katya, Mhari hovered. Not even a re-run of the Game of Thrones Season 8 finale could distract her from the possibility of real-life drama.

"Can I come with you to the meeting?" Zac said, blue eyes doing their twinkly thing. "You've already got an in with the locals. People like you."

They did? Katya wasn't so sure. People like her friend Gaby made friends quickly wherever they ended up—her

128

openness and bright, bubbly personality attractive on so many levels. Katya was more of a slow burn.

"If I come with you and outline the plans for my business, they're more likely to listen and agree," he added.

Or they saw Katya as part of his plans. And didn't like either of them.

Mhari butted forward, squeezing beside Katya in the door frame. "Aye, aye? And what are your plans, Mr Flashy Car Posh English?"

Katya couldn't have put it better herself.

"Astonishing things, Mhari." It only took him a second to two to recover. His eyes met Katya's, not conspiratorial, but pleading this time. He turned back to Mhari. "Why don't you come along to the meeting too. Then you can find out for yourself what I'm going to do."

Mhari flung up her hands in horror. "No! I'm not a saddo. And anyway, I've got four Tinder chats on the go and Game of Thrones so I'm too busy."

Tinder chats?

"Let me see!" Katya held out a hand for her phone, but Mhari whisked it behind her back. Cheek of her. Nosiness was a one-way street as far as her flatmate was concerned.

Outside, Zac fidgeted—part two steps forward, one step backward. Nerves? Funny how he veered from OTT confidence to vulnerability, and Katya found the nervousness one hundred percent more appealing than the Mr Flashy Car Posh English persona. But if he was to talk to the villagers about his brand-new business, she hoped that he'd be able to turn on the well-practised charm.

"Thanks for this, Katya," he said. "Did you get the money for the articles? I paid it straight into your account."

She stopped outside the library. Lochalshie's community library, the setting for this evening's meeting, was in the middle of the High Street incongruously disguised as a house, like many of the public buildings in the village, so it blended in.

"Yes, I did. A pleasure doing business with you, sir.

True. A client who paid straight away went to the top of the Christmas card list.

"A pleasure?" That wolf-like grin again. "That's my mission, you know—pleasuring you."

"Oh, sod off," she said, pushing past him. Hadn't she told him she much preferred the non-flirty guy?

"Sorry, sorry," he said, hurrying after her. "But it's true."

Dating Zac, the pros and cons. Pros—he was right here. No snatched dates and no tiny reality TV stars providing competition for his attention. A big, big plus. He was smart, funny and when he dropped the alpha-male persona, appealing.

Cons. Still to explain what she'd found out about him online. And did that alpha-male thing follow him round all the time, waiting to leap out? Who was the real Zac? Perhaps those glimpses of vulnerability he gave her weren't genuine. He could have read up on the male equivalent of Kirsty,'s dreadful dating website, The Dating Guru.

"Guys! Pretend to cry sometimes. Or say something about you past that makes you sound as if you've suffered. Women LOVE that. They'll be opening their legs for you in no time!"

Huh. Imaginary advice or no, Katya decided she needed further evidence. And when crunch time came, she'd be the one asking Zac out. On her terms.

Chapter Sixteen

Inside the library was far more spacious than it looked from outside. The main area was lined with shelves labelled crime, romance, thrillers and non-fiction. A mezzanine floor housed the section for children and young adults, and a room packed with computers for the public to use was at the back. A small room with a table doubled up as the space used for village meetings.

Dr McLatchie had appointed herself the organiser of the Hogmanay Ceilidh and parked herself at the head of the table. She nodded at Katya and Zac and told everyone to sit down and make themselves comfortable. Space was at a premium in the committee room, and Zac sat too close to Katya, his thigh next to hers radiating red-hot heat.

Gaby breezed in a few minutes later, breathless with apologies for being late. When Jack sidled in after her, Katya swallowed back the old green monster once more. *It's been too long, too long since I last did this.* Gaby's top was inside out, and her cheeks flushed. Katya pinched her friend's arm and muttered about her top. Gaby's mouth rounded in an 'o' of dismay, and she reached behind her neck to tuck the top's label in.

Jolene joined them, the pipe major, a man introduced as Big Donnie (the nickname literal) and a woman called Laney Haggerty who ran a nearby horse-riding school. Most of them glared at Zac, who did his best to disarm them with his friendliest smile. Everyone ignored the smile, studying the agenda in front of them instead.

"Katya," the doctor said, "you're the writer, aye?"

Here it came—the bit where a small committee with no budget asked her to do press releases and articles on websites. Oh well. It might improve her standing in the village.

"Yes."

"Excellent. You can dae the minutes, then."

Ah. She got out her notepad and prepared to take plenty of notes.

The Hogmanay Ceilidh had begun life as a dance in an old barn, the 'tables' bales of straw, the heating provided by braziers—risky with all that straw—and the food provided by the farmers' wives all competing to supply the best soup/stovies/shortbread.

As this year's Lochalshie Highland Games in the summer had taken on legendary status, the stakes for the Hogmanay ceilidh were raised.

The popularity of the event soared when reality star Caitlin Cartier dropped in for the UK launch of her Blissful Beauty company. Attendee numbers rocketed so high the village experienced its first ever rush hour when all the cars tried to leave, driving along the multi-potholed B-roads all at the same time.

The event gave the villagers dining out stories for months afterwards:

"Aye, weil, you'd never believe the money the make-up folks gave me for an end of aisle slot in the shop for a totty wee jar of skin cream and a bit of mascara!"

Or,

"D'ye ken, those lassies that stayed with us who booked through the Airbnb website came all the way fae Texas just tae see that girl!"

Or the most often talked-about bit:

"The Caitlin lassie—when she rode up the High Street on the wee pony just in her birthday suit to prove her skin-care stuff was so good you didnae need tae cover up... I thought I'd died and gone tae heaven."

Not strictly true, the last story, seeing as Caitlin had worn a bodysuit, though it was one that made it clear what kind of bikini waxing she favoured. But it was a story Katya foretold—without Psychic Josie powers—every single Lochalshie resident would bore their grandchildren and great grandchildren in years to come.

Sadly for some of the village residents, near-naked A-listers wouldn't be part of the Hogmanay Ceilidh. January in a Highland village guaranteed hypothermia to anyone foolish enough to leave their house in anything less than five layers. But Lochalshie needed something to attract the people who'd now heard of it and wondered what might happen next.

While the village hall supplied the venue and the Lochside Welcome the catering for the ceilidh these days, at heart it was still the barn dance of old. And more than a few of the villagers wanted to create the same money-making possibilities.

"This year's Hogmanay Ceilidh," Dr McLatchie announced, making sure she looked at everyone one by one, "will be special. Does anyone have any ideas? Cheap ones, but very exciting ones because Katya here will also do us a press release."

She would? So much for asking. Still, the glow of money from the Caitlin offer meant Katya could afford a bit of pro-bono work even if the thought of writing the book made her insides shrivel. The final chapter, 'Caitlin Falls in Love' too dreadful to contemplate.

Jolene pulled a bit of paper out of her bag.

"Um, Stewart gave me some ideas. They might work."

New Zealanders often made what they said sound like questions.

"A porridge-making competition," Jolene said, ignoring the chorus of groans. "Hey, listen up. There are people all over the north of Scotland who would travel far and wide to show off their porridge-making skills."

Katya's mind had already written up the press release intro, which included puns a plenty. Zac took her pen from her and jotted down, "Want to sow your wild oats?", thoughts chiming with hers.

And persistence, you had to give him that.

"Not a bad idea, actually," she told Jolene. "And bound to be a great hit on social media."

Beside her, Gaby muttered "Good grief!", but Zac leapt to Jolene's defence.

"She's right. Food's such a thing online these days. And porridge is healthy, local and vegan too, or it can be. It ticks a lot of boxes for trends."

Jolene blew him a kiss. Doubtless, she'd expected defending Stewart's idea to be more of a struggle.

"Okay, then," the doctor said, motioning at Katya to write everything down. "A porridge-making competition in the afternoon. If everyone has a wee dram with their porridge, folks will hae to stay the night and they might as well come to the ceilidh too. Did Stewart have any other ideas, Jolene?"

"He mentioned a presentation in the Lochside Welcome about coding… I'm kidding. No talks on coding, okay?"

The committee let out a collective sigh of relief, though Katya noticed Jolene strike a line through something on her piece of paper. That coding talk might not have been a joke.

"What about a Pilates class in the school hall?" Katya offered. "A freebie. If it's New Year people usually make a resolution about getting fitter."

And more of you could come along to make it worth my while, the unspoken bit.

Jolene nodded. "Great idea, mate. You can limber them up for the dancing later on."

"Psychic Josie will attend too. Folks will want to know what their future holds at this time of year. The lovelorn want answers." The doctor shuffled her papers. As far as Katya knew, her dual identity was a secret, and the doctor pretended to be the psychic's agent.

"How much will she be charging, Mum?" Jack threw out. As her son, he knew about her side hustle. It was his job to keep it in line. From personal experience, Katya knew the woman charged vast amounts for her phony services.

"A standard consultation is £50, which includes a detailed horoscope for the following year."

"As it's New Year and people will have spent too much over Christmas, tell Psychic Josie to charge £10. She could put fewer details into the horoscopes."

Fewer lies, more like. The doctor muttered about her client not being amenable to people who tried to cheapen her skills. Jack held firm while Gaby hid her head in her hands, trying and not entirely succeeding to hide her laughter.

The details grudgingly agreed, the doctor moved onto the music—a well-known ceilidh band from the next town who'd offered cheaper rates if the village paid their travel expenses and put them up for the night. The Lochside Welcome would provide a temporary bar for the night, which left the catering. Pizzas from the Lochside Welcome. Did anyone have any other ideas?

"Me!" Zac piped up, leaning forward and settling his elbows on the table. "I'd like to set up a stall showcasing the producers I'm working with. It would offer people the chance to try the venison burgers and oysters."

"Oysters gie me the dry boak," Laney Haggerty, owner of the nearby pony-riding school and a cousin of Ashley, piped up, echoing Mhari's words the other week.

"Mainly venison burgers, then," Zac said. "Or normal burgers, if that's your preference. There's a big farm twenty miles from here which makes its own steak burgers, and they are incredible. If you cook them rare, serve them in a freshly baked brioche—"

"As they as good as McDonald's?" Laney butted in.

Zac swallowed hard. "Almost," he said, "but what about if I gave away a hamper? Worth £250? It could be a prize —everyone who buys a ticket for the dance is entered into a draw to win it."

Neat again. Free food almost always trumped everything else.

The doctor frowned. "Seafood poisoning," she said. "If ye're gonnae offer oysters and shellfish and the like," she made it sound as if Zac had suggested flavouring his food with arsenic, "then what about the folks allergic to seafood? We might end up with a projectile vomiting incident."

She shook her head sorrowfully. Gaby elbowed Katya hard. If you looked closely enough at the doctor, it was easy to spot the possibility of mass projectile vomiting didn't seem to bother her too much. Almost like someone who spent her life longing for a big medical emergency where she got to play the starring role.

"I agree," Katya said, deciding it might be prudent to ally herself on the other side from Zac. "Offering shellfish at a community event is too dangerous." And after the Glasgow-Dexter-Lobster incident, if she never set eyes on shellfish again, it would be too soon.

Zac's thigh worked its way closer to hers. He promised Dr McLatchie and the committee he vetted every supplier he worked to an inch of their lives when it came to health and safety.

"You're right, Doctor," he said, his tone respectful. "I'll make sure I put up signs everywhere warning people about shellfish and cross-contamination so that those who have shellfish allergies can avoid my stall."

"I wouldnae bet on that, Zac," Dr McLatchie said, "sometimes the folks wi' the allergies dinnae realise it lurks within them, waiting to erupt at any moment. Like Mount Vesuvius, puking their guts up left, right and centre, and—"

"Laney! Did you want to bring your ponies so people can meet them?" Gaby jumped in. She must have taken pity on Zac, whose jaw had dropped open. The conversation moved on, everyone else keen not to have the image of mass spewing in their heads. Especially those who'd brought sandwiches and cakes to the meeting.

Katya added a line to her notes. 'Zac to do stall.' Beside her, he leant in to read the screen.

"And you."

"In your dreams," she snapped, smiling nonetheless when he feigned heartbreak.

"What are you going to do after the ceilidh?" Laney asked Zac. "Are you going to stay here and can the local farmers trust you not to rip them off?"

Several pairs of eyes swivelled to where Zac sat.

He took a deep breath. "I'd like to stay here for a year. I plan to buy a mobile food van and park it on the loch shore in the summer to attract visitors. Pop-ups are all the rage these days."

Oh. Was this the restaurant possibility thing then? And something he hadn't talked about when she'd interviewed him. Around Katya, a collective intake of breath sounded, and the dissent started. What about Ashley and the Lochside Welcome? The pub relied on tourist income to a large extent.

"I want to work closely with everyone to make the venture a success," Zac continued, battling on in the face of hostility. "And put the village on the map as a foodie destination, ensuring all local businesses benefit, the Lochside Welcome too."

"Lochalshie's already on the map," Laney Haggerty piped up. "The Guardian Lifestyle said the Lochside Welcome did the best vegan pizzas in Scotland. And when I was in there last week, two women telt me they'd come up fae Carlisle just to eat Ashley's chocolate decadence dessert and sit on the same bog Caitlin did."

Murmurs of agreement chorused around the table.

"Of course," he said, blue eyes wide and open. "All I'm doing is building on the fantastic reputation the village already has. The food I'm offering isn't the same as Ashley's. I won't be his competition. And the van won't have a licence for alcohol."

"You've just lost my boyfriend as a customer, then," Jolene said, her comment drawing titters. True, somewhere that didn't offer inebriation plus food would lose a fair few customers. The atmosphere in the room lightened.

"Right," the doctor said. "Well, if you've remembered my warning about shellfish poisoning—it can kill, ye ken—consider yourself appointed as one of the official stalls. Katya, include that in your press release about our afternoon fair and ceilidh. Michelin-starred food on offer."

"Er," Katya began but Zac jumped in and said he had worked for one once. The doctor decided that would do, given that restaurants and not chefs were awarded Michelin stars.

She declared the meeting over and the bulk of the committee grabbed handfuls of sandwiches and shortbread, stuffed them into their mouths and left, muttering about the Lochside Welcome's pub quiz. The quiz was a fiercely contested evening where reputations went to die. Katya had tried it when she'd visited Gaby for her house-warming and was still to recover from the humiliation of temporarily forgetting the name of a Jane Austen book.

Gaby hung back, wittering nineteen to the dozen about all the work Dexter had heaped on her ahead of Blissful Beauty's South Korean campaign.

"God, sorry. I shouldn't mention the 'D' word, should I?" She kept darting glances at Zac, who mooched around the library shelves, picking up books and reading the blurbs at the back. Katya was almost sorry enough to take pity on her. *"Yes, he seems to fancy me, and yes it seems easy and convenient but he's not for me."* As she couldn't yet work out what she felt for him, she kept her thoughts to herself.

Zac wandered over to join them, two books in hand. "Eclectic selection of reading they have here," he said, no wit, no mockery, no flirting. "Can I borrow them, even though I've not joined the library yet?"

Such a statement demanded Katya inspect what he held. She tried her best do it discreetly. Not discreetly enough. He turned the books over, cover up.

The world's most famous self-help book, *How to Win Friends and Influence People* by Dale Carnegie, and *Persuasion* by Jane Austen. If Katya been asked to pick out two books for Zac, these wouldn't have turned up. Bits of him kept pricking her expectations.

"Course you can!" Gaby said, and Brigitte, the village's librarian, materialised at the counter. She handed Zac a form to fill out, gave him the books once he'd done so, and disappeared into the back room.

Gaby's phone beeped, and she shrieked in alarm. "Yikes! I promised Jack I'd join his pub-quiz team tonight! They need me for the celebrity gossip round!"

She grabbed her coat, mouthed kisses and bolted.

"You didn't mention a pop-up van when I interviewed you," Katya said.

"Sorry—but I did say restaurant possibilities, didn't I? A pop-up is something I've been mulling over, wondering if it would work." He took out his phone and showed her a picture of a van on eBay—a rusty old heap that barely looked road-worthy. "I could convert this. Minimal over-heads and all that. And I know I'll need to charm Ashley's socks off, but he has nothing to worry about."

He shifted the books. She watched his expression. Another sincere plea? Who to, Ashley or her? The lights in the place dimmed. A writer couldn't hope for a better setting for romance. Books surrounded them. Brigitte had set up stands all over, themed romance, crime, thrillers and Scotland, and added in corresponding props. The romance table was draped with lace, the silhouette of a couple pictured at the back and plastic roses scattered over the books.

Zac picked one up and handed it to Katya. "Believe me, I want to make a difference here," he said.

She moved to the front door. Brigitte was nowhere to be seen. That didn't mean she wasn't a member of the notorious Lochalshie WhatsApp group, her thumbs moving in double-quick time over the screen as she added updates. *"STOP PRESS—Katya still in library with new guy! They're chatting! Heads too close together!"*

Katya took it back. Librarians did not use exclamation marks lightly. Or for three sentences in a row.

Outside the November chill was all too present. The wind rustled on the surface of the loch, raising white-frothed waves and causing gulls to dip and surge in its lulls and roars. Zac moved closer and threw his arms around her.

"You don't mind, do you? It's Baltic. I need to borrow your body heat."

Katya didn't move. Men who felt the cold. She seemed to attract them. She didn't reciprocate but the warm solidity of him was comforting. When he tilted his face closer, lips seeking hers, she did nothing either. They landed, soft pressure and the heavenly tingle of nerves awakening. *Please, please don't let Mhari see us*, she begged silently, not bothered enough to break apart from him. Finally, as his tongue tried to part her lips open, she pulled her head back.

"I've just broken up with someone. I'm not ready for a relationship. Despite what you might have heard at Gaby and Jack's, I don't jump from one guy to the next."

Katya wasn't someone who said something but meant the opposite. So she told herself. Zac hadn't let her go. He'd moved his hand to the top of her head, pushing it into his shoulder. The other arm was around her waist, the hand hovering above her bottom ready to slide down any second.

Go on, go on, go on... she willed it, subconscious and conscious locked in an epic battle.

"Anyway," she wriggled away from him, taking hold of the hand that had been around her waist. There it was, the faint trace of a white ring around his third finger. A wedding ring had been there once, if not now. "I'm shattered. And off home to bed. Alone."

Said firmly before any eyebrows could raise and unasked-for invites be offered.

"Goodnight Zac."

She felt his eyes boring into her back all the way to the end of the street.

Chapter Seventeen

Katya's Pilates class the following week was busier than the last one—the participants having quadrupled in numbers. All thanks to Mhari. No sooner had the conversation with Caitlin ended, Mhari updated the Lochalshie WhatsApp group. "Katya's gonnae write a book for Caitlin Cartier. About her love life and the billion boyfriends she's had. Find out more if ye come along to her Pilates class on Wednesday."

"Um, a) you promised discretion," Katya told her when Mhari relayed the good news over a cup of tea in their kitchen. "And b) it's not just about her love life." As Caitlin had said nothing about secrecy,

twenty people in Lochalshie knowing the real identify of the book writer shouldn't be an issue, but still.

"Is it no'?" Mhari asked, all fake innocence. "And your ex is Boyfriend Billion and One, eh? Stupid sod."

Katya's one-time project writing for a life coach two years ago came in useful in many situations. Ones where you wanted to burst into tears and wail about men who forgot you oh too easily. This wasn't the place to do so. The world's nosiest woman, while not at heart malicious, found other people's misfortune too fascinating to keep to herself. Best to pretend she wasn't bothered. Fake it till you make it, the life coach said.

Katya plastered a smile on her face. "Could be!" she said, congratulating herself on how breezy she sounded. "Wise of Caitlin to choose someone who isn't in the fame business himself."

As she dragged her mats into the already overcrowded hall that evening, Katya counted heads. Enough people to make a profit this time.

The class took a long time to quieten down, hushed and not so hushed conversations drowning her out as she tried to get them to start. No one wanted to take deep breaths and pull in their cores when they could ask questions.

"So, you'll be writing her life story eh? Willnae take very long, seein' as she's only twenty-one!"

"Are ye goin' to Hollywood, then, tae meet her?"

She palmed people off with vague answers, clapped her hands and promised to answer all questions at the end, hoping an hour's hard work would kill off curiosity.

"Right—let's all take several deep breaths. In one, two, three, out one, two, three!"

Her questioners had, however, raised interesting points. How on earth did you write 80,000 words about someone who'd only inhabited the planet for such a short time? And the practicalities—did she phone Caitlin, ask questions and write it all down? An initial email had already winged its way to her inbox confirming that fat advance payment. The 'deets' were to follow.

"I passed this Land Rover outside Kirsty's old house this morning, the one Zac's renting out," Dr McLatchie said between pants, her legs in the air and her hands beating out the hundred counts of Pilates' most (in)famous abs exercise. "Two women getting oot. Anyone know who they are?"

"Aye, me too," Mhari added. "Rich-looking women and they seemed to know your Zac well, Katya."

"He's not my Zac," Katya said. "Maybe they're going to help with Zac's business or something."

Lois and Angeline, she guessed. Visiting again. Or perhaps they didn't visit him the first time when he wanted Katya to help him entertain them. She kept meaning to look them up, intrigued by their relationship to Zac. And their interest in Lochalshie.

Just as she made the class do the hundred for the third time—an effective conversation-stopper—the door to the hall opened.

"Am I too late?"

She heard the collective intake of breath and caught Gaby's grin. Zac stood at the door, a yoga mat over his shoulder and dressed in work-out gear Katya knew hadn't come from Asda or any of the other cheap chain stores her other class members bought their stuff from. He'd even tied his hair back—the longer blonde strands at the front pulled into a stubby bun at his crown. It attracted stares. The man bun was unknown in Lochalshie. The tiny barber's shop in the next village only offered men a short back and sides.

"No," she said, waving him to the only remaining space at the front. "Though I make late-comers do press-ups as punishment."

"Good practice, then!" he said, hastily unrolling his mat and dropping onto his hands and toes, elbows clamped to his sides. "It gives you stamina for the real thing."

Gaby sniggered. Others joined her.

Katya wandered over to Zac's mat, counting out loud. "One, two, three..."

She put her foot on his back, touching him lightly so his body dropped flatter to the floor. It made the move ten times harder.

"How many?" the question gasped out.

"Fifty," she said cheerfully, and the class laughed. A few minutes later, he collapsed in a perspiring heap on his mat.

He did the rest of the class far more peacefully and hung around at the end to help her put away the mats and blocks. The hour's hard work killed off all interest in Caitlin's autobiography and everyone else in the class vanished as soon as she said, "And we're done". She and Zac had the hall to themselves, Gaby throwing another of those 'Go on, my son!' looks over her shoulder as she hurried out the door.

"So, rumour has it," he said, "you've got a big writing project. Bigger than mine by a long shot."

"Ah. I take it you accepted membership of the Lochalshie WhatsApp group?"

She rolled up mats and stacked them in the cupboard at the far end of the hall.

"Yes, though I left it after a couple of days. That is one lively group. If you don't want to be stirred out of sleep at two in the morning, you need to kick it to the curb. Will you still be able to write for me if I need any more articles?"

She nodded, flattered when he looked relieved. "Yes. I'm a freelancer. I take every job going. And your business interests me. I find it easy to write about."

"Do you?" he said, removing the band from his hair so it flopped forward once more. "I hate writing. When I read the stuff you wrote for me, it was so descriptive I thought it must have taken you hours. Do you want dinner, by the way? I'll make you something meat, fish, egg and dairy free."

He grinned suddenly. "How do you stop yourself farting all the time? After Jack made us that risotto, I didn't leave so quickly afterwards just to chase after you. And in the end I was glad you turned down my offer for a drink. My house stank like a sewage explosion for the rest of the day."

Oh—incoming, incoming... Another flashback. This time, the third time she and Dexter met up. He took her to a jazz cafe that specialised in 'dirty' vegan food—veggie burgers that bled, full hangover fry-ups and kebabs made from seitan. The food, rich and different to Katya's normal fare, made her stomach gurgle repeatedly afterwards.

"That wasn't a fart, by the way!" she'd burst out the fifth time her stomach had complained.

"Are you sure?" Dexter pushed down his sunglasses so he could gaze at her over the top of them, smirk in place.

"Yes!"

Never declare something so forcefully you forget to concentrate on holding onto the sphincter muscles. When the inevitable happened, Dexter's smirk widened into a broad grin.

"I love a dame who's not afraid of flatulence," he said, reaching over to stroke her face. Brave, given that thing's potency.

And I love you, I love you, I love you for that. Farting in front of a new boyfriend could play out many ways. This one convinced her Dexter was perfect.

And now Zac did something similar to her in reverse— joking about farting in front of someone he fancied. She warmed to him.

"Anyone new to veganism experiences the after-effects. Stick with it—if you eat a plant-based diet for a year, your digestive system will forgive you and settle down. Anyway, thanks for helping me clear up but I've got to go."

He caught hold of her hand. "Please come for dinner—a non-date dinner. I'm practising a vegan dish for the van, and I need an expert to tell me if it's any good. Please?"

She looked at his hand—the one with the white mark on the third finger. If she went back to his house with him, she would ask him for sure.

"A non-dinner date. Do your worst."

They'd just reached the house when a huge silver Land Rover pulled up beside them. The front window rolled down and a skinny hand sketched a wave.

"Hello, darlings!"

Zac closed his eyes briefly and said something rude under his breath. Katya recognised the posh, confident voice—Lois. Her presence confirmation of what people had discussed in the Pilates class. The front doors flung open and out she got, Angeline emerging from the other side, the two of them complaining vociferously about country roads, potholes and the inferior coffee one had to put up with outside the UK's cities. They'd been planning to stay the night in the Royal George but had changed their minds.

"Katya!" Angeline. "How delightful to see you. And you've met Zac too. We said, didn't we, Lo-ee-lo, that they would make a lovely pair. You look like brother and sister!"

As a general rule, you didn't look for incestuous analogies when hooking up with someone, but Katya supposed it was true. She and Zac were close in height, blonde and blue-eyed and their faces shared similar bone structure.

"What are you doing here?"

"We had a meeting in the George and then Lochgilphead," Angeline said, referring to the coastal town an hour from Lochalshie. Katya noticed the three people around her exchange glances and wary looks. Spidey senses well and truly wakened, she asked what it had been about.

"Oh, this and that!" Angeline trilled gaily. "Did you know you can take the ferry to Islay from there? I've never been, but we've booked it for next year. How thrilling! Anyway, were you on your way home? Zac tells us you live nearby."

Did Zac indeed? He'd talked about her to them, then.

"We're here for a few days," Lois said, "why don't you pop in sometime?" She smiled warmly. It didn't disguise the 'now piss off out of here' hint to her words. Katya toyed with smiling back at her. *"No, no Lois. I'll pop in now. Zac has promised me dinner, and I'd love to see how that plays out while you and your evil twin tell me what you are up to."*

The non-date dinner. *Which I wasn't fussed about in the first place.*

Zac ran a hand through his hair, the front of it kinked where he'd tied it back for the Pilates class earlier. He met her eyes—apologetic but regretful.

"Sorry, Katya. Another time, yeah?"

"No problem," the woman who hadn't been bothered about her non-date dinner said. She blew him a kiss—so it wasn't just him who got to do all the flirty stuff—and sauntered back to her flat, waiting until she turned the corner into her street to let her shoulders sag.

Back in her bedroom she fired up her laptop and Googled Lois Manson and Angeline Berringer. Unlike Zac, they were easy to find online, although the page she landed came as a surprise. Hammerstone Hotels, the name behind a fair few luxury hotels located in the south-east of England.

Looking through the list of Hammerstone properties, Katya spotted one she recognised—the Staffordshire just off Regent Street with its hip bar, where she'd met Dexter just before he rushed off for yet another marketing meeting. It explained why Lois and Angeline were there. The coincidence had bothered her.

The website had a news page. She clicked on an article in a trade magazine—an interview with Lois where she outlined the company's plans for expansion.

"The modern customer," she told the interviewer, "wants much more from a hotel break these days than sumptuous luxury and a slap-up meal. And do they want hotels at all? Look at the rise in demand for glamping holidays. People adore the idea of getting away from it all but in comfortable surroundings."

Did they? In Lois and Angeline's world, perhaps. Katya reckoned most people were happy to settle for extra-large beds, fluffy white towels and a breakfast and dinner they'd not had to make.

She put her laptop to sleep, still wondering why Lois and Angeline showed so much interest in Lochalshie and how that involved Zac.

Chapter Eighteen

Puzzling over what Lois and Angeline wanted and why Zac had seemed so keen to get rid of her kept Katya awake for several hours, the rest taken over with Dexter regrets.

If I tried harder to take time off. (Why didn't he?)

If I hadn't thrown up in front of him. (Was he that fussed by it?)

If I'd called him a few times afterwards when he left for London/LA. (He didn't call her).

She woke the next day groggy and grumpy. When the text message about a job came in, she weighed up ignoring it. But money was money, and she needed cash soon if she was to pay next month's rent. Showered and changed, she left the house. One afternoon a week, Dr McLatchie ran a weight loss class where a person could stand on the scales, be ticked off and given information on what not to eat. Letting herself into the surgery, Katya met glares. Two women and a man sat in the waiting room, their substantial girths hinting they were there to be weighed.

"What are you doin' here, hen?" the man asked. "You're no' that fat."

"Er… I need to see the doctor about something else," she said, taking the last remaining chair. "And, um, nothing wrong with being fuller of figure."

The two women exchanged glances at that. One of them pushed herself to her feet. "Aye, you're right. You comin', Angie? We can go to the Lochside Welcome and order pizza for lunch and then get some of that chocolate decadence dessert. I'm fair starvin'."

Angie agreed all too readily, and the two of them dashed giggling from the surgery. The man watched them go wistfully before leaving himself seconds later. The doctor's office door swung open two minutes later, Dr McLatchie's voice drifting out behind a shame-faced Stewart clutching a diet sheet.

"No more beers this month, Stewart, and nae chips either. Jolene's the one meant tae be eating for two, not you."

He nodded at Katya and scurried off. From the window in the waiting room, she saw him head towards the Lochside Welcome. If the doctor had just said 'nae chips', he might have obeyed her orders.

"Och, I thought I had more people to see," the doctor's gaze swept around the waiting room. "Come on in, Katya. D'ye want to find out how heavy you are at the same time? I've been reading up about plant-based diets. They dinnae always make ye thin."

A size 14 and more than happy to be described as 'hench' by admirers in the gym, Katya ignored the hint. "You said you had more work for me?"

When they'd first met at the Lochalshie Highland Games, the doctor asked Katya to help build her website presence. She'd offered decent money too. Most of Psychic Josie's business came through stalls at the local shows and fetes and the occasional event in the cities. The side hustle made her a fortune. For Katya, anyone who wanted regular work and paid well made the ideal client. Who cared if astrology was utter tripe?

An opinion backed up by the doctor herself, who admitted that as Psychic Josie she used a combination of social media checks, skilful reading of body language and advice so general it could apply to anyone. On the website, she posted horoscope forecasts where ninety-nine percent of the time people wanted advice on their love lives.

Every time she wrote an article advising all Virgos to stray out of their comfort zone on Tuesday or Aquarians to be careful around the fifteenth of the month, Katya shook her head and told herself what a pile of crap astrology was. But hundreds of comments saying, "Spot on!" or "Psychic Josie, I took a different route to work as you advised and bumped into the man of my dreams!" made even the most fervent non-believer waver.

The doctor waved Katya to a seat in her surgery. "Can ye write me an article for Psychics Monthly magazine? I'll pay double my usual rates. Or…" her expression changed to calculating, "the normal rate and I throw in a wee freebie for you. A forecast. I'm awfy good wi' folks' love lives."

About to refuse, Katya decided to go with it. Hadn't she spent the last few weeks chopping and changing her mind about Zac?

"Okay, then."

The doctor grinned at her and steepled her hands together. "The stars are seldom wrong! Who's the best one to go wi? On the one hand, you've got that pretty American boy. On the other, you've got that bonny English laddie.

Even if none of us knows for sure what he's up tae. Nae wonder you need advice working out which one's the best."

Katya felt her jaw drop. "Dexter? But he's…"

Over me. Too busy working and falling in love with tiny, impossibly glamorous reality TV stars.

"The spirits tell me you are troubled."

Katya curled her top lip. The spirits were weeks out of date. Wasn't it common knowledge Dexter had chosen work over her? Asking the woman's advice began to look even more ridiculous than it had minutes ago. Nevertheless, here she was and the devil on her shoulder whispered, "Ask, just ask."

"Compatibility," she said, "I wanted to find out if Zac and I are suited. And is this one hundred percent confidential?"

"Aye, aye," the doctor said. "I treat my psychic clients the way I do my patients. Dinnae worry. What are your dates of birth?"

Zac had mentioned his birthday when Katya had interviewed him the first time round. She rattled the dates off and the doctor sat back in her chair and smiled.

"He's a Scorpio!" she exclaimed. "And that day too! Look!"

She typed in the address of her website on the laptop in front of her. The site featured a compatibility chart where people could input the dates of their birthday and that of their partner (or about-to-be one). The screen flashed and a pop-up banner exclaimed, 'Bingo! Your ideal match'. Underneath it was the 'flame' rating for sexual compatibility.

NSFW.

"What does NSFW mean?" Katya asked.

The doctor stared at her. "You're the young yin. Dae I

have to explain modern slang to ye? Not safe for work—it means websites you shouldnae look at when you're at work. But I use it to tell folks if sparks will fly. Basically, your birthdate and Zac's make you one of the hottest possible combinations."

"But that doesn't mean he's right for me," Katya protested.

"Might no' be," the doctor agreed. "But if ye can get me the time he was born, I can run a full chart for you and that'll tell ye for sure. I've got the software for it an' all."

"Maybe."

"Aye, and it's only eighty poun—och, free to you, then."

No wonder the woman was rolling in it. And if she wanted her psychic identity to remain a secret, any charts she produced for Katya *would* be freebies.

Ask about Dexter. The devil on Katya's shoulder hadn't finished.

"Um, what about Dexter?" she said. "He was born third August 1990."

"A Piscean and a Leo. You're wasting your time."

The pronouncement made her deflate.

"But you're on the cusp—a Pisces-Aries cusp, which means you're no' that different after all. You're a cusp fire-water sign and he's a fire sign. Magic, eh? I don't suppose you know what time he was born, do you?"

When she shook her head, the doctor sighed. "Pity! I could gie ye all sorts of detailed information then. Water doesnae always destroy fire when signs are on the cusp. D'ye know I was able to tell someone once when she and her man would have their first child even before they'd met. Down to the exact day."

A lucky guess, no doubt. Katya got up, promising the

doctor she'd have the article—*The Star Signs and How They Can Help Our Health*—by tomorrow morning.

Outside, she bumped into Gaby, who said she needed to escape the house, having spent her morning hunched over her iMac doing yet more work for Blissful Beauty.

The two of them watched a car roar past them, Gaby glaring after it.

"I wish people wouldn't drive that fast. Dead dangerous. What were you doing seeing the doctor? Are you okay?"

If she told Gaby she'd had a consultation with Psychic Josie, she'd never hear the end of it. If, however, she confessed to something else, it might distract Gaby completely.

"Promise you won't say anything?"

Gaby nodded. "Cross my heart and hope to die!"

"I kissed Zac the other night. After the committee meeting."

"Did you?" Gaby clapped her hands. "That's wonderful. Oh, Katya I'm so pleased for you!"

"Aye, aye, you didnae say anything about that when you came in."

They both turned. Dressed in her pharmacy uniform and phone held in front of her, Mhari beamed at them. Within seconds, the WhatsApp group would be updated and the whole of the village would know. Katya might as well have snogged Zac in the pub in full view of everyone.

"How…?" Gaby asked. No one knew how Mhari managed to plant herself wherever there was news to be overheard.

"I'm on my vaping break." Mhari held up a thin tube. The pharmacy was only two doors down from the GP's surgery. The truly cautious said nothing out loud within 100 metres of the pharmacy.

"You don't vape," Katya pointed out.

"Aye, well, Alison the boss does so I said it was only fair I got vaping breaks too. Is he a good kisser? And did ye use tongues—"

As one, Katya and Gaby marched off. "Just wait until I get home!" Mhari called after them. Then, the questions would begin in earnest.

Chapter Nineteen

"Hey—what have you been doing today?"

Zac caught Katya coming out of Jamal's shop late on Friday afternoon. She'd finished work at lunchtime and then tackled Maggie Broon's Boobs. Everyone promised the view from the top of the hills at the other side of the loch was spectacular. Maybe it was. When she'd reached the summit, her breath coming in raggedy gasps thanks to the steep ascent, a thick layer of grey cloud swirled around obscuring everything.

Still, the ache in her calves and quads told her she'd exerted herself. Perfect justification for buying a large bag of crisps, some hummus to dip them in and an evening Netflixing in the living room wrapped in her duvet.

"Hill climbing," she said. If she mentioned the local nickname, Zac would respond with innuendo or flirty banter, and she wasn't in the mood. Still, Psychic Josie's name for him, NSFW, flashed through her mind. Difficult to stop all the filthy scenarios her imagination conjured up.

"Can I walk you home?"

"It will take all of five minutes."

She let him anyway.

"What are you doing this evening?"

"A hot date eating crisps." She held up her bag. "On my own."

"So long as they aren't salt and vinegar, right?"

Despite herself, she smiled. Nice of him to remember. And smart of him not to angle for an invitation. That was the thing with a giant bag of crisps—they were best eaten in solitude where you let the crumbs drop all over your top and double dipped.

As they passed the Lochside Welcome, Ashley came out carrying the board which usually advertised that day's pizza specials. *Charity Pub Quiz in aid of Alzheimer's UK*, it said. *First prize—all your food and drink for a week.*

"What's your general knowledge like?"

He'd stopped walking, the wind lifting his hair back from his face. Katya admired the way it highlighted the squareness of his face and then told herself off for fancying an Action Man. Even a NSFW one whose hands and mouth did all kinds of things in those blue-rated fantasies.

"So-so." The Jane Austen temporary memory loss still too humiliating to remember.

"Want to be in my team?"

He always loaded much of what he said with multiple meanings. What team? The pub quiz team stroke the outsiders stroke the potential couple? Still, a charity pub quiz was a community-minded thing to do. And spending a Friday night alone eating crisps was pitiful.

"Okay. I'll get you at your house at eight o'clock."

It was closer to half-eight. The achy calves and quads demanded a bath, and she'd fallen asleep in it, only waking when the water turned cold.

Zac had changed into a brown suede jacket over a turtleneck jumper and narrow trousers with turn-ups. Her tea-dress worn over thick tights and over-the-knee boots meant she matched him for smartness. Hopefully, it wouldn't make them stick out any more than they already did. Gaby said Stewart often showed up to the pub in his pyjamas.

Ashley, manning the door so he could frisk people for undeclared phones, gave Zac a hard look when they came in.

"Aye, aye—Mr I'm Just Here To Do An Online Food Business. A wee birdie tells me that's no' all you have up your sleeve."

Zac plastered on his friendliest smile. "Yes, I wanted to talk to you about that. I've had an idea about a joint venture so we both profit. Can I pop by tomorrow afternoon and tell you all about it?"

"It had better be good," Ashley harrumphed. "Now, hand over all phones. We're no' one o' those modern quizzes. Google has no place here." He took their phones and dumped them in a large glass bowl on the bar.

Just like the first (disastrous) time she'd gone along, the quiz seemed to attract the entire village, and it was standing room only. She and Zac squeezed their way through bodies and shouted conversations, perfumes and after-shave competing with the smell of the turkey and Brie pizza Ashley was trialling for the Lochside Welcome's Christmas menu.

Every table was taken. Gaby, huddled together with Jack, Mhari, Jolene and Stewart, gave her a wave and a smile. When Katya had texted her with the crisp-night plans earlier, she'd messaged back saying, "Please come! It'll be a laugh."

At the bar, she ordered two pints from the barmaid, who rolled her eyes before she headed back to where Stewart had parked himself at the bar and made yet more demands for beer. As she and Zac had got to the pub too late to find a table, they'd need to stay at the bar. Ashley shuffled over and gave them paper and pens. "I'll forgive you your pop-up plans," he said, darting wary looks at Stewart. "If you're brainy. Jolene telt me her man was away on a coding course this weekend. If his team wins, I'll go out of business before the week's out."

"Public school squeezed knowledge into us by hook or by crook. My memory's legendary," Zac told him, scribbling a team name on the top of the sheet.

I was right about the public-school background, Katya congratulated herself. The men who'd attended them were easy to spot. Eton or Harrow were her best guesses—England's incubators for politicians, business leaders and media executives.

"Mine too," she answered. "Without the unearned privilege."

He only laughed. "Come the rebellion I promise you can have me up against the wall."

Back to the flirty banter. "As if. There would be too many other delightful Tory boys to ram my bayonet into."

Across the room Gaby gave Katya the thumbs-up, meant to be unseen by Zac, but he shoved his shoulder into hers when he saw it.

"Gaby likes me, then? She's not on the list of people who'll stab her bayonet into me."

"Nope," Katya said. "Although excusing Jack, Gaby's taste in men hasn't always been spot on."

Ashley rang the bell to start the quiz. Silence descended as the quiz master Big Donnie, who wore a Barbour jacket and matching waxed hat despite the ferocious heat of the place, cleared his throat and began the questions.

"Sports first," Katya said as Zac took up the pen, ready to jot down answers. "Bound to be the round for you, so long as the questions are cricket and rugby related, rather than football."

But it was Katya who managed all the cricket and rugby questions, while Zac supplied the answers for the football ones. He also knew the winner of the last darts world championship. She awarded him extra points for not grinning too smugly afterwards. He had answers for all the questions in the history round too. Katya remembered everything in the literature round, although again he surprised her by knowing the answer to a Charlotte Brontë-related question.

Half time—and in finest half-time tradition, the bar owner offered to send out free snacks and update everyone on the scores so far. The teams mingled.

"You're in second place!" Gaby exclaimed, yelling her team's drinks orders to the harassed barmaid. "How brainy!"

"And there are only two of them," Jack said. "I thought celebrity gossip was your speciality, Gaby?"

"Not mine, Mhari's," she said, "and she got Katie Price's kids' names muddled up with Kerry Katona's."

"Molly, Lilly-Sue, Heidi, Max and Dylan-Jorge," sang out a female voice behind them, its upper-class braying quality all-too familiar. Lois and Angeline. Zac's face fell—their appearance not a delightful surprise for him either. He murmured a 'sorry' to Katya and shuffled off his seat to flee to the loos. Ten out of ten to him for cowardly behaviour and landing a person in it. Katya took a fortifying gulp of beer and turned.

"Lois, Angeline!"

The two women smiled in sync. "Katya, how lovely to see you again. We thought we'd join in the village fun."

Had anyone noticed how they'd aligned themselves with her? Their loudness had silenced everyone anyway—that, and the outrageous outfits. The embodiment of Ab Fab, as they both said. Lois wore a puffa skirt, tragically back in fashion. She'd paired it with a bright pink fake fur and wedged slider shoes, while Angeline's tight white trousers skimmed bony ankles on top of feet teetering on spindly heels. On her top half, she wore what looked like a chain-mail cardigan over a mini slip dress.

Katya turned to Lois. "You forgot the sunglasses. To wear indoors." That set the two of them off in peals of laughter, making her wonder if she ought to consider a side hustle as a stand-up comedian

Lois held her hand up to her mouth to do an exaggerated whisper. "If there's another celebrity gossip round, you're laughing. Angeline and I know everything about the rich and famous. We read Starz magazine avidly."

Mhari didn't bother with the niceties. "Who are youse? What are you doin' here?"

A good question.

Angeline extended a hand. "Angeline Berringer. And my friend Lois Manson. Young Zac here is our prodigy and we're big fans of Scotland. We arrived in Lochalshie a few days ago because we wanted to see what darling Zac is up to. Now we can join Zac's team."

"You're no' allowed to call in reinforcements to your team half-way through," Mhari said.

She folded her arms, bouncer-style. No one else did, but Katya sensed the rest of the pub's regulars lean back against their seats, regard them beadily and nod along. The Lochside Welcome's pub quiz had been going almost twenty years. You mocked or disregarded the rules at your peril.

"Am I right, Ashley?" Mhari called out. Ashley, in the middle of pouring yet another still thankfully paid-for pint for Stewart, shook his head.

"No, Katya and Zac didnae have the full complement to start with. The rules say teams can have a maximum but no minimum. They don't say anything about folks joining in half-way."

And presumably, the more people on a team that wasn't Stewart's, the merrier.

Mhari sniffed and turned back to her team, whispering furiously. Katya did her best to make it look as if she was with her new team members under sufferance.

Zac hadn't exaggerated when he said public school crammed one's head with useless facts. Sport, politics, history, geography, science, film and TV, Netflix's most popular box sets, YouTube's biggest stars—he appeared to know everything, and the few questions he couldn't answer were filled in by Angeline. Katya's hands and feet twitched—always a killer sign of lust kicking in despite the voice that screamed, *Are you sure, Katya, really, really sure?* The evasiveness, failing to mention the one crucial thing she'd found out about him after digging?

But of all the things he could do, the non-stop flow of answers made him shoot skywards in her estimation. The show-off car, the flirty banter, the too-rehearsed speeches about sustainable food production and even the physical contact she'd had with him so far. None of them of them worked on her libido like this.

Be serious, Katya, she scolded herself. *Pub quizzes only test general knowledge and memory. It's not a sign of true intelligence.* But she caught snatches of whispered conversations between him and the two witches. Behind those one-two-word answers she heard substance. Zoom, zoom—the libido revved up further.

The quiz ended, and Stewart rose to his feet, evidence of too many pints there in the unsteadiness. "I need tae walk Scottie here. Dinnae announce the winners till I'm back."

Ashley gathered in all the papers. He promised a strict and neutral marker, handing them over to Big Donnie. Gaby scuttled over to join them, providing Lois and Angeline with a one-sentence description of various villagers when she asked.

Big Donnie gave the sheets back to Ashley, who rang his bell and silence descended once more. "The judge's decision is final," he pre-empted what was coming next—an unpopular result. "And in third place…"

"Hold on," Jolene called out. "What about Stewart? He's not back yet."

"Too bad," Ashley replied. "The rules also say the results must be announced as soon as the judge has spoken. So, in third place, Agatha Quiztie!"

Jack, Gaby, Jolene, Stewart and Mhari cheered. The local rugby team who provided bouncer services for the Lochside Welcome when necessary came second.

"And the winning team is… Big Fact Hunt!"

A second of stunned silence before everyone got the name, titters and then boos and hisses when everyone realised who they were.

Katya put her head in her hands. "I can't believe you called our team that," she hissed at Zac. "How utterly juvenile." Well, a teeny bit funny, perhaps. Lois got to her feet, threw out pink fur-covered arms, and announced that drinks were on the Big Fact Hunt. Boos rapidly changed to cheers.

Katya hoped Stewart hurried back. Missing out on the winner announcement and first prize was one thing, but not being there for a free drink added extra insult to injury. As he presented the team with the vouchers for their free meals, Ashley muttered fevered thanks.

"I was banking on Stewart not turning up and I just about had a heart attack when he came in. You folks can do my quiz anytime you want."

The voucher said they were each entitled to a turkey and Brie pizza, a helping of chocolate decadence dessert and all their drinks for a week starting tomorrow. When Lois said they were leaving in two days' time, Ashley offered to bring her a pizza.

Lois shook her head and sighed. "Love to, dear one, but I only need to look at a carb for it settle on my hips. It's years since I've eaten pizza."

If haute couture was outlandish, the concept of a carb-free diet came across as extremism gone mad. Heads shook in disbelief. But free drinks went a long way towards making a person reasonable, and people gathered around them, wanting to ask the newcomers questions. The two women had mastered the art of appearing bright, bubbly and open without giving anything away. Job inquiries, why they loved Scotland so much, how they knew Zac—everything was expertly deflected. Secretive, Zac said. Not half. Mhari repeated her questions several times, however, the expert interrogator well aware they weren't getting answered.

"Anyway, we must go," Lois said. "Too much excitement for one evening. Enjoy your drinks everyone. Zac—are you coming?"

No invite for Katya then. Why the disappointment?

Zac grabbed her hand, pulling her knuckles to his mouth and kissing them lightly. His eyes glittered. "Did you enjoy your evening?"

No point pretending she hadn't. "You're okay company."

"That bet I made with you? It pains me to say this, but one of the pieces you wrote about me has been picked up by one of the major media outlets and they want an interview."

"We don't get to go out on a date then," she smirked, and he grinned, blowing her a kiss. "Sure that's what you want?" She raised her shoulders to her ears and fluttered her eyelashes.

As she watched him go, Gaby, Jolene and Mhari swirled in to fill the gap Katya's departed teammates left.

"Tell us all—especially about those two skinny cows," Mhari said, "or I'll let myself into your bedroom every morning just as you're waking up and fart. Ye ken I can fart to order, don't ye?"

"She can," Jolene confirmed, "so yeah, spill. Are you and the Viking God an item?"

Gaby nodded, pug-dog style. They'd always confided in each other, but Katya had found it harder to do when Jack came on the scene. Their happiness was so... obvious and ever present, her best friend didn't feel like the best person to talk to any more.

She was about to tell them Mhari's torture threat was useless when Stewart, his shaggy haircut windswept and his eyes wild, burst back in the bar. Scottie added to the effect, barking his head off. Katya clasped Jolene's arm.

"Gaby! It's Mena, your wee cat," Stewart blurted. Katya closed her eyes. She knew where this was going, and it was nowhere nice.

"She's on the road," Stewart said, tears welling up. "Some eejit's knocked her down."

Gaby paled, her face losing its normal pretty pink glow, and she grabbed her coat from the back of her seat.

"Jack, Jack," she gabbled. "Come on. That vet in Ardlui will take her in as emergency."

Katya's heart flipped over for her friend. "Gaby…" she began, Jack saying her name at the same time and gently touching his girlfriend's arm. Stewart flung his arms around her. "Ah'm sorry, Gaby!" he said, tears running down his cheeks, "but she's deid."

Chapter Twenty

Stewart's news silenced everyone, making his and Gaby's sobs all the louder.

"What happened?" Katya asked Stewart, who gulped back tears long enough to say Scottie had sniffed out Mena's little body hidden behind a hedge just off the main street. As there was blood crusted on her nose, he reckoned a car knocked her down and she'd managed to get up and stumble to the hedge and died there.

The description proved too graphic for Gaby, who thrust her fist into her mouth. She attempted to put her coat on once more. "I'm going to get her," she told us all. "Poor little Mena can't…"

Jack took her hand. "C'mon. We'll pick her up and I'll bury her in the back garden wrapped in one of our nice blankets."

He dropped a kiss on Gaby's head, and Katya welled up too as she watched them leave. Stewart shuffled off to the bar, the trauma too much for him.

"A pint," he called out. "And a whisky chaser. Ah've had

an awfy shock." Scottie put his front paws up on the stool. Whatever the doggie equivalent for a pint and a whisky chaser was, he looked in need of it.

No one had asked the obvious question. "Who did it?" Katya piped up. "Someone hit the cat and left her. You don't bump into a cat in your car and not notice."

True. Her mum had done it once when Katya and her sisters were little girls. The five of them howled for hours afterwards, the sickly thump of it too easy to recall. Nice people owned up; however difficult such a confession was. Mena wore a collar that said where she lived.

"Mmm-hmm," Jolene answered. "Must have been a tourist—someone passing through and taking the road too fast."

"Rotten luck," Mhari said. "Poor wee pussy."

Everyone drifted off, the night spoiled. Mhari told Katya she was off to her mum and dad's, having run out of clean clothing once again and not willing to risk trying the washing machine in the flat.

Back at the flat, Katya phoned Gaby, who was still sniffling, asking endlessly, "Do you think she suffered?", and telling her about the poor little stiff body she and Jack picked up off the pavement before the foxes got her.

"No," Katya said, crossing her fingers it was true. Animals weren't sentient beings, so they didn't fear or know death but that didn't rule out pain. Hopefully, poor little Mena hadn't lived that long after the car hit her.

And who, who, who could have been as heartless to knock over poor little Mena and not stop and try to find the cat's owner? A hit and run, Gaby solemnly declared, and didn't people go to prison for that?

"Yeeessss," Katya said, "but I'm sure that's for humans only. Sorry."

"Jack's mum said she'd pop in tomorrow. Apparently, Psychic Josie uses spirit animals from time to time, and she reckoned she might be able to contact Mena on the other side and find out if she is okay."

In the background, Katya heard someone snort.

"It's okay. She means well. And much as I like the thought of Mena telling me she didn't feel any pain and thanking me for looking after her, I'm not at the stage of believing anything Psychic Josie says. No offence, Jack."

"None taken."

"Although part of me wishes there was something in that rubbish, so the spirit of little Mena haunts her killer for the rest of their life."

Quite. Promising she would pop round the next day too, Katya hung up.

An evening that turned out unexpectedly enjoyable and then ended so horribly. Katya didn't want just herself for company. If only she'd managed to persuade Mhari a washing machine only needed a person to put clothes in, add powder to the dispenser, select a programme and press 'on'. God knows, she'd tried plenty of times. They could have snuggled up in Katya's bed under the maximum-tog duvet, electric blanket going full blast, and found a horror film to distract them. Mhari, like Katya, loved horror. No matter how rubbish your life seemed, it was unlikely to be as bad as being chased through a dark empty building by some unknown blood-thirsty monster. Films like that always cheered one up.

A longing for Dexter struck her. He'd have found something comforting to say. Katya doubted anyone else in the world knew this, but apart from the Blissful Beauty and several influential beauty vlogger accounts, Dexter's YouTube subscriptions comprised cat and dog rescue channels. "Not manly, is it?" he'd remarked when she caught him once, engrossed in the story of a starving cat found in a dumpster. "I guess I should watch car test drives, or sports stuff."

"Better you don't," she smiled, and tucked the info away securely. Someday, it might come in useful.

"And the cats are super-cute," he added, pulling her in so she could see the clip too. She couldn't be sure, but he might have wiped away a tear when it ended, the starving cat now fat, fluffy and purring his head off as he curled up on his new owner's lap.

She'd forgotten to put the electric blanket on before she got into bed. When Gaby had lived with Mhari, this had been her room (the smaller one, as Mhari ensured she bagged the biggest and best one), the electric blanket a welcome gift left for Katya. Even though she'd kept her socks on, the bed's iciness when she slid between the sheets made her shiver. She resigned herself to not drifting off for at least an hour, her mind playing over dead cats and the nagging worry that Lois, Angeline and Zac were up to something.

She got her phone out, determined to find distraction. Experts didn't recommend looking at your phone after eight o'clock at night but as she was wide awake anyway, where was the harm? The email notifications showed the latest one came from Madeline. Mentoring did marvellous things for Katya's mental health. Every single email Madeline sent cheered her up, whether she was making suggestions or telling Katya how brilliant her work was. And wasn't it kind of her to send a message this evening? She'd warned Katya that emails might be tricky for the next few weeks as her company was going through a terrifically busy time.

"How has your week been, honey?" her message said.

"Fantastic job with Caledonian Brewers. They told me that content plan you put together for them for their social media accounts was a-may-zing." (A direct quote.)

Madeline, Katya decided, was so nice she wouldn't mind if she shared the cat story with her. Gaby's face when she realised her cat was dead was too easy for Katya to recall. And she hated the thought of some heartless git knocking the cat down and not stopping.

She typed out the message, telling Madeline all about it and how upsetting it had been. The minute it disappeared from the screen, she regretted it. The woman ran a high-powered recruitment company and made a ton of money. What would she care about a cat being run over in a remote village?

But a reply came back straight away.

"Honey, that's awful. I'm so sorry. I'm a cat lover too. I hope your friend recovers. And you."

Madeline shared a story too—a personal one about a cat she'd had as a child. The cat had been her pet from a young age, but her family circumstances weren't great. When her father abandoned the family, and her mother was forced to move, the cat got left behind.

"I never knew what happened to that cat and it still bothers me. My job means I have to travel a lot as otherwise, I'd love to have a cat."

Me too, Katya thought, startled by the immediate reaction. A cat, a steady boyfriend—the two of them waiting for her when she came home... Boy, she'd turned into a sap. Did Madeline have a partner? The clues weren't there. She mentioned no one, but perhaps people at that level didn't. And maybe that was why Madeline seemed to have thrown herself into helping Katya. Whatever. She was grateful.

Madeline signed off with kisses. Again, Katya was taken

aback. Gaby always ended her emails and texts with kisses, even the ones she sent to her boss, Melissa. "That's what we do," she said when Katya asked. "Our generation are much more open about our emotions. We're not stiff and formal like people in their 40s and 50s."

Katya didn't include herself in that category, but Madeline's kisses touched her. She sent her one back and Madeline replied, "Goodnight, honey. Send me an email when you're feeling better and we can talk about your work plans and anything else you want."

Cheered, Katya took her phone into the living room to charge. Perhaps Madeline could advise her about Zac too, the last thought she had before turning off her bedroom light and snuggling down to sleep.

Chapter Twenty-One

"Your phone's been going crazy," Mhari told Katya the next morning when she stumbled out of her room after a lousy night's sleep.

Katya had woken at 4 a.m., the jumble of thoughts from last night still plaguing her. Those worries segued into general woe about the state of her love life—the all-too-familiar why, why why she and Dexter hadn't been able to work things out and his insultingly quick ability to move on.

Stupid question, Katya—you've met Caitlin. Can you blame him? Inner pep talks, she found, rarely worked. Even if you bombarded your emotions with logic, they didn't listen or bother to feel better.

Mhari, ready for work in her pharmacy assistant uniform of a white tunic with green braiding over dark green trousers, handed the phone over.

"Have you looked?" Katya asked, ticking herself off for having let it out of her sight. Experts recommended not sleeping in a room with a charging phone, but she should have known better. Granted, Katya hadn't told Mhari her

PIN code, but she never underestimated her flatmate's ingenuity. She must have managed hacking phones by now.

"No, no," Mhari said, all faux innocence, "but there's a text fae Mr Flashy Car Posh English, Gaby's sent a few messages and Madeline's emailed ye."

Katya gritted her teeth, vowing to turn off all notifications so those with too much of an unhealthy interest in others weren't able to read them on the lock screen. Gaby asked her to come around asap. Zac's text was apologetic. "Sorry! Hadn't realised they were planning to return last night. See you soon, yeah?"

Madeline's message was far more interesting. "Katya, hi! I hope my email finds you well. Your work continues to dazzle everyone I refer you to—a fantastic recommendation for my company. Thank you. Can I make another suggestion? How would you feel about writing skincare and beauty articles for a company about to launch in South Korea?"

Heavens, did she mean…?

Mhari still hovered, awaiting an update. "Won't you be late for work?" Katya asked, her flatmate too expert to take heed of such an obvious hint.

"No. Gonnae tell me what Zac said?"

"Mr Flashy Posh Car English wanted to know when you won't be here this week so he can sneak round to the flat and shin his way up the ivy trellis to my bedroom where I let him in after he taps out the SOS sign in Morse code. Then the two of us make mad, passionate love. All without you knowing a thing."

Mhari blew her a loud raspberry. "Whatever. I'll find out, ye ken."

Threat uttered—and lessened somewhat because Katya's laughter followed her as she stamped her way down the stairs—Katya found herself alone and able to read Madeline's message in peace.

"The company is Blissful Beauty—the one owned by Caitlin Cartier. And I guess it ties in neatly seeing as you will be writing her autobiography in the near future! They are about to launch in South Korea, a huge market for them, and they desperately need content. It would mean hard work but in the short term only and would tide you over. What do you think, honey?"

I think, I think I want to do it.

Even if the marketing manager in charge had dumped her so ignominiously. Not something to tell her mentor. Madeline was a professional. Personal feelings didn't come into it. Anyway, she would mull it over. In the meantime, she had Gaby to cheer up and the mystery of Lois and Angeline to solve. And Katya wanted answers.

———————

The Gaby who opened the door was red-nosed and piggy-eyed, Jack hovering in the background.

Katya hugged her and dug out the article she'd printed out about coping with pet bereavement. Too much, she might have said a year ago. But that was then and this was now. Reassurances given—no, no Gaby felt dreadful, but she wasn't suicidal. Her almost-mother-in-law had asked too and had appeared disappointed when Gaby said no. Dr McLatchie had just completed a mental health first-aid course and was desperate to practice her new skills. She'd looked forward to communing with Mena's spirit and that offer of help had been firmly knocked back too.

The house smelled of baking. Once she and Gaby sat down, Jack brought out tea and plates of freshly made shortbread—another margarine, vegan-friendly version he'd made on Katya's behalf. "Promise me you will enter the Great British Bake Off," Katya repeated, the shortbread melting in her mouth. An attractive, softly spoken red-headed Scotsman—he'd win the people's vote if nothing else. And no matter what placing he got in the competition, someone somewhere would offer him a TV show or his own YouTube channel afterwards.

Gaby's iMac screen showed the templates for the Blissful Beauty South Korea website. She spotted Katya's glance at it and apologised.

"It's okay. I'm doing work for Dexter. Through an, um, agency, though he knows I'm doing it."

Funny she'd not wanted to mention Madeline to Gaby. Was it she was scared she might sound too fangirl and Gaby wouldn't like it? Their friendship had changed. Hardly surprising, given that until recently Katya and Gaby had lived close to each other for years. When Gaby's ex had vetoed his girlfriend going to art school too far away where she might meet guys one hundred times nicer than him and get up to all sorts of shenanigans, Gaby had persuaded Katya to join her in Norwich.

Katya had moved to Lochalshie too, and partly to be with Gaby, but Jack was a different kettle of fish to Ryan. He was nice, for a start. A person a girl found easy to confide in or talk about anything, such as the things she used to save for her best friend. And Gaby loved spending a lot of time with him. But Katya missed her and Gaby's one-time super-close friendship. And the increasingly personal emails she sent Madeline were because of this. Still, she would not admit this to Gaby and not today of all days.

"Are you okay working for Dexter?" Gaby asked, her green eyes blinking at Katya. The concern touched her.

"It's fine. These days, he's so important a minion briefs the writers, so I'm not in contact with him. And Blissful Beauty pays so well."

"True. I've been slaving away for him for weeks now," Gaby said, pointing at her screen with its too recognisable pink and silver glitter Blissful Beauty branding.

"Which brings me on to next weekend," Gaby threw in, hyper-casually.

"What?" Katya said, brushing the crumbs off her fingers.

"Jack's had this offer from the VisitScotland people in Oban. He tries out one of the restaurants there and one of the Airbnb properties so he can recommend them and take tourists there as part of his Highland Tours. He said it would be the ideal thing to cheer up a bereaved, over-worked graphic designer."

The hyper-casual mention? Katya suspected another ulterior motive.

"And?"

"And there's a ceilidh in Oban that evening too, so we could go along. Good practice for we Sassenachs, Katya. We've no idea how Scottish dancing works and we don't want to make fools of ourselves on New Year's Eve."

"And?"

"So, the Airbnb property sleeps eight. Might as well make a trip of it—me and Jack, Stewart and Jolene, you and Mhari."

"That's six."

Gaby prodded Jack.

"S'pose we could invite Zac too, eh?" said Jack.

Gaby must have roped him in, reckoning the not-so-subtle suggestion would sound better coming from him than her. Just as Gaby was a hopeless liar, Jack made a terrible matchmaker. The words had come out through gritted teeth.

"Gaby—has your interference in my love life ever worked?" Katya asked, arching her eyebrows. When she'd been with Ryan, her best friend had been forever trying to set her up. She'd included most of Ryan's friends, all of whom were as big a douche bag as him.

"Granted. But he seems ever so keen. And he's here, he's fit—not a patch on Jack but if you like blue-eyed blondes, he's ideal."

Time for the big reveal.

"I did some digging when I first met him. He's married," Katya said, watching her friend's mouth round in surprise.

"He doesn't wear a ring!"

She gave Gaby the look that remark deserved.

"But he's not anymore, is he?" Gaby said. "Um, I have seen no one else at his house…"

Another 'oh c'mon' look.

"I know, I know. Make allowances for me. Grief has turned me stupid. How did you find out he was married? Did he tell you?"

Jack caught Katya's eye and smiled ruefully. He didn't mean it nastily, but she took it as an agreement that yes, her friend's grief resulted in daft questions or perhaps she needed coffee instead of tea. He got up and headed for the kitchen, while Katya told Gaby what she'd found out.

Katya had checked Zac out online soon after they'd met. Didn't everyone nowadays? He'd put enhanced privacy settings on his social media sites, but page six of Google's results included a link to an obscure society photographer's website. In it, a couple so glossy-looking they could only be from the top of the privilege pile grinned at the camera. A younger Zac, his blonde hair much shorter than it was now, but Zac, nonetheless. Under the picture, the caption confirmed the names and date the marriage took place. The pictures were dated several years ago. The woman's wedding dress with its long sleeves, fashionable at the time thanks to the Duchess of Cambridge's choice for her 2011 nuptials.

"He must have got married when he was twenty!" Gaby exclaimed. "And I thought I was too young getting engaged at twenty-six, remember?"

The aforementioned douche bag Ryan. He of the Little Ryan notoriety.

"Does he hide his phone from you, or take calls in private?" Gaby asked.

Yes he did but given that she still had to find out what he was up to with Lois and Angeline she suspected the calls more likely related to that than to a mysterious wife. Katya looked her up too and found a woman in Brighton running a restaurant. She wasn't called Cavanagh but that meant nothing. Many women no longer took their husband's name when they got married.

No mention of Zac there, but Natasha Wrayworth was definitely the wearer of the long-sleeved wedding dress.

"Have you asked him?" Jack said, plonking a full-to-the-brim mug of coffee in front of her and his girlfriend. He'd added a cute stencil to the top, a leaf floating on the foam.

"He should have told me!" she said. "It's a biggie, isn't it? 'I am married', or 'I was married but now I'm divorced.' And even if he is divorced, it is still worth mentioning."

"Totally!" Gaby cried, backing her up. "Why do men not tell you things so then you…"

"Second-guess their every move because you haven't asked outright, make up your own reasons for them and then get upset about it?" Jack sipped his coffee and pretended innocence. Gaby had made all sorts of assumptions about Jack before they got together—the main one that he was hung up on his ex because he held on to a painting of her. The real reason? He'd painted it. He was proud of it. End of.

"Oh, you!" she said, mock-slapping him on the knee. "It's a fair question, though, Katya. Why not ask Zac outright? If he turns out to be a lying toe-rag, we'll all hate him and find you someone else. Won't we, Jack?"

Jack looked as if he'd rather have teeth drawn than do any more Gaby-imposed matchmaking, but he nodded anyway.

"Back to the Oban ceilidh trip, then!" Gaby said. "Do we invite Zac or don't we? Remember, this is a serious cheer-up Gaby mission. If my best friend comes along with a lovely man in tow, my cheeriness levels will skyrocket."

Katya reached for the last remaining bit of shortbread, promising herself she would get up as soon as it was light the next day and run around the loch twice to compensate.

"Can I think about it?" she said. "I haven't decided if I like or trust him enough yet."

"Of course," Gaby replied, her expression too earnest. Whether Katya liked it or not, she suspected an invitation would wing its way to Zac, anyway. After that, it was up to Katya to decide if she wanted to take advantage or not.

Chapter Twenty-Two

Outside Zac's house, Katya stopped in front of Lois and Angeline's huge silver Land Rover that hogged half the pavement and a good bit of the road.

A tourist or someone from out of town driving far too fast down a narrow road... Weren't the best candidates witches one and two? She bent down to inspect the bull bar for stray spots of blood or fur. Nothing, but who was to say they hadn't wiped it clean afterwards?

"What are you doing?" Zac inquiry was mild. She stood up too quickly, the move bringing her so close to him she felt his breath tickling her cheek. His fingers brushed her arm. And even if it wasn't bare, the touch burned. Physical attraction overrode many logical objections to a person. It made your body scream, *I do not care in the slightest.* Even when plenty of gigantic reasons said she should.

"I thought I'd dropped something."

He crouched to the ground, inspecting the tarmac. "What was it?"

"Nothing. I found it. Anyway, did you hear what happened last night?"

He got up again, shaking his head. When Katya told him, he murmured, "Poor Gaby," but there was no substance behind it. Not an animal lover, then. Though to be fair, Katya wouldn't have counted herself or Gaby as cat lovers this time last year. A lot could change.

He rocked on his heels—a man steeling himself to say something. Katya got in first.

"What might have happened last night if your Fairy Godmothers hadn't turned up?"

"After the quiz ended, I would have done my best to persuade you I'm an okay guy."

He said it straight up—no banter, no flirting, no over-the-top cocky confidence.

"Maybe I might have been persuaded," she replied, thrilled that his eyes lit up when she said it.

He started to say something else, but the door opened, Lois on the threshold, her outfit as outlandish as ever. She wore a golden-yellow fur—Katya hoped it was fake—gilet over skin-tight jeans, a peony pink cashmere jumper, and blingy jangly earrings which definitely weren't fake.

"Katya! How lovely to see you. Are you coming in? We adored what you wrote about Zac's new venture. You made the whole business come alive! I'll make you a coffee," she sang out, voice too loud for its surroundings, as usual. "Zac's got a proper cafetière and a bag of the ground beans too, so none of that ghastly instant stuff."

Jamal, owner of the general store and seller of vast quantities of instant coffee, scowled from his position outside the shop where he swept the doorway and set out the newspaper display.

Better get them inside before Lois made any other gaffs.

"Yes please," she said, "and perhaps you could tell me what makes you and Angeline so fond of visiting Zac here in Lochalshie. I'm dying to know."

Lois flashed her a smile. If it was supposed to make her look innocent and straightforward, it was wide of the mark.

Inside, the house looked far tidier than her last visit—all dirty dishes and mugs cleared away, surfaces gleaming with polish, the laminated floors dust-free, the carpets freshly vacuumed and the place reeking with the clash of plug-in air fresheners and expensive perfumes. Katya stifled back a cough and then sneezed ferociously, anyway; her nose had always been over-sensitive to chemical pong.

"Bless you, darling! This piece," Lois waved a sheet of paper in the air—a printout of an article Katya had written about Zac's new business. "The Sunday Times want to run it in their travel section at some point. And a few specialist food websites have been in touch wanting more detail and some pictures. Marvellous work."

"Thank you," she said. "I hadn't realised when I wrote the article that you planned to use it as a press release?"

Zac handed her a coffee. Papers on the coffee table caught her eye—a council logo at the top and the words 'planning application' there too. Zac spotted her noticing it. He sighed, his eyes flashing first to Lois and then back to Katya.

Creepy, Katya thought, two people inspecting me so thoroughly, waiting for me to work out…

Angeline, so far absent, wandered down the staircase that dominated the open-plan house, her outfit as outlandish as the one her business partner wore—a garishly patterned silk wrap, too thin for Scotland in the winter, worn with a pair of fluffy mules. The straight-out-of-bed hair stuck out in tufts at all angles while her eye make-up seeped into each tiny line around her eyes. Seediness personified.

"What time are we meeting that council officer at the Royal George, Lo-ee-lo?" she asked, stopping at the bottom of the stairs to reach her arms above her and stretch, a move that afforded Katya a glimpse of too much bony chest.

"Katya!" Angeline blinked a moment later. "Didn't see you there. How splendid."

Things began to stack up. Hammerstone Hotels and their new direction—glamping holidays? Hotels that offered more than sumptuous luxury to the modern, demanding customer? Zac, the man setting up an online business and building relationships with local food suppliers. The as-yet non-existent pop-up food business he promised was not a threat to local business.

Katya stood up, folding her arms and adopting her best glare, directing it at the man who'd only admitted to a stupid pop-up van.

"Git," she mouthed at him. A wasted gesture. He'd decided the floor was terrifically interesting to study. Lois took her seat and sipped coffee, while Angeline leant against the door frame to the kitchen area, both of them watching her.

"Hammerstone Hotels have bought the Royal George— the other, not-so-popular hotel in Lochalshie," Katya said, ticking off the points on her fingers. "They plan to turn it into a boutique hotel—whatever that is—specialising in food, retreats, blah, blah, blah. Zac here is your man on the ground and has been busy pretending to the locals he's here to help them."

"He is!"

"I am!"

She couldn't make out whose indignant cry came first.

"Katya!" Once more, Zac was in front of her, taking her hands.

"Reinvigorating the Royal George will help Lochalshie, I promise." Hot hands gripped hers while wide-spaced big blue eyes fixed on her face. "There will be jobs there and the Royal George's mission statement is to buy food that comes from a 50-mile radius, so all the local farmers and producers will benefit. Hundreds of people will flock to Lochalshie. They'll spend money in the general store, they'll pop into the pharmacy, they'll…"

"And the Lochside Welcome?" she snapped. It was the question all the locals would ask.

"Won't have anything to fear!" Lois got to her feet, putting a hand on her shoulder. She and Zac had boxed her in. Katya resisted the temptation to shove her elbows back, one thrusting into Lois's torso and the other into Zac's.

"The locals are so loyal," Angeline added. "And we're planning boot camps at the George too, so no doubt they'll get the escapees—the people who can't cope with a week of hardcore exercise and not much food."

Scorn at the idea.

"Pizza and chocolate cake will be like a red flag to a bull."

She chortled. Katya didn't. Nothing convinced her so far. Hammerstone Hotels had tons of resources at their fingertips, advertising budgets and everything else that could make a hotel in the middle of nowhere succeed. Succeed—and drive out tiny little businesses that didn't have tons of money to spend on marketing.

Was the Lochside Welcome's status as top vegan pizza producer in Scotland and location of a toilet Caitlin Cartier once parked her pert posterior on enough?

Katya had had enough. "I'm off. Good luck with the hotel. I hope it fails and you tossers go back to London where you belong."

It wasn't her finest line, but the tension she'd been holding since Angeline asked what time they were to meet the council planning officer left her body with the softest pfft. She got to the front door before Zac reached her.

"Katya, please! I promise we're not here to decimate local businesses. We can co-exist. The Lochside Welcome can cater for the locals and people doing day trips. It's a great place for lunch and overnight stays. We're doing something completely different. I'm sorry I wasn't upfront with you from the start."

"He is!" someone offered from the background.

Zac rolled his eyes. "They're too much, I know."

He took her hand again, gripping her fingers so tightly her rings dug into the skin. She snatched it away. Hint taken, he backed off, holding his hands out in supplication. "Sorry, sorry! But this is true, I promise."

He dropped his voice, leaning closer to murmur the words in her ear. "I don't want to do anything that makes you dislike me, Katya. You're amazing."

In their short time together, Katya had grown used to Dexter. Hyperbole didn't excite her. A guy who came out with 'You're amazing' did not guarantee she roll over puppy-style, tummy in the air begging to be stroked. She let the seconds tick by. Zac did too, wise enough to keep silent. Blue eyes met hers. She blinked first.

"You three will tell the villagers what you are up to and reassure everyone that it won't harm the village businesses?" she asked, raising her voice so the two witches would hear her. "No bullshit about how you're just here to source online suppliers or stupid pop-ups?"

"Yes."

Another shout through from the living room. "All in good time. We've got community meetings planned to do so."

"Are we okay?" Zac whispered.

"Mmm-hmm," Katya said. "Goodbye."

As she walked past the Lochside Welcome, gales of laughter sounded as the door opened, and another smoker let themselves out the door. Saturday evenings were always busy—even in November.

Nobody would laugh when they heard about the plans for the Royal George. Katya hurried past so no one would catch sight of her coming out of Zac's. Her head whirled with it all, and despite the temptation to stomp to Gaby's house and pour it all out, she held back.

———————

What was she to do about the Oban trip? When Gaby had asked, Katya thought Zac's secret was his marital or otherwise status. The Royal George business made the situation more complicated. Did she really want to take him along, knowing what she did—her an unwilling co-conspirator in the plans for the hotel?

As she mulled it over the following day, her phone rang. Zac. Could she come to the Royal George on Wednesday? When Katya asked why, he said he wanted to show her what they were doing there so she could see for herself the plans were no threat to Lochalshie.

"And there is a pop-up van, I promise. The van was always part of my plans. They're delivering it then. Please, please, pretty-please? I'll throw in free food and drink too. I need someone to try my food and tell me if it's okay."

EMMA BAIRD

Persuasion, Katya thought, when it was so persistent and delivered in an attractive package, made him difficult to resist. And she'd tried. Where was the harm?

"Okay—but I want you to tell me the truth. Why you ended up here and everything else. I think you've still got stuff to tell me. About your personal life."

She heard the pause. Someone who'd worked out what she knew.

"Yes, Katya. I'll tell you everything. Promise."

Chapter Twenty-Three

Now Dexter was back in the States, Courtney invited him for Thanksgiving—determined they celebrate this, the most of American of holidays, in style.

Style meant money—and Courtney had little of it. She'd phoned Dexter two days before listing all the dishes she intended to make and ending with, "Hey, can you pick up the groceries, hon?"

"No, Courtney. I've got work to do. No, Courtney, I already hand over a decent chunk of money every month. Can't you budget right and find greenbacks that'll pay for all this instead of asking me again? No, Courtney, I can't take any time off for Thanksgiving anyway…"

He said none of it, handing over the list to his temporary marketing assistant, asking her to order all the food from Whole Foods and get it delivered to his sister's house. She raised her eyebrows. "How many people are you feeding? And I hate pumpkin pie, by the way. You can skip ordering that."

Dexter's new assistant, aka his niece Flower. He'd persuaded Courtney that interning at Blissful Beauty would work wonders for her. Not that Courtney's opinions swayed Flower. As soon as he'd mentioned it, Flower had jumped on the opportunity and glared at her mother as if daring her to object. She didn't.

Flower made an enthusiastic intern, even if she needed close supervision. She'd been desperate to help with the management of Blissful Beauty's social media accounts—a non-stop deluge of updates and comments the full-time PR team of ten struggled to stay on top of. Her first response to someone who dared to say, "Hey, that glow serum is, like, not that great…" had been along the lines of "Die, bitch die." It had taken all of Dexter's considerable persuasion skills to convince Blissful Beauty to keep her on. And Flower that she wasn't yet ready for social media management.

Flower worshipped the ground Caitlin walked on. She'd spent much of her first day in his office whipping out a compact mirror every few minutes to check her make-up was perfect. If your hero was famous for her beauty and skincare company, it stood to reason you looked flawless when you met her. When Caitlin came into Dexter's office, she spotted Flower hovering in the background right away and threw her arms around his niece.

"Hey you! I'm super stoked you've joined the team." When she stepped back, Dexter noticed Flower trembling. Caitlin peered closely at her.

"Is that my sequin stars you're wearing?"

Blissful Beauty's latest release was a set of reusable silver stars you could stick on your cheekbones. A smart product choice, as they were perfect for Instagram posts.

When Flower nodded, Caitlin flung her arms around her once more and ordered Dexter to take their picture. Uploaded onto the social media account, the likes flooded in, and Flower found herself followed by people in their thousands. It was, she told Dexter later, "the best, no Uncle Dexter really, the best" day of her life.

Food ordered, Flower sat back. "So, is Caitlin gonna come for Thanksgiving?"

If she did, would that replace their initial meeting as the best day of Flower's life?

"Nope," he said, keeping his eyes fixed on the imagery the graphic design team had pulled together for the South Korean launch. "You watch her show. You know what she and her family do at Thanksgiving."

True. The day before Thanksgiving, the Cartier clan piled into their ginormous vehicles and drove to the hills where they owned a large, sprawling villa complete with a basketball court, swimming pool, outdoor bar, indoor cinema and endless rooms. Mom, step-dad, sisters, husbands, boyfriends, kids and various hangers-on congregated and drama—often manufactured for the cameras—ensued. Last year, Caitlin had pushed one of her drunk brothers-in-law into the pool. He couldn't swim.

"Still," Flower said. "It would be awesome, huh? Have you ever gone to hers for Thanksgiving?"

When he'd first started working for her, he had, although he and the other Blissful Beauty employees weren't filmed, considered too dull for the show. He'd found the experience... weird. Just as people tended to be smaller in real life when you met them in the flesh, so too did that villa. The whole place felt plastic-y like a film set. If he pushed a wall with the tip of his fingers would it fall down?

"No."

If he told Flower, she'd hint like mad for him to wangle her an invitation. Knowing Caitlin, she'd say yes straight away, and it would suck his niece into the crazy Cartier morass. She was too young for it. Dexter still found the constant scrutiny the Cartiers attracted challenging.

Take those photos that had appeared online and were then splashed all over the magazines.

How did people live like that all the time? He told himself Katya wouldn't have seen them. As far as he knew she didn't subscribe to any of the celebrity gossip sites. Or read the trashy magazines, because they offended her feminist principles thanks to their obsession with women's appearances. Still, a friend of hers might and have pointed them out to her. And much as he couldn't bear to hurt her it wasn't his concern anymore, was it?

By the time Thanksgiving came around, he found himself at the office once more. The current marketing head had come up with a bright idea for Black Friday at the last minute and he'd volunteered to work, one eye on his boss's job, the other on escaping the chaos at Courtney's house. The sale was due to start at the stroke of midnight on Thursday night/Friday morning, and he was still putting the finishing touches to the social media ads at eleven that night. Blissful Beauty's offices weren't deserted but the whole area was spookily quiet—the usual traffic and siren noise dialled down.

"All work and no play…"

"Caitlin! What are you doing here?"

She looked stunning—cut-off shorts, the top button open and tanned, taut abs on show. Her hair rippled down her back and the crop top hugged the plastic-surgery tennis-ball shape of her breasts. Ironically, she didn't seem to be wearing make-up and her olive-tinted skin glowed.

"My family," she said, allowing her shoulders to express whatever those two words really meant. Disdain, frustration, something. "I still haven't told them about… you know."

She started Dexter's treadmill—Blissful Beauty being the kind of company that encouraged employees to keep gym equipment in their offices, all the better to keep them in there for obscenely long periods of time—and hopped on. The movement made her quads ripple. Caitlin was tiny but perfectly in proportion, so her legs looked long.

"If I tell them, that's it," she said. "My mom will see it as perfect for the TV—the 'Caitlin brings her new boyfriend home and introduces them to the family' episode."

She smiled at him. "Even if they have already met him when he came for Thanksgiving two years ago."

Dexter smiled back. "There you go."

"I have thought about it, though. I'm gonna tell the world in my book. D'you think that is okay—the final chapter, 'Caitlin Finds Love'? I thought people might find it interesting. I'm just like anyone my age. Insecure, worried that guys only like me because I'm super-rich."

Not really, Dexter thought, but he found her admission touching. And, like him, Caitlin didn't have positive role models for how relationships should work. Her mother and step-father were about to divorce, her oldest sister was on her third marriage and the second one was splitting up yet again from the Twitter meltdown guy.

"Of course. That'll be the reason everyone buys it."

She stopped the treadmill and flew into his arms.

"Dexie—you are the greatest, I mean the greatest. When was the last time I told you I loved you because whenever it was, it was too long ago. I love you. Times a billion."

Chapter Twenty-Four

The early morning's rain and dark clouds had given way to icy-blue skies and bright sunlight by the time Katya let herself out of the flat the next morning. By ten in the morning the loch, its colour changing constantly according to the weather, reflected the pale blue of the sky. And miraculously, the wind failed to make its presence known. The loch's surface barely flickered—the reflection of the surrounding hills in the water crystal clear.

The Royal George was covered in scaffolding as small teams of men carried out lichen removal and gutter clearing. The improvement was striking. No one in the village had mentioned the hotel and what was going on, but the work must now be obvious to everyone. Lois and Angeline's huge silver Land Rover was already in the car park, despite Zac's house being a mere 500 metres away.

The hotel's front door—a grand, thick wooden structure complete with a huge cast-iron knocker—swung open. Zac, phone held at his ear, cut off the conversation as soon as he spotted her, frown changing to delight in double-quick time. He wore a dark green puffa jacket branded with the Hammerstone Hotel's HH logo picked out in gold lettering, the tag line *Luxury Lifestyle and Leisure*. Naturally, it matched his blonde hair and blue eyes perfectly.

"Hey!" He took her hand. "I want you to see this. Come on."

He steered Katya towards the side of the hotel, bolting when Lois's cry of "Zac!" rang out behind them and forcing Katya into a run. When he halted behind a large beech tree out of the line of sight of anyone in the car park, she bumped into his back and the two of them dissolved into giggles.

"Are you skiving?"

"No. They've been on my back all morning. If I don't escape now, I'll throw them both in the loch."

Katya shuddered. At this time of year, she reckoned they'd last ten seconds before hypothermia set in. As it was, she'd put on a vest, thick sweater, padded coat, scarf and gloves this morning, her blonde hair tucked neatly under a wool beanie. Even so, Zac's body heat penetrated the layers. If she asked him now about his marriage and he decided to tell her all, pressed tightly against her and whispering the words into her ear, Katya would not complain.

"Look!" he pointed at something behind her ear.

Parked at the side of the hotel was the burger van he'd shown her on eBay. It was barely recognisable. The original version—a battered ancient vehicle that had toured industrial sites in Glasgow punting grease-laden bacon butties and cheeseburgers to workers in industrial estates—had been transformed into something street-food hip. Alloy sides gleamed, signs for Zac's Fabulous Fish and Food decorated each side and the front window opened out onto a flat serving area. A chalked-up slate outside the serving window listed the dishes on offer and their prices. In front of the van, four tables and chairs offered customers a lochside view.

"Take a seat," he said, leading her towards it. "I'll get you something hot to drink. You won't freeze, I promise."

To back up his words, he took a heater out of the van and switched it on. It blasted out waves of hot air—doing dreadful damage to the environment no doubt—but Katya's scarf, hat, gloves and thick coat did the bulk of the warming-up work.

She eyed the van cautiously. An online food business, a hotel offering specialist mini breaks AND a van with minimal overheads. Despite the promise of no harm, did Hammerstone Hotels intend to take over the entire village?

Zac placed two mugs of steaming hot chocolate on the table, promised her it had been made without milk and sat down in the chair opposite, his legs spread wide in that universal male entitlement to space that always irritated Katya.

"Drink your chocolate before it cools," he said, raising his own mug in a toast to her. He must have used almond milk, as the chocolate tasted smooth and creamy, top notes of vanilla offset by nuttiness and...

"Is there booze in this?" She set the mug down, pushing it towards him.

He shoved it back. "A bit of brandy. It's a chalet thing. No one in Switzerland would dream of making hot chocolate without a heft—I mean, tiny drop of the hard stuff."

Good grief, the stuff was lethal. But ever so warming at the same time. Every molten drop of it slid down her throat, spreading warmth, well-being and willingness for anything. On an empty stomach, though? Katya, a habitual breakfast skipper, felt her head float off the top of her body, her thoughts so wild and scattered even a loch dip where she and Zac ran naked into its freezing waters suddenly seemed do-able. Desirable, even.

Jeez. How much brandy had he put in that mug? Still, if alcohol lowered inhibitions, it was time to ask direct questions, such as the one Jack suggested. Hang on a minute, though—he'd mentioned Switzerland. The playground of the rich and famous. That figured.

"Don't tell me. You spent a gap year or two in Switzerland?"

A half-smile flitted across his face. "That would fit with what you think of me, huh? Not quite."

The floodgates opened. Brought up the only child of two high achievers—father a top journalist later college lecturer, mother a doctor stroke heiress, there was only ever one way for Zac to go. To the top. As far as the upper-middle classes were concerned, doctors, professors, lawyers, politicians, industry leaders and university professors were the only respectable professions. Zac, despite his general-knowledge prowess, couldn't manage exams. He left school with minimal qualifications and headed for Switzerland to work in chalets. Then, he'd embarked on business idea after business idea with his—

Unable to wait any longer, she butted in. "Zac. Are you married?"

Blue eyes rounded and widened once more, and his hand lifted to rake through his hair. The movement wafted the scent of his shampoo in her direction—something pine, lemony and masculine.

"You're ahead of me."

"Fine. You have thirty seconds to convince me you're not a serial liar and a two-timing cad to boot."

The more she sipped of the chocolate, the less she noticed the burn of alcohol at the back of the throat. Sitting lochside on a cold winter's morning, the skies icy blue but clear and the only sound muffled building work and the call of birds on the loch, was gloriously peaceful. And Zac's words were so soothing, the way he kept his eyes on her face the whole time, the earnest entreaty there...

"I'm separated."

Praise be.

"Have been so for six months—minimal baggage, I promise. That's partly why I'm up here. I wanted a new start."

"Why did you split up?" She stopped herself before she threw in the word 'cheating'. Maybe Zac's wife had been the unfaithful one.

He blinked and then sighed. "Never get hitched just to piss off your mater and pater. It counts as one of the worst reasons in the world. They didn't come to the wedding, predicted it wouldn't last, and they were right. Natasha and I fancied each other like mad, but once that wore off we had nothing in common."

So, the confident smiles in the wedding photographs she'd seen online. Not as care-free and happy as they made out.

"And don't marry someone you then make your business partner," he added. "Especially the last. That works out expensive in the long run."

Definite bitterness—words that belied his promise of minimal baggage. Still, it rang of the truth.

"How old were you when you got married?" she asked, keeping her eyes on his.

"Twenty. I know, no one gets married that young these days."

Too right they didn't, unless they belonged to weird religious cults. Katya conjured up her twenty-year-old self, at the time obsessed with a lecturer on her course and doing everything she could to engineer meetings with him. She hadn't considered herself grown-up enough to leave home, let alone embark on a life partnership.

"I met Natasha in Switzerland while we were both working in the chalets." He lifted his mug of hot chocolate and sipped it. "When they show it in films, it looks fun. A bit of cooking, tidying up and skiing in your free time. Spoiler alert. Chalet work isn't like that. We put in 70 to 80-hour weeks, and when we collapsed into bed at night, we fantasised about escaping. I suggested getting married, and she said, 'Let's go into business together.' I was infatuated. We both were—probably too tired to think straight."

"And now there are no more surprises left?" Katya asked. "Because so far, you haven't been upfront with me and call me old-fashioned, but I like honesty in a person."

He ran his hand through his hair again. "Fair point. Though I never lied outright, did I?"

No. Lies through omission instead. Just as she occasionally did. Still, she could tell how much that business failure rankled. Did the collapse of his marriage cause the same pain? And didn't men feel failure in a different way—toxic masculinity and its strict rules that men must succeed in everything they did?

She put her mug down. Cold, an empty stomach and a booze-laden hot drink made a potent combination. "Can I have something to eat?" she said. "This stuff is... awfully strong."

"I was hoping you'd ask!"

The too-heady hot chocolate didn't seem to have bothered him. He leapt to his feet—legs steady, movements assured—and clambered into the van, leaving the back door open so he could continue to talk to her. She heard things being switched on, the clattering of pots and pans and the swoosh of gas as rings were fired up.

"The thing is... I want you to try something that's not vegan."

The one hundred percent of Katya who believed in sticking to one's principles said, 'no thank you'. But brandy overrode everything, firing up hunger and greed. She held back the 'feed me whatever it is NOW' demand but only just.

"What is it?"

"A venison burger—locally sourced, ethically killed. The deer in this part of the world have a fantastic life and you're doing the environment a favour eating them. They destroy the forestry unless they are culled. Come and see what I've made."

"Okay, but only if you are prepared for an honest, possibly even blistering review."

The World Wildlife Fund was going to need a substantial donation in carnivore offsetting. In her head, she promised them money she would add to their fundraising efforts that evening.

Whatever the brandy had done hadn't affected her movements. She stood up and sent prayers to whoever when she stayed steady and upright climbing the steps into the burger van. Inside, the shiny, clean chrome echoed the feel of the outside. The hob sat alongside a griddle while fridges and cupboards lined the space at the back.

"Wow," she said, peeling off her coat. "It's warm in here."

The griddle was turned full on, its all-encompassing heat batting back the cold air that tried to creep in the back door. That and the brandy-helped insular central heating forced Katya to take her coat off. Tipsy on brandy, she flung it out the back door. It sailed past the table and chairs and drifted down to a graceful halt just before the beech tree. Off came the gloves, the hat and scarf, similarly discarded.

Zac, whose attention had been glued on the burgers frying on the griddle, turned to her and widened his eyes.

"Don't stop now! If you want to do the full stripper thing, I'll whack the heating up even higher."

Katya pirouetted—a movement tricky in a confined space. The brandy-heated stomach was now in charge, making her do very stupid things.

"No, no, it's not your lucky day. But hurry up with those burgers."

He prodded the one in front of him and swivelled so he could see her side-on.

"Coming up. I promise this is worth breaking your principles for."

He was right. The burger he presented seconds later with an ironic bow was sandwiched between a soft white bun and garnished with fried onions and a thin layer of mayonnaise. Her mouth took in the second heavenly Zac creation of the day. It tiptoed then stamped flavour on her tongue. Katya hadn't eaten meat in years. Principles took a person so far, but tofu, Quorn and seitan could never match the iron-rich taste and the way meat made the molars work.

"I hate it. It's the worst thing I've ever tasted," she said, jamming the last too-big bit of it into her mouth.

At that, he wrapped his arms around her, grinning as he watched her chew furiously. When she swallowed the last piece of the burger, all super-smooth mayonnaise, sugar-sweet onions and the long savoury linger of caramelised red meat, he leant forward and kissed her lightly on the lips.

"Do that again. It's the horniest thing I've ever seen."

The proof was there. Pressed this close against him, he did not need to tell her how horny he found it. Katya wriggled closer. She brushed her lips against his. The encouragement spurred him on. She found herself pressed up against back of the van as lips and hands explored, tentative at first and then bolder. She tugged at his shirt, pulling it up so she could run her hands over his back. The air crackled and they were just in the process of finding out what you could manage in such a confined space when a flash went off.

"There you are!" Lois exclaimed, the man at her side rapidly shooting a dozen more pics. Katya willed him to stop. A gob-smacked expression suited no one.

She held a hand out, obscuring her face. "Did I agree to photos?"

The photographer lowered his camera and heaved his shoulders to his ears. Lois beamed. "Didn't Zac tell you? We're here this morning to take some publicity pictures. Would you mind awfully being in them? You could pretend to be a punter, leaning into the van to try some of Zac's delicious food. It's marvellously good, isn't it?"

She sounded too knowing—as if she might have witnessed Katya's undignified burger consumption.

"I…"

"I thought we'd got all the pictures you needed?" Zac said, glaring at Lois.

"A picture of someone eating your food will make them much more exciting."

He turned to face Katya and rolled his eyes apologetically. "Please, Katya—would you mind? If you are in the pictures, they will be amazing."

He was careful to make it sound factual, rather than praise. The photographer broke off from fiddling with his lenses and nodded earnestly too.

"If I must. But I'm not going outside the van. It's far too cold." Now Zac no longer had his arms around her, Katya shivered.

"Terrific!" Lois said, and the photographer started snapping once more. He told Zac to fry more burgers while Katya looked on. She wasn't sure what her role was meant to be. Zac's assistant? When Zac slapped the second burger into another bun and handed it to her she got it. Zac meant her to re-enact the earlier ecstasy. It felt like being on the set of a porn film, the camera snapping away intrusively as she faked a reaction.

"I'll make it up to you," he muttered under his breath, dropping the 'for show' smile for a second. "Just pretend this burger is the best thing you've ever eaten."

Oh, what harm could it do? Katya shut her eyes and opened her mouth. He let the burger rest there as the camera clicked furiously. It was so ridiculous she couldn't help the ginormous grin that lit up her features when she opened her eyes once more.

"Bravo!" Lois exclaimed. "That's our shot of the day, right, Neil?"

Neil gave Katya a far too knowing wink.

The unfamiliar food and the brandy gurgled in her belly ominously. She had to get out of there before something dreadful happened, and all that food reappeared. Time to leave.

"Gotta go! See you soon."

She dashed from the van, hastily retrieving her coat and scarf from where they'd landed earlier, Zac's cries of "Katya, wait!" unheeded.

It was a close call, but she made it back to the flat just in time. Up came the burger and the chocolate, far less appetising second time round. Pale and shaky, she let herself out of the bathroom and flopped on her bed.

You ought to know better—sensible Katya sounded stern. She was right. If someone who hadn't eaten meat for years wolfed down a burger in record quick time on top of booze-laden chocolate, what did they expect? At least this time, she had not thrown up in front of the man she was with. Or a whole crowd of people either.

Her phone bleeped. Zac. "Are you okay?" And then another. Madeline.

"Thanks for that skincare guide you wrote. Blissful Beauty loved it. How are you, anyway?"

The brandy must still be in her system. Otherwise, why type out a long and detailed reply where you told a super-professional, high-achieving woman you aspired to be the truth?

"Sick. Compromised by something I know about that the villagers don't."

"Seafood poisoning?" the reply asked. "It's nasty."

"No, not that," although even thinking about what had happened with Dexter in that fancy hotel made her nauseous once more. And because further explanation was needed, she ended up telling Madeline everything. Zac, who'd flirted with her from the outset. Zac, who hadn't admitted to having been married until she pushed him on it. Zac, who hadn't told the truth about what he planned. Zac, who…

"…I find madly attractive, and I'm so flattered by the attention. I dated a workaholic previously who had no time for me, even though I still miss him like mad now, but I'm desperate to have a normal relationship where we live near each other, see each other all the time, go out together and all the other ordinary things."

"Tough call," the reply came back, "but trust is mega important. You deserve an amazing guy—do you think Zac is the right one?"

No, yes, no? Yes, yes, yes.

She sent thanks for the advice, put her phone down and headed out for a walk, hoping the fresh air would clear her head. She met a tearful Gaby, bag in hand.

"It's not the same going into Jamal's store," she said, "now that I don't need to buy any f-f-food for M-M-Mena."

Katya hugged her. Two white vans sailed past them. Katya recognised them as the ones that had been parked outside the Royal George earlier that morning. As both advertised their building and repair services on their sides, it must be blatantly obvious where they'd been and what they had been doing. Luckily, Gaby didn't seem to notice them.

"So… the Oban trip? Jack says we should set off as soon as Mhari finishes work on Friday—4 p.m. Is that okay?"

The unasked question—and will Zac be coming?

NSFW. The perfect match, according to the stars. Flatteringly persistent. Definitely about to be divorced. In the here and now. Hadn't the universe given her enough signs? Time to move on.

"Great," she said. "I'll ask Zac if he's free."

The smile lit up Gaby's face. Her best friend was ridiculously easy to please. "Fab. We'll have a brilliant time, promise."

Watching her go, Katya took her phone out. She sent Zac a message, his acceptance of the invitation coming back flatteringly fast.

"God, YES. I can't wait to…"

The rest of his reply made her blush to the roots of her hair. She'd set something in motion. Fingers crossed Zac proved to be worth it.

Chapter Twenty-Five

When Friday arrived, the mini-bus turned up outside the flat just after quarter past four, beeping its horn. Katya and Mhari grabbed their rucksacks and headed out. Everyone else was there, Gaby waving enthusiastically from the front and Jolene making those meant to be discreet and never were gestures pointing behind her where Zac was.

Katya sat down next to him, the mini-bus's wide, velvet covered seats much more comfortable than those bus and coach journeys usually supplied. Stewart, armed with a huge cool-bag, passed out cans of lager. Zac took one and popped the tab, passing it to Katya. He didn't take another one, to her relief. It would be a long enough night anyway.

"What music do you want?" Jack asked, and seven different suggestions were offered and argued over. Gaby suggested a sing-along, which was met with derision, while Stewart argued for an obscure metal band no one had heard of. In the end, Jack tuned into Radio 1 and Scott Mills' run-down of the charts.

The pulse and beat of the dance tune at number thirty

did funny things to Katya's body—throbbing and pulsating music that originated in her solar plexus and spread throughout.

"We won't be dancing to these later," she said, and Zac smiled. "No." He shifted himself so he could move closer to her. She'd sat beside him so often now. Waiting for planes, on planes, in pubs, around dining tables and in meetings. Tonight, they'd dance together. A first. The night promised possibilities that made her shiver in anticipation.

"How did the photos work out? Where will you be using them?"

"Fine—you looked beautiful. Look."

He took out his phone and brought the picture up, zooming in to frame her face.

Goodness, it was... revealing. The picture expertly conveyed greed, gluttony, want, desire and more. The old marketing cliché, sex sells. She pinched her fingers together, shrinking the photo back so she could see him too. The message already loud and clear, doubled. In the picture, adoration shone from Zac's eyes.

"So, Lochalshie... Do you see yourself staying for a while?"

Her 'yes' was hesitant, but when she said it, he squeezed her thigh. "Good. If you're here, living miles from anywhere will be much better."

Zac's phone bleeped again, as it had been doing repeatedly ever since they'd pulled out of the village.

"Do you need to answer that?" she asked, remembering Gaby's point about phone calls he took in secrecy. He took it out of his pocket, glanced at it and shoved it back in.

"No need. I'm on holiday as of now. Back to you and me and the end of this evening. What do you think will happen?"

He'd dropped his voice, but Katya sensed five people in front of them ear-wigging.

"Depends on what kind of dancer you are," she whispered back. "How a guy dances often tells a girl everything she needs to know."

"Aye, that's true," came a shout from the front. Mhari and her bionic ears. "Ask Jolene. She and Stewart first got together after the time we held a Valentine's Day dance in the village hall."

Gaby turned in her seat so she could catch Katya's eye and the two of them exchanged disbelieving stares. The question they always asked themselves: what did Jolene see in Stewart? Gaby had once speculated he must be dynamite in bed and they both pulled faces. Maybe she had been right all along.

"I'm brilliant," Zac said, grinning. "At dancing, that is."

Back to the hyper-confident flirty Zac, who made every sentence sound filthy. He let his forearm rest along her thigh. That hand burned red hot and reminded Katya of Psychic Josie's daft flame ratings for compatibility. The heat was literal, then.

By the time the bus arrived in Oban, everyone bar Jack as driver and the four-months-pregnant Jolene was tipsy. Katya and Zac hadn't shared more than two cans, but the label revealed the alcohol content to be much higher than standard lager. And there had been a few too many toasts to Scotland which Katya, Gaby and Zac as incomers felt duty-bound to acknowledge.

Jack parked the mini-bus in the town's car park. As Jack had booked the restaurant for 6 p.m. and the ceilidh started an hour and a half later, they had no time to drop the bags off at the house. The group followed him to the restaurant on the town's high street, its large front window looking out to the water. It was done out in different shades of blue with wooden panelling. A sign advertised it as Scotland's Best Fish and Chips three years in a row.

"That was five years ago," Zac pointed out, but the tang of chips and malt vinegar scented the air all around and the queue for takeaway snaked down the street and around the corner. The accolade must still count. Inside, the tourism people had reserved the party a long narrow table at the front. Dim lighting and candles added ambience, and a woman came forward to take their coats, expressing huge thanks to them for coming all this way.

Zac took the seat opposite Katya, his knees knocking against hers. Candlelight added sharp planes to his face, turning him from attractive to knock-out gorgeous. Katya felt her groin tighten in response.

"Anything to drink?" Another too-cheery waitress handed out menus, superfluous for most customers. Who needed choice in a fish and chip restaurant? Katya requested a diet coke at the same time as Zac asked for two bottles of white wine on the wine list, promising everyone it was an "out of the world variety that will blow your minds."

Food ordered, and to Katya's astonishment the restaurant included a decent-sounding vegan option, Zac poured everyone drinks. He managed not to object when Stewart took the still half-full bottle from him and emptied it into a pint glass.

"Cheers!" Gaby said, raising her glass. "Here's to the memory of my wonderful little cat and ventures new in Oban."

"To Mena and adventures new in Oban!"

Zac, Katya noticed, only joined in the bit about adventures.

"Whatever form those adventures in Oban might take!"

Gaby added. Everyone looked at Katya and Zac and echoed her words once more. Zac tapped his glass against hers and blew her a kiss, which got them a chorus of 'aah's.

She was half-way through her food—the fish bit made from pressed tofu wrapped in nori seaweed sheets coated in beer batter, and convincing—when Zac's foot touched her calf. He was busy talking to Jolene next to him about New Zealand and a holiday he had there years ago, but he'd somehow managed to remove his shoe and the foot edged its way up to her knee.

Katya hadn't realised her knees were an erogenous zone, but the foot-stroking made every nerve cell in her body quiver. She gulped down wine, suddenly unable to eat.

"… yeah, we ended up in Hamilton at one point. Beautiful gardens there, as I remember…"

He leant back, and the foot landed on her lap, the heel pushing at her crotch. Then, the toes ended up there, and she opened her legs. Zac had remarkable toe dexterity, all of them wriggling independently and pushing at the seam of her jeans so it rubbed up against the sweet spot.

"… and we did a wine tour of Blenheim. That's where I picked up a taste for this stuff." He shoogled his glass and turned his head to look at Katya.

"What do you think, Katya? Delicious, isn't it?"

"Fantastic!" she said, her voice squeaky, which prompted Jolene to ask her if she was all right.

"Anything wrong, Katya?" Zac chimed in, straight-faced and his upper body still as his foot continued its miraculous movement. Unbelievable. If he didn't stop soon, she would…

The urgent telepathic message she signalled, *stop it, stop it, it's too nice*, didn't work. The toes kept going and seconds later, she dropped her head, groaned as quietly as she could, slapping her hand over her mouth and turning it into a not very convincing cough.

Once again, everyone looked at her. "Are you okay?" Gaby called from her end of the table where she and Jack appeared to be locked in a battle of who ate whose remaining chips.

"Fine, fine," she said. "Food went down the wrong way."

Zac reached for her glass, smirk in place. "Here, take a mouthful of this. Climax in a bottle, I reckon."

Not safe for work indeed.

Stewart, now on his second pint of the stuff, nodded. "Too right. I dinnae usually like wine, but this is no' bad at all."

The food finished and the restaurant owner waving aside contributions to the bill even though the wine had been the priciest one on the list, Jack said they needed to get to the ceilidh, which was taking place in the town hall on Dunollie Road.

Outside, the night had turned bitterly cold. Katya dropped back and Zac joined her.

"Where did you learn to do that?" she asked, "and thanks a bundle for embarrassing me in public."

He huddled in closer to her. "Oh, it's a public-school trick. I was at a mixed-sex boarding school, and they closely supervised us all the time, so you had to come up with sneaky ways to do things."

He dropped his voice to a whisper. "Wait till you find out what I can do with my tongue."

Lord. She took his hand in hers, enjoying the roughness of it and imagining how his fingers and palms might feel rubbing over the more delicate bits of her. Whatever the sleeping arrangements were in the house Jack had booked, she hoped there was an out-of-the-way bedroom they could claim once the dance was over.

Ahead of them, the rest of the party had reached the town hall. Light flooded out the front, picking out plenty of people coming and going, and pipes sounded. Inside, the woman at the front desk waved them through without paying once again and pointed at the stairs.

The place heaved and the band, all dressed in kilts, was just visible on the stage over the top of heads crammed together. The air reeked of alcohol, perfume and sweat. A woman, also in a kilt, barked instructions that were only just audible above the whiny nasal drone of pipes. Gaby had promised Katya pipes were an acquired taste, but when you got it the sound sent shivers down your spine. Katya resisted the impulse to plug her fingers in her ears. She was yet to be convinced.

At last the dance they'd stumbled upon ended and people moved from the main floor to the sides. She was shoved back against Zac, and his hands burrowed under her top, warm, rough skin scratchy against her waist. She wriggled her hand behind him about to sneakily undo his zip and return the favour he'd done her earlier, when the music started up again.

"Eight-some reel," Jack said. "We'll find a stray body to make up the eight."

And that was that. Katya whirled everyone in the set round and regretted the beers, the wine and the too-big portion of chips. When Stewart—who proved to be an amazing dancer and once more Gaby and she exchanged stares at that—was flung too hard across the room by Jolene and fell flat on his face in the middle of someone else's eight-some, hysteria ensued.

Dance followed dance. None of them complicated, but

with so many about turns, romping up and down and circling around, Katya ended up hopelessly muddled. Gaby threw herself enthusiastically into each new dance, getting every step wrong and falling over. Mhari—sensible woman —sat most of the dances out, too entranced by whatever was on her phone.

Zac managed each dance flawlessly. He glided through them, never mixing up left or right and steering her to ensure she didn't go too wrong.

At least the energetic moves detoxed her. By the end of the evening, she was stone cold sober once more and knackered.

"Right," Jack said. "Let's see what the house is like. I hope it's got plenty of bedrooms." Gaby held a hand up, the first two fingers crossed.

"Let's bag the biggest one," Zac whispered in her ear. "This house better have great sound-proofing otherwise your friends won't get much sleep."

Katya stifled her inner old lady—the one who begged, *I just want to collapse on a bed and sleep for a week.*

The streets were busy, the ceilidh attendees heading back to their homes and too-loud conversations all around them. The Edwardian townhouse, Jack said, had been done up, so it had all mod cons—central heating, power showers, fridges with ice makers and Wi-Fi. The central heating news was welcome. Away from the muggy heat of the hall, the wind coming off the water blew straight through Katya. Would she ever get used to the Scottish climate?

Key retrieved from under the plant pot at the back of the house, Jack opened the door to the house.

"I'll just check the bedroom situation," he said, sprinting up the stairs at the back of the hallway. Katya snuggled up to Zac once more. Everyone else now seemed to accept them as an item. Perhaps even Katya herself. *Move on, Katya, for heaven's sakes. Dexter is long gone.*

Zac rested his head on her shoulder and Mhari held her phone up. "I'll take a pic of you for the WhatsApp group. You look cute."

Her camera flashed and everyone's phone pinged with the update.

Jack trotted back down the stairs; the smile he wore sheepish.

"Er... I think there's been a mix-up," he said. "There's only one bedroom."

"Whaaat?" Jolene and Zac synced their replies.

"I'm sleeping for two," Jolene said. "I need a bed."

Jack nodded. "Aye, fair enough. Does everyone agree?"

As Zac started to say something. Katya stood on his toes. They couldn't take the bedroom from a pregnant woman.

"What is up there?" Gaby asked.

"A huge bedroom—double bed and two couches so four people could go in there. And the living room looks okay."

He pushed open the door of a room to his right. It had two sofas and two big armchairs, all of which looked comfortable. Except that three people would be in there. Zac might not mind performing clever tricks under a table, but Katya drew the line at attempting anything covert while Mhari was in the room. Her flatmate would know, film them secretly and share it with the WhatsApp group.

A discussion ensued, where everyone agreed Jolene and Stewart got the bed, Gaby and Jack took the sofas in the same room, and Zac, Mhari and Katya fought it out for the most comfortable options downstairs.

Gaby shrugged apologetically at Katya and headed up the stairs with Jack, followed by Jolene snapping grumpily at

Stewart who was so drunk his eyes crossed and he had difficulty putting one foot in front of the other. Katya guessed he would snore like a walrus. Downstairs might not be so bad after all.

Mhari rustled around in her bag, pulling out several bars of chocolate. "Want one?" she asked. As Zac and Katya nodded agreement and reached forward to take her offerings, she handed them over and darted into the living room, plonking herself down on one of the sofas. Neat. They were big enough for one person to stretch out. Two would push it.

Zac pulled at Katya's hand, whispering, "The mini-bus. We'll be on our own there."

"I need to get my rucksack from the bus!" Katya said. Mhari shot her a sharp look, letting her know she wasn't fooled. Still, it gave her a room all to herself and she stretched out, a blanket pulled over her and head rested on the cushion. Katya doubted she would be awake if or when they came back.

Outside, the silliness of creeping out of a house and along the streets to get up to all kinds of shenanigans in a mini-bus was so daft it made her giggle. Zac joined in, taking her hand in that rough one of his and musing about what the space in Jack's mini-bus allowed.

He started up on all the things he would do to her. Not to be outdone she reciprocated, running through all the things on her sexual repertoire, some of which made him widen his eyes and say he didn't think they were possible.

The car park appeared around the next corner. Only a few vehicles remained: two cars, a rusty old van, a camper van and...

No mini-bus.

Chapter Twenty-Six

"He parked there, didn't he?" Katya asked Zac, pointing to the empty space at the front, one of those marked out for buses and coaches. He nodded and the two of them paced the car park, hoping to spot a mini-bus hiding behind a stray tree or something. There was no sign of it.

"Do you think the council towed the mini-bus because it was in the wrong place?" Zac said, the southern mindset so ingrained he thought it the obvious answer to a missing car. In London and the south east cars were towed all the time.

"Nope," Katya, "I think someone's nicked it. And—"

"That means we need to go back to the house and tell Jack," he finished.

A worthier thought than hers, as she'd meant to say, "Let's find a hotel and pretend in the morning we never saw this." But Zac was right. If it had been stolen only a few hours ago the sooner Jack reported it to the police, the better.

"Is the universe is trying to tell us something?" she

asked, suddenly convinced she'd read whatever signs and omens wrongly.

He sighed, running his hand through his hair. "No," and with that, he pulled her to him, lips seeking hers. She liked his mouth, the way it moved, firm and confident, and when she parted her lips, the tongue that met hers set off shivers all over her body. Everything about Zac was hyper-physical —the rough hands, the assured dancing, the feet capable of incredible things and now the lips, teeth and tongue that all grazed hers.

Psychic Josie, maybe you're not such an old fraud after all...

They broke apart, though he kept hold of Katya's hand as they walked back to the house, the streets deserted now and the wind howling a gale that froze her hands and feet. Back at the house, she argued with Zac about whose responsibility it was to tell Jack.

"Yours," he said. "You've known him longer."

"Yours," she replied. "You can do that manly sympathy and understanding thing."

Just as they were about to toss coins for it, Gaby appeared at the top of the stairs.

"You guys!" she said. "Is everything okay? Comfy enough? I'm happy to swap. It's a bit... noisy up here."

Gaby had left the bedroom door open—from it, the sound of decibel-breaking snores.

"Jack?" Katya whispered, and Gaby pulled an outraged face. "No, Stewart!" Katya's oldest friend was, and always had been, criminally easy to wind up. Behind her, a tousled-haired Jack emerged, blinking in the light.

"Um, Jack," Katya said, "did you move your mini-bus at any point tonight?"

He shook his head, puzzled and still half-asleep.

"It's not where you left it. Zac and I needed to get something from it." Gaby lifted one eyebrow. "And when we got to the car park, there was no sign of it."

Jack swore, the sleepiness banished in an instant. He mouthed something to Gaby, retrieved his phone from the bedroom and vanished into the bathroom where a muffled conversation took place.

"So, um, had you left anything valuable in the minibus?" Gaby asked. Katya knew what she really meant, and her shake of the head confirmed the question. *"Yes, Zac and I sneaked out to the minibus because we wanted some privacy to..."*

"Coffee, anyone?" Zac said. "We might as well. It'll be a long night."

Gaby came down the stairs. "All right, then. Don't worry about tomorrow. Jack knows people. We'll get transport back easily enough."

The kitchen was fully stocked. The house might not have the ideal sleeping arrangements, but the food in the cupboards and fridge was spot on. Fresh bread, eggs, bacon, milk, cereals, proper coffee, tea, hot chocolate and even Katya's favourite brand of peanut butter. Zac put the kettle on and popped slices of bread in the toaster. Jack joined them a few minutes later.

"It's sorted," he said.

"What, reported to the police?" Katya asked, and he gave her a 'don't be daft' look. "Lachlan Forrester. He knows all the robbing, thieving scumbags round here and the van will be back in place tomorrow. Fully valeted too."

Mhari wandered in, attracted by the noise and the smell of toast. When she heard Lachlan Forrester would be there in the morning, she flushed. Gaby flashed Katya a triumphant grin. At last—something they could tease Mhari about—or info to hand over to the WhatsApp group.

Zac slathered toast with olive oil spread and peanut

butter, and handed slices round, saving the last piece for Katya and taking a bite out of it first before sticking it in her mouth. By this point, it was 3 a.m., and she was dead on her feet. When Jack suggested they all try to get some sleep, she was so relieved she could cry. Zac and Mhari followed her into the living room as Gaby and Jack headed back up the stairs.

"I'll take the armchair," Katya volunteered. It looked comfy enough.

"No need," Zac said, dropping gracefully into it. "You and Mhari have the sofas."

Neither of them argued. Katya pulled the sofa's cashmere throw from the back and wrapped it around her. She was asleep minutes later.

A horn's beeping woke her in the morning. As Jack had promised, when she got up and looked out the front window, the mini-bus sat outside the house, gleaming. On the couch opposite her, Mhari opened her eyes and sat bolt upright. "Is that Lachlan? He's early," and with that, she jumped up and ran out of the room, taking her bag with her.

Zac stood up from the armchair, tipping his head from side to side and rubbing his neck. The armchair couldn't have been comfortable. As he turned side-on, she spotted the not-very-subtle morning glory.

"Um, you might want to get rid of that before Mhari comes back."

She got a sizzling look in return. "Well, there's one obvious way…"

Footsteps clattered down the stairs. "Zac, Katya—are you up?"

Foiled again.

Two hours later and they headed back to Lochalshie in a mini-bus that was much cleaner than it was yesterday, the inside vacuumed and smelling of lavender. They were one person down. Mhari had wangled a lift back from Lachlan in his mud-encrusted Jeep. Katya had never met the mysterious Lachlan before, and he'd come as a surprise. From all the talk—the illegal licence plate schemes and knowledge and influence in the criminal underworld—she'd expected a bearded skinhead complete with tattoos all the way up his arms and on his neck.

But Lachlan Forrester was thin, wiry and absent of tattoos or at least any you could see. Polite and well-spoken too. He'd shook everyone's hands, apologised for their inconvenience and hid his dismay when Mhari asked for a lift home. Lachlan looked like a man who treasured peace and quiet, and the company of his own thoughts.

No one wanted to linger in Oban, the theft having put a dampener on everything. Miraculously enough, Stewart and Jolene had slept through everything the night before and the first they knew of it was Lachlan's arrival first thing. Stewart and Lachlan exchanged high fives when Stewart heard he'd got the mini-bus back.

"Was that Joe and Andy who nicked it, then?" Stewart had asked. "Ye'd think those two eejits woulda recognised the bus and no'…"

Jolene slapped his back hard. Better none of them knew the full extent of Lachlan's criminal activities and acquaintances.

Next to her on the bus, Zac rested his head on Katya's shoulder as the bus made its way out of the town heading north-west. The winds had given way to periwinkle-blue skies and a sun that hung so low in the sky it dazzled and forced Jack to put on sunglasses so he could drive safely.

"What shall we do when we get back?" Katya asked, sure of what she wanted. Talk about delayed gratification.

A heartfelt sigh. "Lots of things and all of them involve you and me naked. But I've gotta go down south."

"What for?"

"Work stuff," he said. "I've got to help Hammerstone Hotels out with their pre-Christmas retreats. I booked the flight weeks ago."

"How long are you away for?" Ah well. As they'd waited so long already, what was another few days?

He straightened up. "Two weeks. Sorry."

She worked the dates out. Two weeks would mean he was back two days after Christmas. Katya had promised her mother she would go back to Great Yarmouth for Christmas and her mum had demanded she stay until the Friday after as that was her youngest sister's birthday.

"I'll be away," she said, explaining what she'd be doing. "I won't be back until at least the thirty-first."

Zac squeezed her hand. "Imagine what will happen at New Year," he dropped his voice. "All good things come to those who wait."

Chapter Twenty-Seven

When Katya opened the door the following morning at an hour far too early to be civilised, the sun was only just up, promising a bright but cold day.

"I want to hear all about you and Zac." Katya's best friend, ringer of the too-early doorbell, greeted her bright-eyed and far too cheery. "Are you an item now? And did you do the deed when you got back to Lochalshie on Saturday? Where's his car, anyway? I went past his house just now and it's not there."

She glanced around her, no doubt seeking it out. He would have needed to hide it well. That flashy red motor stuck out a mile.

"He's away for two weeks. That's a lot of questions, Gaby. Which one do you want me to not answer first?"

"Oh, you meanie! You're supposed to tell your best friend everything. The doing the deed one, I suppose."

"I've never asked you about Jack." Katya let the point sink in as Gaby screwed her face up. "Oh, okay, then."

But she couldn't resist the Oban restaurant story, enjoying Gaby's incredulous reaction.

"In public? Goodness. If that's what he can do when you're both fully clothed, imagine what will happen when you're not!" She grinned. "How on earth are you going to wait until he returns?"

Katya raised an eyebrow and made it clear what she'd be doing. As well as being a cinch to wind up, Gaby was easy to shock. She must be the only woman left in the world who had never owned a vibrator.

Startling revelations over and done with, Katya took in Gaby's outfit—leggings, a hoodie and trainers, and pointed at them.

"Mmm," Gaby said, "I thought I'd better take up jogging. It's good for your mental health, right? After you've suffered trauma? And I'm seriously unfit. It doesn't help Jack keeps force-feeding me his home-made shortbread."

"Force-feeding?"

"Oh, okay, then. I keep scoffing it. He goes to the tin, sees he's run out and makes more of the stuff. I can't win. I wondered if you would take me out for a run with you and we could catch up on all your news."

To show willing, she jogged on the spot doing that high knee thing and then kicking her butt with her heels. Katya ran two or three times a week, but on her own. She knew Gaby would set off too fast, exhaust herself after five minutes, complain for another ten and then give up.

Still, why let the lesson of experience (times ten) stop her now? And Katya wanted to mull over things. Confidential chats were much easier when you weren't face to face with someone; panting alongside each other and needing distraction from the physical pain helped.

"Give me a few minutes to get changed."

By the time she came out, Jolene, also wearing exercise gear, had appeared, her long-sleeved top covering her four-month bump. Stewart was there too, Scottie by his side, the dog wolfing what looked suspiciously like shortbread from Gaby's hand.

"Are we all going jogging?" Katya asked. It was lovely to have this level of interest, but she'd wanted a chat with her best friend, not a group confessional session.

Stewart shook his head. "Naw. Running is for eejits. Nae offence lassies, but it's only useful if ye're trying tae get to the pub in a hurry. I just wanted to check ma Jolene was okay."

Jolene patted him, sending him stumbling forward. "Yeah, I'm fine, eh? Off you toddle to the pub and I'll catch you later." He took her at her word, hurrying off so fast he proved perfect qualification for the morning's jogging group.

Katya made Jolene promise she'd got the all-clear for jogging from her midwife, and they set off. She'd forgotten how fit Jolene was. Katya's plan had been to set off at a snail's pace so Gaby would last more than ten minutes, but Jolene flew off, so fast Katya and Gaby were both panting hard by the time they got to the loch shore, Jolene ready to run around it. Gaby bent over, hands on her thighs.

"Last-night-then," she said, the words coming out in between gasps.

"Did you and the Viking God finally get it on?" Jolene added, her voice unaffected. As she waited for Gaby to recover, she started doing squats. Katya watched awe-struck as she lowered her bottom almost to the ground before pressing up again.

They were too near a group of walkers for discreet conversation. Katya indicated they move off, walking so

Gaby didn't collapse, her friend nudging her gratefully in response. Once they reached the far point of the west side of the loch, Katya started jogging once more, going at a slow pace so Gaby could keep up.

"Do you promise you won't tell anyone the next thing I'm about to tell you—especially, especially, especially not Mhari?"

Gaby promised and Jolene nodded. "My lips are sealed. Cross my heart and hope to die."

"I… er, asked Psychic Josie for her advice."

At that, Gaby and Jolene stopped and howled with laughter, so much so Katya had to shush them, the noise attracting attention from the walkers.

"Katya," Gaby said when the laughter subsided, "if you'd told me three months ago you'd believe in a psychic you know to be a total fraud, I'd have eaten my hat."

"Mate," Jolene added, "Psychic Josie offered me a reading at the Highland Games and predicted travel. Unlikely, given my current condition, huh? And we all know who she really is. Worst kept secret in the Highlands."

Neither of them was aware that Katya administered Psychic Josie's website. All those articles where people told the psychic her advice was spot on. Aggrieved, Katya set off running once more. If Gaby was out of breath, it would stop her laughing so much. Not that funny, surely?

"Now you have to tell us what she said," Gaby said, forced to run to catch up with Katya and Jolene and panting hard.

"Apparently Zac and I have an NSFW compatibility rating."

"Ooh!" Obviously, Gaby and Jolene had a better grasp of internet slang than Katya. "Lucky you. Though of course I don't believe in that rubbish," Gaby said.

"And obviously, I asked Zac outright if he was married, like Jack suggested," she said, "and he is."

Her audience booed, panto style. Katya threw in a quick explanation for Jolene, though her lack of surprise indicated she already knew about Katya's internet search. Gaby and her runaway mouth. She'd better keep the not-telling-Mhari promise.

"But he's separated." Cheers this time.

She repeated what he'd told her—emphasising the bit where he said they'd only got married to annoy their parents and he hadn't seen his about-to-be-ex-wife in months.

"I like him," Jolene said. She jogged on, her conversation so normal that you'd never know she was exercising at the same time. By this point, they'd reached the south-west point of the loch. Gaby yelped in delight and stopped—an excuse Katya knew. She pointed at a tiny head dipping in and out of the water. "An otter!"

She and Jolene spent five minutes ooh-ing and aah-ing. Katya couldn't comment, not yet native enough to recognise one or spot it that far away.

"You like Zac?" Katya asked once they'd moved on, the otter having decided he'd done enough entertaining humans for the day.

"I like all newcomers," Jolene said, "having been one myself." True. She'd come from New Zealand five years ago on a working holiday and for some inexplicable reason fell in love with Stewart and decided to stay. "It's my duty to make them welcome."

At that, she elbowed Gaby, the one-time newcomer. Except, this being Jolene, her elbow tap sent Gaby tumbling forward onto the sand.

Katya extended a hand to help haul Gaby back to her feet.

"But what about Dexter?" Gaby said, brushing her hands over her hoodie and leggings to get rid of the excess damp sand. "I must admit, Katya, I didn't see that one coming, but you were so…"

Ah, the dot, dot, dots. And once again, a memory surfaced so fast it punched her in the face.

Dexter and Katya, a few weeks in and she had challenged him on his fitness.

"Plank on top of you!" she'd said, rolling out of their hotel bed. They'd spent the weekend in yet another luxurious place paid for by him, eating and drinking too much. The food and drink weighed heavily in her belly, and he'd been talking about yoga, how awesome it was, how it made you super-strong, etc.

"Bet I can beat you!"

'Plank on top of you' was a feature on a radio show she listened to where the host asked his celebrity guests to do the plank on top of him for as long as possible. The plank— body resting on forearms and toes—was okay for about ten seconds. After that, the stomach, back, bottom, arms and everything else started to complain. Doing it on top of someone made it twice as hard as the minute you let your belly sag, it touched them. And awks, because you were face to face staring at each other, aware that the collapse of abs meant at any minute one body would be pressed too tightly into the other. On the super-soft hotel room carpet, she positioned herself on top of him and grinned—a challenge.

She only made it to the thirty second mark, giving in not because her abs waved the white flag of surrender but because the sight of him, dark eyes fixated on hers and the cock that prodded her belly, made it too difficult to maintain the separation. He lasted less than three minutes; her two and a half later when he—

"Katya?" Gaby asked, whisking her back into the present.

"I can waste the best years of my life thinking what if? Or I can concentrate on the here and now."

Jolene started running again, turning around so she jogged backwards and could face them.

"That's always been my motto."

When Katya and Gaby gawked, she burst out laughing. "What, you thought Stewart was my number one choice? Jeez."

She ran backwards over the sand, bits of grit and dust flying up in the air until she was by Katya's side. "Stop looking for your soulmate, mate. It's a dumb idea. Reach out for what's in front of you."

Gaby stopped once more, the pace far too fast for her. She bent over, straightened up and placed her hands against the small of her back for support.

"Oh, I dunno," she said, tipping her head back to look up at the sky so she could stretch out her lower back in full. "I like a soulmate. Maybe Dexter was never yours all along."

So said Gaby, so said Psychic Josie. Leo and Pisces do not work, she warned. Even if Katya was on the cusp or whatever rubbish that meant.

"Anyway," Gaby continued, "if we've finished running?" Katya and Jolene nodded, and Gaby let out an exaggerated groan of relief. Jolene checked her watch and said goodbye.

"Want to come back to mine for a cup of tea?" Katya asked Gaby. The flat was nearer than Jack's house. Gaby nodded enthusiastically, and they set off, walking at a faster rate than Gaby had managed jogging earlier on.

"Shush," Katya put her finger to her mouth as she opened the flat's front door. "Mhari's having a lie-in. Let's not wake her up."

Gaby got that instruction straight away. No Mhari meant not needing to take care with anything you said. They took their trainers off and crept into the kitchen, closing the door with exaggerated care. Katya boiled the kettle and took out two large mugs and slotted two thick slices of bread in the toaster.

"What do you want on it? Butter, jam, Marmite?"

"Butter and Marmite, tons of. I've earned it."

Toast and teas made, they edged into the living room.

"Dexter called me the other day," Gaby said the words super casually, but Katya's head whipped round, and her heartbeat started double time.

"What?" So much for quietness. She heard someone in a bedroom nearby stir herself.

"Well, as you know, I'm doing tons of design work for Blissful Beauty for the South Korean website," Gaby added. "Dead hard doing something when all the content is in a different language. And he's such a control freak, he likes to oversee everything."

Not my writing, though. He leaves that to Madeline. The air deflated out of Katya. She'd longed for the call to be about something else. Wasn't that greedy—the here and now, remember? Zac wasn't here at the moment, but he'd be back soon and his future in the village and her life looked assured.

"He spoke to me on Friday morning, but I haven't had a chance to say anything to you about it until now," Gaby added. "I thought I needed to speak to you when we were on our own."

And you didn't want to put me off Zac, did you? Katya

thought. Her friend, she could tell, was waiting for her to ask more about the call. Good job Katya was much better at psychological warfare than Gaby.

"Oh and he asked after you!"

See?

"Did he?" Katya said, adopting the super casual tone she'd used earlier, even if she wanted to get up and do a dance of joy.

"Yes, wanted me to tell him how you were. Like, really. He didn't want me to be British and say 'fine' if I meant something else."

"You didn't..."

"No, I said nothing about Zac as I didn't think you'd made your mind up about him."

Whereas now it seemed Katya had and therefore it was safe to tell her such things? Anyway, Dexter was still in LA, still a workaholic, still possibly (probably) dating Caitlin.

"He said something about—"

The living-room door opened, and Mhari walked in, toast in hand and a rolled-up magazine under her arm.

"Are youse talking about Katya's love life? Gaby, did she tell you Zac diddled her under the table at that restaurant in Oban, in public like, while we were all—"

"Shut up, Mhari," Katya spat at her, horrified that her flatmate had somehow found out what had gone on. Was there no end to the woman's skill at whittling out others' secrets?

Gaby, snorts barely suppressed, stood up, beckoning Katya over. Katya got it straight away. Revenge, at last. She grabbed hold of one of Mhari's arms while Gaby took the other. They frog-marched her to the sofa and forced her to sit down.

"Tell us EVERYTHING," Gaby demanded. "You and

Lachlan Forrester yesterday. Now. Or we're never letting you out of here."

"None of your business!" Mhari said sulkily, making her companions jeer derisively.

"Shall we tickle her to death?" Katya asked.

"Too right," Gaby said. "I'll hold her. You get her under the arms."

She was about to make good the threat when Mhari pulled the trashy magazine out from under her arm and waved it front of them.

"Oh no you don't," she said, handing the magazine to Katya. "I need to show you some pictures."

Katya suspected she didn't want to see the pictures at all, but flicked through the pages anyway, the usual guff where women were slagged off for having tiny bits of cellulite on their otherwise perfect bottoms and endless speculation that someone might be pregnant because their stomach wasn't washboard flat.

The centre pages were different, though, the headline as lurid as the rest. *EXCLUSIVE—Caitlin's new man! Engagement pics!* Katya tutted at the use of exclamation marks two sentences in a row, but the all-too blatant pictures made her eyes blur. As Gaby and Mhari were in front of her, she couldn't throw the magazine to the ground and trample on it.

The two-page spread features had re-run the Instagram pics, along with another one—a blurry shot of a couple in the back of a car snogging. It didn't show either of their faces, but dark hair that looked too similar to Dexter's was clearly visible. *IS CAITLIN ENGAGED?* the tag line screamed, various headings adding 'dates in top restaurants', 'man thought to be employee', 'commitment ring on left hand', and another blurry shot of Caitlin's hand, complete with the so-called commitment ring.

The article did the usual, 'a source says', 'a close friend agrees that Caitlin is head over heels in love this time', and 'The man works all the hours God sends for her and he's devoted to his boss', words that sounded oddly familiar. Caitlin had received advice earlier in the year from a well-known psychic—Dr McLatchie would love that—the close friend added. She'd been advised to avoid her usual choice of boyfriend and here she was totes loved up and totes happy. The close friend said the might-be fiancé worked for Caitlin's skincare and make-up company.

So much for Dexter's heartfelt questions after Katya's wellbeing. Or maybe he worried the about-to-be-announced news would send her over the edge.

"That ring's well vulgar," Gaby said, resting her hand on Katya's forearm. "The Cartiers have yet to work out that money doesn't buy taste."

Bless her for her loyalty. The ring, a narrow band of platinum dotted with tiny diamonds, was okay. It could probably pay Katya's rent in Lochalshie for the next million years, but it wasn't obvious bling. Mhari snatched the magazine back from her and studied the ring pic.

"Totally disgusting," she said, getting to her feet. "But you've got Mr Flashy Car Posh English now, haven't ye?"

Katya's phone rang. An unknown number.

"Katya Bukowski?" the voice sang out. She said "yes" warily. In the background, voices shouted behind the woman. She must be in an office somewhere.

"I'm Lacey Bloom from Starz magazine. Have you heard of us?"

Another wary yes. Mhari's trashy magazine. Gaby and

Mhari stilled, everyone listening to hear what the woman said next.

"We want to talk to you about Dexter Carlton, your ex-boyfriend, right? Did you see the article in our magazine this week? We're running a follow-up article next week where we reveal Caitlin's new man's identity. Want to tell us more about him? He dumped you in record-quick time, didn't he? Sounds shallow, right?"

Mhari's mouth rounded in an 'oh' of surprise. What astounded Katya was the next move. Her flatmate grabbed the phone from Katya, turned it on speaker mode and held it in front of her mouth. There followed a selection of choice swear words, all of which sounded much scarier when said in a broad Scots accent. She finished by referring to her audience as a nosey old bitch and a sad, lonely loser, and hung up.

"Thank you." Even if Mhari's actions counted as 'pot, kettle, black, rearrange the words into a popular phrase', her defence touched Katya.

"Nae problem, flatmate. I'm off to my mum's for breakfast. See ya."

And with that, she was out the door, leaving Katya and Gaby staring at each other and shaking their heads in disbelief.

Chapter Twenty-Eight

Finally, Edmund Morris & Co sent through the 'deets' Caitlin had promised weeks ago when she spoke with Katya about her autobiography. Five days before Christmas, the email arrived red-flagged and requesting a 'read' receipt.

I do not want to do this. Think of the money, the money, the money, the money...

The message had so many instructions and links to files to download it took Katya hours to work through. The level of detail shouldn't have shocked her. She was untried. The agency could more or less guarantee a bestseller with Caitlin's name alone. But to make sure the reviews weren't all one star, they needed the story to be compelling and the writing crystal clear.

And aimed at people who didn't read books. Katya ticked herself off for being so uncharitable to Caitlin's fans. Many of them might be Booker Prize-winner readers who liked celebrity gossip on the side. Didn't she find herself on the Pop Glitter app too often than was healthy? Or rather had. These days, she steered clear. Who wanted yet more pictures of Caitlin's commitment ring or the official photos where she and Dexter stepped out in front of the cameras and dazzled the world with their glamour?

The agency had drawn up an outline of how the book was to be structured which went on for fifty pages, almost book-length itself. They'd included transcription files of conversations with Caitlin where someone else had interviewed her—clearly not trusting Katya to ask the right questions. There were plenty of links to existing interviews online too.

The job appeared to be more of an admin task than a creative one. Would the fans be happy about reading re-hashes of interviews they'd probably already seen? And so much for Caitlin wanting a writer who understood every fibre of her being. She wouldn't be in contact with her at all.

Think of the money. The email promised the agency had paid the first part of the advance into her account. A quick check on her bank account made her refresh the screen several times, the noughts that showed there unreal. She had more money than she'd ever possessed. What a change it would make not having to worry about Christmas, scrimping on presents she was sure everyone donated to the charity shop come 27 December. No, this year it would be cashmere sweaters, Chanel toiletries, LK Bennett heels and those daft scented candles that proved the adage 'money to burn'... Even then, the spending spree wouldn't dent her current account too much.

The exact instructions for how to write, picky as they were, made the prospect of producing 80,000 words less daunting too.

Page thirty-nine of the document made her pause,

bracing herself for pain. She rewound back to the discussion she'd had with Caitlin two months ago.

"You know what my final chapter is!" An announcement, not a question.

"Um, no? What is your final chapter?"

"It's the best Katie, the best! The one my fans have been waiting for all their lives!"

Katya mumbled her name was Katya, but Caitlin wasn't listening.

"It's where I find lurrrve," she purred.

At that, Mhari sat bolt upright. Katya's giggles dissolved, seeping out of her body so quick it was as if someone had punctured her stomach.

"That's why I wanted you too," Caitlin burbled, the bubbliness a contrast to the iciness that crawled its way over Katya's skin.

"Because when I visited Lochalshie, the most amazing psychic told me what I needed to do to find the man of my dreams! And she was right. Lochalshie's, like, this special place for me. The psychic told me the truth, and I'm gonna pursue it with…."

"… every fibre of my being," Mhari mouthed, the phone uttering the words in sync.

Katya braced herself. "Have you found the man of your dreams, then?"

"Oh, yeah!" Caitlin's voice sang out, breezy and cheerful, oblivious to a heart breaking nearby.

"He's amazing, and he's been under my nose all the time. It will make such an amazing story for my autobiography—and exclusive, only for people who buy the book."

Here were the instructions for it now. Katya took five fortifying deep breaths. Entitled 'Caitlin finds love title tbc', it included several paragraphs dictating how she write the piece to make it as romantic as possible and include the key events which led to Caitlin's realisation that the man who had been there all along was The One. The outline referred to the Psychic Josie consultation—the doctor would need to hang up her stethoscope and take up fake astrology full time —and the man's work history with Blissful Beauty.

"Discuss lab meeting with Donal. See transcription 62."

Lab meeting with Donal? Curiosity piqued, Katya dug out her headphones and hit 'play' on the Mp4 file. She had to wade through endless 'Hey beautiful, how are you? No, how are you? You look A-MAY-ZING. No, you look FANTASTIC. Is that my strawberry lip plumper you're using? Yeah, how did you guess?' comments before the interviewer asked the crucial question.

"So, Caitlin... Rumour has it you're in love. Can you tell us more about him and how you met?'

More excruciating comments. Caitlin seemed determined to squeeze 'amazing', 'fantastic', 'just the best', 'the greatest', 'I'm so super happy' into every sentence, often multiple times.

Then, the killer words. "He's like no-one I've ever dated before. Donal doesn't want fame or to be rich. Y'know he gets cross with me if I buy him anything that's like more than $50? Isn't that the cutest?"

Donal??? She re-wound the interview and played the sentence again. *"Donal doesn't want fame or to be rich."* Change a few vowels in a word and see what it did to a gal. At the realisation that Caitlin's secret love was Donal and not Dexter, Katya's heart pitter-pattered so hard she put her hand to her chest.

Donal and not Dexter. Not Dexter!

In her head, Katya had conjured up a meeting in a top-secret lab where Caitlin met Dexter and the mysterious

Donal, a shadowy, white-coated man holding two test tubes and asking Caitlin to choose between them. Katya's knowledge of how beauty products were made was shaky. She assumed that was how they were produced.

In this scenario, Dexter caught Caitlin's eyes across a Bunsen burner—he would have to drop his eyes half-way to the ground given her tiny height and his six-foot-plus status—and the shadowy Donal melted away, his murmurings about Caitlin agreeing on other product formulations unheard.

Was the mysterious man who melted away Dexter, not Donal?

"And you've known Donal for ages, right?" the interviewer asked.

Absolutely, Caitlin said, throwing in a few more amazings and awesomes. Once upon a time he'd worked at this tiny lab creating all-natural skincare. When Caitlin's business-savvy mother suggested her daughter buy a beauty and skincare brand she could then promote to her millions of online fans, the nineteen-year-old stepped in with an offer the company wasn't able to refuse. On condition Blissful Beauty kept its original employees, all five of them.

"I noticed him from the start," Caitlin continued, her voice dreamy. "So serious, so devoted to his work. I didn't think he'd be interested in me—y'know, I'm kinda… shallow, I guess, compared to him."

If you read the words, Katya mused, you'd assume she was being coy. But listening to them, they held the ring of truth. A young woman experiencing the universal teenage-girl feeling—not good enough for the person she wanted more than anything. The challenge for Katya was to ensure she made Caitlin come across as shy and unsure of herself when millions of people believed the opposite.

And Katya found she wanted readers to sympathise with and love this version of Caitlin. Particularly as she'd just experienced a 180 degree flip in what she thought of her.

"You've kept it quiet, though," the interviewer probed.

Yes, Caitlin said. She wanted to respect Donal's wishes. She couldn't help that websites and magazines jumped to conclusions. They'd been doing that all her life. But she had a few tricks she used—having her agent 'leak' details from time to time if she was with a male friend to send paparazzi photographers down the wrong path.

A male friend, hmm?

Katya got to her feet. Adrenaline flooded her body, making her pace the floor. She should phone Gaby and share the news. About to do so, she changed her mind. Better to wait until something happened. But Caitlin's book took on new meaning. Now, it would be a pleasure to write, knowing that the final chapter she pulled together did not involve the man she thought would be there.

Oh, Caitlin, I will make you so lovable in your book. Even your critics will read it and be convinced of your wondrousness!

The good mood lasted Katya until the evening. Mulling it over as she lay in a bath full to the brim with bubbles— best thing for banishing the cold—did this change anything? No, yes, no. Apart from her thinking much more fondly of Caitlin, Dexter was still the man too eager to put his job first. And lives thousands of miles away. Blast him and the way he lingered in her head, popping up all the time when she tried to move on.

You could/should phone him. Find out for sure.

I'm too scared.

Bath finished and dressed in her favourite pink velour PJs, she decided to phone Zac instead. So far since being away, he'd called her twice, apologetic but frantically busy helping out in one of the Hammerstone Hotels running a pre-Christmas retreat for people with thousands of pounds to spare. He'd sent plenty of WhatsApp messages. Many of them most definitely NSFW.

Propped up in bed under two duvets and a fleece blanket, she rang the number. Straight to voicemail. From one workaholic to another? Still, he phoned back five minutes later, breathless with apologies. In the background she heard chatter, music and laughter—a party, a bar or what?

"Where are you?"

"A launch thing—terrifically dull."

"Launch of what?"

"Hammerstone Hotels celebrating a new direction/profitable partnership. See? Boring. I'm here under sufferance. Where are you?"

"At home in bed." As you might expect, calling someone at 11.30 p.m. on a Tuesday night.

"Oh?" He drew the word out into multiple syllables. "Want to tell me what you're wearing?"

"A lacy, see-through negligee that only just covers my bottom—no, of course I'm not. I'm in my oldest pink pyjamas tucked up in bed with a good book and a cup of tea."

"When you should be tucked up—"

"Zac, darling! Hurry up!"

"God, wherever I am, Lois is two steps behind nagging me endlessly."

He dropped his voice, more whispers about bed and how being tucked up in one with her would be a dream come true, and that he couldn't wait for New Year and all the excitement it promised.

The phone call ended. She was still not tired enough to

sleep—wired thanks to the Donal/Dexter revelations and all that lovely money sitting in her bank account. The book hadn't felt real until this point. As a freelancer, Katya had put in her fair share of pitches to jobs where a client or agency nodded eagerly only to have them forget who she was a week later. And even if Caitlin had made that personal call way back in November, what say did she really have in hiring the out-of-sight minions whose job it was to further Brand Cartier?

Now, the job took on shape, corners and outlines solid and reassuring.

I must tell Madeline. She was the one who started this off. The thought jolted her out of more money splurge daydreams. "Madeline, I'm so thankful. Today, Edmund Morris & Co got in touch, and the advance money is in my bank account. I can't begin to thank you. I'd love to meet up so I could tell you in person..."

Two minutes after sending the message, she regretted it. Too icky? Too soppy? And as she'd sent it so late at night, would Madeline suspect she'd sent it while drunk—heaven forbid, there was the irony. Katya, the woman who favoured the stiff upper lip, reduced to over-effusive emails to a woman she'd never met. Her phone pinged—an email fresh in.

She opened the message gingerly.

"Katya, honey! I'm so pleased. I knew you were the perfect writer for them, and my confidence has paid off. Tell me, are you gonna spend too much of that advance buying Christmas presents?! I hope everything else in your life is working out. What's the update on the Zac guy? Did you decide he was suitable boyfriend material? If so, I hope he makes you happy.

"Anyway, looks like I was wrong about living in Lochalshie. A successful PR guru and writer can build a life anywhere. Makes me wonder what else I've been wrong about, but keep…"

A long message, but Katya read it over three or four times, cheered by the champion who kept cheer-leading her. "Lochalshie is wonderful," she typed back, "and I can make a life here. I'm still not one hundred percent sure about Zac but maybe it's better to take a chance than not do anything because you're too scared of risk?"

As she settled down to sleep, something struck her. Madeline had guessed what Katya would do with the advance. Sometimes, late at night or in the wee sma' hours when anxiety stirred her awake, Katya wondered if the real soulmate she sought was not Zac, nor the long-gone Dexter, but Madeline.

245

Chapter Twenty-Nine

The Christmas-present spending splurge took place sooner than Katya expected. Deciding she'd left it too late to buy everything online despite what the companies promised, Gaby came to the rescue a day later, having the done same thing herself.

Jack needed to go to Glasgow to meet with the Visit-Scotland people there ahead of his tours the following year. Did Katya want to come with them? She and Gaby could hit the shops while Jack discussed marketing and hawked giant cut-outs of himself around the tourist information centres. He apologised profusely for them when Katya got into the mini-bus the following morning.

"Not my idea," he mumped, ordering Gaby to flatten them. Heaven forbid the villagers saw them as the bus left. Too many Jack heads popping up in the windows would be disconcerting. Or the villagers might think he'd developed too high an opinion of himself, a crime that outdid murder in the eyes of most Scots.

"Mine!" Gaby said, unrepentant. "I told Jack giant cut-outs of him looking like Jamie Fraser are the best advert for Outlander-themed Highland Tours. The fans will flock to book them."

Katya's last trip to Glasgow had ended disastrously. She told herself she was in a far better place now as the bus slowed, hitting the queues of traffic on the M8. Career established, devoted potential boyfriend waiting in the wings, too much money in her bank account... The appreciative person counted their blessings and considered themselves fortunate.

They did not, did not think of the Zac pros and cons list where the word 'untrustworthy' kept appearing at the top of the cons, no matter how often she rubbed it out.

Buchanan Street bustled with crowds determined to out-prove theories online retailers had killed the high street. Bags knocked against Katya's legs repeatedly. When she caught up with Gaby two hours later, both of them swore never again.

"I hate cities now," Gaby said, dumping her bags on the seat next to her. They'd chosen the coffee shop above one of the huge stationery chains at the top of Buchanan Street where floor-to-ceiling windows allowed you a view of the masses. Beyond the street, the Christmas lights and a giant Ferris wheel were just visible in George Square.

Gaby wrinkled her nose at the brightness and clashing colours. "It's as if someone swallowed the Christmas spirit and threw up, isn't it? I wanted to talk to you about Christmas, though."

Katya sipped her Christmas latte, all cinnamon, nutmeg and orange oil. "What about it?"

As this was her first December in Lochalshie, Gaby wasn't returning to Great Yarmouth, though her mum and brother were travelling up there for the occasion.

"You could come to mine," she said. "The more the merrier. We've got Dr McLatchie and Ranald, Stewart and Jolene too. If Jack has to cook for lots of people, that suits him. It means he can hide in the kitchen drinking wine, getting slowly plastered and avoiding my family."

Gaby's mother and brother were lovely, but the three of them together were full on. As an only child, Jack wasn't used to the noise and chaos, she said. He needed sane people to balance the day out.

"I promised my mum I'd go back for Christmas," Katya said. True, but what if she wriggled out of it, and told her mother she wanted to do something different this year? Her family Christmas was never fun. Inevitably, two of her sisters fell out or one of them brought her latest obnoxious partner, and he or she insulted one or all of them. They then spent the evening quarrelling about what to watch on the TV and fighting over the Quality Street chocolates.

"I'd need to come up with an epic excuse to tell my mum," she said, already thinking them up and rehearsing saying them on the phone in her head. Food made for her, not far to stumble home afterwards, the company of her best friend, other people she enjoyed spending time with...

Versus five people shrieking at each other as if it was the end of the world while one of them scoffed all the toffee logs and pink-wrapped fudges.

"Yes, that would be lovely."

Gaby grinned at her. "You kno—oh sorry, I keep forgetting I'm not supposed to say that in front of you, my fussy friend, but sometimes I want to pinch myself. Nine months ago, if someone had told us we'd both end up in a tiny village in Scotland with the men of our dreams and deliriously happy, we'd have told them to do one!"

The man of Gaby's dreams, who'd just joined them, rolled his eyes and sat down.

"Gaby, you're starting to sound like my mother," Jack said, helping himself to the last of her coffee. Katya smiled. Those two did their super-cute thing—the continual exchange of surreptitious looks at each other, as if exclaiming, "How did this happen and is it real?"

She stifled envy. Zac, remember? Flirty, full on and into her. Bring on the New Year and the start of a new chapter.

———

Back at the flat, Katya wrapped up all the presents, managing to hide Mhari's just before her flatmate returned from work via her mum and dad's. Mhari, she imagined, was the kid who'd always searched for and opened her presents way ahead of Christmas Day.

She decided to listen to more of the recordings. The agency's instructions for the writing meant delivery of the first chapter was due midway through January, the second two weeks after and so on. It was a punishing schedule, but they were paying handsomely for it. If she listened to most of the recordings and read the interviews as soon as possible, it would put her in a good place to write come 2 January.

Donal interview part three. Katya braced herself for more awesomes and amazings. The first fifteen minutes of the interview delivered them in bucket-loads. Writing about Donal and making the whole love affair not sound vomit-inducing would be another challenge.

"When you're in love," Caitlin purred, having run out of awesomes and amazings, "you kinda want it for everyone else in your life. Do you know what I mean?"

Grr. Katya's least favourite phrase.

"You wanna sprinkle it like glitter all over the people around you, right?"

The interviewer murmured agreement, asking if Caitlin meant her sisters. The oldest one dated serial cheaters with drug problems, while the second one was on her third marriage, the latest to a Donald Trump fan who kept having meltdowns on Twitter.

"Oh, I guess so. But I'm talking about my friends too. Like Dexter, y'know? He's the marketing manager for Blissful Beauty and a brilliant dude, but boy he works too hard. He was with this British chick."

Katya stopped the recording, heart pounding against the front of her ribs. Did Caitlin know about her and Dexter's relationship? Doubtful. People in her position rarely thought about the people below them.

Katya hit 'play' once more. "But they split, and he's been so sad since. Like, crying every day."

Take back your words, Katya Bukowski, and stop being mean about someone you don't know.

"Really?" The interviewer sounded as sceptical as Katya.

"Like, no?" Laughter. "He's a guy. I mean guys my age are in touch with their emotions. Dexie's too old to be." A mere eight years older than her "But hey, he's super grumpy. And too inhibited to do anything. I wish I could help…"

Catlin snapped her fingers. "Hey, wouldn't it be cool if she heard this interview?"

Katya jumped back from her laptop, the message so personal it was as if Caitlin was in the room—that teeny-tiny fizz-bomb of energy who had the power to light a place up. The heart thumping continued, worse than ever, making her hands shake as she reached for her phone. Proof positive he wanted her, hmm? And given a nudge in the right direction by Caitlin of all people? Bless the woman. She was a saint.

And Zac? She said sorry to him out loud. Dexter had taken up too much headroom for so long, she couldn't do anything else.

The dial tone sounded for an age. Just as her courage began to fail her, it stopped.

"Hey!"

Ridiculously cheery. Wrong gender too. Unexpected, but she pushed past sinking feelings.

"Is Dexter there?" her best haughty voice, the Queen's English she sometimes used to make people act quickly.

"Like, no?" the young woman at the other end drawled, reinforcing the point with some choice swear words. "Don't call again, like ever. Okay?"

Katya put her phone down. Adrenaline still flooded her body, though this time the kind that told you to run and hide rather than hurtling to meet whatever. She checked the date on the recording—its three weeks ago recording signalling the last nail in the coffin.

Caitlin had meant well. She just hadn't figured out what might happen in the intervening period. Some young, undoubtedly LA-sleek and glamorous woman had crept into the space and had no intention of letting Katya back in. Maybe he had found their split upsetting, but had he done anything about it or got in touch?

Workaholic. Can put his feet flat on the floor when he does down-wards-facing dog. Says awesome far too much. She repeated the points from the Dexter cons list over and over, a mantra against other thoughts that crowded in where she railed against unfairness once more.

Later that evening, she checked her phone. "Can't wait till New Year!"

Zac had added a Christmassy photo to his message. He wore a Santa hat, tinsel draped around his shoulders—and wrapped around another bit—and not much else.

I don't want this. No, I do, I do, I do.

At least she had time to make her mind up. New Year was still nine days away.

Chapter Thirty

"Merry Christmas, flatmate." Mhari pushed open the door on Christmas Day armed with two mugs of tea. "Where's my present?"

Katya rolled over and pulled the gift out from under her bed. She hadn't been daft enough to hide the gift there in the lead-up to Christmas Day, but had reckoned last night it would be safe enough. She handed it over with a smile.

Post the Dexter phone call, she'd resolved to be cheery. No-one wanted a moping, miserable moaner at the Christmas table. And the reasons-to-be-grateful list included a slap-up meal with lovely people instead of squabbling siblings, for a start. Then there was Zac's return and whatever the New Year brought with it. The other night's silly doubts didn't bear up to morning inspection. Ask Gaby, ask Jolene, ask Mhari, ask even Madeline—wouldn't they all say, *"Your Zac is a prince. Go get him, princess!"*

Mhari handed over one of the teas and perched herself at the bottom of the bed. Not a natural expresser of gratitude, her eyes narrowed and then widened when she held up what Katya had bought her—a pure silk blouse, the turquoise-coloured shirt the perfect match for her auburn hair. Also, because Katya couldn't resist it, Roger Hargreaves's cartoon book Mr Nosey.

Mhari tossed that aside contemptuously as soon as she saw it. She clung onto the blouse, though, and asked Katya if she thought it was the kind of thing people wore for New Year ceilidhs if there was someone at that dance they quite… liked.

A rotten flatmate would take advantage and tease her like mad. Payback for all the times Mhari had poked her nose into Katya's business over the last few months. But as it was Christmas Day, Katya let it go.

"Yes," she said, "it would look amazing with skinny jeans and over-the-knee boots. You can borrow mine seeing as we're the same shoe size. Plus I've decided Enisa could do with more of our business. I'll book her in for the works on New Year's Eve—waxing, a facial and a manicure. If you want to get yourself tarted up at the same time, I'll pick up the bill."

This time, Mhari's face lit up. She took her blouse and scurried out, face hastily turned away. If Katya hadn't known better, she might have thought her flatmate brushed away a tear.

Niceties over with and obligatory phone call to her mum made—the squabbling in the background told her she'd done the right thing—Katya decided to go for a run. Having never experienced one, she'd hoped for a white Christmas. Outside, the weather hadn't obliged but the whiteness of the over night's hard frost decorated Maggie Broon's Boobs, dazzling them in the low winter sun.

Lochalshie was deserted. Even the dog walkers were absent, and she saw no sign of Stewart and Scottie. The freezing air made it tricky for her to adjust her breathing but the cool freshness of it flooded her lungs after a while, and she fell into a rhythm. She headed out half-way around the loch and then turned back.

The end brought her to Zac's house. To her amazement, the French windows opened, and he emerged. He'd said he'd be back on the twenty-seventh. Those Christmas retreats needed top-quality chefs so people paying to escape their families could relax in style.

"Hey."

"Hey yourself," she called out, trying to decide if his surprise was of the very pleased variety. Yes?

"I wasn't expecting you." They said the sentences together and laughed.

"Come in," he said. "It's freezing. You can tell me why you changed your mind. Lois suddenly decided she owed me too much overtime, so it was cheaper and easier for her to find someone else instead. And I couldn't face the family Christmas."

"Me too. I've spent twenty-six Christmases with my family," Katya said. "I wanted to find out if other people always fight on Christmas Day."

"Same," he said. "Last Christmas, my ex and I screamed at each other all day. Anyway, can I get you breakfast?"

Oh, those twinkly blue eyes... Inside, he'd made an effort to make the place Christmassy—more so than Katya and Mhari had at their flat. An arty silver tree stood in the corner and cards lined the shelf over the fireplace. Freshly baked bread smells drifted from the kitchen and the coffee machine gurgled. Katya felt as if she'd wandered onto the pages of a lifestyle magazine or website.

"Just a cup of coffee," she said, taking off her shoes and

sinking into the armchair. She curled her feet under her legs and imagined the caption for the picture.

Katya and Zac, whose luxury home makes the most of its lochside setting, spend their Sundays drinking proper coffee, eating home-baked bread and congratulating each other on their smugness.

Cheery, Katya! Kindness and good wishes to your fellow man instead of cynicism and catty thoughts. Say something nice to make up for your inner meanness.

"This time next year, though, you'll be running a new, successful business," she volunteered.

Suddenly, he was in front of her. "With a hot, sexy girl-friend who never shouts at me by my side."

He bent and took her face in his hands and kissed her lightly on the lips, letting his lips linger there a while. "I fantasise about the last time I kissed you all the time. Except in my head it goes a lot further."

The blood in her veins fizzed in response. Zac, the man who'd promised good things came to those who waited. Why not give herself a much-anticipated Christmas present, rather than wait for the New Year? That top bedroom in the house offered glorious views of the loch. The idea of doing it in front of such a view, curtains left open, thrilled her.

The Thoroughly Modern Millie always scratched the itch. Sometimes it was a mistake. Sometimes it wasn't. Mr NSFW had his astrological reputation to live up to, the Psychic Josie promise sparks would fly. No regrets—well, one. Enisa's full body waxing and beautifying services were booked for six days' time. Nature had taken its course since the last waxing and hair sprouted everywhere. Would he notice?

"I mean it, Katya," he said, coffee breath warming her

cheeks. "I'm serious about you. I know you think I'm a joke or untrustworthy but I'm not, I'm…"

The Thoroughly Modern Millie also acted responsibly. Katya hadn't left her flat that morning expecting encounters with men she fancied. When she asked Zac if he had condoms, he gave her one of those half-smiles he did so well.

"No. I don't carry them around 'just in case'."

That, more than anything, convinced Katya. Zac took her seriously. Ironically, she had a packet at home gathering dust, as they hadn't been used in some time. But it was now noon, and she was due at Gaby's in an hour's time, complete with the vegan dish she'd promised to bring.

"Later, then," she said, getting to her feet and throwing her arms around him, happier than she'd been in a while—the fresh start ahead of her shiny and dazzling. Zac gave brilliant hugs, their similar heights pushing together all the corresponding bits of their bodies. She nestled her chin on his shoulder, resting it against soft blonde hair and breathing in warm skin, shampoo and bread. His hand cupped the side of her head. She turned, pressing her lips against his cheek.

"Gaby and Jack won't mind an extra guest," she said, apologising to them in her head. "Especially if you bring food and drink."

He saw her to the door, the half-smile banished and a wide grin in its place. "Ah. Gaby invited me when she bumped into me last night. She forgot to mention you'd be there too."

"Forgot."

"Best surprise in the world. Go off and make yourself beautiful."

Chapter Thirty-One

As expected, Jamal's general store was open. Christmas Day, he told Katya when she popped in on her way back to the flat, allowed him to take advantage of supermarkets' closure when almost everyone realised they'd forgotten a key ingredient for lunch. He didn't bother to celebrate, but he shut the shop at six instead of eight, figuring that most people would be slumped in front of the TV comatose by that point.

"What d'ye need?" he asked, conjuring up a dusty tin of peeled chestnuts from the depths of one of the over-packed shelves as soon as she asked. "And what about these?" He waved a packet of Rennies at her. "In case o' the indigestion."

"I don't plan on eating or drinking too much," she told him in her head, *"seeing as I'm going to get naked with someone later this evening."* Chestnuts purchased, she had forty minutes to shower, shave her legs, get dressed, apply a ton of make-up AND come up with a main course for herself.

Red dress on, tummy held in with mega-control pants

that made breathing tricky and make-up in place, she got to Gaby and Jack's twenty minutes late and without a main course. Oh well. Christmas dinner always included lots of potatoes and veg. So long as Jack hadn't cooked them in goose fat she should be okay.

"Oh, you look fabulous! And I'm totally under-dressed!" Gaby opened the door, blasting Katya with the smells of roasting turkey and mulled wine.

Katya's friend wasn't underdressed—or not for her, anyway. She'd exchanged the usual track pants and hoodie for a tightly belted woollen dress pulled over leggings. It was a pity they were covered in cat hair, even though poor little Mena was no longer there to shed her hair.

Inside, too many bodies in a confined space made the heat suffocating. The doctor perched on an armchair, lecturing Jolene on what she could and couldn't eat from today's menu. Jolene shot Gaby a 'rescue me' look, the latter saying Jack had made a pregnancy-friendly menu, so she did not need to worry. Jolene gulped down a small glass of fizz in record time, telling the doctor women in France drank through their pregnancies and wasn't the French population happy and well-adjusted? Next to them, the mysterious Ranald McLatchie sipped mulled wine, his cheeks blowing out air every so often. He was someone who spoke as if words were taxed; this full-on Christmas party must be an ordeal.

Gaby's mum Mandy pushed her way through the crowd and hugged Katya, telling her daughter at least one of them had made an effort to dress up. Gaby's older brother Dylan was engrossed in conversation with Stewart. Gaby caught Katya's stare. Yes, Stewart had finally found someone— apart from Jolene—who didn't mind the ear bashing. Snatches of their chat drifted over. Coding. Dylan shared

Stewart's fascination for all things HTML, SQL, Binary and jQuery.

The doorbell sounded again. All the guests looked at each other as if to say, "Where on earth is someone else going to fit in here?" Ranald backed himself up against the wall, gulping the rest of his wine.

"I'll get it," Katya said, the nearest person to the front door.

"Please do!" Gaby piped up. This was the bit where she was supposed to be surprised. Katya decided to play along.

"OMG!" she burst out as she opened the door, and Zac, his face already prepared for politeness, broke into a much broader smile when he saw her. His eyes ran up and down her body, lingering on her chest, the red dress moulded tightly to it.

"Wow. You look incredible."

He wasn't so bad himself, dressed in black straight-legged Levi's, a lumberjack shirt over a black tee shirt and floppy blonde hair touching his shoulders. "I made you something," he said, holding out a foil-covered dish. "I didn't think you'd have time."

She could kiss him. Gorgeous, devoted, responsible, thoughtful...

Not Dexter.

No, not Dexter but better. *Better, better.* Say it enough and her subconscious should get the message.

"Thank you!" She took the dish from him and kissed his cheek. "It's hot as Hades in here. Expect to get much closer to people than you've ever been in your life."

Following her, he pinched her bottom. "Good."

Inside, the guests greeted him, with cheers doubling them when he held up a plastic bag of rattling bottles.

"We made canapés!" Gaby exclaimed, coming out of

the kitchen bearing two trays. There was a cough behind her. "Well, Jack did. But I plated them up because I'm the designer and I know how to make things pretty."

Everyone cooed appreciatively, and the food was passed around—Brie and cranberry pastry twists, potato cakes with smoked salmon and cream cheese, and hummus-loaded celery sticks. Zac helped himself to a handful of everything and held one of the celery sticks in front of Katya's mouth.

"Go on," he said.

"I am not a performing seal."

But the run and the skipped breakfast persuaded her hunger was more important than dignity. She opened her mouth, and he popped it in. The doctor gave her a discreet wink, a reference to the NSFW reputation. Anyway, none of that mattered now. Katya had just tasted the best hummus she'd ever had. She'd eaten plenty of the stuff over the years. Nothing matched this one—the sharpness of the lemon, the velvety-smoothness, the nutty sesame seed tahini, garlic and chickpeas.

Jack made his way into the living room, regarding the invading hordes to his living space and hanging back so Mandy didn't pounce on him.

"Jack, this hummus…" Katya said when he made it to their side.

He shook his head. "Zac brought it round earlier. Awfy keen on supplying the vegan options."

She nudged the man next to her. He nudged her back.

"I hope the turkey replacement is out of this world," she said, and he promised it would be.

"A blistering review, remember?" she added.

He grinned. "Do your worst."

No one sat down to dinner until an hour later. The booze had flown, but the canapés kept coming too.

Hummus-topped celery sticks weren't the only option, unfortunately for Katya's belly. Tiny flat-breads topped with baba ghanoush followed and home-made potato crisps with an aioli drip made from silken tofu instead of eggs. A clumsy attempt was made to clear the living room, so the extendable dining table fitted the space, and the guests gathered around. Katya landed on her seat with a thump, bread, crisps and too many rich sauces and dips plummeting her onto the chair.

Zac, naturally enough, sat down beside her. "I'm too full," she moaned, rubbing her stomach and regretting the control pants that dug in mercilessly. "It's your fault. I'll never manage the main course. Or the pudding."

His thigh pressed against hers. "Bet you will."

Gaby insisted on a group photo for Instagram, checking with Jack who thought social media the devil's tool. He gave in gracefully and everyone leant in closer for Gaby's pic. Katya sneaked her arm around Zac and seconds later, the photo was online. Multiple beeps sounded as the Lochalshie WhatsApp group cottoned on.

One member of that group, anyway.

"Happy, I mean... Merry Christmas. Soz, 2 much vodka-irn-brew, I mean, bru! Katya, are ye an item with Pac, no Zac?"

Everyone in the room bar Mandy, Dylan and Zac were the lucky recipients of Mhari's message. Nine pairs of eyes moved from phone screen to Katya, and she put on her best neutral face. Honestly. Once upon a time, she'd done a job for Norfolk CID where she had to write a guide for trainee detectives about how to spot liars in interview-type situations. She'd picked up lots of useful tips.

Hands and feet. Stillness was unnatural. Move them slightly. Do not rush to say anything. Dead giveaway.

"Yes," Zac said, kissing her. Oh well. Most people thought they were together already.

Jack and Gaby brought out the main courses, the obligatory turkey, gravy, roast potatoes, stuffing, Brussels sprouts and parsnips done in parmesan. Jack went back to the kitchen and emerged seconds later, presenting a dish to Katya with a flourish. Everyone else 'oohed!' in appreciation. In front of her, pastry puffed itself up, supporting a topping of caramelised red onion and beetroot studded with thyme leaves and surrounded by rocket dressed with balsamic vinegar, olive oil and wholegrain mustard.

"Can I have that instead of turkey?" Mandy said and immediately looked contrite. "Sorry, Jack, love. But I've never liked turkey that much."

Three others made the same plea. Zac did his best not to look smug.

The Lochalshie WhatsApp group beeped once more. "Your dinner looks nice! Can I come round for seconds?"

The chorus of no's equalled the ones of yes.

"Mhari," Katya explained to Mandy and Dylan, "resident of Lochalshie, my flatmate. Nosiness personified and suffers from FOMO all the time."

She was on her way round anyway, Katya was willing to bet, well before anyone said, "invite her over". The doorbell sounded five minutes later, proving her right, and that familiar 'I dinnae want to intrude' speech started.

The doctor asked after her mum, dad and older brother, and Mhari dismissed them. They were about to curl up and watch the Coronation Street special on the TV. Mhari fancied she might find excitement elsewhere. Which elicited a warning about too much excitement at Christmastime and the number of festive-invoked heart attacks the good doctor had dealt with in her years as a GP. Mhari muttered that it was just as well her ma and pa did not believe in excitement and looked around her for a space to sit down.

Why was Katya surprised when she sat herself opposite her, prime viewing for anyone who wanted to eyeball the couple in front of them? Mandy shouted across the table. "Mhari? You're a local here? Will my daughter be dismembered for being a dirty Sassenach?"

Gaby jumped, dismay clear in her eyes. If you wanted to make a good impression on the locals and, more importantly, your boyfriend's family, fingers crossed that ill-advised remarks about England-Scotland did not surface.

Zac stretched across the table, expensive wine bottle at the ready, and topped up Mandy's glass. "Mandy," he said, "and I can't believe you're old enough to be Gaby's mum. I thought you were her sister." She fell for it too, tilting her glass and letting her fringe fall forward in front of her eyes. Jeez. "Your daughter is in good hands. Everyone here adores her."

Jack brought in yet more plates of delicious food and leaned in to kiss the back of Gaby's neck so everyone awwed in admiration. Mhari said she'd eaten too much but then took a plate. Forks and knives were picked up and silence descended.

Katya took a mouthful of what was the best vegan main course she'd ever had. From the expression on Mandy's face, she agreed. Katya decided a second helping was doable if she went to the loo and removed the control pants. Mission accomplished, she returned to her seat only to discover all that remained of the tart were a few pastry crumbs.

"What happened to the pie?" Mandy, Gaby, Jack and Jolene looked sheepish.

"Sorry, Katya," Gaby piped up, "it was just so delicious."

None of them were vegan. They could have tucked into extra stuffing or bacon-wrapped chipolatas. But no. They nicked the dish Katya had just removed her knickers for.

"A blistering review of my dish, yet?" Zac asked as she sat down. "I can take it."

The others rushed in to tell him how wonderful it was, and amazing that a recipe without meat, fish, cheese, cream, eggs, butter etc., tasted so fab.

"My complaint is the same as what I said last time. You didn't make enough."

No one wanted pudding—a chocolate bombe stuffed with ice-cream that had small chunks of Jack's home-made millionaire's shortbread running through it. He pulled a 'suit yourself' face and said he, Gaby, Mandy and Dylan would eat it for breakfast the next day. The crazy things people did at Christmas.

Zac's leg moved closer to Katya's. She returned the pressure. As others cleared the table, he used the distraction to whisper in her ear. "Promise you'll come back with me later?"

Hardly a surprise that he asked. And she'd spent the afternoon admiring how he looked in those cute jeans and the way the shirt sleeves moulded to his arms. He'd taken the time and effort to make her the best food she'd ever eaten and if she stood up now and announced they were going back to his place for some serious shagging, everyone would probably cheer.

It was enough to banish all thoughts of workaholic, too-quick-to-move-on Americans from her mind.

Almost.

In the here and now, she whispered back a 'yes' and

placed her hand where it was impossible to mistake the intent. His head was still close enough for her to be the only one who heard the groan. Not safe for work indeed. That thing was rock hard.

"Shall we go to the pub?" Gaby announced. "Jack says Ashley has a Christmas karaoke, which should be fun."

Below the table where only Zac could see it, Katya waved her hand from side to side. Yes, they'd be cat-called when they announced going back to his house or her flat, but a few hours' quiet beckoned. Why not take advantage?

Zac grabbed her hand, crushing her fingers tightly. Agreement, then. Coats on and the table and kitchen a bomb site, everyone moved out. The cold air was welcome after the heat of the house and Katya held back, determined she and Zac would peel off as soon as they got to his house as discreetly as possible, so no one noticed they weren't there until they were in the pub.

Outside his house, he paused, jangling his keys, and they slipped in the front door, unnoticed by the group who'd gone into the Lochside Welcome arguing about what the best Christmas song was. The Pogues and Kirsty MacColl —Fairytale of New York. No question, surely?

Zac's house was cold, and he apologised, turning the thermostat up to its maximum.

"Um… want to get under the duvet?" he suggested. "Fully clothed until we warm up?"

"Yes. Let's."

Funny how confident she sounded when her mind told her she was eighty percent sure, and twenty percent racked with doubt. Another thing struck her—she and Dexter got together for the first time at the Lochside Welcome right next to Zac's house. And it felt like betrayal to do this so close by.

Silly, Katya, she told herself. *It's not betrayal and even if it was, does the location matter?*

Upstairs, darkness hid the view from the full-length window—the one she could have enjoyed earlier. She took off her shoes and got in beside him when he threw up the duvet. The bed was enormous and his duvet maximum tog like hers. He wrapped an arm around her shoulder and pulled her side-on to him, his fingers stroking the side of her head.

Her stomach growled loudly, making her squawk, "That was my stomach!" Heaven forbid he mistook it for anything else.

"You can't be hungry!"

"I'm not... I'm... just a bit full."

She moved so she was flat on her back in the bed and Zac shifted too, propping his head on his elbow. His hand shifted, fingers gently stroking her throat and making their way onto her breasts. When his mouth landed on hers, she tasted red wine on his tongue. He dropped butterfly kisses along the line of her throat and took both her hands above her head, pinning them there. Goodness, working in kitchens made you strong. But the powerless thing had its bonuses. If she didn't take such an active role, did this make her guilt-free when that irrational sense of betrayal kept surfacing?

When he let go of her hands, she slipped them under his shirt, tugging it loose and pulling at his waistband. Guilt, it seemed, sat alongside plain ol' lust. On the plus side too, her stomach had settled down. All the nerves and cells in her body focussed on pleasure and what was going on all over her body.

Furious banging sounded at the front door. The house

was a new build and its insulation amazing but the shout outside came through loud and clear.

"Zac, open the door, you lying, murderous git!"

Gaby.

The wandering hands came to an abrupt halt, the words an ice-cold wind that blew into the room. Next to her, Zac's face registered many things. Irritation and disappointment, yes, but guilt and dismay there too. Those last two the most prominent.

Another bout of fierce rattling on the door.

"I know you're in there, you utter jerk, open up or I'll call the police!"

Chapter Thirty-Two

"You know what I'm going to say."

Dressed in a white coat that didn't close properly at the back and naked underneath, Dexter shifted in his seat and hoped this would be quick. He had three million and one things piling up in the office and he needed to get back there asap.

The doctor, one of those super-expensive ones whose sole business was corporates and employee health insurance, steepled her fingers together and sat back. The office radiated luxury befitting its Harley Street location—from the gleaming wooden furniture to the tasteful prints on the wall and the super-soft seats.

"You're working too hard. No vacations in, what," she checked the folder in front of her, "two years and an average 70 to 80-hour week?"

The doctor's appointment hadn't been Dexter's choice but after he'd collapsed when he and Caitlin had flown to London following a whirlwind pre-Christmas PR tour of South Korea ahead of the launch, she'd insisted. The collapse couldn't have been more dramatic either; Dexter hit the tarmac as they exited the Cartiers' private jet at Gatwick. A flurry of excitement ensued. Waiting photographers saw the private ambulance and decided it must be Caitlin herself. Doubtless they were disappointed when they saw her head for her gigantic car minutes later. The world's first Cartier death would have been headline news.

Stress, the doctor said. He'd suffered a sudden drop in blood pressure thanks to a vasovagal response brought on by a strong emotional reaction. Had he been worrying about work and everything he needed to do? It didn't help that he was underweight too. Not a common problem in first-world countries these days, the doctor said, tapping her own rotund girth, but he didn't have the same resources to draw on people with more pounds on them had.

"Corporates generally employ me to weed out employees trying to pull a fast one," the doctor continued. "But I tell them I take the Hippocratic oath seriously—first, do no harm. You need serious time off. That's the recommendation in my report."

She tapped the edge of the folder against the desk.

"Serious time off?" Dexter asked, his heart sinking. Time off now was impossible. They were at the most crucial part of the launch—the three-month beforehand period when PR activity ratcheted up to frenetic.

"Uh-huh," the doctor said, "no less than eight weeks. But you are under no obligation to follow my recommendations."

At this she stopped and eyed him beadily. "Young man —is telling people to buy more lipstick that important?"

Ah… yes? As a twenty-one-year-old graduate, he'd written his ten-year plan as per his university's career-coaching recommendations. On it had been the goal, the dream. Be the marketing manager of a huge global corporate by the time he hit thirty. The Forbes list was around then too, but he hadn't put that on the list until later. Whisper it, but he pictured the front cover with him on it, sharp-suited, moody-faced and tag lines that screamed his achievements. Managed multi-billion-pound marketing South Korean launch. Profits that surged by millions of dollars in less than a year. A LinkedIn profile with hundreds of thousands of followers. Other marketing managers who frothed at the mouth awaiting his cleverly crafted posts…

… which he wouldn't have time to write. He'd need to outsource them to a talented freelancer.

Katya, say.

Back in the UK HQ—these days based in London rather than Glasgow—he let himself into his office, the doctor's letter clutched to his chest.

Courtney had wailed when he phoned her and said he wouldn't be back for Christmas or New Year. He used the work excuse, not wanting to worry her with the collapse thing. Flower grabbed the phone off her mother and said, what did this mean? Was she still supposed to go into the LA office and work?

"No, Flower," he said, "you've got school and exams. Pass them and come back to me afterwards. I'll find you something that makes the most of your super-talented skills."

"Ooohhhh," she said, and argued vociferously for a while against it before giving in.

"But you've no idea how much I did for you, Uncle

Dexie!" she finished. "I took this call the other day from this snooty Brit cow trying to get hold of you."

The words knocked him for six. Did this mean…? Could it, dare he think it…?

Caitlin broke through the introspection, bounding into his office to say goodbye before she flew back to LA for the Cartier family Christmas, another much-televised event where the family proved it was possible to out-bling Christmas.

She plucked the envelope from his hand.

"It says here you need eight weeks off to recuperate."

He opened his mouth to object and closed it again.

"I'm your boss, right?"

Caitlin's eyes bored into him. An impressive feat for someone that much shorter. He thought about how much he loved her—the teeny-tiny fizz-bomb of energy who'd exploded into his life and then taken it over. Completely, absolutely and utterly.

"You are. The best boss in the world. And I've been considering something. Flexible working, Caitlin. What do you think?"

Chapter Thirty-Three

Katya hurriedly got out of the bed and pulled down her dress. Zac sat up, making no move himself.

"Aren't you going to answer the door?" she asked. "What does Gaby mean, anyway?"

No answer. He sighed and heaved himself up, tucking his shirt back into his trousers.

"It's a mix-up. It must be. Wait here. You don't need to do anything." He took her in and let out another heavy sigh. "And I don't need to answer the door."

Katya paused, struggling to pull her hand through mussed up hair. And to stop her imagination remembering a night some months ago when an American glided across the floor, took her brush in his hand, and pulled it through, soft, gentle strokes.

Dexter. A pesky man for popping up left, right and centre when a girl had done her best to embark on a different course.

"Sooner we get this misunderstanding cleared up, the sooner we get back to this," she said. Was the interruption a relief? Zac always presented her with too many conflicting emotions. If she analysed it fully she'd say the lingering one was a sense of something not quite right.

"Let me in, you ass-wipe!"

"Wow," Katya said as she followed him downstairs, almost crashing into his back. A guy in no hurry to open that door? "Did you steal her silverware when you left the house?"

He didn't laugh.

Gaby wasn't the only one at the door. Jack stood there, the pair of them grim-faced. Katya had known Gaby many years. Quick to anger wasn't a description she'd ever used for her friend. Gaby's face was tear-streaked and the eyes panda-like thanks to mascara and eyeliner that had not lived up to its waterproof claims. (Blissful Beauty. Guilty again.) The tip of her nose was bright red, and two spots of high colour dotted her cheeks. Behind her, Jack's flint-eyed stare took in Zac and her.

"My cat!" Gaby shrieked, poking her finger onto his chest. "You murdered poor, defenceless little Mena!"

"I don't know what you are taking about."

Vehement denial but Katya heard its hollow ring. She stepped back, conscious of a small audience of people who had come out of the Lochside Welcome. Did this count as the Lochalshie EastEnders special? The long-running British soap opera was notorious for a Christmas episode that always ended in tears or a fight. This doorstep confrontation might include both.

"Um… Gaby, do you want to come in? Perhaps Zac can explain better when we are inside?"

Gaby pushed past them both. "I don't think he can, but we might as not entertain the whole village."

By some miracle, Mhari hadn't appeared. She must

have returned to the excitement of her family's Christmas celebration. Missing out on this little show would count as an awful mistake in her books.

Jack stomped past them both too, pausing as he brushed past Zac so they could do that 'stags eyeing each other up' thing. Inappropriate as it was, the sight almost set Katya off laughing. Oh, the ridiculousness of it all! Five minutes earlier, she'd been snuggled up under a duvet, her and Zac's attempts to get down and dirty interrupted once more and now two men jostled for alpha male status while Gaby paced the floor, arms folded. All she needed to do now was come out with a terrible cockney accent, and the East-Enders comparison would be perfect.

"You ran over my cat after the pub quiz. You never told me!"

Inner hysteria banished and replaced by dismay, Katya watched Zac. He blinked and said he hadn't. He'd been nowhere near her cat. Didn't even know what the stupid thing looked like.

At that, Jack stepped forward, flint-faced still and fist curled. "Not a stupid thing. Like Gaby said, a poor defence-less animal that stood no chance against a flash car going too fast down the High Street. Jamal got it all on CCTV. He spotted it when he needed to check something."

Out it came. Jamal was sick and tired of finding dog shit outside his shop. In the last few months on four separate occasions he had begun the day faced with a steaming pile of poo close to his doorway. He'd tried the local Facebook group—a post headlined *Shop-keeper Shames Shit-leaving Dog Owner*, hoping that might deter the offender or encourage someone to come forward. No luck.

As Christmas Day had been quiet, he decided to go back to check the CCTV. The only time the camera had been working—shoddy systems were much cheaper—had been the night of the charity pub quiz. A distinctive red motor caught on screen at 8 p.m. driving down the street at a speed far north of 30 miles an hour and a cat scuttling across the road.

Dot, dot, dot for what happened next.

Jamal hurried to the Lochside Welcome and told everyone what he'd seen.

All those signs of lying… What to look out for when someone is lying, according to those brochures Katya had once written for Norfolk CID trainee detectives. A person who tries to hold your eye for too long to convince you of their sincerity.

As Zac did with her now. "Katya," he pleaded. "If I hit her, it was an accident. I didn't mean to. And I don't remember it. I would have known if I'd hit something."

Hadn't he been on top form that night? Flirting with her, coming up with a dirty name for their team and promising an exciting end to their evening? Knowing he had run over her friend's cat and not saying a word?

Who *was* this man?

Three people awaited her judgement. Best friend and boyfriend, expecting her to take their side. Prospective boyfriend. Trying to persuade her on slim evidence he was a good guy. Oh, Zac… blue eyes met hers. Could you reek of sincerity? He did. At the time of the accident, she'd said you know when you've run over something. Perhaps you didn't.

"I'm foibles personified, aren't I?" she cast the question to the universe, rather than the room. *"Ergo, I forgive those who also make mistakes."*

The pros and cons list did its amazing reappearance act. Zac pros—here, into her (not yet literally), amusing, attractive. Cons—bit of a liar (or at least needs a lot of prodding to volunteer anything) and has probably run over my best friend's cat. Plus, my best friend and her boyfriend hate him.

The scales jiggled.

Katya grabbed her coat from the hook in the hallway.

"Goodnight, Zac."

Outside, Gaby shifted from foot to foot. "Sorry about that. But when Jamal told us what he saw, I hit the roof."

Katya pulled her coat closer around her. The snow hadn't started but the gleam on the pavement suggested they would wake up tomorrow to a hard frost. Thank goodness Mhari had lost interest and gone back to her parents' house. (Hopefully.)

"I don't blame you," Katya said.

Jack wrapped an arm around Gaby. "No offence, Katya, but your taste in men is utter... shite."

He grinned at that, the smile making his eyes gleam, and Gaby giggled, protesting half-heartedly. "It's not so bad... Dexter was...."

"A total workaholic? A man who thinks pushing lipsticks and serums is the be all and end all in life?"

"Oh. I'spose so. Are you okay—do you want to come to the pub?"

Katya shook her head. "No thanks."

She watched them go, still cuddled up together and bickering affectionately about whose Karaoke performance had been the better one. At least she'd have the flat to herself. Answering Mhari's three hundred and one questions would be too much to bear. And when you found yourself once again questioning your judgement and wondering why your man choice skills were as terrible as Jack put it, quiet moping all alone was the only thing to do.

Chapter Thirty-Four

Boxing Day dawned and Katya decided to start on Caitlin's book. Her phone, which she'd switched off last night, showed eight missed calls from Zac, and a message he'd sent beforehand.

"I didn't run over Mena. Promise. It's complicated."

Intrigued, Katya called him back. If he was not the person responsible for the accident—and she could convince Gaby of it too—didn't that give their relationship the green light? Or an amber one anyway. It'll need to be a very good excuse, she told herself. Short of the car zig-zagging out of control, what else could have happened?

But his phone went straight to voicemail. Whatever. Perhaps the two witches had whisked him off to the Royal George to plan the hotel's launch. Give it a few hours and he'd be back in touch. She replayed the Oban trip and last night and shivered. Goodness, anticipation intensified lust.

The fridge in the flat was empty—not even any almond milk for a coffee. Mhari arrived back from her parents, wandering into the kitchen and opening the cupboards. Katya regarded her warily. No mention of the cat. By some miracle, no-one had thought to update the WhatsApp group.

Mhari leant against the table. "If you get us bread, I promise I willnae ask any questions about you and the Viking God and what you got up to last night."

Hmm. A temporary let-up in questioning only. Just wait till she found out.

"Deal."

"Today, anyway."

Katya poked her tongue out. One day of relentless questions missed was the best she could hope for. She found a bag for life and jogged down the stairs, setting off for the general store.

The streets were quiet; most people were spending the day after Christmas in front of the TV, although she could see a group of walkers struggling their way up one of Maggie Broon's Boobs at the far side of the loch. Across the road, Laney Haggerty walked two of her giant German Shepherds, the dogs practically pulling her arms out of their socket. Katya raised her arm to wave, taken aback when Laney glared at her and pointedly looked away. Even her dogs joined in, one of them growling and straining at the leash.

How rude. Someone must have got out of bed the wrong side that morning.

Inside the shop, Stewart leaned on the counter, engrossed in conversation with Jamal.

"Aye, well ah've never liked that place," he said. "The money they charge for a pint in there and they dinnae let me take in Scottie." Contrary to health and safety regulations, Jamal allowed the dog in his shop because Stewart claimed he was an assistance dog vital for his owner's mental stability.

Jamal spotted Katya and cleared his throat. The stares both of them gave her were not welcoming or friendly. She picked out a carton of almond milk from the fridge and a loaf of wholemeal from the shelves and took them to the counter. There, on the surface in front of Jamal was one of the bigger Sunday newspapers, its glossy weekend section open. A photo of Zac dominated the centre spread, arms folded and that grin he always managed to make look as if filthy thoughts were running through his head. Behind him, the Royal George towered—the photographer having captured its Victorian splendour without making it look as shabby as it usually did.

Jamal tapped the second page. Oh, heck... There she was, having said 'yes' weeks ago to appearing in publicity pictures for Zac's new business, the one where he held a venison burger to her mouth, her eyes closed in what was clearly ecstasy. The camera had zoomed in on their faces, the picture intimate and intrusive at the same time.

"Well," Jamal said, taking the almond milk carton from her, "you willnae be needing this, will you? Seeing as you seem to have thrown aside all your plant-based principles. And every other one at the same time."

"But... but..." The hostility puzzled her. Was Katya not being a vegan such a big deal? A quick glance at the feature's headline told her there was a lot more to this than a woman eating venison when she'd told everyone a plant-based diet was best for the planet. Unable to face buying the newspaper, she muttered an apology, returned the bread to the shelf and fled back to the flat where she could check the story out online.

In the living room, Mhari's phone beeped furiously—

her flatmate in the shower. The Lochalshie WhatsApp group must be very cross with Katya for eating venison. She'd find out soon enough. Mhari, her hair wrapped in a towel, wandered in and swiped the phone, asking Katya if she wanted toast.

Katya nodded absently, forgetting to tell her toast-making was out the window seeing as they had no bread. She opened her laptop and searched for the newspaper, swearing once she realised the article lay behind a firewall. Still, the prospect of returning to the general store and buying the paper daunted her. She opened her PayPal account and coughed up the subscription. Voila—the article appeared in front of her.

Oh. Oh. Oh, dear.

"Make your own toast!" The shout came from the kitchen and Mhari stormed past her, phone in one hand, a large mug sloshing hot liquid over the top in the other. The bedroom door slammed behind her, and she heard a hissed and furious phone call take place.

"Aye, vegan my arse!"

"A traitor in our midst!"

But if the villagers felt betrayed, so did Katya. A pop-up food business that would complement the Lochside Welcome? Not so. Zac was to be the new executive chef at the Royal George, currently undergoing extensive renovation. The aim was to turn the place into a boutique hotel, run by Hammerstone Hotels, whose proven success in turning lacklustre establishments to dizzyingly profitable places was bound to succeed.

"The new breed of boutique Hammerstone Hotels," Lois outlined in the article, "will offer experiences—from silent retreats, to sober gatherings for the new booze-free millennials, dog-pampering weekends, and yoga. We are even offering dating boot camps led by the one and only Christina the Dating Guru and Lochalshie local girl, who will coach people through what it takes to make a relationship succeed."

And yes, they were confident this concept would work outside of London and the home counties area.

Zac's biography was there—his years of private cheffing and how well equipped he was to deal with the new-style business model for hotels. Yes, there would be exclusivity and weekends that offered the stressed-out executive yoga, gourmet food and hill walks. But the time had come for the Royal George to compete for the local market too. Fish and chip Fridays, Taco Tuesdays and...

... wood-fired pizza Wednesdays.

In addition, Hammerstone Hotels had applied for planning permission. The company wanted to extend the hotel and use the field behind it for a glamping camp site. The extension would eat up public land behind the Royal George—the old playing fields where the Highland Games usually took place.

And Katya stood next to Zac, eyes closed in ecstasy and appearing to endorse what he was doing. Little wonder everyone hated them.

Something else pinged into place. The 'interview' in Starz magazine where a 'source' said "Dexter works all the hours God sends for Caitlin and he's devoted to her..."

No wonder the flaming words sounded so familiar. She'd said them to Lois and Angeline all those months ago. Them pumping her for information about anything they thought could be of profit.

Her phone went. Gaby.

On top of the cat revelations, the latest news compounded Zac's crimes. Katya listened as Gaby called him every rude word she could think up. And a few more besides.

"I didn't know!" Katya exclaimed. "Honestly, Zac told me he was doing a pop-up business. When those pictures were taken, he was vague about that photo and where it would be used and I didn't question it."

Mhari had wandered back through, and she sat down opposite, top lip curled contemptuously. Small, out-of-the-way villages often contained generations of people going back decades who were all inter-related. Mhari was a second cousin once removed (or something) to Ashley.

"But the Royal George," Gaby said, and the guilt surfaced. Katya couldn't claim complete ignorance. She'd known Lois and Angeline wanted the Royal George. They'd said nothing about making it the Lochside Welcome's competition too, and that Zac was part of it all along.

Boutique hotels and an adjunct pop-up van business—that was what she understood about the acquisition of the Royal George. No one mentioned yoga retreats, dating boot camps (run by Jack's ex-girlfriend and the woman who'd spectacularly failed to find anyone herself) and, worst of all, targeting the local market too.

Even if the Lochside Welcome's regulars boycotted the Royal George as she expected they would, they didn't make up a substantial number of people. Visitors, tourists, incomers. All of them would come to Lochalshie, see the splendid, refurbished Royal George with its wonderful fish and chips, pizza offers, etc., and be seduced.

"I didn't think…" she began but got no further as her best friend hung up on her. The first time she'd ever done so in all their years of friendship.

Bleeps and pings from Mhari's phone continued to pierce the silence. Luckily for Katya, nosiness motivated

Mhari every time. And as she doubled as the village oracle or town crier, it would be useful to get her onside.

"Well?" Mhari said, wandering back through and making it clear that this would not be easy. "What did ye know?"

"Lois and Angeline—Hammerstone Hotels—told me they wanted the Royal George," Katya. Complete honesty from now on was best. "But I thought they wanted to turn it into a boutique hotel, a place where rich tossers hung out. I didn't think they intended to provide any competition for the Lochside Welcome."

"You should have said," Mhari sniffed.

"I know, but Zac said Lois and Angeline wanted to tell the villagers themselves. I took it for granted he meant having a meeting where they told everyone in person, rather than an article in a Sunday supplement."

"Aye," Mhari said, her voice softening slightly. "Kick in the teeth, isn't it?"

And Zac? Katya's first concern had been the hotel and what the company had planned for it. But the man who'd been chasing her for months, talking in that sincere voice of his about wanting to make a difference, sustainable food production, blah, blah, blah... had obfuscated at every turn.

Surprised, Katya? the inner voice said. The man who didn't admit upfront he was still married. They'd had conversations about her relationship history, its path strewn with disasters. Why didn't he pipe up then? *Oh, yeah... bad splits. I know all about them. I've been married.*

Every opportunity to tell her why he was really in the village had been there. Not a word.

It didn't matter now what he said about Mena and the accident. This was too much.

"I said he was an eejit right from the start," Mhari said,

fierce scowl still in place. "Turning up here in that poncy car of his, revving his engine and everything. I bet he sent you dirty pictures. And he used Photoshop to make it look bigger."

"Um…"

"Knew it. All big co—"

As she talked her fingers flew over her phone screen, nails click-clacking, and Katya leapt to her feet ready to snatch it off her. "You aren't telling everyone about that, are you?"

"No!" Mhari tucked the phone by her side out of Katya's reach. "I'm saying he's a smarmy liar. And you didnae know the half of it."

Not quite how Katya would have put it, but Mhari's updates might dig her out of a big hole. She'd only been in Lochalshie a few months. She didn't relish returning to Great Yarmouth and El Crappo Villas tail between her legs.

The doorbell sounded and Mhari jumped up.

"Don't answer it," Katya said, "or tell whoever I'm not in. It's probably a lynch mob."

"A what mob? Okay then, I'll say you've left town."

But she didn't, returning a minute later, hard-faced scowl back in place and Zac in tow, hair tousled as if its owner had run his fingers through it so many times he'd created static electricity. He shot her a desperate look.

"Mhari, please," he said. "Can I talk to Katya alone?"

As if. Whatever he wanted to say, Katya told him, he could say in front of Mhari, her dear, loyal—emphasis on the second word—friend. But, and this must be a first, Mhari shook her head and said she was going out. Destination the Lochside Welcome, Katya guessed, where people would have gathered to reassure Ashley they would never abandon his establishment for the Royal George. As Katya's flatmate, they'd want the gen from Mhari, the woman who loved being the bearer of top-quality gossip, good or bad.

"Don't tell them," Katya pleaded as she left. What? That she was in the flat alone with Zac and that they were welcome to storm the building and burn it down with them in it?

"I willnae," Mhari said. "You're not the..." The rest of the description was so colourful, Zac turned red and muttered something about it not being his fault either, a statement Mhari greeted with derision. To further her point, she slammed the door on her way out.

Alone with Zac, Katya turned to face him, taking him in —ratty hair, the sweatshirt and jeans that looked thrown on and haunted eyes. Or where they shifty? Perversely, he'd never looked better.

Katya said nothing. It was not her job to make things easy for Zac. When he sat down on the couch next to her, she got up and took the armchair opposite.

"It's not what it looks like."

Katya snorted.

"Okay, it is. I got myself into a mess earlier a few years ago—a real mess. Natasha and I were brilliant chalet chefs. We took it for granted, we could pitch up in London, open a restaurant and make it work. You can probably guess the rest."

Katya was reminded of her words to him months ago— the food industry, notorious for failure. Especially for anyone trying to set up a restaurant in one of the most expensive cities in the world. It astonished her he'd managed to find the backing to finance it in the first place. The question must have shown on her face.

"As you probably worked out, we're both from wealthy families," he said, shifting forward so he could rest his forearms on his thighs, and taking his phone out of his front pocket. "I'm the proverbial 'selling snow to the Eskimos' guy. We talked a lot of people into investing in us. Then, we made every mistake people who have never run their own business make—miscalculating food costs, so we didn't charge enough. Not allowing enough money for food orders and the payroll, so we didn't have enough money for wages. Not paying our taxes."

She winced at that.

"It limped on for two years," he continued, staring out of the living room window. His cheeks had tinged pink, and she realised he found this shaming. It couldn't have helped either that the money they wasted came from family and friends.

"Everything was in my name, so I ended up declaring myself bankrupt."

"Which rules you out from starting up any other business in your name or borrowing money without the permission of the courts."

He nodded. "Yes. Natasha did, though. She runs a smaller-scale version of the London restaurant at a Hammerstone Hotel in Brighton. It's wildly successful because she learned from our mistakes. We did it back to front. I should have started somewhere like this first and then moved it to a bigger city."

"And that's why you have to work for Lois and Angeline."

"Yes," a half-smile there, bittersweet. "I moan about them, but my godmothers were among the original investors, and they wrote the debt off. Since then, I've worked for their hotels all over. When they said they wanted to start a new venture in Scotland and offered me the chance to be part of it, I jumped at the chance. They suggested a pop-up and offered me the position of executive chef cum pop-up manager. They wanted to expand their portfolio, and they said why not make a brand-new start away from everything? They offered me free rein. I'd be the one running the business. I couldn't say no."

"Why weren't you upfront from the start?" Katya butted in. "Wouldn't that have been better?"

He sat back in the chair, hands resting on knees. "I meant to be. No, I did," when he saw her expression. They'd shared the flight to Scotland when he'd first moved to Lochalshie and then several hours in a car. The perfect opportunity for truth and explanation, Katya would have said.

"Lois and Angeline didn't want the villagers to know. They banged on and on about keeping it quiet until they were ready to let people know. They had credit arrangements to put in place, so it was important not to jump the gun.

"I thought they meant leaflets or to go around people's houses and tell them. Or even hold a meeting in the library where they stressed the Royal George wouldn't hurt the Lochside Welcome."

Katya's own thoughts earlier.

"There are big investors involved," he added. "Russians. The Chinese. That's why the article was in the Sunday Times. That sort of thing impresses them."

He got up and walked over, crouching in front of her.

"Lois phoned me this morning to say the article was in the paper. I hadn't expected it to go in so soon, but the feature meant to be there was dropped at the last minute, so they replaced it with the Royal George piece because it was already written."

Katya's words from the press release neatly interspersed

throughout because the journalist had been too lazy to do anything else.

He placed a hand on her knee. She shifted it off.

"Katya, when I saw it I wanted to cry."

Clear blue eyes fixed on her. A plea for understanding and/or forgiveness.

"I've wanted you right from the start. I saw the article this morning and thought, 'I've blown it—I've blown it yet again.' I'm so sorry."

Genuine tears. And guys crying counted as one of Katya's weaknesses. When her mother wasn't too busy falling for losers and moving them in, Katya had grown up in an all-female household. And five women often turned on the tears easily. She still subscribed to the school of thought that men didn't cry. When they did, its unfamiliarity felt much more powerful.

"And Mena?" Katya added. "You said you had something to tell me about that."

"Lois was driving. She wasn't insured. If that had come out..."

"You shouldn't have covered for her."

"I know."

He tipped his head forward, so his forehead rested on her knee. She stroked his head. What lies mattered and what ones didn't? Dexter hadn't lied to her, but if actions spoke louder than words (thanks, Gaby's nanna for the home-spun wisdom once more) he had not tried to spend much time with her either. Zac kept trying.

"The journalist took the competing for the local market bit out of context. And I can persuade Lois and Angeline the Royal George shouldn't try to nick the Lochside Welcome's customers."

Said oh-so sincerely.

"And we'd make an amazing couple," he added, the words warm on her knee. "I can't, I mean couldn't wait to…"

The words stopped, and the mouth fastened on her knee, a cloth-covered kiss that still set off sparks. And he'd got form for doing miraculous things to her through her jeans. She should stop him, but she froze. The mouth moved further up her leg and his hand sneaked under her, caressing her bottom. She kept up with the hair stroking, locks of it soft and thick in her hand. He moved to her waistband, fingers sliding from the back to the front and stopping at the button of her jeans. He unfastened it and tugged at the zip.

Months of pent-up frustration, exquisite sadness when Dexter disappeared to LA and didn't bother getting in touch, loneliness and the years of single-dom that seemed to label her a loser… They mingled and frothed together in a potent mix. Common sense left the building.

Katya raised her bottom, allowing Zac to pull her jeans down and she yanked at his too, trying not to flashback to when she and Dexter used to do this and how easy it was to persuade him to part with his. Zac's body was a complete contrast to Dexter's, stocky and muscular and a scar on his leg he told her was caused by spilling boiling water down it a few years ago while working in a chalet in Zermatt. She touched it lightly, the skin there bumpy and shiny compared to the rest of him.

By now, they were on the floor, the carpet scratchy underneath her. She slid her hands up under his shirt and admired the hardness of his chest. Zac kissed her lightly, moving from her face to her throat and making her arch her back. Once more, it was heavenly, enough to make Katya consider offering Psychic Josie free web copy in reward for her prediction about Zac's NSFW status.

… oh dear heaven, she was this close to…

Lois and Angeline. The planning application she'd seen on the coffee table in Zac's house. The one they'd let her believe was about Hammerstone Hotels acquiring the Royal George. Not expanding it. Not encroaching on land nearby and erecting posh tents for nob-ends with too much money who wanted to pretend they were at one with nature.

She pushed him back. "The expansion? The glamping?"

Trousers unbuttoned, shirt out and deep breathing, the warmth of him intensifying that smell of his, a heady blend of expensive after-shave and baking bread. He ran his hand through his hair, the front of it messily flopped forward. And then all movement stopped.

Hands and feet still. A tiny flicker in the eyes as he observed her. Wide and blue—weren't people always led to believe that blue eyes were clear and innocent, owned by those who tell you the truth?

"I didn't realise that's what they had planned." The fingers that rubbed together almost unconsciously told her this might not be the truth. Liars, as that leaflet she'd written for the Norfolk CID years ago said, tended to fidget.

His eyes ducked from hers. "Katya. I want the Royal George to succeed big time. Need it to. But when you turned up here, I thought I'd hit the jackpot. Here I was in the arse-end of nowhere but with this vision in front of me. Everything I was doing suddenly felt so right."

Oh words, words, words. And Gaby's nanna popped up again. *"Actions!"* she wagged her finger. *"Speak louder than words!"*

What was Zac's version of right and wrong? Different

from everyone else's—a world where you kept quiet about so many things? Mr Not Safe for Work was not safe for anything else either. Katya grabbed her discarded jeans and pants, shoving her legs clumsily into them. Zac watched her for a few seconds and then did the same.

"Please, Katya. I'm—"

"A lying, cat-killer!"

Ah, Mhari back once more. Katya thanked the stars she had her clothes back on. Minutes earlier and this would have been very embarrassing. And it sounded as if someone had filled her in about the incident Jamal had seen on CCTV. Katya opened her mouth to correct her and then closed it. Zac did not deserve her help.

"I'm not!" Zac got to his feet, turning to appeal to Katya, wide blue eyes unblinking, and hands held out. "Come on, Katya. You know the truth—and you know the Royal George will not harm the Lochside Welcome, so long as Ashley's not so stupid as to—"

Too much for Mhari—Ashley's cousin once removed. She drew her hand back and punched him, her fist landing in his crotch and making him double over, groaning.

Katya stood over him. Violence was the answer to nothing. Nothing. But the lies, heaped up on top of each other, took their toll.

"Mhari," she said. "I'm not sure that is allowed under the Marquis of Queensberry rules."

"Aye? Never heard of the fella. Does he have any other daft rules about no' kicking someone when they're down too?"

Katya put her hand in front of her. "I don't know but I do. Even if he deserves it."

She held her other hand out to help Zac to his feet. "Off you toddle, sunshine. And have a dreadful life."

He cast her a last despairing glance and left, Mhari shouting "Good riddance" as they listened to him hasten down the stairs.

A sudden realisation pulled Katya up.

"Gaby," she said to Mhari. "Was she in the Lochside Welcome when you convinced everyone I didn't know that much about what Zac and Hammerstone Hotels were up to?"

Mhari shook her head. "No, they weren't in the Lochside Welcome. But mebbe if you go round to their house, you can tell her yourself and sort out your wee fall-out."

An excellent idea. Katya hugged Mhari, told her she was a fab friend and hurried off, determined to at least set that relationship right.

Chapter Thirty-Five

Jack opened the door and made to close it as soon as he saw her.

"Can I come in?" Katya asked. He'd folded his arms and planted his feet on the doormat as if he expected to have to block her from sidling past him. "So I can explain."

Behind him, Gaby emerged from the kitchen—her face as stern as her boyfriend's. "Let her in," she said, "I'll listen to what she has to say."

At that, Jack stood aside, following her through to the living room where cat detritus still littered the place—the bed, a fishing rod toy and a cat tree where she'd perched to watch the wildlife from the comfort of a warm and cosy home. Gaby still hadn't cleared any of it away.

"I knew about the pop-up van," Katya said, "and that Lois and Angeline wanted to buy the Royal George. I did not understand their plans for the place were so ambitious. When I'd asked about the pop-up van and if it would be competition for the Lochside Welcome, they all promised it wouldn't be—that the two businesses could exist together."

"And the photos?" Jack barked. So far, he hadn't offered her coffee or tea.

"Zac said they were publicity pics for the website. And that Hammerstone Hotels would hold a meeting where they told the villagers about the plans. The big spread in the newspaper came as a surprise to me too."

The seconds ticked by. Katya thought back to her and Gaby's last argument, working out it had been ten years ago. At the time, Gaby had just started seeing Ryan the douche bag and Katya made it clear how much she disliked him. The two of them blew up—shouting and screaming at each other in Katya's bedroom. As screaming matches were a regular feature of the Bukowski household, no-one in her house noticed. But Gaby stormed out, and they didn't speak to one another for a week. It counted as one of the worst weeks of Katya's life. They made up when Katya extended the olive branch and admitted (lied) that Ryan wasn't that bad. She managed to keep quiet about his faults from then on.

Gaby stood up. "Mhari believes you. She told the WhatsApp group he's a liar—or words to that effect—and you're as much a victim as the rest of us."

Katya swallowed. "Is that what you think?"

Gaby sat down beside her. "Yes."

"Jack?"

"So, he comes here, tells a lot of lies, runs over my girlfriend's cat and threatens to put the village pub out of business. Please be pickier about your friends in future!"

She could tell them the truth about the car, but would it make any difference? Anyway, Gaby had started to giggle—titters at first, then laughter that quickly turned hysterical. When Katya added the story about Mhari and the literal ballsy punch, Jack joined her.

"Gosh," Gaby said, wiping her eyes. "I wish I'd seen that."

"I'm sorry, Katya. I got mad." Gaby held a hand out.

"I'm sorry too. I fell for an idiot."

Gaby hugged her tightly. "We all do that sometimes. At least you didn't spend ten years with him. And New Year's Eve is always a brilliant time to meet someone new—a hunky, kilt-wearing man with magnificent knees."

Sweet of her. But here she was, single yet again and hit by a bolt of loneliness, the bitterness of it piercing her. Katya. The world's worst judge of character.

Gaby sent her a message the next day. Why didn't she come with her and Jack to the Lochside Welcome for a coffee? Might be a good idea to show herself there.

As she waited outside for Gaby and Jack to appear, Katya swallowed nerves. Laney had been so hostile the day before, she imagined pushing the door open and the pub falling silent. It strengthened what she'd been considering ever since Zac had turned up at the flat.

"It'll be fine," Gaby appeared, wrapped in a huge, padded jacket to counter the cold. Next to her, Jack smiled and pushed the door open.

As it was only two days after Christmas, the pub wasn't busy, although its most regular customer sat at his usual stool next to the bar. He waved a hand in welcome, yesterday's unfriendliness towards Katya forgotten already.

There were stares and whispers from the few people dotted at the tables round about, and when Ashley emerged from the cellar where he'd been changing one of the barrels, Katya braced herself.

The hotel owner eyed her speculatively, wiping his hands on a towel.

"What's it to be, folks? I'll warn ye—venison burgers are no' on the menu." At that, he grinned, and Katya let out a sigh of relief. She was off the hook.

"Is that what they mean by food porn?" Stewart called out, making Katya cringe. The villagers didn't hate her, but she would never live those photos down. "Ashley, mebbe you should get some photos of Katya eating your pizzas."

"Or the chocolate decadence dessert," Gaby piped up. "No, scrap that. Get photos of me eating your pudding, Ashley. I promise I'll make them look X-rated."

And with that, everyone laughed. Ah well. What did a little teasing matter?

"What about that hamper, though?" Katya asked. "Zac promised a hamper for the ceilidh. Everyone who bought a ticket was to be entered in a prize draw to win it. And he was supposed to have a stall at the afternoon event."

Jolene, coming out of the bathroom and muttering about the number of times a pregnant woman had to pee, took the stool next to Stewart.

"He dropped by our house this morning," Jolene said, "and gave us the hamper. Said he's clearing out of town for New Year."

"Mebbe the lack of a warm welcome will scare him and those terrible women off," Stewart added. Sage nods all around. Katya doubted it. She sensed steel ran through Lois and Angeline underneath that fluffy exterior and all those 'darlings'. Though Zac might not be the one heading up the team at the Royal George. Jolene said he was leaving and neither his nor Lois and Angeline's vehicles were parked outside the house.

At home in the flat later that day, she opened her laptop

and researched flat rents in other parts of the UK. It was time to move on. She didn't belong in Lochalshie, wonderful as those few friends she had made were. She'd moved to be closer to Dexter. When that hadn't happened, she stayed to explore what might happen with Zac.

Even her best friend being there didn't make it the attractive proposition it had once been. Gaby had Jack and was blissfully happy. Katya should take herself off to another town or city and build a life for herself there—the kind she should have made when she was eighteen or when she'd graduated, instead of staying in the place where she'd grown up and then following pathetically in the footsteps of her friend, hoping Lochalshie's enchanting setting would work romantic magic on her too.

New year. Fresh beginnings.

She could start with Norwich, which would mean she was closer to London. Madeline would approve. Perhaps she might even meet her online mentor at last and offer profuse thanks for all her wonderful support over the last few months. She owed the woman a great deal.

"Hi Madeline," she started an email to her, "thanks so much for everything you have done for me over the last few months. It's been so helpful. I'm thinking of moving to Norwich or perhaps even London because…"

She poured out the whole story—the discovery of what Zac, Lois and Angeline planned, and the revelation of the cat killer, and ended her message with an earnest plea she and Madeline finally meet up so she could express her thanks personally.

"Yes," the reply pinged back. "Let's."

Chapter Thirty-Six

"I'm going to London for New Year, so I won't make the Hogmanay Ceilidh."

Gaby had arrived at the flat the following morning dressed in her exercise gear once more and wanting to go for a run. She'd spent the last few mornings eating chocolate bombe surprise and toasted turkey and stuffing sandwiches for breakfast. Something had to be done, she said, before she exploded out of her clothes.

Luckily for the two of them the weather was mild enough for this to be possible, though freak storms had hit further south-west, causing flooding and power cuts. Once they got to the loch shore, Katya told Gaby her plans.

Madeline had not only said yes to meeting up in London, but suggested Katya come down for New Year. Edmund Morris & Co held a legendary New Year's Eve party for clients and writers every year, she said. They could pop in for a couple of hours early evening and then go out for a meal. And why not come down the day before so they got to meet up beforehand?

"My treat," Madeline said, and also offered to pay for Katya's hotel room. "No need," Katya replied, telling her she now counted as one of the well-off thanks to what Edmund Morris & Co had given her. The habits of a lifetime kicked in anyway and she booked one of London's more reasonably priced hotels instead of Madeline's five-star option.

The arrangements confirmed, excitement mounted. Wouldn't it be wonderful to finally meet this woman, the two of them having shared so many confidences over the last few months?

"Who exactly is this Madeline?" Gaby asked, her tone narky. Katya had forgotten she'd never told Gaby about her —or how Madeline had come to replace her as a soulmate. When Gaby had been with Ryan, their friendship worked differently. Now Jack had replaced her to an extent. Katya didn't blame Gaby, but it did leave her needing someone else to talk to, and Madeline had proved ideal.

She explained Madeline as tactfully as she could—a woman who was mentoring her and who had shared lots of useful advice, as well as landing her the Caitlin Cartier writing job. Plus, when Gaby's cat got killed the lovely Madeline had sympathised and told her the story of her own childhood, the pet she'd had to leave behind.

They reached the lochside, its sandy shores adding challenge to the run.

"Can-we-stop?" Gaby gasped, having done what she always did and set off too fast.

Katya slowed to a walk, and they headed to the far side beneath the shadow of Maggie Broon's Boobs.

"But New Year here will be fantastic," Gaby said once she'd got her breath back. "Jack told me all the young farmers from miles around love the ceilidh. You could meet a decent chap and end up a farmer's wife, writing your articles in the kitchen while he rounds up his sheep or milks the cows."

"Or I could be in London at a party where absolutely no one talks about porridge, meeting hipster guys starting up their own breweries or vegan cafes and making useful contacts for the future."

She also wanted to avoid that sinking feeling at midnight where everyone kissed each other, and she blinked back a stray tear and wondered why everyone else seemed to find relationships easy.

"You were going to do a Pilates class in the afternoon," Gaby reminded her as they started to run again. "To limber everyone up for the dancing. Everyone will be very disappointed to miss it."

Katya doubted that. Besides, when she'd suggested the idea originally, she'd meant the free class to be an advert for those wanting to take up Pilates in the New Year. Now she wasn't sure she was going to stay in the village beyond January. Though that would be a conversation with Gaby for another day.

"I'll ask Doctor McLatchie if she can do it," she said. "I'm sure she'd love to. If she can kid on she's a psychic, I'm sure she can fake core-strength training easily enough."

Fifteen minutes later, having run but mostly walked, Gaby begged to stop. Katya insisted they do an extended stretching session before heading home. Otherwise, Gaby was destined to wake up tomorrow stiff as a board.

"Must we?" Gaby grumbled, looking around her. There weren't many people about, but Jamal, sweeping the ground in front of his shop, stopped to watch the stretches, shaking his head in disbelief.

"Do you think there will be lots of famous people at Edmund Morris & Co's party?" Gaby asked.

Katya pulled a heel to her bottom to stretch out the quads. "I guess so. And hopefully all looking for a talented ghost writer to pen their autobiographies for them at some point. Madeline says it's a super-amazing party and bound to be beyond awesome. That's a direct quote. She's fond of hyperbole is Madeline."

"What?" Gaby said sharply, dropping her leg. Jamal, still sweeping, lifted his head—an instinctive reaction to possible intrigue.

Katya repeated what she'd said, puzzled.

"Oh no, nothing," Gaby said hurriedly. "I've just been thinking. It's an excellent idea for you to go to London and meet her. It'll be fabulous. You'll have fun. We can phone each other on the dot of midnight to say happy new year."

Calf stretches done, Gaby smiled. "Well! Must go. Let me know when you're off and I'll come and say goodbye."

And with that she was gone, hurrying home at a much faster speed than she'd managed running earlier.

Weird, Katya thought, but at least she had her friend's approval to spend New Year elsewhere. As Gaby said, it would be fabulous. She couldn't wait.

Trips to London from Lochalshie were not easy. Katya planned to take the first bus to Glasgow, which would get here there just before lunchtime and then a flight to the capital the day before New Year's Eve. Even then, the whole journey was likely to take six or seven hours and would not get her to her hotel until 5 p.m. at the earliest.

Gaby and Mhari saw her to the bus stop on Thursday

morning, Gaby insisting on carrying Katya's rucksack for her and banging on and on about what Katya planned to wear. She'd arrived at the flat half an hour earlier and insisted on picking out what she said were Katya's best outfits.

"It'll be very smart," she said. "You know what London parties are like."

No, Katya thought, *and nor do you seeing as neither of us have ever been to one.* Still, it was nice for her to show this much interest.

"Aye," Mhari said, "ye need to wear your best or all those snotty London women will look down their noses at you."

When Katya had suggested Mhari come with her, thinking she might appreciate the experience, Mhari shook her head in horror.

"London? Is it bigger than Glasgow?"

Katya solemnly confirmed it was.

"Far too big. I dinnae like cities."

The bus didn't arrive when it was supposed to, but as this was a regular feature of village life Katya didn't worry. She did, however, when there was no sign of it fifteen minutes later. Unless the bus got here in the next two minutes and then did its best to make up the speed on the way to Glasgow, she would miss her flight.

Mhari held her phone up. "I dinnae think that bus is coming," she said. Sure enough, the sign at the front of the bus stop changed from 'Delayed 15 minutes' to 'Cancelled'. A news report showed the freak storms at the Rest and Be Thankful had caused a landslide. The road was closed, a two-hour diversion in place for all traffic heading south which would be in place for the next couple of weeks.

Katya swore loudly.

"I'll ask Jack," Gaby jumped in, whipping her own phone out. "He can drive you there and we'll get to Glasgow in time for you to catch the 4 p.m. flight instead, and then we can drive back so we're in Lochalshie by…"

"Nine," Katya finished for her. "No. I can't ask you to do that for me." Even if she really, really wanted to.

"It's no problem!" Gaby said, suddenly unflatteringly keen to get rid of her best friend for the weekend.

Katya shook her head. "No, it's okay, honestly. I'll message Madeline and let her know, and we can meet up early in the New Year once the road is no longer blocked."

"Okay, then," Gaby said. "Well, we'll see what we can do. Need to go—I'm helping the committee set up the stalls in the hall. See you later."

She dashed off, having failed to remember Katya could now do her taster Pilates class. Katya decided not to remind her.

Mhari watched Gaby go.

"I just sent Enisa a text," she said. "She can still do the both of us tomorrow if ye want."

Katya had forgotten all about it—her booking of Enisa's mobile beauty services when she'd been expecting exciting things to happen with her and Zac. Now it seemed pointless, but if the booking was still in place, why not? She'd cancel the hair removal and have a facial and a massage instead, and she and Mhari could enjoy an afternoon's pampering.

Her New Year plans hadn't worked out as she'd expected a week or even a day ago, but she resolved it signalled something—a goodbye to Lochalshie and new beginnings ahead.

Chapter Thirty-Seven

So much for the relaxing afternoon in the lead-up to the New Year's Eve ceilidh. The pampering session turned out not to be pampering at all—Enisa and Mhari weirdly determined Katya stick with her original booking where Enisa waxed her from head to toe.

"I've bought my wax 'specially," Enisa said, holding the container up. "I'll dae it that quick you willnae feel a thing."

She was right about her speed, if not the lack of pain. Still, she also insisted on doing Katya's make-up. She had a new mineral range she wanted to try out—tons better than that Blissful Beauty muck, she promised—and Katya loved what she did.

Her eyes looked brighter and whiter, her skin gleamed and the subtle lip gloss plumped her lips. Mhari, owner of thick, wavy hair, was a whizz with tongs, and she put Katya's hair up for her, arranging tiny ringlets that fell around and framed her face.

Thanks to Dr McLatchie, Katya didn't need to worry about spoiling the effects sweating it out in a Pilates class.

EMMA BAIRD

The doctor promised she would take it over, rubbing her hands together gleefully. Anyone attending was about to have their pelvic muscles pummelled and their abs battered. Katya's Pilates class was fine, she said, but nowhere near challenging enough. Folks needed to pant far harder if they were to get the benefits. Katya hoped she wouldn't put attendees off Pilates—or any form of exercise—for life.

She'd wanted to phone to cancel Madeline, but the woman had never handed over any contact details apart from her email. As soon as Katya sent her a message, however, she replied, "Honey, that's such a shame. But we'll meet soon!"

When she drifted into the hall later that afternoon, stalls and local businesses promoting food, handcrafts, Highland Tours and more crowded the room. The number of people milling around suggested attendees in their hundreds. The committee must be delighted.

Jolene, hand behind her back to stretch out pregnancy ache, called her over. She and Stewart were judging the porridge competition, three tiny stoves set up so competitors could work three at a time, furiously stirring bubbling pots of oats. So far, a neighbouring villager raced ahead with his deluxe chocolate, sultana and brandy version.

"Want to try this one?" Jolene asked, handing over a small paper cup of steaming oats and a teaspoon. "It's the vegan, super-food one."

Katya took a mouthful and choked. The competitor had added chillies, Goji berries and coconut milk and been too heavy-handed with the chillies. The combination was unlikely to catch on.

"Er... no."

Jolene nodded, and Stewart declared the chocolate,

306

raisin and brandy porridge maker the winner, awarding him a gold sash and hand-carved wooden spurtle.

Thanks to the masses of people, the hall was far too hot. Katya wandered outside. It was only four o'clock but dark already, the village street lights not making that much of a dent on coal-black starless skies. The sounds of the loch drifted over—gentle waves lapping against the shores. But they were only just audible above the chat and laughter coming from the hall and faraway noise of bagpipes warming up. There were wooden benches on the grass bank next to the loch. She sat on one, determined to banish the doom and gloom mood.

Pluses. Her career was on the ascendancy. Yes, the Caitlin book was short term, but such a high-profile project would lead to more work. No worries on that score. Norwich or London beckoned. Plenty of possibilities there.

Minuses. Alone again once more… A biggie, no matter how often she told herself a partner wasn't the be all and end all of life.

"Katya?"

Gaby appeared, laying a hand on her shoulder. "Are you okay?"

"Fine." She reached her hand back to touch her friend's. "Do you need my help with anything?"

"The ceilidh starts at six," Gaby said, "so the committee is looking for volunteers to clear the hall."

"Okay."

Inside the hall, tables and stalls were moved aside. Gaby found a supermarket trolley, and she and Katya carted over endless crates of beer from the Lochside Welcome to put behind the temporary bar in the hall.

When Gaby's phone chirped for the tenth time, Katya

put her crate down. "Do you want to answer that? It's driving me crazy."

"No!" Gaby said, her smile frenzied. Katya eyed her suspiciously.

"I hope you're not matchmaking. Jack's friends are bound to be a heck of a lot better than Ryan's, but I'm not in the mood."

"No, no. I'm not doing that, promise!"

Methinks the lady doth protest too much. Gaby's lying skills had not improved in the time she'd lived in Lochalshie. Tonight, a ruddy-faced muscular bloke who whiffed of dung would ask her to dance while everyone watched. At midnight, he'd pucker up and... urgh. Was it too late to plead a sore tummy and spend the evening under her duvet watching the latest series of *Jessica Jones*, the kick-ass woman her aspiration for the future?

"What are you wearing tonight?" Gaby asked, picking up her crate of bottles once more, dumping it in the trolley. "Not that."

"Seriously, Gaby? You're critiquing my clothing choices?"

Her friend wore leggings, one hole in the knee, the other perilously close to her crotch. And one of Jack's Highland Tours fleeces. She looked like a Weeble.

"No, no—though Jack loves me whatever I wear, don't you, pet?"

'Pet' walked past, carrying several bottles of whisky. He winked at Katya, a slow sweep of eyelashes over the top of sharp cheekbones. "Gaby, your dress sense astounds me every day."

"See?" she said. He winked again, unseen by Gaby. "But Katya, what about that lovely designer dress you were going to wear to the party in London? That would be perfect. Shall we pop back to yours and dig it out?"

Wow. Gaby stopped at nothing in her mission to prepare her best friend for a dung-reek young farmer. Katya owned one designer dress, The Vampire's Wife outfit she'd had the enormous good luck to spot in a charity shop. The dress featured printed pink and red wild roses overlaid with gold lace, three-quarter length sleeves, a fitted bodice and a tiered hem. Beautiful indeed, but she suspected no one else would be that formal.

Still, the outfit got few outings. Why not?

As it happened, she never got the opportunity. By the time they had cleared the hall and set it up for the ceilidh, people began to arrive, waving tickets and chattering excitedly. January was a dull month in the north of Scotland, the nights too long and the weather dreich, Jack told her. Everyone partied hard on Hogmanay to make up for it.

To avoid any young farmers, Katya took up position at the front table, taking money from everyone who came in. Jolene joined her, Stewart too busy flinging himself into dancing interspersed with frequent trips to the bar.

"We took heaps of money this afternoon," Jolene said. She had to shout to make herself heard above the bagpipes. "And loads of people ended up in the Lochside Welcome for lunch, so Ashley is happy."

"Has everyone forgiven me for Zac?" Katya asked, stamping someone's hand so they could come and go into the hall.

"Not your fault, mate," Jolene said. "And I liked him. Stewart didn't want me to say anything, but it is only fair. When Zac came round to drop the hamper off, he looked terrible. He made me promise to tell you how sorry he was and that his marriage is long dead."

She dug around in her handbag, pulling out a scrap of paper and handing it to Katya. An address in London. "He's going back there to work for Hammerstone Hotels. If you are ever in London, he hopes you'll look him up."

Katya screwed the paper up, about to lob it in the waste basket next to the table and then changed her mind. Maybe when she was back in the city she would take him up on his offer. And meet up with him a few times to work out who the true Zac was. She stuffed the paper into her pocket.

As the queue of people waiting to come in had died down, she left Jolene at the table and peeked into the hall. So far, this year's ceilidh broke all previous records for attendance. There were far more people than the original licencing application specified. A good job all those employed by the local council pretended not to notice. A caller yelled the moves, but movement was restricted because of the numbers.

Dr McLatchie joined her. "D'ye want me to cast your horoscope for the year ahead? I see great things for you."

Katya raised her eyebrows. "You do? Shall we start with Zac? Not safe for work indeed. And how come the stars didn't tell you he and the truth do not enjoy close acquaintanceship?"

The doctor pursed her lips and flapped a hand. "Aye, well. Sometimes the stars make mistakes. But no' this time. I sense amazing, wonderful, awfy—"

Katya smiled and let the rest of the sentence drift over her head. Thanks to the overwhelming noise of bagpipes, laughter and chatter, she didn't hear the din outside at first. But when the doctor tipped her head to one side and pointed to the doors, she caught it—the roar of an engine and the unmistakable whop-whop-whop whirl of blades.

She headed outside, the commotion drawing out others, all of them joining Katya to stare at the skies in disbelief.

"Is that the air ambulance?" someone asked. The crowd exchanged glances as if trying to work out who the ill or injured person in need of emergency medical services among them might be.

"Naw," Dr McLatchie replied. "The air ambulance is bright yellow. That yin's pink wi' silver stars."

Mhari, her phone held high above her head, as she filmed the chopper coming in to land, swung around to face Katya.

"What? Are ye still here? Off you go, you silly mare. Madeline decided if the mountain wouldnae come to Mohammed, Mohammed would go tae the mountain."

Chapter Thirty-Eight

All the 'Hi honeys', not being able to find Madeline online, the bending over backwards to help her and the emails that became increasingly personal...

Chink, chink, chink—the sound of pennies dropping. And Katya, who prided herself on being far savvier than Gaby and Mhari, who'd already worked it out. Or even arranged it. Who knew, who cared? In a few minutes' time, a helicopter would land in a field in Scotland and the door would swing open and a dark-haired head pop out. And that was all that mattered.

She wasn't the only one in the field. Villagers had made their way there too, joined by the people who'd come to the village for the ceilidh. Perhaps they thought an unexpected helicopter appearance was part of the entertainment. The lights from the helicopter beamed out, picking out faces in the crowd. The whirl of the blades blasted Katya's hair back from her face and ruined Mhari's efforts.

Oh well. She wanted to jump up and down anyway and as it was, Lochalshie's off-duty community cops acting as the landing crew and waving the helicopter in had to stick their arms out to stop her coming any further forward.

"No further in, hen!" the older one of them said. "We dinnae want ye getting decapitated."

"Too right," his colleague added. "Think of all that paperwork we need tae fill in."

Heaven forbid a Scotsman didn't get to spend his evening whirling unwitting partners around a dance floor and drinking too much whisky.

The blades seemed to take forever to stop and the helicopter's door to flip up. Behind her, someone whispered, "I wonder what this Madeline looks like?" Gaby, the conspirator in the miracle that had managed to overcome all obstacles, the literal roadblock. The non-stop phone pings and the insistence on leg waxing explained.

"I have my suspicions," she whispered back, "but I am very grateful to my best friend and very excited. That comes with five exclamation marks, by the way."

Gaby giggled. "We'd better go. I've been roped into woman-ing the bar and making sure we don't run out of anything. See you later, right?"

"Right," Katya nodded, her head still fixed to the front, terrified she might miss the exact moment the door opened.

And then it did, and the dark head came out crown first, moving slowly until his face was directly opposite her. Everything else vanished—or appeared to. Did the villagers all melt away? Did the engine suddenly die and darkness lighten so two people were able to walk the ten long metres and then fling their arms around each other?

Not quite, but that was how it felt.

"I can't believe…"

"Caitlin was disappointed when you didn't take the hint

from her interview for the book. She insisted I take the helicopter when she heard the road to Lochalshie was blocked."

"Please tell Caitlin that I plan to write the best celebrity autobiography ever."

They stood back from each other. Just like the last time she'd seen him, Dexter looked exhausted, all dark smudges under the eyes, limp hair and fine lines sketched around his mouth and eyes. No sign of an LA tan—impossible to get when you spent all your time working—and yet, her libido reacted as she had then. Lord, he was beautiful.

"I've got an empty," she said. "Mhari is at the ceilidh. We have hours and hours to ourselves. That's if you're not too tired?"

His eyes gleamed. "No. Let's go."

Two tiring but amazing hours later, Katya finally got out of bed, pulled on her robe and went to fetch them something to eat, waiving her usual rule about eating in bed.

A gigantic stack of peanut butter-slathered toast between them, Dexter explained the events of the last few days, including the enforced time off which had come at an opportune time...

"Gaby worked it out," he said, "the Madeline thing. I wasn't sure—I thought you were gonna make a go of it with the Zac guy, and I didn't think it was fair to interfere. But when I heard about what happened, I decided to suggest a meet-up as Madeline. You beat me to it."

He bit into the toast, the peanut butter spread so thickly he left teeth marks.

"You didn't mind me interfering in your career by pretending to be Madeline? I always thought you were super-amazing, but I started it because I wanted to help and persuade you to move to London when the company relocated. Then events got in the way."

Katya wiped away a bit of peanut butter stuck to the side of his mouth and kissed it. Any excuse.

"No... I don't mind. I enjoyed the Madeline chats. Especially when they got personal. At one point, I remember thinking my true soulmate might be Madeline."

He squeezed her hand. "When your bus to Glasgow was cancelled, I spoke to Caitlin, and she lent me the helicopter. You have to jump through a lot of hoops to get flight permission at this time of the year. I let Gaby know. Did she really manage to keep it quiet?"

Katya laughed. Her best friend had dropped plenty of clues, but Katya didn't notice. Too busy feeling sorry for herself. Still, who cared now?

Dexter picked up another slice of the toast and fed it to her. Katya would have mocked all this cutesy stuff normally. Now, she lapped it up. At this rate it was only a matter of time before she and Dexter fixed on icky nicknames for each other.

Oh, but... what was he doing back in this country, anyway? The South Korean launch was scheduled for spring next year.

"I'm thinking of moving to Norwich or even London," she said, "I know it's still a long-distance relationship, but not quite as long distance as Lochalshie."

He slid the robe off her shoulders and pushed her back gently onto the bed, clambering over the plate of toast and lying on top of her, propping himself up on his forearms so he could look at her How, how, how had she been able to forget this and how powerful it was? Tomorrow—or whenever—she would tell Psychic Josie her lousy website had no idea how to figure out a couple's NSFW status. Turned out Pisces and Leo far out-sizzled Pisces and Scorpio no matter what her astrology software said.

"That's a pity," he said lightly. "Seeing as I've negotiated a super-cool new working arrangement with Blissful Beauty where I get to work remotely—wherever the hell I want. Leaves a lot more time for a relationship, I guess."

"What?"

He bent his head to her and kissed her. "Yup. Turns out I'm indispensable. So I call the shots. If you can do the digital nomad thing, so can I. And if I say I'm not gonna work all the hours God sends, they agree."

There was another thing she'd forgotten—that silky smooth voice. And one hundred times nicer when it said words she'd always longed to hear.

"But the money," Katya said. She'd never asked how much Dexter made, but she guessed it was substantial, a six-figure kind of deal. Not that he ever did anything with it. When you worked 70-hour weeks and took no vacations, it left no time for spending sprees.

"I've got a lot of savings," he said, confirming the suspicion. "Wanna to try living in London? Or we could live in a tiny Scottish village where the weather is atrocious, it's criminally cold ten months of the year and the locals poke their noses into your business all the time."

"When you put it like that... But it does have the best vegan pizza in Scotland. There's a Pilates class too, where stressed marketing managers can chillax."

"And admire what the teacher can do with her legs and fantasise where they might end up later. It's also the place where I met the most super-awesome, amazing, beyond brilliantly beautiful woman."

Hyperbole? You could learn to live with it. Love it, even. This time, she brought her head up to kiss him.

"I phoned you," she said, remembering the call and how it had screwed with her head. "After I listened to Caitlin's not-so-subtle hints."

He propped himself up on his elbow and smiled. "That was Flower—my niece. Also an intern at Blissful Beauty."

"Niece?" she said, struck by the things she didn't know about Dexter. All this was to come, then. Dexter and his family, Katya and hers—the details you didn't bother with in those heady early days. And now they had the time to find out, to question and explore.

"Yeah. My older sister Courtney started young. Flower's her eldest and kinda protective of me. I was getting loads of calls from magazines about the so-called relationship with Caitlin. Flower thought you were a journalist from one of the British trashies when you rang. She happened to be alone in my office. I didn't make the connection until days later."

He rolled onto his side, resting his hand on Katya's torso where it moved up and down and they watched it circle her belly button, and edge downwards.

"I've supported Courtney for years, but it's time for her to stand on her own two feet."

Katya had assumed Dexter's piles of wealth sat in a savings account somewhere gathering interest and dust. But it turned out he gave it to his family instead. "What a prince!" as Gaby would say. Katya murmured a half-hearted protest. Was he sure? She didn't want him to feel guilty.

"I'm not going to. When she found out about you, Flower turned into another person, telling me I had to go after you. She also told me I was an enabler—allowing her mother to drift and not take responsibility."

"I'd like to meet Flower."

"She'd love to meet you too. But if we've finished all the explanations…?" The hand had found its way between her thighs and his fingers did magical, sparks-flying things.

One last thing.

"Zac."

"Shush." Lips landed on hers once more. He pulled his head back. "You don't need to explain."

Just as they were about to explore the far-most reaches of human pleasure, the flat's front door opened, and a shout came up the stairs.

"Katya? Dexter? Are ye decent? We decided we might hae a wee party in the flat to celebrate the new year." Footsteps—a few of them—clattered up the stairs, accompanied by chat and laughter.

Katya groaned. The ceilidh was supposed to finish just after midnight. For the sake of decency, they might have waited.

"Dexter," she stood up. He grinned at her. "Welcome to village life."

When they emerged from the room, clothes hastily pulled on, Mhari, Gaby, Jack, Jolene and Stewart by now ensconced in the living room and dispersing drinks, cheered. Ribald comments followed, along the lines of good things came to those who waited and a marvelling at the powers of the village to kick-start romances.

"Aye, aye," Stewart said, Scottie wagging his tail furiously by his side. "Look at me and ma Jolene. Five years together and a bairn on its way. Mebbe that'll be you next, Gaby."

Jack shook his head. "Can you imagine Gaby having to

cope with pregnancy *and* my mother? It would be the high-light of her medical career. She'd never leave your side, Gaby."

Another knock at the flat front door. Seconds later, the doctor, whose ears must have been burning, came in with Ranald. "How're, how're," she said, nodding at everyone in turn. "The ceilidh's going full pelt, so Ranald and I thought we'd spend the bells wi' the ones we love."

She turned gimlet eyes on Katya. "Did I no' promise you amazing things, Katya?"

Katya stifled a smile. And then let it out anyway. Gaby, Mhari and Dr McLatchie all had permission to take respon-sibility for tonight's overwhelming bliss.

The doctor sat down next to Gaby, Ranald taking up his usual position near the door so he could hide in a corridor the minute someone tried to talk to him. The doorbell sounded again, and Katya shot Mhari a filthy look at the same time as she gave Dexter an apologetic one. He didn't seem to mind the non-stop troop of folks. Stewart had button-holed him, determined to discuss the porridge-making championships that had taken place earlier the day. Dexter seemed happy enough to talk about it, even if the super-food vegan version he might have favoured had ended up in last place.

Downstairs, a man bounced on his toes nervously.

"Ah... Katya, isn't it? Um, is there a party here tonight?"

Lachlan Forrester. Rescuer of people stranded when their mini-bus was nicked. Also mad crush of Mhari's. He wore smart clothes—pristine clean jeans, a dark green roll-neck jumper and a blazer with its sleeves rolled up. A man who'd put in effort. He shivered with nerves—someone on the verge of bolting. He carried stuff too—a rucksack that clinked glass together and a basket that wobbled from side to side and meowed.

Lachlan looked at the basket. "Wee pressie for Gaby."

"Mhari!" Katya yelled up the stairs. "Someone to see you!"

"She's a gigantic pain in the butt," she said, watching the corners of his mouth edge upwards in response. "But special too. You won't regret it."

Ah, love. As Caitlin said, didn't it make you want to yell to the rooftops? Or at least make sure those around you felt its blissful warm blanket too?

Upstairs, Dexter winked at her. Lachlan set his basket on the floor, and the cat, a ninety percent ginger ten percent white, nosed her way out. Scottie tried to say 'hello'. The cat immediately hit him on the nose with her front paw, forcing him to retreat, cowering, under one of the armchairs. Satisfied the space was now safe, the cat wandered over first to Dexter, who tickled her under the chin, and next to Gaby. Obligingly, she leapt onto her lap. Someone started up the music—a Spotify playlist aimed at encompassing all tastes. Tricky, given the party attendees, but a cheer went up when the Proclaimers started up, determined to walk their 500 miles and back again.

Privacy tonight, of all nights, might have been nice but time, the luxury that had eluded Katya and Dexter in their first few months together, now bolted itself to their side. Oh, the endless days, evenings, lunches, dinners (breakfasts) together that stretched out in front of them... Pilates classes, walks by the loch, pub-quiz evenings in the Lochside Welcome... They could even climb Maggie Broon's Boobs and take photos of each other in front of the nipple cairns.

With all that alone-together time ahead of them, who could begrudge a dark winter's evening gathered in a flat far too small for that many people as they talked about Stewart's porridge judging, Dexter's helicopter descent, the money Psychic Josie had taken, the sales of shortbread, the numbers of people who had signed up for next year's Highland Tours and the overwhelming success of the Lochalshie Hogmanay Ceilidh?

"Better put the word out, Mhari," Katya said, crossing her fingers every single member of the Lochalshie WhatsApp group didn't turn up. "Ceilidh post-mortem at our house. Can we get Ashley to send us take-out vegan pizza and chips?"

Muttering "Aye, he'd better" and adding in "vegan pizzas with bacon and cheese" (Katya told herself she could pick the offending bits off), Mhari's thumbs moved up and down over her phone screen.

Sat next to her, Lachlan retrieved his rucksack. "I also liberated these," he said, fishing in the bag and pulling out a plastic bag that clinked—the telltale rattle of glass hitting glass. "Zac forgot he'd left them out the back of the car park at the Royal George, so I took them."

He made his way into the kitchen, saying he was on a mission to find crisps, shortbread and anything he could turn into a sandwich.

Dexter retrieved one of the bottles from the plastic bag and whistled. "Um, Dom Perignon Vintage 2004... should we be drinking this?"

Katya took the bottle from him, opening it with that soft pfft bottles of fizz were meant to give when opened by those who knew what they were doing (or who had plenty of experience). She swigged from it. "Yes. If fools want to pay hundreds of pounds for this stuff and think that's impressive, we should drink it in an ordinary house, in an ordinary place and at an ordinary time."

"Except," Dexter accepted the proffered bottle from her and knocked back a decent amount himself. "You're extraordinary, and I'm beyond excited, super-thrilled that we're embarking on this fantastic adventure together and jeez, if that ain't worth celebrating with overpriced, stolen champagne, I don't know what is."

Quite.

Katya squeezed Dexter's hand. He squeezed hers back. "Village life," she whispered. "You urban metrosexual you. Are you sure you want this?"

She was ninety-nine point five percent sure of the answer, but it thrilled her anyway. "God, yeah, Katya. Bring it on!"

Ten, nine, eight, seven, six…

And with that, he kissed her—mouths meeting, lips bumping and tongues dancing together, the two of them oblivious to the cheers that started behind them.

Happy New Year.

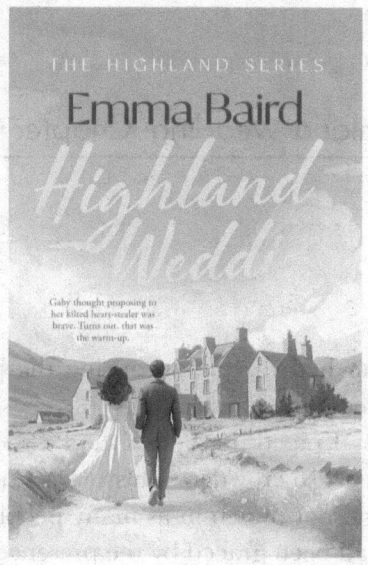

vinci-books.com/HighlandWedding

She popped the question. Now comes the chaos.

When Gaby proposes to Jack, he says yes—but so does the entire village. As wedding fever sweeps Lochalshie, pressure mounts, plans go awry, and a charming newcomer stirs things up. Can love survive the guest list?

Turn the page for a free preview…

Highland Wedding: Chapter One

"Yes!" Jack punched the air, surprising the people around him who jumped back in alarm.

"Yes what?" I piped up. We'd found a spot in the field's edge which wasn't so crowded. This year's Lochalshie Highland Games had not drawn in as many people as last year's event, which had been graced by the presence of one of the biggest reality TV stars in the world, but it was still busy. Mother Nature had granted us a warm, sunny day too, rare in the north-west of Scotland.

From where we sat, I could see the tops of heads as dancers competed on the stage and the queue that snaked all the way around the park as people waited to see Psychic Josie, international medium consulted by all the stars. (As she herself put it.) From time to time, the bagpipes sounded. Earlier that day, the local pipe band dressed in regimental tartan marched down the High Street to start the games, and a few of them hung around piping tunes for the dancers and hammer throwers.

"The results are in!" Jack showed me his phone. As a

long-time resident of Lochalshie, Jack held the record for best caber tosser in the area. And, as I often told him, the best-looking caber tosser. Shockingly judgemental of me to say so, but the competition wasn't high. Meeting any of the other contenders on a dark night guaranteed nightmares.

Jack's screen showed the Lochalshie WhatsApp group—the first and often the only source of up-to-date news for the area. Angus had sent out a rude message questioning the accuracy of the result but was one hundred percent certain the village's biggest tosser had won.

"I've regained my pride," Jack said. "First again."

Last year, he didn't win—distracted thanks to his pursuit of me. He was back in the game this year. The sun caught the red in his hair and made it gleam. I fell in love with Jamie Fraser's far more handsome and younger brother, and I still tingled when I looked at him. The Games competitors all looked the part—kilts, Timberland boots and tight T-shirts. Biased I know, but no-one wore a kilt better than Jack. He had the knees to carry it off. And the biceps to show off a skin-tight black T-shirt, and the calves that displayed socks to full adv—

"Gaby?"

I snapped to attention. Tempting as it was to sneak off home for a little tumble, we were committee members. Our job today was to help organise the Highland Games and ensure everything ran smoothly.

I ruffled his hair. "Good," I said. "I only date winners." Whispered, "Sleep with."

He laughed and leaned over to kiss me, a tiny peck on the lips that took me back to our first kiss on this same day one year ago. Once upon a time, I lived in Great Yarmouth with my boyfriend of ten years who was, not to put too fine a point on it, a douche bag. Chance took me here—the village in the middle of nowhere—when I signed up for cat-sitting services. As a fanatical Outlander fan, I'd been delighted to discover the village contained Jack, Jamie Fraser's (better-looking) double. We didn't hit it off at first, but the path of true love never does run smooth as the cliché goes. When we got together months later, it was all the sweeter for the wait.

And what a year it had been.

"What's the prize, oh champion tosser?" I asked Jack. "One thousand pounds?"

That was the cash prize last year. In my head, I'd spent the money already starting with a long weekend in a luxury hotel somewhere in the city where I rediscovered retail therapy and the two of us romped on a bed we didn't have to make afterwards.

"Ah... ten pounds and a wee dod o' shortbread."

Oh well. Last year's generous donation was a one-off. Though it seemed cheeky to force the winner to make his own prize. Yes, my boyfriend not only tossed cabers with aplomb, but he was also a dab hand in the kitchen. His shortbread had won the best bakery entry overall in the village's version of the Great British Bake Off, which had taken place earlier this afternoon.

"We'd better make our way over there," I said, "so you can have your picture taken receiving the prize for best caber toss." And then upload it onto the village website and Facebook page. If it's not on social media, it never happened right?

The Games were almost finished. The crowds had drifted away, and the stallholders were packing up. I'd seen plenty of people carrying bags brandishing the names of local companies—those selling soap, candles, hand-knitted jumpers, food and everything else artisan and craft-sy. Jack's stall advertising his authentic Outlander (ish) tours of the Highlands had taken sheet-loads of sign-ups to his mailing list, which promised a good start to next year's tourist season.

We picked our way over the field. Torrential rain the week before had turned it into a quagmire. The sun had come out today and the day before, making them the best ones of the summer so far. A miracle. The muddiness was due in part to building work going on nearby. The Highland Games took place in the large greenfield area next to the Royal George hotel. It had been bought last year by a company determined to expand. And the field was under threat. Next year, we'd need to find somewhere else to hold the games.

"Jack!" Angus waved us over. He sat at a table in front of the roped-off area for the actual games. Kids mucked about, trying to turn over the smallest of the tractor tyres. A few of them managed, which was more than could be said for me. I tried taking part in Highland Games activities once—the result a broken windscreen on an expensive car thanks to losing control of a too-heavy hammer.

"Fancy a go at the tug of war?" Angus said, standing up. I had to strain my neck to look up at him. He was also a rugby prop—a truly terrifying prospect to face. No wonder he doubled up as a bouncer at our local pub.

Jack squeezed my hand. "Nah. Gaby and I were going to head home and—"

Just what I'd been thinking too. But Angus butted in.

"New team put themselves forward. Calling themselves the Royal George champions."

Rivalry between the Lochside Welcome and the Royal George, the two pubs that bookended the village, had always been fierce. This year it was worse than ever. The

expansion of the hotel threatened the Lochside Welcome—
our favourite pub. The George never usually bothered with
the tug of war. This year they must be trying to prove something. Honour was at stake.

Jack turned to me, eyes glinting. Often, I had to pinch
myself. My mind would feverishly run through his many
plus points. Red-head! With lovely knees! Jamie Fraser or
rather Sam Heughan look-a-like but better... Then, I'd give
my mind a ticking-off for being so shallow and make myself
list the good points that didn't relate to his appearance.
Kind! Maker of fantastic shortbread! Considerate! Fun to
be with.

...a-may-zing between the sheets.

We'd seen little of each other during the past week. It
being August, the tourist season was in full swing, and Jack
left most mornings at sparrow's fart, not returning until nine
or ten o'clock at night. He was off tomorrow, and we'd
planned to sneak away from the games early and...
catch up.

"You go," I said, prodding him forward. "And make me
proud."

He and Angus exchanged eyebrow-raises—an 'as if!'
thing I guessed. The Highland Games champion caber
tosser and hammer thrower along with the other rugby
boys, and Stewart who fuelled himself on industrial quantities of lager and porridge. What could the Royal George
team throw at that?

Jolene wandered over to join me, baby clamped to her
front. Macmillan Junior was a month old and—luckily for
him—had inherited most of his mother's eight percent
Māori genes. A tiny dark head nestled against Jolene's chest
and snored gently. She'd put those baby headphones on him
to protect against the bagpipes.

"How's Tamar?" I asked, resisting the impulse to stroke his little head. As a later in life cat lover, I wasn't sure what you did with babies, but I assumed they didn't enjoy being stroked the way cats did.

"Fine," Jolene said, reaching her arms behind her so she could stretch out her back. "Though I wouldn't mind heaps more sleep at night, eh?"

Like many New Zealanders, most of what Jolene said sounded questioning.

"And is Stewart…?" Pulling his weight. A delicate question. Stewart's second home was the Lochside Welcome. I didn't know how much that had changed since the arrival of baba. Or if his attendance there had increased—a reluctant father too eager to leave the demands of parenthood to the woman.

She grinned—large straight white teeth gleaming, and the movement highlighting the dimples she had on each cheek. "Devoted. Tamar's his perfect audience. He doesn't mind listening to Stewart for hours at a time. Works a treat to get him off to sleep."

Oh to be a baby! If you nodded off when a person started banging on about the mysteries and marvels of coding as Stewart loved to do, no-one considered it impolite.

"Blast it!" Jolene's tone changed. Alarm. She pointed across the field.

I followed the direction of her fingers—the Royal George and a line of people who'd walked out of it. The tug of war wasn't always about bulk and size but having heavyweights on your team was an advantage. Every man swaggering out of the hotel was three times the height and width of a normal person. Except for the end guy who looked familiar though I wasn't close enough to see.

"Right," Jolene said, unbuckling her baby harness. "He's been fed and changed, and he's fast asleep."

To my dismay, I realised she meant me for me to hold Tamar. Oh heck. Before I could mutter, "Gosh, are you sure?", she strapped the baby to me, dropped a kiss on his head and strolled over to the Lochside Welcome team.

That was the thing with Jolene. She was far fitter than your average person and stronger too. All the way through her pregnancy she jogged and weight-lifted—all the better to pop your baby out in under two hours, as her GP (and my almost mother-in-law Dr McLatchie) told me later.

The team members lined up, eight on each side, one behind the other and a thick strand of rope lying to the side of them. Word must have spread. Those crowds drifting off home drifted back inside the park gates. Whistles, cheers, boos and catcalls started up.

I booed myself when I worked out who the Royal George's end man was. Zac Cavanagh, one-time resident of Lochalshie, would-be boyfriend of my best friend and murderer. Come on, the Lochside Welcome team!

"The rotten, sodding cheats," Laney Haggerty hissed beside me. Owner of the local riding school and a cousin of Ashley, proprietor of the Lochside Welcome, she had skin in the game. "Channel 5 is filming the World's Strongest Man in Inverness. The Royal George has bussed them all in. I hope their steroid-filled biceps explode under the strain."

I could hardly bear to watch. These monsters dwarfed Jack, Angus and the others. The teams picked up the rope, the centre line above a marking on the ground. Jolene, face grimly determined, was third in line. Jack was behind her, his face equally so.

Big Donnie—and even he looked tiny next to the George's team—held a whistle and conferred with the teams' drivers. He positioned himself at the line marked on the ground, raised his arm in the air and dropped it, blowing the whistle at the same time.

The teams' drivers yelled instructions. "It's no' just about big bulging muscles," Laney said, eyeing the other team in their wife-beater vests with distaste. "A team needs rhythm too, so they harmonise their traction power."

I nodded as if I understood what she meant, my eyes fixed on the middle of the rope as it moved one way then the other. The whistles, cat calls and jeers grew louder. Laney gripped my hand and Tamar stirred, his little mouth opening and shutting before he twisted his head the other way and returned to baby snores.

A faint cheer but a much louder boo sounded as the George's team yanked the Lochside Welcome's four metres over the centre line.

"Best of three!" someone yelled, and the teams nodded.

Second time round, the driver's pep talk must have worked. After what felt like the whole field willed on the Lochside Welcome team to "heave!", the George's over-grown athletes stumbled over the centre. Tamar's baby headphones did their job. The ear-shattering cheer that went up didn't disturb him.

So, one-all. Laney started muttering the Hail Mary under her breath.

Once more, the teams lined up, feet dug into the ground and scowls all round. Jack twisted his head and blew me a kiss. I blew him one back and concentrated on bargaining with everyone—God, the universe, Big Donnie even, any old Celtic god whose spirit still hung around.

Please. Let. Them. Win.

And if they did... An idea took root. What about if I...?

Yes, yes, yes! The team's win would be a clear sign from the universe. Approval, even.

The George's too-big crew hauled the rope over to their side so easily, our team fell forward—the ground yanked out from underneath them. The boos rose once more. I cursed, upset because the universe had just signalled disapproval for my plan. The omens had seemed so promising too.

Laney shook her head. "No way," she said, ducking under the rope that fenced off the field. She marched over to Big Donnie. He blew his whistle once more and called both teams back.

"What did you say?" I asked when she returned. "Those rotten cheats cheated again," she said. "Did you notice the guy second at the back? He had the rope over his shoulder. Not allowed!"

Big Donnie conferred with the teams' drivers. Both sides gesticulated wildly, but another cheer went up when every team member returned to their positions. A replay then. Beside me, Laney muttered, "Hail Mary, full of grace, the Lord is with thee…"

The ground wouldn't help the Royal George. Those overgrown heavier than average bodies were ankle-deep in rain-sodden soft soil. The cry, "Heave!" started up once more, and both teams grasped the rope and pulled.

Laney bargained. She'd resume regular chapel attendance; even get up at 8am to attend mass every morning. "What are you going to do, Gaby?" she asked as we watched the rope nervously. "Give up pizza and chips for two months?"

"No! I'm going to do something much better."

"… blessed art thou amongst women, and blessed is the fruit of thy womb, Jesus… Oh aye? What are you going to do?"

I tapped my nose.

This time, the universe listened. Seconds later, the George's giants fell forward and everyone around us exploded—yelps, hoorays, claps and wolf whistles. Time to fulfil my part of the bargain.

I ran and then slowed, mindful Tamar might stir (he was still, miraculously, asleep) towards the victorious team. Jolene got to me first, her poor hands red raw and the palms bloody but the smile lighting up her face showing she felt no pain. I offloaded Tamar and Stewart joined us, mono-loguing about porridge and its amazing capabilities.

Everything flew over my head. There was only one person I had eyes and time for. And there he stood... again, the sun catching the glint of his hair, longer than usual but a perfect length to run your hands through. The sun that back lit him and set his profile in sharp relief. And those dark eyes when he turned towards me...

The perfect place to ask, right? The modern woman did not wait for a man to make his move. She jumped in and asked what she had been thinking about for... ooh, an age. Circumstances now presented me with the perfect moment. Universe approval, remember?

"Jack! Will you do me the great honour of becoming my wife—husband, husband, slip of the tongue!"

Jack's brow wrinkled. I watched two emotions chase their way across his face. Puzzlement and... oh, was that dismay?

"Did she just ask Jack tae marry her?"

Argh—yikes. The crowds had died away, so the small number of people around us had heard me loud and clear. An audience hadn't been part of my original plan for good reasons. My phone pinged. Easy to guess the cause—the Lochalshie WhatsApp group updating with the news. I couldn't see her, but the WhatsApp number one updater must be nearby.

In the background, a lone piper sounded, and traffic noise drifted over as cars made their way out of the village. All I heard was silence.

A man who didn't impulsively yell, "Yes, yes, a thousand times yes!" and punch the air.

Tamar chose that moment to wake up, loud cries that pierced the air.

You and me both, Tamar. I'd misread the situation completely. Was it possible to recover from such a public proposal when someone turned you down...?

Highland Wedding: Chapter Two

My phone pinged once more. The wretched WhatsApp group. A speech bubble hanging on the screen: "He's no' said aye!" and "Why no'? She's a lovely lassie!" The thing where people pretend kind concern while at the same time revelling in your misfortune and embarrassment.

I cringed and considered my options. My best friend is a style-it-out expert. I channelled her. Nothing came through. Jack faced me, his expression back to a blank. It looked neither pleased nor displeased. In the days before we were an item, I reckoned he would make an expert poker player.

He took my hand. "C'mon, Gaby. Let's go."

Let's go? LET'S GO?! Around us, people murmured, asking the same question I did, I guessed. Dude, you've no' answered the lassie's question. Are ye gonnae marry her or no'? Out of the corner of my eye, I spotted Zac—Lochalshie's one-time resident. He raised his hand to wave at me. I ignored it. I make a point of not acknowledging murderous scumbags.

Jack tipped his head to the side, gesturing towards our

house a mere three minutes' walk away. I nodded gratefully. Perhaps he wanted me to do the proposal properly—get down on one knee and ask. At which point, he'd punch the air and say, "Yes, yes, a thousand times yes." Throw in, an "Are you sure, Gaby? I don't know if I'm good enough for you."

Stewart, who had yet to develop social awareness skills, jogged behind us followed by Scottie his West Highland white terrier. "Are youse off the pub?" he asked. "Jolene says Ah can have one pint if Ah promise to change wee Tamar's nappies for the next ten days."

"No!" I snapped. "We've got stuff to talk about."

When Jack smiled, fingers squeezing mine, relief washed over me. Thank goodness. Yes, he longed to settle down to a detailed discussion about wedding venues, menus, cakes and whether or not I opted for the full meringue dress-wise.

Someone called out Jack's name. Ashley. The Lochside Welcome had done a roaring trade so far today on half-price pizzas and cocktails invented especially for the games. He didn't need our custom. I pulled Jack's hand, still unnerved by the non-answer to my question.

"I'd better see what he wants," Jack said. "Sorry."

As we headed over, Mhari sidled up. The Lochalshie WhatsApp group updater extraordinaire. Mhari was one of the first people I met when I moved to Lochalshie. Her nosiness was legendary. There wasn't a single aspect of a person's life Mhari thought worth ignoring.

"What's happenin'? Are you getting married or no'?" she asked. her face arranged into what she thought invited a person to confide.

"None of your beeswax," I snapped back. Impulse took over. "We're off to the Lochside Welcome to celebrate."

Might be a celebration—might be a drink to drown my sorrows. Another hand squeeze.

"Bad news," Ashley said when we reached him. His normally friendly face looked strained, and he shot killer looks in the direction of the Royal George. Extensive refurbishment of the hotel had been carried out at the beginning of the year, finishing only the day before. Once a shabby Edwardian place favoured by coach parties of touring OAPs making the most of their free bus pass, these days its car park was chokka most of the time.

"I'll tell you about it in the pub," he added, dropping his voice. "Free pizza and chocolate cake thrown in."

Ten minutes later and a large helping of Chocolate Decadence in front of me—created in honour of the reality TV star Caitlin Cartier and utterly delicious—Ashley told us what he knew.

'Us' being Jack, Stewart, Jolene and Tamar, Mhari and I. We'd taken up stools at the bar. Tourists and visitors occupied the tables at the back, Ashley's staff running back and forth delivering the wood-fired pizzas the Lochside Welcome specialised in. Mhari and Jolene had nabbed their own teaspoons and kept trying to swipe bits of my cake. What was it with women not ordering their own? I guarded it as well as I could.

"The appeal's been overturned," Ashley said as he poured Stewart a pint. "So those evil witches get their way."

Those 'evil witches' was how everyone referred to Lois Berringer and Angeline Manson, the millionaire property moguls behind Hammerstone Hotels and new owners of the Royal George. Last year, they'd come to the village and pretended their acquisition of the place would be a brilliant thing for everyone.

Spoiler—it wasn't. The only beneficiaries were Hammerstone Hotels who appeared to be on a mission to edge out all the local competition. Already, they'd pinched a lot of passing trade. Now, they'd be able to up the ante. Their first planning application had been to convert part of the field/playing park into a glamping site for stressed millennials and Gen Y-ers. After a lot of shrieking and shouting, we had persuaded our local councillors not to pass it. The application went to appeal.

Doom and gloom.

"I'll never drink there," Stewart declared supping his pint. Admittedly, Stewart spent more than your average punter but what difference would it make?

"And I'll make sure every coachload of tourists I pick up gets dropped off for lunch here," Jack threw in. He helped himself to a blob of fudge icing from my cake. At this rate, I'd be lucky to eat half of it. I dropped a bit and Scottie dived for it. Stewart whisked it away before he ate it seeing as dogs and chocolate did not go together. When he stuck what he had recovered from the floor in his mouth, only two people shook their head in disgust. We were used to him.

"They're planning this big launch," Ashley fumed. "So I've heard. Celebrities and everything. Those glamping tents are so warm you can even camp in winter!"

Gosh. So far, I'd experienced one Highland winter. Jack's heating bills shot through the roof. As a former soft southerner, I found the Arctic chill unbearable. And anyway, in the meantime, WHERE WAS THE ANSWER TO MY PROPOSAL? The phone in my pocket vibrated. A hundred or so people asking Mhari via the WhatsApp group, "Well? Has he said 'aye' yet?"

"Gaby," Ashley said, moving along so he stood opposite me. His eyes gleamed. "Would ye like another bit o' cake? Or what about some chips?"

Jack nudged me. Once upon a time, in our pre-dating days, we'd come to the Lochside Welcome for food and ended up in a chip-off. It's like a boxing match only uglier. People pretend they are happy to share chips. When they are as good as Ashley's. this is never the case. I crammed ten of them all dipped into garlic mayo into my mouth at once to win the competition. Did Jack now remember this fondly? Or did he think to himself, "Hmm. Can I spend the rest of my life with a woman who will always nick my chips?"

"No thank you," I replied, passing the remains of the cake to Mhari.

"I've had this idea," Ashley added, "to bugger up their launch."

Jack turned his head my way. The paranoid bit of me— all of me at present given that he still hadn't answered my question—detected full-scale panic in his eyes. They'd widened, his eyebrows signalling a warning and his mouth stayed straight—no upturn of corners or the flash of teeth that showed when he was happy or pleased. He must have worked out what Ashley was about to ask, as had I...

"We've no' done weddings before," Ashley continued.

I blinked. Jack did too.

"Dunno why," Ashley pointed at the view in front of him. The Lochside Welcome's beer garden sat right on the edge of the loch, as you might expect from its title. On a nice day—though there weren't that many of them— wedding pictures would be superb.

"If you two got married here and invited the entire village, which would be a kick in the teeth for the George.

And show off the Lochside Welcome as the best wedding venue in the area? I know you're supposed to get married in the lassie's home town, Gaby, but wouldn't you rather do it here than Great Yarmouth?"

Oh heavens... so now, not only did I have a boyfriend I'd proposed to and put under pressure by doing it publicly, but we were also duty-bound to marry to save the Lochside Welcome. Stewart, Jolene and Mhari loved the idea. They threw in their own suggestions. Lachlan Forrester could provide the wedding car. (Stolen, probably.) Mhari could do my hair. Ashley could create a wedding cake in my honour this time, instead of Caitlin Cartier, aforementioned reality TV star...

And still no answer from Jack. None of them seemed to have noticed that. No point in a wedding if only one person turns up, hmm?

Jack grabbed my hand. "C'mon," he whispered. "Let's talk."

We slid from our stools. Mhari moved too as if to follow us and I glared at her. Outside, the sun had sunk in the sky colouring it a lovely pinky-orange shade. We took the furthest away table. I felt four pairs of eyes on our backs—our friends, pushed up against the window and trying to listen in.

"Not the end to the day I'd planned," Jack said, and my heart sank.

"Listen, don't worry. I'm sorry it slipped out. Didn't mean for it to happen that way and it doesn't matter, and we can come up with another plan for Ashley. How about dirty tactics, I start spreading rumours that anyone who stays at the George gets food poisoning. I mean, Katya threw up after eating Zac's food, so that might wo—"

When I'm anxious, my mouth runs away with itself. The

kiss silenced me, taking me back to our first time. Also beside the loch, also just after the Highland Games. Lips light at first and then demanding. My mouth parted underneath his and I surrendered to the here and now; jolts of electricity firing off in all directions—my throat, my chest, further down…

A kilt makes a man much more accessible. I was just about to reach under it when Jack broke apart, grin in place. "That's more like the end of the day I planned," he said. "Thought I'd get us warmed up."

STILL no answer. Even if the interlude had been extremely pleasant.

"But, but…" I hated how feeble I sounded.

"Oh? Don't actions speak louder than words then?" A sly wink and a grin. He'd been winding me up all along.

"You!" I said, planting one hand on his chest and shoving him away. "Are the biggest, rottenest bas—"

Another kiss, and this time his arms enfolded me, crushing me tightly to that T-shirt and kilt.

"Of course I'll marry you! You pipped me to the post. I had this plan where I asked you at the end of the tourist season. We went to a hotel, one of those ones with a big log fire, I got down on one knee all traditional like, and said, Gabrielle Amelia Richardson, will you—"

Relief can make you giddy. When he kissed me again, my head spun.

"Get a room!" someone called out. Jolene, I decided, and we didn't need to because all too soon we would head back to the house where marvellous, mind-blowing things would take place. After which, I *might* casually bring up the idea of a themed wedding. An Outlander one.

Ashley ran out bearing an ice bucket and a bottle of champagne. He stopped at the table next to us and wiped away a tear. The rest of our friends rushed outside to join us.

"So, so?"

"It's a 'yes' from the mean and moody one," I said, earning me a dig in the side.

"I'm so happy for youse both!" Ashley said, whipping off the foil top and wire cap. The bottle opened with a soft pop. Stewart downed what was left of his pint and held his glass out. Ashley ignored him and poured champagne for me and then Jack.

"Aye, so," he said, once I'd taken a fortifying gulp. My emotions had zig-zagged all over the place in the last couple of hours. "The Royal George's launch and your wedding?"

"Mmm?" I murmured, distracted. The groom-to-be had slung his arm over my shoulder. Out of sight of everyone else, his hand did discreetly clever things, fingers gently brushing against the super-sensitive bits of me.

"...so that gives you just over three months. Plenty o' time, aye?"

Jack and I snapped to smartly.

"What?"

"The launch of the Royal George," Ashley said. "It's December 21. When you get married here. I can't wait to create a pizza 'specially for it!"

Despite our best intentions—and all that anticipatory action we'd built up earlier in the day—we didn't stumble out of the Lochside Welcome until well after ten o'clock.

When Ashley told us the date of the Royal George launch, Jack and I exchanged horrified grimaces. Engagements were all well and good, but they were supposed to last ages. We'd hold a party for our friends, everyone would bring us a present (hopefully), we'd hashtag #engaged all over the place, plan our wedding in perfect detail three years ahead of the event and bang! We got married. Three-and-a-half months—or fifteen weeks—must miss out a lot of those key steps. Bad form, for example, to ask people to come to an engagement party (armed with pressie) and then demand their attendance at your wedding a few months later (again armed with pressie).

Greedy acquisition stuff aside, didn't wedding organisation take longer than twelve weeks? Like, a lot longer. Didn't photographers get booked up a year in advance? And weren't you supposed to take months searching for the perfect dress? My proposal had not even included a ring. Mhari had already noted the absence of anything on my left hand.

Jack tightened his hold on my hand. "Aye… okay, Ashley. The Lochside Welcome it is!"

A cheer sounded. Everyone had been listening in, and all those who'd been inside drifted out to join us. Cameras flashed left, right and centre, making me feel as if I was a celebrity. Every single app on my phone beeped—even the BBC weather one (felt like) as folks reacted to the news. Someone pointed out the length of time it had been since the last wedding—years, decades even. Funerals, on the other hand…

Ashley said the champagne was on the house—for me and Jack anyway. He whisked the bottle out of reach of Stewart, who only ever drank out of pint glasses no matter the drink. But everyone kept toasting us and it was only polite to raise our glasses when they did so. Jack's mother appeared too—once the village's GP and now in demand as self-proclaimed Psychic to the Stars, Caroline McLatchie.

"Jack! Gaby!" she exclaimed, throwing her hands in the air. "You've made me the happiest woman in the world!"

Fresh from her packed stall at the Highland Games, she still wore her psychic costume—long tasselled skirt, peasant-style smock top and her hair tucked under a turban. Caroline had kept her side line secret for years. But ever since Caitlin Cartier outed her as the source of amazingly accurate advice, she was proud to tell everyone about her lucrative sideline. I say 'amazingly accurate' because my (almost) mother-in-law once confessed to me she made it up as she went along. Modern life made it easy for the would-be fake psychic. All she needed to do was check out people on social media, read their body language and say she sensed pain and indecision. Worked ninety percent of the time.

"Didn't you see it in the stars then, Mum?" Jack asked. He took a dim view of his mother's activities and often had to rein her in. This year at the Highland Games, for instance, she wanted to charge people £50 for a ten-minute consultation in her tent. Psychic to the Stars prices and all that.

She flapped a heavily ringed hand. "I never use my powers to look at my own family members."

Convenient.

Ashley's promised pizza never materialised so by the time we left, my feet appeared to be working independently of my brain.

"I love you, you know," I said as we headed back to the house, darkness around us. "And I'm the luckiest woman alive!"

"I know. And watch your st—oh, too late."

Crap. Literally. I'd trodden in it—a heap of steaming dog poo outside Jamal's General Store. Despite his combing through his CCTV footage looking for the culprit who made a habit of this, the irresponsible dog owner had never been identified.

"How romantic!" I wailed, wiping my feet back and forth on the grass. "Just as I was declaring my love. And by the way, aren't you the luckiest man in the entire world?"

He winked and grabbed my hand. "C'mon. The luckiest man in the world wants to—"

My phone buzzed—a tinny ring sound I'd given my best friend so I could prioritise her calls and messages.

"WHAT THE..."

Choice expletives followed. Oh dear. Despite leaving Lochalshie months ago, Katya must still be a member of the Lochalshie WhatsApp group. Or our friends' social media posts hashtag GabyJackEngaged gave it away and all before I'd spoken to her. My phone showed eight missed calls.

By this point, we'd arrived back at the house.

"Katya," I mouthed to Jack as he opened the door, and I pressed the call back button. Mildred, waiting behind the door, miaowed angrily, her fluffy ginger and white tail waving huffily in the air. Her name was nothing to do with me. We inherited her when her previous owner needed to go into an unenlightened nursing home that did not allow pets. She liked me. Jack she tolerated. Just. That was the deal with cats. If dogs think they are human, cats regard themselves as gods.

"Sorry-sorry-sorry-sorry times a million trillion billion," I said as soon as my oldest friend picked up. Jack rolled his eyes and retreated to the kitchen followed by the still-complaining Mildred, miffed because we were so late feeding her. "But aren't you pleased for me?"

"Marriage is a sorry institution that props up an outdated patriarchal system."

"Thanks, Katya."

"Kidding—well, half-kidding. I'm delighted for you. Have you set a date?"

"Ah, now there's a thing," I dropped onto the comfiest armchair in the room and tucked my legs under me. The phone call would take a while. Jack's expression had changed back to inscrutable, and I wished yet again that I'd done the proposal differently. In private. Nowhere near a landlord with a desperate plan. He pointed to the upstairs bedroom and left again.

There was another wish. In my proposal fantasy, I said the words, he punched the air with joy, and we then spent the evening in bed doing filthy things. When I'd first met Jack, I entertained an intriguing fantasy where I imagined his body half-naked and wrapped in a pristine white towel. When I first got to see it, reality surpassed my expectations. Every time I saw him in the buff now; he still made me gasp.

"Twenty-first December," I told Katya.

"Good stuff," she said. "We can have your hen night in September, and you've got more than a year to do Pilates three times a week, so your pelvic floor muscles are in excellent shape for a honeymoon that—"

"Katya. It's December this year."

The silence lasted far too long.

"OMG. Why? Are we living in 1922? Are you pregnant and you're marrying so your shame doesn't show too much as you walk up the aisle in a baggier than normal dress?"

"No!" I squawked. "I am *not* pregnant!"

Upstairs, a bang sounded. If bangs could sound part horrified part terrified part relieved that one did.

Mildred butted my hand with her head wafting stinky cat food breath my way. I adjusted position so she could sit on me.

"So why?"

I outlined Ashley's offer / emotional blackmail plea for us to marry in the Lochside Welcome to knock the shine off the Royal George's official launch. And mentioned that I'd seen Zac.

A hiss. "How is the lying git?"

"I didn't speak to him. I don't, as a rule, talk to murderers."

"But your wedding. It's so soon," she said. "I mean… well, I had something to tell you. Dead important in terms of career development."

"Aren't you already wildly successful?"

True. Katya had ghost-written Caitlin Cartier's autobiography stretching it out for 80,000 words despite Caitlin being a mere 22. She'd received a fat fee in advance. The book was due out anytime now, and Katya had negotiated royalties too. She was about to hit the stratosphere. Caitlin now considered Katya a bosom buddy, thanks to the autobiography. They exchanged DMs all over the place. I might have been jealous, had Katya not told me Caitlin considered 750 other people who also worked for her in some capacity as close mates.

"Not me. You."

"Me?"

She explained. I listened, excitement mounting. Gaby, the underpaid, underappreciated graphic designer finally getting the recognition (and money) she deserved. I ended the call.

"Gaby, please hurry up! I want to celebrate properly!"

I raced upstairs. An unbelievable opportunity… How it fitted with me walking up the aisle in three months' time was another matter

---

"So you'll be finished at seven, right?"

"Yup. They're spending the day on Skye and then we'll be back on the mainland for six o'clock. I'll drop them at their hotel, and I'll meet you at the Plockton Inn at seven."

Mildred sat on my small suitcase and eyed me balefully. She knew an owner who was about to disappear for two days when she spotted one. But our two nights away now were a necessity. Two weeks after I'd proposed, and Jack and I had spent ten hours together if I didn't count sleeping —him zonking out as soon as he got in at night.

To be fair, Jack had warned me from the beginning the tourism season was bonkers. And this year, he'd been busier than ever. So busy, I'd yet to tell him what Katya had said to me on the night of the proposal. When we finally ended up in bed that night, amazing things happened just as I hoped. Breaking the mood would be such a waste.

"Tonight's the night, Mildred," I said. "And, um, can you shift off my case so I can put my super-sexy underwear in it?"

Ever tried reasoning with cats? It rarely works. I picked her up for a consoling cuddle and she scratched me in return. Mildred hated being left on her own. I'd arranged for Mhari to look after her, even if I risked having her poke her way around the house looking for anything secretive. I'd hidden as many incriminating items as I could. She wasn't able to stay tonight but she could do tomorrow. Mildred must have realised a night alone was on the cards.

When Jack had said last week he'd be away yet again at the weekend, I stamped my foot. A day later, he sent me a message with a link to the Plockton Inn. "Fancy a night here, gorgeous?"

Too right. Set in a sheltered bay overlooking Loch Carron, Plockton outdid even Lochalshie with its village charms. I'd plugged the location into my phone and Google maps was about to take me there now. I had previous for taking too long to get anywhere in Scotland—the views distracted me—so I set off in plenty of time.

Just as well. Eilean Donan Castle demanded I stop the car, get out and visit it. Then, a group of Americans caught my attention chattering excitedly about Outlander and if the castle had been used during filming.

I bustled up, keen to show off. "No," I said, "but it was in Highlander—the film with the sexy Frenchman and that woman Beatie thingie who has never been in anything since!"

And then didn't it only turn out 'that woman' was leading the tour, the imaginatively named Scottish Film Locations. "Five seasons of Poldark!" one of her party snapped at me. I spent the rest of my visit to the castle ducking out of sight every time she and her group appeared.

Still, the road to Plockton was enchanting weaving its twisty way through tiny hamlets and farmland. Highland cows, their horns scarily long and pointed, sat on the road and didn't seem inclined to move. I peeped the horn and waited. And waited. By the time I got to Plockton it was five past seven. The inn was the first hotel as you drove in. Jack's minibus was nowhere to be seen.

I checked in and headed up the stairs. The room looked onto the high street, beyond which you could see the loch. Signs at a jetty for a seal tour promised your money back if said seals didn't appear. I dumped my suitcase on the bed. "Perhaps," I told my reflection, "I should ask Highland Tours for my money back for the non-appearance this summer of my boyfriend!"

Last year, the tourist season was tailing off when Jack realised I was the woman of his dreams. (He'd been slow on the uptake.) As soon as October kicked in six weeks later, he was all mine for months. Goodness it had been fun. In theory I was working, having negotiated a remote working deal with my boss at Bespoke Design. When your boyfriend dangles keys in front of you and says, "Hey, shall we drive out to Oban and get some fish and chips?" who says no?

Or even better, he dispenses with the keys and dangles himself. "Gaby, I'm bored… shall we go to bed for a while?"

This year, the summer season began gently, but then the bookings stacked up. Throughout May, June, July and August we'd spent so little time together, Mildred sometimes hissed at him when he came in, arching her back, her fur all puffed out. Who was this stranger? Don't get me wrong. Those end of the week get-togethers were exciting. But for the past two weeks we hadn't talked about the wedding once. Or Katya's revelation. And yesterday I'd only gone and said 'yes' to it…

"Think of the money," Katya said when I umm-ed and ah-ed again. "And how brilliant the job will look on your CV."

"Room service!"

I'd recognise that deep, gruff Scottish voice anywhere. I ripped off all my clothes. This must be one of those role-playing scenarios. Plockton was about to reignite our relationship in a wonderful way. I pulled the bobble off my ponytail and shook my hair out. No time to apply make-up but at least I'd shaved everything in readiness.

"Come in!" I thrust out my arms. "Ta da!"

"Your boyfriend sen—"

Difficult to know who was the more horrified—me or the teenage boy holding an ice bucket and champagne. He flushed the exact colour of his scarlet waistcoat, and I discovered that yes when you blush, it can go head to toe. I crossed both hands over my chest, realising too late that left everything else on show.

"Ahem."

Jack materialised behind the teenage waiter who appeared to have frozen to the spot. If he'd been half a minute quicker, this would never have happened. I fled to the en suite and bolted the door. My heart hammered in my chest as I prayed that the lad got temporary but total amnesia covering the last five minutes of his life. Or he was struck dumb and illiterate from this moment forth, unable ever to describe what he'd seen.

I heard Jack and the traumatised teen exchange murmured words, and the bedroom door closed as someone hurriedly made their way downstairs.

A knock sounded on the door. "You can come out now."

I sat on the bath, its porcelain doing a grand job of cooling down my still burning hot in embarrassment skin. Yes, bottoms felt shame too. "I think I'll just stay here."

His voice dropped to a whisper. "You can't. I've just seen the best view in Plockton. If you don't open the door right now, I'll have to batter it down."

An offer I couldn't refuse. Still, Jack might have put more effort into stopping the upward tilt to his mouth. He kept straightening his lips, but the corners moved upwards of their own accord as he watched me edge out, worried Teenage Room Service boy might have hidden himself under the bed.

Jack pulled the naked me into a bear hug and laughed like a loon for far too long.

"Gaby, the look on your face. That poor fella's shell-shocked."

"Shell shock!" I squawked, my face pushed into his shoulder. As I began to recover from the indignity, it struck me there were advantages to this being naked already lark. Hands, for example could make the most of it, moving up and down leisurely and slowly, making the tiny hairs on my skin stand on end.

"Aye, the family that run this place are God-fearin' souls. You might be the first in the flesh naked woman he's ever seen. You've done the lad a huge favour," Jack said. His voice changed, the words becoming laboured. "And now, seeing as you are..."

Later, we sat up in bed sipping the champagne. "Do you want to order room service?" Jack asked, turning on the TV. "I dunno if I can be bothered moving. Though if we do, both of us will be fully dressed when the food arrives."

At that, he gave me one of those sideways glances. I knew the story would be dredged up for the rest of my life. The time Gaby mistook an 18-year-old waiter for her boyfriend and swung open the door buck naked. Heck, he'd probably even tell it—

"You're *not* to mention this at your stag night," I said. "Or, absolutely not three hundred times no, at the speech you make at our wedding."

He turned onto his side and propped his head on his hand. "Not fair! It's the best story ever."

I thumped him, then ran my finger down his nose, moving gently over the slight bump where he'd broken it at the Highland Games a few years ago.

"Is this all moving too quickly? We, um, don't have to get married. Well, I'd like to eventually, but we can wait."

Time to check in with my intended. Why had neither of us mentioned the 'w' word since my proposal? Part of my reasoning behind the 'spur-of-the-moment' ask at this year's Highland Games had been something that happened the week before. Jack had come in after work and caught me watching a repeat of *Don't Tell The Bride*, the programme where the groom-to-be has to organise the entire wedding including choosing the dress. (Always the most contentious bit.) I'd whipped the remote control from underneath me and offered to change channels, but he waved the offer aside and sat down.

"Nah, I quite like this programme. Just out of interest, what kind of dress would you want? And what's your favourite cake?"

I took that as my green light. He likes *Don't Tell The Bride!* He's asking me marriage-related questions! Ergo—he can't wait for me to walk down the aisle towards him. I should ask him soon.

And then he threw me by winding me up after the all-too public proposal. Imagine the cruelty of making a girl wait so long for her answer!

"I want to get married too Gaby. I just… now it's a bit like a runaway train. Every time I go into Jamal's shop, someone tells me they're fair looking forward to our wedding, and do we have a wedding list yet so they can buy us something before all the cheaper presents get snapped up and they're left with the thousand pound telly or something."

"We wouldn't do a wedding list." That seemed the easiest thing to say. 'Runaway train' alarmed me.

Suddenly he was on top of me once more, his body heavy, familiar and comforting. I stared up into those brown eyes I loved and watched a lock of auburn hair fall forward onto his forehead.

"And we do need to help Ashley make the Lochside Welcome the venue of choice for all brides to be."

He kissed me. "Though I doubt any of them will be as daft—I mean, delightful as you."

More kisses, in part to stifle my protests at that character assessment. M'lud, I'm as sensible as the next woman. My best friend testifies to that. When she isn't telling me I'm bonkers.

As he seemed to be in an agreeable mood, I cleared my throat.

"So, I have this thing to tell you." Spit this out as quickly as possible, Gaby, I told myself.

"Dexter has offered me a job with Blissful Beauty in London. Big promotion, tonnes of money for things like weddings. Isn't that amazing?! But he really needed an answer. Like, yesterday and I said yes."

Grab your copy…
vinci-books.com/HighlandWedding

About the Author

I'm in my 40s, married and 'mum' to a very spoiled cat. I live in Dumbarton near the bonny, bonny banks of Loch Lomond, and by day I'm a communications officer/freelance writer, by night an author. My biggest dream come true would be to be able to write full-time.

About the Author

The Grateful Thanks Bit!

Thanks to Caron Allan and Kimberly Lynn who were very encouraging on Wattpad, particularly grateful thanks to Caron for her last-minute double-checking. (*Really* last minute…)

Kristien Potgieter made an excellent job of beta reading and then proof-reading my manuscript—she's a cat lover too so we bonded quickly—and Enni Tuomisalo. (Is it weird to admit I have a mad crush on the Dexter vector?!)

Thanks to you for reading. We all lead busy lives these days, so it means a great deal to me that you decided to take the time to work your way through my book. I hope you feel your efforts were rewarded.

Lochalshie is loosely based on Arrochar in Argyll & Bute. It is a beautiful place so if you find yourself in the west coast of Scotland, please visit. And I have a wee plea to make… if poor little Mena has inspired you to get your own cat, please adopt, don't shop. There are hundreds of cats in shelters desperate for a forever home. I also have a soft spot for *Cretan Cat a List*, and the work they do on the island to trap, neuter and release/re-home cats.

Apologies to Jill, Fiona and Lorraine for allowing an unqualified Pilates teacher to star in my book. I know from lessons I've had from these ladies that thorough and extensive training is a must.

The biggest bit of thanks goes to Sandy, who supports

me as a writer, putting up with the so-far poor remuneration and his lady wife disappearing for hours at a time to tap away on her keyboard. Some day, my sweet, we *will* be able to afford to shop at Marks and Spencer's for our food instead of Aldi…